~

One dollar from each sale of this book reported to the
author will be donated to *La Casa Hogar*, a non-profit advocacy
and educational agency for farmworker families
in Yakima, Washington.

~

María Juana's GIFT

BOOK 2 OF THE AMERICAN TEACHERS SERIES

T. Lloyd Winetsky

Third Edition

P

Pen-L Publishing
Fayetteville, Arkansas
Pen-L.com

Maria Juana's Gift
Copyright © 2015 T. Lloyd Winetsky

Although there are some real places and historical events referred to in this novel, the towns of La Cholla and Sofia are inventions. The characters in this book are fictitious. Any similarity to real persons, living or dead, is coincidental and not intended by the author.

Printed and bound in the United States of America.

Cover design by Nick Shipley, Warhorse Studio.
Photographs by Nick Shipley and Micah Sol Winetsky.
Photo credits: p. x, author's collection; p. 78 by Micah Winetsky; p. 158 by Nicholas Shipley

ISBN: 978-1-942428-23-7

Acknowledgments

Vital to the completion of this work were constructive comments by Kathleen Ruth Nelson, first reader; Carl Kleinschmitt, reviewer; Jesús Lemos, professional interpreter and editor of the Spanish text and translations; Dr. William Cox, reviewer of the novel's 1975-6 medical terminology, and Kent Lundgren, U.S. Border Patrol (retired), author of *Tracks in the Sand* and reviewer of Border Patrol information in the story. Also key were professional critiques and edits by Victor West of Pacific Literary Services, and Karinya Funsett of The Editorial Department. The author also thanks Duke Pennell of Pen-L Publishing for his knowledge, support, and the idea to group the author's books into the "American Teachers" series.

For Anna W., and to the person she would have become.

PART I

Anne S., Jake Dylan and
Jake Dylan Friend, 15 Months
("Constance," the Gower Street Theater, 1951)

1

The old woman was less than five feet tall and not even a nurse's aide, but it was obvious to Jake that she knew what she was doing. One moment he would see María carrying out heavy bags of trash, and minutes later he observed her holding the baby with an authority and tenderness that gave him some hope.

He watched her now, but the pink blanket in her arms didn't move—no wiggling, no crying, and María had stopped acting as if the baby were responsive. Jake and his student who lived with them, Ben, had just visited Tina for a few minutes in her room at the end of the ward. Her reticence led Ben to excuse himself to wait in the truck.

Jake knocked lightly on the nursery window so he could talk to María, who was returning the baby to the incubator for more oxygen. She met him at the glass door, leaning on it hard because of pressure from the air conditioning; Jake pulled it open for her.

María's pale-brown face was drawn and grave. "¿Señor Fren, el doctor?"

Frowning, Jake told her he hadn't found him.

"Señor, la niña, she is worse. She breathes faster," she said in Spanish, pointing up at the speaker near the ceiling. "I heard there was an emergency; the doctor came."

"What? ¿Cuándo, señora?"

"Maybe a half hour."

"I'll be damned," Jake mumbled to himself, already hurrying away from the nursery into the hall toward the small emergency area. He passed the closed administrator's office and saw the door to the doctors' lounge was ajar. Jake stopped, opened it and called, "Hello?" A dark suit coat and blue tie were draped over the top of a leather recliner; he assumed the clothes were Serna's. Jake left and turned a corner, but he had to stop to keep from colliding with a custodian who was dry-mopping.

"See the doctor go by here?" Jake asked.

The heavy man, a bit startled by this unexpected redhead in a beard, baseball cap and Bermudas, finally said, "*El doctor*, he go."

"*Gracias, señor.*" Jake hopped over the wide broom and ran to the bench by the back door where many times in the last day he waited futilely, trying to catch the doctor when he left.

Jake went right out into a blast of dry, hundred-degree air to the nearly empty staff parking area. He ran around the corner of the hospital and saw the vintage white Corvette convertible easily take the steep hill, a passenger in the seat next to Doctor Serna.

"Damn it!" Jake shouted, not far from the grey stone face of Mary holding baby Jesus. He ran for the visitors' parking lot and could already see Ben, waiting in the front seat of Jake's old truck.

Doctor Serna and his cousin, the mayor, had no idea someone was pursuing them; the doctor's high-powered engine easily conquered another incline while several blocks back Jake's forty-horse motor strained, balking like a mule.

The Corvette disappeared from Jake's sight; he yanked his gearshift all the way down to second. "Crap, Loretta," he grumbled to the dual-cab Volkswagen he had been refurbishing for years. *Swear to God, you're sold if the damn doctor gets away.*

"¿Maestro?" the teen said, a quiver in his voice.

"It's okay, Ben, I just need to talk to the jerk." *And take him back.*

The pickup slugged onward past some carbon-copy three-bedroom ramblers up to the summit where the afternoon sun struck Jake in the eyes. He reached for the visor, forgetting he had yet to repair it, and instead pulled down the brim of his Chicago Cubs cap. Ben blocked the glare with his arm.

Three blocks ahead at a stop sign, he could see the doctor's Panama hat and the mayor's bald head. To Jake, they looked like tourists at the border, basking in the sun as if it were provided by the gods just for them. He hoped they would stop at the doctor's office, but Serna drove by well above the speed limit.

He's going home, Jake thought, but the Corvette didn't turn into La Cholla Gardens, where the doctor lived; he was heading to town. "Hold on!" he called out to Ben.

His student's dark skin blanched a shade as Jake ran the stop sign. Ben ducked, slouching his gaunt frame below the windowsill. On the down slope, Jake accelerated almost to fifty, the trees and houses blurring by.

"Maestro, you leave me here?"

"What?" *He saw someone back there.* "Okay—this next hill, when I have to slow down."

"*Está bien.*"

The truck hit the incline and started to labor; Jake released the gas pedal, stopping their forward motion. He yanked the hand brake to keep from rolling back, and saw the passenger door was already open. Ben jumped out, waved, and ran down an alley; Jake struggled on up the hill in first gear.

At the next summit, he saw his prey had lengthened the lead to about a half-mile, but Jake was less than a hundred yards behind by the time he sped down to level ground near the fruit warehouse at the outskirts of La Cholla. Doctor Serna parked behind a ceremonial black and white '51 Ford squad car at the head of a line of disparate vehicles.

The friggin' parade. Two Cadillacs idled behind the Corvette, then a fire engine, six antique autos full of war veterans, a farm tractor pulling a hay wagon swarming with Brownie scouts, and four teams of Little Leaguers in station wagons. Eight horses followed, mounted by glittering Mexican *charros* in wide sombreros, then came a hobo clown with a shovel cart, and a tiny red Nash Metropolitan stuffed with three more clowns—one red, one white, and one blue. Every child held a patriotic helium balloon, and some of the adults had dressed up as sons or daughters of the Revolution.

The high school band was near the end, thirty strong, in stifling, clashing black-and-orange uniforms. The teens stood in the shade by a semi's trailer, sullenly unpacking instruments in front of a green tractor that pulled the town float. Sitting up there on star-spangled stairs beneath a white umbrella, the stout 1976 Miss La Cholla primped her puffy black coiffure, gazing into a pocket mirror. The town's tall yellow street sweeper, draped in flag bunting, was the last in line. Its driver, impatient for the parade to begin, was making the square vehicle spin slowly in place like a robot.

There were no curbs this far from downtown, so Jake just pulled off the road by some other cars near the fruit warehouse, not far from Miss La Cholla. He got out of his truck, then ran in starts and stops toward the front of the queue, not noticing a police car slowly following him a half-block behind.

As Jake dodged around participants and gawkers, he recalled that the parade would cross the border and loop through old La Cholla. *No wonder nobody's marching; they don't want to get stuck in Mexico.*

He passed the clowns, who were opening boxes of goodies to throw to the kids—baseball card packs on this side, then athletic socks and hard candy below the border. Jake saw some citizens fooling around with bunting and a sign for the doctor's car: GRAND MARSHALL—MAYOR "RICO" RANGEL. *He can just find another damn driver.*

3

Sixteen months before the parade in La Cholla, Jake gazed out at a sign in San Diego—OLD TOWN BAKERY AND PANADERIA. He was thinking that some warm *pan dulce* with margarine melted on top sounded good. Fog and the evening rush hour had extended their trip to nearly three hours.

Armando drove two more blocks, circled another, and turned the school district sedan into a parking lot. Except for snoring from the two veteran female teachers in the back, the last fifteen minutes of the drive were quiet; Jake and Armando had run out of things to talk about.

The uneven black letters on the bright sign outside the hotel read, **WELCOME mIG/BIling Ed/eSl**, adding to Jake's certainty that his third dreary state conference wouldn't affect anything important in his life.

"Why the frown, Skip?" *Skip* was a recent addition to Armando's exuberant vocabulary, but Jake didn't mind. The fledgling teacher was doing well in their alternative classroom for secondary migrant students, although the previous summer Jake had to convince the principal to hire Armando.

"Not frowning," Jake said, intentionally loud enough to wake the women. Armando parked; they all got out and entered the lobby with light baggage. The hotel had already begun to decorate for the Bicentennial—nothing elaborate yet, just a tall poster of a smirking George Washington and some strings of tiny U.S. flags around the door of the small gift shop.

While Armando and the two rumpled women checked out the tourist junk, Jake handled the purchase order. He made sure their room was far away from "the two ol' bags," as Armando referred to them. The four teachers then registered at the conference table, all but Jake obediently pinning on a two by four-inch rainbow-bordered name badge.

At the third floor, the women glared at Armando before leaving the elevator; the young teacher shrugged and punched the "7" button. Predictably, he and Jake looked up at the indicator as they passed the fourth floor.

Armando Tapia had chestnut-colored skin and dense, raven hair that matched his brows, moustache and long sideburns. Unlike his mentor six feet away, Armando's regular smile gave the impression he was content even when he wasn't. He and Jake had one physical similarity, they were both two inches or so shy of six feet tall.

Jake, a "fat kid" through puberty, developed in his early twenties a preference for walking and biking whenever he could, but the benefits of his exercise sometimes lost out to a daily "beer or two." Now almost twenty-six, his waist had a two-inch fold of adipose; he outweighed lean Armando by about thirty pounds.

A shade darker than a classic redhead, Jake was fair but didn't look blushed, and his constellations of freckles faded over the years. His slowly receding hair and a sporadically trimmed full beard had darkened from rufous red almost to brown. Jake's most obvious feature, thick auburn eyebrows, furrowed, arched or flattened with any serious thought that crossed his mind.

Both men waited for the elevator in garb typical of what they wore in class—Armando in pressed half-belled blue jeans, black loafers and a brightly printed shirt; Jake in coarse suede shoes, dark-brown jeans and a short-sleeve light-blue dress shirt, never a tie.

The seventh-floor bell "dinged" and Jake turned to Armando, who carried one worn cardboard valise; his black guitar case stood next to him on the elevator floor.

"Far enough away, are we?" Jake asked, grinning.

"Yeah, Skip, thanks. Those two would cramp my style for sure. We're not eating dinner with them, right?"

"We're on our own," he said as the door opened.

Armando twitched his rakish moustache and broadened his smile as he lifted the luggage. "The room's still mine for tomorrow night; you're at your brother's, right?"

Jake hefted his grey canvas bag as they exited, searching for numbers. "My cousin's." He turned a corner. "You're *that* sure you're going to score?"

"Can't miss *con mi guitarra*." He raised the black case and "yipped" as if he were singing a *ranchera*.

"Geez, don't get us kicked out the first night."

Armando put a forefinger over his lips. "Got it, Skip, play it cool."

They walked ahead, reading door numbers. "Where did you come up with *Skip*?" Jake asked.

"That's what we called our coach. You're the Skip of our little team, man."

"Great." They turned down a hall. "So, you'll be trying to date a teacher?"

"You nuts? If they're not old like those two," he pointed down, "they act like 'em. I'll be checking out teacher's aides. What about you?"

"The women here are too young, too married, or still into Elvis."

"You gotta be lookin' for something."

"Yeah, I found it." Jake pointed at room 725; Armando already had his key out; he opened the door and rushed in. All the lights were on by the time Jake plopped his bag on the first of two queen beds.

Armando drew back the white curtains. "This is perfect, Skip; check out the view."

Jake looked out at downtown San Diego. The fog had lifted to overcast; a flashing airliner seemed to be making a suicidal descent right between glimmering office buildings.

"Damn, how can they do that?" Armando said, not expecting an answer. The room had the typical small coffee pot, plastic ice bucket, and sterile wrapped glasses. On the wall above the dresser, a metal-framed print portrayed a generic sailboat on the ocean that was actually several miles from the hotel.

Jake smiled. "First time this high, Mister Tapia?"

"Yup, this beats those dumps on Highway 99. Let's see how the TV works." Armando lifted a boxy remote control attached to the nightstand.

The news came on, the announcer blaring, " . . . Revere's kitchen table in 1775—your Bicentennial Minute for Wednesday, February twenty-sixth, nineteen seventy-five."

"I can't wait to learn the name of Paul Revere's horse," Jake said.

"Yeah, let's eat. I'm starved." Armando muted the sound and checked some other channels.

"Do you want to go out or eat downstairs?"

"Downstairs—easy pickin's." He turned off the TV.

Jake looked at him askance but didn't care enough to ask what he meant. After they washed up, Armando put on a white Filipino shirt; Jake didn't change. About ten minutes later, they entered a half-occupied restaurant decorated with fishing nets, blue glass floats, swords and seahorses. They stood by a Neptune dummy that held a sign in the shape of a treasure chest: PLEASE WAIT TO BE SEATED.

"Where's your name tag, Skip?"

"In the room."

"It's okay, I've got mine." He patted his badge.

"So?" Jake replied just before a young peroxide-blonde hostess in a jaunty sailor cap walked up to them.

"Two?" she asked Armando.

"We're meeting some friends. If we don't find them," his smile widened, "maybe you could find us a table."

She literally flapped her artificial black lashes. "Anything I can do to help, sir."

They walked into the seating area; Armando half-winked back to her.

"Well, I think you already scored," Jake murmured.

"Not really my type, but who knows?"

"I thought you didn't want to eat with those two."

"You're kidding, right?" Armando scanned the diners as they walked.

"We'll eat alone before we do that."

"Then who are you looking for?"

"We just passed a good possibility. Back, Skip."

Jake turned and saw two women, not ten feet away, slightly slouched and reading their menus at a table set for five. They were both at least Armando's age; one had medium-length curly brunet hair and strikingly dark oval eyes. To Jake, her attractiveness was compromised by ponderous silver earrings, a matching gaudy necklace, and the rank cigarette smoke she kept waving from her bronze face.

Armando started toward them; Jake lagged behind, thinking the second woman was unremarkable. She wasn't homely or even plain, but her pale, serious, rounded features had no help at all from Revlon, and unlike her friend, she wore no jewelry. He thought she had average looks and was twenty-five, at most. *God, but look at that hair.* It was long and honey-blonde, natural, he decided, cascading by her slender neck and over her shoulders like clear water, even in the dimmed light.

She could pass for Amish—great. Following Armando up to their table, Jake glanced at the rainbow badge on the blonde's buttoned-up white cardigan: ~~CHRIS~~TINA LINN, VISALIA, BILING ED. CERT., the first five letters struck through with black marker.

"Man, you guys are from Visalia? I'm from Fresno!" Armando blurted, slapping his conference badge. Christina Linn's face was blank, but Jake noticed her eyes. They looked soft to him, and root beer brown; he liked the contrast with her resplendent hair. Jake couldn't tell if she was bashful or angry, but he thought she did deserve to be pissed off by the interruption.

"Fresno, no kidding?" the other woman said, as if it really were a coincidence. She smiled fetchingly; her breasts distended the badge on her white blouse: ORALIA MEDINA—VISALIA—TEACHING ASSISTANT. Oralia doused her smoke and presented long fingers and crimson nails to Armando for a delicate handshake. "I'm Orie; this is Tina. You're a teacher?" she added, clearly impressed by his status.

"*Armando Tapia, a sus órdenes.*" He nodded to them, then away. "This is Jake; we team-teach in Lemon Branch. Would you ladies care for some dinner company?"

Orie grinned toward Tina, who raised her fair brows ambivalently. Jake stood there looking sheepish and wishing they had gone out for beers and Mexican food.

"Sit down; we're about to order," Orie said, snickering. "Tell us where Lemon Branch is." Armando sat on her other side, leaving Jake the chair between the two women.

"Lemon Branch, Orange County," Armando beamed, "just a hop from the Magic Kingdom." He bragged a minute about their program and then asked, "So you guys teach ESL?" Tina looked to Orie as the hostess arrived with more menus, giving Armando a surly glance.

"And some other things," Orie answered, still smiling.

The next hour was small talk over large margaritas. The conversation covered the dinner fare, Disneyland, the San Joaquin Valley and Tijuana, mostly two-way banter between Orie and Mando, who had confessed the nickname. As they ate, Tina mostly listened, Jake commented briefly and chuckled; Orie and Armando got louder by the time everyone had dessert. Jake was impressed that Tina understood when they switched to Spanish a few times. All but Tina started on a second margarita while Armando finished telling an energetic joke about seven retarded dwarves, all named Dopey, who couldn't figure out what to do with a willing Snow White.

Tina and Jake sat straight faced.

Orie forced a smile. "Sorry, baby, but that's more cruel than funny."

Armando turned from her to Jake, who looked back at him with a laugh and said, "Don't look at me, maestro, she's right."

Armando slurred a little. "Yeah, guess so."

"Look, Mando," Orie said, "I didn't tell you we work with disabled kids—Bilingual Special Ed."

"Hey, I'm all for *that*," Armando said eagerly, "except when they dump kids in there just because they don't know English. Right, Skip?"

"Of course." Jake made a half smile.

Orie looked at Tina, and then spoke for them again, this time proudly. "Tina doesn't let that happen in our class. The kids need to have some learning problem besides English."

"Yeah, that's what I'm saying." Armando was pleased he had everyone in agreement. "Hey, my stupid joke got us talkin' school—two whole days for that. Let's order a drink; get into music or movies or something." He had no takers for another round but still looked for the waitress.

"Okay," Orie said, "let's see, I just saw a John Wayne movie, *Micky-D*, something like that. Wasn't very good, cops and robbers, but I do love his cowboy movies."

Armando laughed at Jake. "Another vote for the Duke."

Jake shook his head. "You heard the lady, he's not even versatile enough to play a cop."

"Ladies," Armando said, pointing his thumb, "right here's the only guy in the U.S.A. who doesn't like John Wayne movies."

"You don't like his politics, Jake?" Orie asked.

"No, I don't care about his opinions."

Armando smirked. "Now you gotta explain, man."

Her pretty eyes wide open, Orie waited for the explanation while Tina slanted her brow, looking puzzled.

"Okay, short and sweet. My dad was an actor—after work, weekends; I grew up around legit actors who loved the stage. You'd think people in L.A. would get used to movie stars, but they treat them like gods. To me, they're nothing unless they can act and don't sell out—Gregory Peck, Katharine Hepburn, Brando; damn few others. John Wayne just plays himself; he's a star, not an actor." Embarrassed that he got so carried away, Jake was flushed.

Tina cleared her throat, creasing her forehead. "Uh, sorry, I don't think I've heard of him."

They all stared at her for a few seconds; Jake's jaw felt unhinged.

"John Wayne?" Armando said, starting to snigger. "You *are* kidding, right, Tina?"

"No," she answered quietly.

Orie kept herself from laughing. "Tina, you've been here six months now; you must've heard of him back in college, or after that."

"No, I went from Kentucky right back to Africa."

Trying not to stare rudely, Jake said, "Africa?" *And no John Wayne?*

"Yes." Tina looked at him with a shrug and a very slight grin, transforming her face for a moment.

Jake saw her brief and comely smile. *What was her family doing over there? Diplomats? Doctors? How does she know Spanish?*

Armando, still chortling, was telling Tina how John Wayne was number one at the box office.

Orie jumped in. "Tina, get this, he's been married," she showed three fingers, "*tres veces, a tres hispanas.*"

Tina returned a diffident half smile, again enchanting Jake, who watched her furtively while they filled Tina in on John Wayne's movies and his real name.

"Enough with the Duke," Armando finally said to Tina, still amused by her cultural naiveté. "I want to ask you about Jake's favorite singer, and you gotta tell us the truth."

"All right," she said, looking down self-consciously.

"It's Elvis Presley." Armando's tone was gleeful. "You can't tell me you never heard of *him.*"

She barely closed her eyes, like a long blink, showing a bit of pique. "Yes,

I know about Elvis." Tina looked at Jake apologetically. "I don't like his music very much."

"Bingo!" Armando shouted, then laughed. "Tina, before he starts telling you how much Elvis sucks, have you ever heard of—?"

"That's enough, Mando," Orie broke in, eyes daggered. Her interruption barely precluded one from Jake, who looked at Orie appreciatively.

Armando put both arms up helplessly, like in a movie stick-up. "Okay, okay, sorry. Relax, everybody; the night is young."

Orie yawned. "Not for me it isn't. We drove half of California and shopped all of Tijuana—afraid I've had it."

Armando stood, his mind working on a way to finish his move on Orie. "Should I order coffee?" He searched for the waitress again.

Orie smiled, shaking her head. "Not before bed, baby."

Either *bed* or *baby* seemed to put Armando in a frenzy; he sat again, proposing to play her some music.

Jake smiled at Tina, who attempted to ignore Armando's nearby pleading. Before Orie could end the conversation with Armando, Jake tried to summon his nerve. *What the hell, give it a shot; ask her.*

Fifteen minutes later, Jake and Armando sat at the small table in their room and looked out, this time at a propjet flying even more precariously past the modest skyscrapers of San Diego. Jake had picked up two beers downstairs; they sipped from the cans, watching the view.

"Look at that crap," Armando said. "I'm never goin' up there."

Jake scoffed. "You'll fly before you're twenty-five."

"Feeling pretty smart, aren't you, Skip?" His question was rhetorical. "Man, I can't believe it; you score for tomorrow night, and I strike out."

"Yeah," Jake replied, needling him, "I think I could've had a date with either one of them."

"You're getting carried away now, man." Armando shook his head. "I never would've guessed Orie's three years older than me."

"Like she wasn't surprised by *your* age?"

"I shoulda' faked it. It was goin' good until then."

Jake couldn't hold back a snicker. "Yeah, maybe so."

"It isn't funny. I heard that line you used on Tina: *¿Le gusta los mariscos?* That's horrible, and way too formal. She probably hates seafood, but she bought it anyway. She's into you, man."

Jake tried not to smile at that reassuring news. "And how do you know that?"

"Shit, I know. So, you take the room tomorrow night."

"And scare her off? No, I like her."

"Jesus, aren't you the guy who was going to the border to check out *las putas*?"

Jake's light complexion reddened a shade. "We were just going down there for, uh—"

"Yeah, yeah," Armando interrupted. "Won't your date mess up the deal with your cousin?"

"I'll call, and see him on Friday night. The room is yours."

"Works for me." Armando stood up. "I'm gonna brush my teeth, get the ol' *guitarra*, and head downstairs for the social."

Jake grinned. "Back on the trail?"

Armando started across the room. "Yup. You coming?"

"Nah, I'm finished for one night."

"Tina's cool, Skip; and I know you dig that hippie hair, but you just met her." Armando laughed, stopping near the bathroom. "You sound like an ol' married man."

"Yeah, sure. Just go have fun, Mando," Jake chided.

"I will; bank on it," he called back from the sink.

Regardless of the joking around, Jake thought about what Armando said, admitting to himself that he didn't know Tina at all. *Acting like a smitten adolescent.* He looked out the window at the lights, finishing his beer. *Then again, she seems like one of a kind.*

2

Sweat pouring from his forehead, Jake approached the doctor and mayor in the Corvette; they laughed to each other about something. The mayor had donned a ridiculous white ten-gallon Stetson; his gut jiggled where it hung below his red cowboy shirt. The school band cut loose with a discordant blast of *It's a Grand Old Flag*, the horses jittering from the clamor.

Jake tapped the back of the sleeve of the doctor's red-and-blue-striped white summer shirt. "Doctor Serna!" he shouted over the racket.

The young doctor turned around with a wide smile; the portly mayor was shaking hands with Ben Franklin and simultaneously leering at a busty Betsy Ross. Serna distorted his light-brown face into a squint and removed the Panama hat to block the sun, revealing a full head of neat hair, dark and reflective as plain coffee.

"Oh, uh, Mister Friend," the doctor called out. "Good, you finally got out of that place—happy Fourth."

The band's practice medley was now on *Yankee Doodle Dandy*, so Jake and the doctor had to keep yelling.

"I'm not here for the parade, doctor; you know I've been trying to reach you. I want you to come with me to the hospital." Jake pointed back. "I'm parked just over there."

"What? I don't think so, Mister Friend." His smile vanished only for a moment.

"My daughter, doctor, she—"

"Listen, she's in good hands. Now please leave me to enjoy my Sunday," Serna said, not as loud. He turned away and put on his hat, assuming the matter was finished.

"*You* listen," Jake shouted just as the bandmaster signaled for immediate silence, "our baby's sick!" Those within twenty yards of the Corvette stopped yammering to gawp at Jake and the doctor.

"Jesus, man, shut up." Serna spoke under his breath through a toothy grin, looking around as if Jake were not there. After a few silent, awkward moments, the parade participants mumbled, and then resumed the loud gabbing.

The doctor spoke to Jake again, still without eye contact. "All right, spit it out; keep your voice down."

"Fine. Yesterday the nurse told me something wasn't right with Emma; I've been trying to catch you ever since."

Serna finally looked at him. "That was *you* at my house again? This is getting ridiculous," he added in a low grumble. "All right, here's the deal, Mister Friend."

Teeth clenched, Jake glowered at him. "Okay, tell me."

"I came back yesterday for morning rounds and checked them both; they were fine, and I know you've been told since then that the baby's levels are normal."

"Have *you* been told that McNally isolated her, put her on oxygen, and she's still breathing too fast?"

"I heard about the oxygen," he said with a trace of a scoff. "My colleague was just taking precautions."

"He was trying to help. You could've come by and checked her when you were there this morning."

"Mister Friend," he said, smiling and snarling at once. "I was taken out of mass for an emergency that *wasn't*. I'll see your wife and baby on regular rounds first thing tomorrow."

Jake shook his head. "No, that's not good enough."

"What? Who do you think you are?" The doctor caught his rising tone mid-sentence and smiled at a Minuteman walking by. Serna turned, glaring at Jake. "Who said she was worse, that old woman?"

"Yes, that's right."

"For God's sake, man, her job is to change diapers and clean up. You couldn't understand her, anyway."

"I speak Spanish, Doctor."

"Doesn't matter. These people think she's, uh . . . a cure-a-dera—whatever they call it."

"*Curandera.* What matters is that María knows the baby's sick."

"Ridiculous. The charge nurse would've contacted me if there was a real problem."

"She said you were too busy."

"Exactly right; she deserves a raise." He waved to three tardy band members.

13

"My wife knows something's wrong; she just stares at Emma when they bring her."

"Mister Friend, your baby is big and healthy, and your wife is uh, stoic, like these wet—uh, migrants."

Schmuck. "I know my wife; she *should* have been crying." Jake tried to calm himself. "Look, I'm just asking you to go and take another look at Emma. If we're wrong about this, you'll have my personal apology."

"You know where I'm going? To old La Cholla."

Overhearing his cousin, the mayor stopped glad-handing and swiveled his thick neck. "Is there a problem, Eddie?"

"Nah, Rico, he's just leaving."

Jake opened the door of the Corvette part way. "I am, and I'm still asking you to come with me. The cops can drive him."

"Last time, Mister Friend," Serna said through his teeth again, "I'm not going to the hospital."

Jake prepared for the first day of the convention by cutting up a paper sack to cover the novel he was reading. He woke up Armando, showered, and then got dressed in the same pants with a clean white dress shirt, the sleeves rolled up to the elbows. He put on his badge because it also served as the lunch ticket. Jake headed for the elevator with his book and the conference folder.

Downstairs, the educators were assembling for continental breakfast in the hallway outside the cavernous main room that would host the keynote speech. The corridor was wall-to-wall with conventioneers jabbering while nibbling from plastic plates held in one hand. Some of them carried their belongings in SAN DIEGO or TIJUANA shopping bags.

Jake figured about three-fourths of them were teachers, mostly women, but he wasn't surprised to see some men who were very much into "Sunny San Diego," wearing Bermuda shorts and florid short-sleeve shirts, although it was again a cool day.

Their mean age, he guessed, was around thirty-five, mostly born during World War II, only a few years his senior. Jake thought many of them belonged to a society whose day had passed; he dismissed their generation as the last one that would grow old with the champagne music of Lawrence Welk. He believed the majority had ignored the sixties and were now chiefly motivated by acquisition or greed. Most egregious of all, he concluded that for way too many of these teachers, students were a low priority.

After seeing one man make a spectacle of himself with an oversized souvenir sombrero, Jake looked for Tina at the breakfast tables. He found Armando; the two of them sat through a self-congratulatory keynote address by a man named Muñoz, a high-level bureaucrat in federal education.

Following the speech, Jake spotted Tina in the hall making coffee; he started over to her. She seemed an inch or two shorter than he recalled from the night before, probably about five-five. She wore sleek dark slacks and a different cardigan, this one was pink and buttoned only at the bottom; he couldn't help but notice that her breasts formed a nice taut line in her white blouse. Tina carried an over-the-shoulder purse larger than a grocery sack, printed in three vertical colors—green, red, and yellow, with a yellow star at the middle of the red band.

She doesn't look Amish today. He walked quickly the rest of the way. "Morning, Tina."

She looked up with an unimposing smile, but to him it was radiant. Tina read his badge.

"Morning, Jake. Your last name is Friend?"

He noticed her faintly penciled brows. "Afraid so."

"Is that an unusual name?"

"Not really; I'll tell you its fascinating story tonight when we have some time."

They quickly firmed up their plans to taxi out for seafood, but Jake worried that she sounded unenthused, even for her. He hoped Armando was right, maybe she just didn't like fish; later he could suggest something else. They arranged to meet again during the second break in a room provided for publishers to display their books.

Jake's first session was a mandatory one on Migrant Health, which turned out to be even more of a waste of time than he expected. His book hidden in his conference folder, Jake started to read, chuckling at the story so loud once that the presenter stared him down.

After the hour droned to a close, Jake walked to the coffee tables, hoping to run into Tina. His next session was flexible; he could choose from anything, even Bilingual Special Ed. Jake perused the schedule and looked around for her at the same time, oblivious of the goofy smile on his face. He poured coffee and cheerily greeted a male server, who told him, "I can see, sir, I don't need to wish *you* a happy day."

Embarrassed, he left for a presentation by Armando's favorite teacher at Fresno State. To Jake, Professor Rivera, a small man with a black Wyatt Earp moustache, passionately stated the obvious: "When our kids walk through that

15

door, they bring the language and culture they learned at their mother's breast. Our schools often treat it like a deficit, sometimes even for kids who are literate in their own language. The latest name for this is 'English immersion,' an insidious idea that assumes the brain of a second language learner is *tabula rasa*, a blank slate.

"Immersion is actually the drowning of our students' language, and is taught by many Anglos *and* Latinos. The good news is, I'm about to show you how some English teachers honor the home culture, and I don't mean piñatas and Taco Tuesdays. Now, if I've ruffled any feathers, you're still welcome to stay. Those who can't handle my spiel, I'll make it easy and fix my overhead. Have a nice life." He turned away; three Latinos and four Anglos left the packed room. From Jake's perspective, they missed out on what was the most practical workshop in three conventions.

At the break, Jake was waiting to talk to Rivera when he remembered Tina and hustled downstairs. He saw her on the far side of the room, chatting with Orie and some other women near a publisher's table. Wondering what he might learn by watching her for a moment, Jake stopped.

Tina listened intently or courteously but didn't respond even one time while Jake watched. He noticed the women all had some kind of curled or processed hair while Tina's, now in full light, seemed even more lustrous than the night before. He broke his reverie and approached them.

As he came closer, Jake heard Orie say, "Here's Jake, Tina, you can find out about that session."

He stiffened his face, consciously trying to hide his crush on Tina. "What session?" he asked matter-of-factly, but she reacted with one of her reserved smiles, melting Jake's resolve into a display of all his front teeth. Before Tina could speak, some sort of body language passed from Orie to the others, which sent the women on their way, half of them giggling. Tina blushed as she removed the convention folder from her huge woven purse.

Jake was determined to be more upbeat after his rant about John Wayne. "I like your purse," was all he could come up with.

"Thanks. That lady laughed at it, said it was a 'Hate-Azberry bag.' Do you know what that means?"

"Yeah, Haight-Ashbury's a neighborhood in Frisco. She meant a hippie bag." Jake scowled. "*Pendeja*," he added under his breath.

"What did you call her?"

"Sorry, my L.A. Spanish."

"C'mon, Jake, I need to know the bad words."

"*Pendejo*—uh, pubic hair. It's used like *jerk*, a tad stronger."

16

"Oh," she said in a bland tone. "And, uh, Frisco is San Francisco?"

"Yeah, only in L.A." Jake smiled. "They don't appreciate it up north."

"I see. You must think I'm pretty slow."

"I do not." He didn't disguise very well how much he disagreed. Jake pointed at her purse. "Is that design from an African flag?"

"Yes, Cameroon." Tina looked into her folder. "This is the session, Jake. I think it's one of yours."

Tina moved beside him, pointing at the schedule and accidentally brushing his forearm. The light touch of her soft skin scintillated him like the first time he held hands in junior high; he couldn't focus on the words.

"Which one again?" he asked, sounding annoyed.

"You okay?" Tina answered, touching the page.

Pathetic, Jake. "Yeah, fine. Uh, the NMAS update? Yes, it's mandatory for me—two hours, probably the driest session here. You're going?"

"After reading this, I was hoping they could somehow help me get my student records sooner."

"What?" Jake chuckled. "Oh, *do* come along; you'll never have to waste your time on it again." They walked around scores of educators gabbing at full volume, and then moved down the hall, heading for the staircase to the second floor, where most presentations took place.

Starting up the wide stairs, Jake remembered their earlier chat. "Uh, Tina, do you really like seafood?"

"Yes, but I've already had my quota of fancy restaurants."

"Okay. Maybe we'll just wait until later and see what sounds good." She returned another demure smile, all the answer he needed.

They entered the same room Jake was in earlier for Migrant Health, but the partition was moved to accommodate about thirty rows of the hotel's ubiquitous scarlet red, padded convention chairs—stacked in some rooms up to the low ceilings.

Behind and above the long table at front, there was a ten-foot white plastic banner, professionally produced with an enlarged version of the same colorful logo that graced the convention badges—a family of six light-skinned, grinning Latino farm workers, the parents and two young children in work clothes, proudly holding up green stalks. A male teen stood at one end of the family, a female at the other, each wearing a mortarboard and holding a diploma. Above the logo it read:

NMAS
NATIONAL MIGRANT ARCHIVE SYSTEM
Jacksonville, Florida

Jake led Tina to almost the last row, where they sat and watched a middle-aged black woman in glasses and a red suit pull a screen down over the banner; all you could see then was NATIONAL and SYSTEM. The large room was about a third full, a few stragglers walking in.

"This is the *real* fun part," he said to Tina, who was reading from the ten-page handout. Jake had already skimmed the pages, stuffed them away and was now situating his novel behind the flaps of the convention folder.

In a southern drawl, the presenter asked someone to lower the lights halfway; she turned on her projector and faced the audience. This was the third time Jake had to listen to her. He thought she resembled Shirley Chisholm, the congresswoman who ran for President, but without the smarts.

The lady welcomed them then wasted five minutes saying she only had an hour to cover a lot of material. She pre-scolded everyone and said, " . . . questions are to be saved for the panel in the second hour." Though most of the audience was experienced with migrant forms, she insisted that some changes required a complete review. After she proceeded to remind everyone that a student's last name must be written over "LAST," a few participants began to disappear for feigned potty breaks. Tina turned to him; Jake was even charmed by the slight scowl she made toward the presenter. As the lady from NMAS continued with one inanity after another, Jake opened his book.

"What are you reading?" Tina whispered without looking at him, like a kid cheating on a test.

"*Milagro Beanfield War*," he murmured. "About a guy named Joe Mondragón, and his pinto beans. Hilarious, but it really has—"

"Excuse me, sir," the presenter said. "If you're discussing form Two-B, kindly do it more quietly or wait for the panel." Several severe faces turned back to Jake.

"Oh, sorry, right, I'll do that." He grinned to Tina. She propped the conference folder on her lap and extracted needles and yarn from her purse. Tina shrugged and started crocheting; Jake went back to his book, thinking about her; it took minutes for the words on the page to mean anything.

During the break, he answered a couple questions that Tina had about the forms. After a bathroom visit, they returned to the room five minutes late for the second hour. The NMAS banner was visible again; most of the audience was back from the first hour along with some new people, including a cosmopolitan-looking group of NMAS officials settling in behind the front table, all of them in suits.

A tall man at the podium said he was Manuel Barajas, Director of California NMAS. Jake thought he could pass for a Mormon missionary in his crew

18

cut, dark suit, black tie and white socks. The man thanked the Shirley Chisholm look-alike; Jake knew they had heard the last from her. Barajas welcomed the panel: two Hispanic men and two women, one Asian and one Anglo. After the first three panelists explained their roles in California, the fourth, a chalky-faced woman whose husky frame strained the seams of her fastidious brown suit, said she was Ida Swanson, the National Director of NMAS from Jacksonville.

Tina took out a spiral notebook, looking surprised that Jake was attentive to the panel.

"Let's see if anyone asks a real question," he whispered to her. The director concisely answered three inquiries about the migrant forms; not even pretending that her assistant had adequately explained the same topics in the first hour. Jake shook his head, then occupied himself by doodling and re-tracing a short phrase on his folder.

Two rows away, a tall, bearded man in a tweedy sport coat raised his hand and stood, identifying himself as an administrator from the Imperial Valley. "My question is also for Ms. Swanson," he said. "NMAS has been up and running now a few years; when do you expect the system will be of any *real* use for teachers who work with migrant students?" Jake saw some of the audience turn and sneer at Imperial Valley as if he had crashed a party. Jake and a couple others lightly applauded in support of the question. Eyes open wide, Tina looked around, gauging the friction in the room as Ida Swanson cleared her throat to answer.

"Thank you for the question," Ida said over her glasses, folds forming in her chubby neck. "Since you've already decided that the system is useless, sir, please tell me what doesn't work."

"Nothing works," he said, "and the fact that you don't know, speaks volumes." In response to the man's criticism, grumbles rippled across the audience.

Ida Swanson smirked, knowing she had the support of most of those present. "Since you offer no specifics, sir, is there anyone here who can explain how *nothing* works with NMAS?" A wave of sniggers passed through the room as the educators looked around for someone foolish enough to disparage the agency that paid part of their salaries. No one spoke up right away, but as Swanson looked like she was about to go on, Jake got to his feet.

"Yes, sir," she said confidently, assuming Jake would start a new topic. "Your question, please?"

"The same as his; I'll give you some specifics. My name's Jake Friend, I teach in Orange County; this is my third year of watching your records fill up our file cabinets. They arrive a month to six months after the students, if they come at all. The records that do show up are blank, inaccurate or out-of-date—to put it plainly, useless."

"With all due respect," Ida countered, "I believe you're exaggerating, sir. In fact, our main goal this year is to improve outgoing data by holding nationwide in-services to help schools send out information properly."

Jake was shaking his head. "Yeah, you sent one of our elementary school secretaries to L.A."

"Yes, she will need to share the information with the other secretaries. As you know, her main job is to get educational information from teachers, combine it with health and other student data, and then send it off to us."

"No, her *main* job is to run a school, and mine is to teach. If the day comes when migrant teachers in Texas and California can directly exchange useful information, we'll have something. Until then, you and your bureaucrats have job security."

"I assure you, we are dedicated to improving NMAS. After all, uh, Mister *Friend*," she smirked again, "we don't want *enemies* in the classrooms."

The jibe at the expense of Jake's surname brought appreciative chuckles from much of the audience, deflating some of the tension.

"Very funny," he said, then paused; the group hushed. "You know, Ms. Swanson, laughter is a great thing unless you use it to hide your real problems." Jake sat down, his arm shaking a little after the adrenaline rush from confronting so many people. As if nothing had happened, a woman stood to ask about NMAS health codes. When Barajas fielded the question, Jake saw Imperial Valley and three others head for the doors.

For the second time in half a day, Tina had been off Jake's mind. He turned and couldn't figure out her blank expression. *Maybe the conflict upset her; that's understandable. What if she disapproves of me hassling them? That'd be too damned bad. See what she does.*

He nudged her arm, showing Tina the retraced doodle he made: SO, IDA, ADIOS. "As usual, this is a waste of time," he said not very quietly and got to his feet. "I'm going." *What about you?*

Not hesitating, Tina stood up and stuffed her notebook and conference folder into the large purse. She turned to him resolutely and they left, Jake grinning at her seriousness. As soon as they were in the hall, she raised her eyebrows and quietly said, "Yes, it was a waste, but you were wrong about one thing—that last part wasn't boring at all."

3

The mayor hailed an officer who had just exited the driver's side of the old Ford in front of the Corvette. In a tan uniform, sunglasses, but no hat, the trim Latino cop walked up to Jake and put a hand on his shoulder. "How's the new dad, maestro?" he said, and then faced the mayor. "What can I do for you, sir?"

The mayor eyed the officer suspiciously. "Sergeant, this man seems to be bothering the doctor."

Limping up from behind in a formal uniform, a thin, graying policeman with sunburned cheeks overheard the mayor's complaint before the sergeant turned back to Jake. "Uh, Mister Friend, so what's going on here?" the younger cop asked in a more official tone.

"I was asking the doctor to come to the hospital. Our baby's sick, Jesús."

"Sorry to hear that," the sergeant said, his face turning grave. He looked at the mayor. "Sir, Mister Friend here is my neighbor; his wife was my kid's teacher. I'm sure if he says—"

"I'll take over here, sergeant," the frail senior officer interrupted. Jesús backed off just enough to avoid insubordination.

"Captain LeBlanc," the mayor said with a huff, "this man—"

"Yes, sir, I already heard." The captain looked across the car to Jake. "I'll need your license, sir."

"License, what for?"

"A stop sign and speeding, and I have a question about that green truck of yours." He started to hobble around the front of the Corvette.

Shit. Jake felt all his pockets. *Double shit.* "Uh, sorry, officer," he called as Le Blanc approached. "My wallet's in the truck."

The captain shuffled up to him. "Of course."

"Look," Jake pleaded, "I'll bring my wallet and pay the tickets right after the doctor sees our baby. Sergeant Ramos will vouch for me." He turned to Jesús, who nodded to his boss.

21

"Is this an emergency or not, doc?" the captain asked, looking down into the convertible.

Serna scoffed. "It certainly is not, captain."

"I see." Leblanc raised his white eyebrows. "This is the same guy Corporal Sanchez saw at your house."

Serna grinned confidently. "Yes, I know."

"I left when I was told to," Jake said, grumbling.

"Whitey," Serna said with a put-on magnanimous smile, "Mister Friend here got anxious about his baby; happens all the time. He just needs to leave; you can forget about the business at my house."

"Whatever you say." Leblanc turned to Jake. "You still get the traffic tickets. By the way, who was that Mexican kid in your truck?"

Damn. "Just one of my students."

Leblanc sneered doubtfully. "Bring your registration and driver's license over to me, sir." He pointed back at his light blue squad car, idling near the fire engine.

"Fine." Jake jogged down the line and around some Brownies who were complaining about the dirty hay wagon. He slipped on the gravel, slamming a knee into the Nash Metropolitan's headlight as the blue clown started the motor, frowning at Jake through his painted-on happy face.

He limped on, hurrying by the last tractor, its engine also starting up. The pain in his leg subsided, and Jake ran faster past the community float before scrambling into the front of his truck, sweat stinging him in one eye. The wallet wasn't there; Jake searched the glove compartment and all the crevices, scratching his arm when he groped into the springs under the seat. "Piss up a rope!" he yelled loud enough that Miss La Cholla heard the oath and wrinkled her bulbous nose. Jake got out, slamming the back door as the band struck up some George M. Cohan, and the parade started to move.

Enough screwing around, find the old doctor. He got behind the wheel, started the engine and inched away from all the hubbub in first gear. Drying his perspiring face with the cleaner side of a filthy oil rag, Jake came to the end of the block and saw police lights flashing far behind. He turned left, "gunned" his weak motor, and made for the top of the hill.

He'll catch you—won't help the baby if you're arrested. Come up with something, quick. Let's see, uh, captain—crap, you better stop. In his rearview mirror, Jake saw the blue squad car start up the hill, but the flashers went off as it approached. Jake took a left at a side street and pulled over just beyond the first small frame house. The La Cholla P.D. squad car made the turn and parked about twenty feet behind him in direct sunlight. Because of the glare, Jake couldn't even see the captain, who stayed in the car.

Doing his cop stuff on the radio; you have to wait. Damn, how the hell did it come to all this?

Jake and Tina came to the stairs and started down.

"We have some time before lunch, Tina; I have at least two questions I'd like to get off my chest."

"I have one, too. What's with *So, Ida, Adios*?"

"It's a palindrome, the same both ways."

"S-O-I-D-A-A . . . " She stopped spelling aloud. "Hm, right. We did them in freshman English, like *radar*."

"Or Hannah, my sister's name; she's really into them. Last year at NMAS, some other bored guy showed me *So, Ida, Adios*—it was the highlight of the morning."

"I can see how it was," she said, stepping off the last stair with him. "Okay, Jake, your two questions. The first one's Africa, right?"

He grinned at her as they started across the busy lobby. "I take it you get that one a lot?"

"Yes, but I can't guess your other one."

"Spanish, how you learned it over there." Jake figured that Tina wouldn't talk much until they had some privacy. They entered the main room; only a few people waited for lunch while a squad of mostly Latino workers in kitchen whites arranged hundreds of place settings on crimson tablecloths. Tina and Jake sat at a table for ten; he looked around the room, recalling that he chatted in Spanish with the crews from the previous conferences. Jake wondered how many of the same workers were still there.

"The people we serve, serving us," Tina said.

He turned to her. "Yeah, that's right. Are you trying to get me talking?" He wagged his finger a little bit. "Uh-uh, Christina, I'm waiting for *you* to begin."

"I actually don't use Christina much."

"Oh? Why is that?"

"My mother wanted Jesus in my name one way or the other. Now just she and the government insist on it."

"Keep Christ in Christina."

"Right. My big brother, Jimmy, told me that my dad called me Chrissy when I was a baby; she'd have none of it. Around Mom, my brother is James, like the disciple."

23

"That sounds, uh, pretty hard line."

"Yes, that's my mom." She explained that her mother came from farm country north of San Francisco; her father, who had passed away, was from southwest Oregon. Tina said that all her ancestors were from northern Europe. She sighed. "My mom and dad were missionaries."

Man, Amish wasn't far off. Trying not to show any dismay over her religious background, Jake said, "So now I know why you were in Africa; what about *where* you were, and the Spanish?"

Tina told him that she and her brother grew up with a fondness for the forests and fields near their town in southern Cameroon. They learned a Bantu dialect from the other children and sometimes got in trouble with her mother after playing for hours with the kids on the cassava, cacao and yam farms. Her father, under the guise of keeping them out of mischief, would often make a case for bringing Christina and James along to the outlying villages to help with his community development projects.

At each transition in her narrative, Tina paused, her body language communicating, *Is that enough?* Jake would just smile and say, "Go on," or prompt her with a question. As she continued, Jake felt privileged to listen because he was sure it was unusual for Tina to talk about herself. He also wasn't surprised by her succinct but thoughtful explanations; Jake had already attributed the old saying, *still waters run deep*, to Tina Linn.

She told him that she attended an international high school in Yaounde, the Cameroon capital, and was entranced by an island, Fernando Po, twenty-five miles off the coast. Po was part of Equatorial Guinea, the tiny country below Cameroon, which was called Spanish Guinea before gaining independence from Spain in 1968.

"There's a Spanish-speaking country in Africa?" Jake asked, a bit ashamed that this was news to him. She spoke fondly of the Equatogineans living in Malabo, a town of less than fifty thousand on Fernando Po. Malabo was the nation's capital, though mainland Equatorial Guinea was ten times larger than the small island.

"You won't believe this." Tina put her hand to her mouth as if to share something risqué. "The island is named after a Portuguese explorer, *Fernao do Poo.*"

"Poo? You're kidding."

"I told you." Tina chuckled slightly. "The Spanish changed it to *Fernando Po*, but the government is talking about changing it again." She saw Jake raise a brow. "No," she quickly added, "not back to *Poo.*"

Tina had actually grinned a little; he counted it as her third or fourth smile of the morning. Jake was charmed again, wishing she'd talk all day. "Go on, you're not even out of high school yet."

She resumed the scanty, low-key autobiography and told him that during vacations she visited the beaches near Malabo with some other girls. Tina became involved with the people there and was fascinated by their languages, which included Spanish, a pidgin English, French, and some Bantu dialects. She switched from French to Spanish in school, and during summer volunteered to teach English classes in Malabo for the Catholic Church. Then, at her small college in the hills of Kentucky, she majored in Special Ed. and minored in Spanish. Despite protests from her Protestant mother, Tina went back to Malabo to teach English with the Catholics.

"So, what brought you here?" Jake asked as a few more hungry conventioneers filed in. Tina said she had only been teaching a year in Malabo when the nation's ruler declared himself President-for-Life, beginning a brutal dictatorship. Not long after that, her father, diagnosed with advanced prostate cancer, came back with Mrs. Linn to the university hospital in Eugene, Oregon. Tina returned to help out; he died soon afterwards. After helping her mother move back to northern California, Tina applied in Visalia, the closest job opening in Bilingual Special Ed.

Jake stumbled through condolences for her father's death and began a convoluted inquiry about Tina's uneven awareness of U.S. culture. He stopped when the hall became raucous with herds of nattering educators, many of them playing a game of *Where should we sit?*

Tina tried to speak over the din. "Your two questions are up." Her mouth formed a slit of a smile. "When do I hear your story?"

He didn't try to answer as the workers pulled back some dividers to expose more tables, already set. They opened a nearby curtain to reveal two long tables on a platform, the place for the bigshots to eat. The room transformed so quickly that Jake and Tina sat there, wide-eyed for several moments, taking it all in.

A large group of women from Bakersfield descended on the couple to claim the eight open seats. A teacher in matronly glasses turned to a cluster of her cronies. "I see some chairs over there, Rhonda," she called, ignoring Tina and Jake as she and the others sat down.

"We're right near the front," Jake said. "Shall we make these ladies happy and join the wallflowers?"

"Yes, let's." Tina stood up. "Your story tonight," she murmured to him as they walked away.

Jake heard the Bakersfield teacher shout, "Rhonda, there's two seats over here now!"

While they ate, Tina and Jake listened to a man explain how he had his students using cameras for language arts. Three women at the table criticized the concept as "too wild." Tina whispered to Jake that they were ganging up on the teacher and his good ideas. When she didn't speak up, Jake said to the man, "Well, both of us like your approach," and then turned to Tina, who quietly defended the camera enthusiast by explaining a similar method she used.

One skeptic stopped the discussion by declaring lunch was over, but Tina and Jake chatted with the man for a few more minutes. They thanked him and walked out to the bustling hallway, stopping between the elevator doors and the stairs, where it wasn't so noisy.

"Tina, are you upset with me for goading you into coming to that guy's rescue?"

"No, I'm glad you did. They were so narrow-minded."

"I was impressed by your argument. Where did you come up with using a portable TV camera?"

"One of my profs recorded our teaching; I learned how to use the equipment. I use it with my kids a couple times a month." She raised her brows. "Thanks to that teacher, now I have some more ideas."

"Your classroom must be a trip, Ms. Linn," he said, smiling. "Very liberated of you."

She scoffed. "Right, that's me—Ms. liberated."

"You are; you try new ideas." He paused. "Tina, it was really hard for you to speak up like that, wasn't it?"

Tina sighed. "You can't imagine." She turned away. "Jake, I need to go upstairs before the next session."

As they headed for the elevator doors, he decided not to pursue the shyness question. "What do you have this afternoon, Tina?"

"Two special eds. You?"

"Another NMAS, if you can believe it, and one open."

Tina looked at him, almost glum. "Uh, in that kind of situation," she glanced back to where they ate, "I get extremely nervous. It's different with my students—we're sort of on the same level."

"Wait a sec, I don't buy that last part," he said, unintentionally brusque, just as the elevator chimed.

"That's me, Jake."

It wasn't clear to him if she was referring to herself or the elevator. "Sorry, Tina, I didn't mean to be pushy."

"You weren't. See you at six." She entered with three others, turned around and lowered her chin.

To Jake, she seemed downcast. *Your fault, klutz.* The door closed; he opened his folder, but the page seemed blank for several seconds.

Jake spotted Rivera's name and decided he couldn't stomach another dose of NMAS, so he went down the hall to a panel discussion on "National Goals." Large enough for a hundred people, the room was only a third occupied, not half the number of participants who crammed into Rivera's earlier session. There were eight on the panel, six administrators and two teachers—Professor Rivera and a male P.E. specialist from San Diego named Acevedo.

While the officials commented on the first educational goal, Jake scolded himself for how he spoke to Tina, worrying he might have blown his chances with her.

Up front, they asked the P.E. teacher to respond to the goal. He smiled and said, "Yes, I think it's very good; after all, the kids are our future." Rivera had his turn and offered four clear and sensible reasons why the goal was nonsense. The panel, looking as if they had soiled their drawers, mostly ignored the professor after that.

Disgusted after a half hour, Jake left for the elevator. He got his jacket from the room, went out and walked around the city, releasing some of his hostility for the convention. He stopped at a tavern for a couple of beers and started anguishing about Tina, wondering if Armando was actually right about her being "into" him. Jake returned to the room, rested a while and showered.

Not wanting to arrive too early and too dressed up for their date, he walked out of the elevator at five fifty-five wearing a fresh long-sleeve yellow shirt, his Cubs cap, an unlined navy blue windbreaker, and the same jeans and sturdy shoes.

They had planned to meet at the gift shop; he ambled over there and noticed some pastel plastic eggs with hotel logos, interspersed now between the tiny U.S. flags.

Have your Easter cake and eat the Bicentennial too. Enough, Mister Sarcasm. Someone tapped him on the shoulder; he turned and saw Tina frowning a little at the mixed decorations.

"Pretty tacky," she said.

Jake chuckled. "Yeah." *God, she looks great.*

4

L ike Jake, Tina was more prepared for an outing than a restaurant. She wore a long wool poncho woven in rich shades of brown; Jake thought it complemented her dark eyes and shimmering hair. The heavy wrap covered Tina's small frame nearly to her ankles, where he saw low-cut sneakers and the cuffs of tapered blue jeans. Her hand escaped the thick material at one side, holding a small, colorfully beaded purse.

"Nice, uh, poncho," he said.

"They called it a *gabán* in Tijuana; smallest one they had in these colors." She sounded apologetic. "Orie told me I really am into the hippie look."

"Her too?"

"She meant it nicely."

"Well, it works for you," he said, but she looked down. *Don't embarrass her, putz.* "Tina, what sounds good to eat?"

She raised her chin. "I'm not very hungry yet. You?"

"After all the junk I ate today, not really."

"Do you want to go for a walk?"

"Sure, where?"

"The ocean?"

"Great. Let's find a taxi."

"Do we need one?"

"We could walk to the bay, but the ocean's too far."

"What's the bay like?"

"More city; a lot of boats, docks, military stuff, but there are places to eat."

"Oh," she replied neutrally, but Jake thought she was unimpressed by that option.

"Okay," he said, "*el Océano Pacífico* it is. There should be taxis out front."

They left the lobby and Jake waved at a solitary lime green cab in the taxi zone. Jake zipped up his thin coat as they waited at the curb, facing an office

28

building. Regardless of San Diego's tropical reputation, the night was chilly, the overcast again threatening to descend as fog.

"Hi," Jake said to the driver as Tina climbed into the back of the sedan. "We'd like to get to the ocean, not the bay, with maybe a restaurant within walking distance."

"See what I can do," the cabby said with a faint southern accent. About Jake's age, the thin man had angry pimples on his chin, a sunburned left arm, and he wore a faded black and red letterman's coat with his new Dodger's cap.

Jake settled on the bench seat a foot or so from Tina. *Geez, should I touch her? Don't force it, Romeo.*

The driver exited and spoke loudly before Jake could say anything to Tina. "So you like the Cubs? When's the last time they won it all?" He turned the dispatch radio and music down low.

"O-eight; they lost it in forty-five," Jake called to him. "Then Durocher's four good years."

"And now they stink again."

"Yeah, afraid so. So you like the Bums?"

"They ain't bums no more."

"Except to the A's."

"Yeah, but Sutton beat 'em once. Like to see that Reuschel from your Cubs throw for L.A."

Jake laughed. "No way." He turned to Tina. In the uneven glow from the lights outside, she shrugged as if she had been listening to gibberish.

"Baseball talk—sorry," Jake said to her in a much lower tone; the driver attended to the traffic.

"It's okay." She glanced at his blue cap. "Where did he say that your team is from?"

"I don't think he did; you are priceless." Jake smiled, touching his hat. "The Chicago Cubs."

"But you're from Los Angeles."

"Just one of legions of Dodger haters."

"Why?"

"Okay, you asked," he warned. "Near to where I grew up, there was a settled community of Mexican immigrants in this big pastoral area right in the middle of L.A.—truck farms, sheep, the whole deal. The city cleared out most of them for urban renewal, and then they sold the land to the Dodgers. A lot of people despise them for that."

"Including you."

"Yes, and I have another reason. My heroes played for the L.A. Angels in

29

the minor leagues. When the Dodgers came from New York, some of my favorite players moved up to the Cubs; I stayed with them and the team ever since. The Bums still get my money; nothing better than watching the Cubs beat L.A. in person." Jake smirked after he said those last few words loud enough so the cabby would hear.

"Believe it or not," Tina said, "I know somebody else who doesn't like the Dodgers."

"Really, who?"

"My brother; he lives in New York."

"Please tell me he's not a Yankee fan."

"No, he likes some other team."

"The Mets. Yup, a lot of their fans hate the Dodgers for leaving."

"Hey, sorry to interrupt all this Dodger hating," the driver called back with a grin. "I'm heading for the public beaches north of town, but I don't think there's any place to eat close by."

"If there's a pay phone, we can ride back later to eat," Jake told him, looking to Tina to see if she agreed.

"They have a phone there," the driver answered.

"Jake," Tina said, "we could just pick up a sandwich."

"You sure?" Her suggestion gave him an inspiration. "Let's have a picnic."

"Really?" she asked, her brows raised.

"Yeah, I used to do this with my parents." He looked up at the driver, raising his voice. "Uh, we just need five minutes at a market—any market. Okay?"

"Sure, I'll find you one." He turned his music higher to give them some privacy.

"Okay," Tina said, "while he's looking, it's your turn to start. So you're the youngest in your family, too?"

"Yeah, afraid so. I was such a butterball that the sisters called me Baby Huey." He groaned. "Still call me Huey."

Jake explained the plump comic book character, then told her a little about "the sisters," as he sometimes referred to them, who all lived within fifty miles of Los Angeles. Caroline, the youngest, was a married biology teacher, no kids; then Hannah, an injury lawyer and single. The oldest, Joyce, was a suburban mom who made her siblings into an aunt or uncle four times over. "They're stinkers, but pretty good little stinkers," he said.

Tina grinned. "Does Uncle Jake see them a lot?"

"Unc, that's what they call me; I see them when I can." *Is this a test?*

"Why, Tina?"

She thought a moment. "Um, I don't know. Was I too personal?"

Paranoid, Jake. "No, not at all."

"When you mentioned Hannah's work, you frowned."

"Man, I'm *that* easy to read?" He sighed. "Hannah's partner sued my mom's hospital for negligence; it's hung up in the system. She died four years ago, when I was still at home; I'm supposed to be a witness. I hate the whole damn thing, but Hannah will never let it go." Jake turned away and watched the blur of lights come into focus as the taxi slowed in front of NACHO'S DELI-MART/GAS.

The cabby lowered the music again. "This place handle it for you?"

"This'll be fine," Jake told him.

"Okay, say hi to Nacho," he said, parking by a red air dispenser. Jake and Tina got out; the driver was already loosening the little black cap on a front tire.

"My parents called this a 'sperm picnic,'" Jake told Tina as he shoved the heavy door open.

She raised her faintly lined brows. "What?"

Jake chuckled. "I'll explain later." He saw right away that the grocery was more of a deli than he expected. There were two employees, a Latino couple in their thirties. The short, bulky dark-haired mom waited at the register, bright piñatas over her head. A baby slept in a crib behind her, cocooned in blankets.

In a stained butcher's apron, a heavy man about five-eight with a trimmed black moustache worked behind a long counter. It doubled as a display case with loaves of wheat, white, and rye on top. Behind the glass, Jake saw a gastronomical meeting of cultures—from roast beef to chorizo, sharp cheese to headcheese, and potato salad to pico de gallo. Three pots steamed away on a stove below a wall menu listing burritos, deli sandwiches, and hoagies. The burritos were available in REGULAR or GRANDE, and with BERTA'S HOMEMADE FLOUR TORTILLAS.

A tall black man waited for an order while his young daughter perused the candy by the register. The proprietor handed a bulging brown sack over the counter, grease marks streaking the paper. "Okay, CJ, enjoy; you have a good evening," he said with no accent.

"You too, Nacho," the customer answered, starting over to the woman at the cash register.

Jake turned to Tina. "What looks good to you?"

"Not sure—whatever you have."

"How're you tonight?" Nacho asked them with a broad smile.

"Fine, thanks," Jake answered. "Our taxi driver said to say hello."

"Oh, green or yellow taxi?"

"Green."

"Max." Nacho chortled around a twitch of his moustache. "He was here for lunch; but say hi back. What can I get for you folks?"

"Uh, we'll have two chicken burritos, grandes. And a pint of fruit, the *pico de gallo*."

"You said that good." Nacho turned to stir a pot, still looking at Jake. "*¿Hablas español?*"

"*Más o menos, señor.*"

"Okay then, you want them *norteamericano, mediano, o picante?*"

Jake looked at Tina. "*¿Mediano?*"

She nodded. "*Por favor.*"

"*¿Tú hablas español también, señora?*" the storekeeper asked.

"*Sí, señor,*" Tina answered quietly.

"Well, I'll be." Grinning, Nacho looked over at his wife as he began preparing the food. "*Berta, the redhead and blonde speak the language,*" he yelled in Spanish.

"And they understand, Ignacio," she called back in English with a heavy accent, tsking.

Nacho winced. "Sorry, didn't mean nothin'. You guys teachers?"

"It's that obvious?" Jake replied with a laugh.

"No, no, no." As he worked, Nacho asked about what they taught and where they learned Spanish. Tina watched Jake explain a little about their backgrounds.

"*¿Sí, señora?*" Nacho said to Tina. "I didn't know there's a country in Africa where they speak Spanish."

When Tina just nodded again, Jake said, "Yeah, me either."

"Well, good for you two; good for you." Nacho's smile beamed with satisfaction as he put a sack on the counter. "Anything else you need?" he asked Jake.

"Uh, if you don't mind, we're going to eat picnic style. Maybe a couple plastic spoons—"

"Get you all set up." Nacho disappeared below.

Jake turned to Tina, raising his brows. "All set up, señora," he said softly, emphasizing 'señora.'

"Very funny," she whispered. "He's so nice."

"Yeah." Jake turned to the grocery aisles. "Let's see, it's traditional to have beer, cocktail peanuts, molasses cookies, and baloney; we'll pass on the baloney." He began to walk away. "Tina, unless you want a beer, choose something to drink, okay?"

Jake returned after a few minutes with his items as Nacho put another sack on the counter by a bottle of juice Tina had left there. Jake peeked into the non-food bag and found paper plates and cups, plastic utensils, napkins, and condiment packets.

"Uh, thank you very much, Nacho. By the way, I'm Jake; this is Tina."

"Good to meet you; come by whenever you're in town," he said with another wide grin. "You two enjoy your dinner."

After Tina left Nacho one of her reserved smiles, they carried everything over to the register. Berta had a sack open; Jake took a twenty from his wallet and handed it across to her after she finished packing the hot food, beer, juice, nuts and cookies.

"You pay only the grocery," she said.

"What do you mean?" Jake asked.

"Ignacio, he likes somebody, first time free. *¿Loco, no?* But they come in always to talk and buy gum, maybe eat." She gave him his change.

Jake held the money. "But we don't even live here."

Berta smiled. "Please enjoy the food."

"Okay, if you're sure." Jake picked up the large sack, Tina the picnic supplies; they turned to thank Nacho, but he was gone into a back room. They thanked Berta in Spanish and went out to the cab.

"Depending on traffic, maybe ten minutes to the beach," the driver shouted back as they settled in.

"Thanks, no hurry. Nacho said hi, Max."

"Nacho and Bertha's good people." He drove out the driveway, raising the radio volume again.

Jake turned to Tina. "Well, that was something."

"We could find them tomorrow to uh, 'talk and buy gum.'"

"Yeah. Maybe we can find something for our kids."

"Good idea." She glanced out where the tall buildings had given way mostly to one-story businesses and stucco apartments. "Okay, so your parents always had peanuts, cookies and baloney for these picnics?"

"That's what *I* ate; maybe some fruit. For them it was mostly deli stuff—blue cheese, dill pickles, sardines, liverwurst, onions, salami, even pickled pig's feet, for God's sake. They'd spread all this gross food out on paper plates like it was a smorgasbord; make sandwiches on crackers or rye, and wash it down with Regal Lager, their favorite beer. Oh, Regal Lager is another palindrome Hannah discovered."

". . . L-L-A-G-E-R," she said, finishing her thought aloud. "Glory, it sure is."

"Anyway, they'd buy the quart bottle and pour it like fancy champagne into those little glasses that cheese comes in. He was a drinker, but not an alky like most of his family. Mom kept a small suitcase in the car's trunk; it just had a blanket in it, those glasses, a paring knife and a can opener; everything else came from the grocery." Jake saw the cabby turn onto the freeway toward Los Angeles.

"So why was it, uh, a *sperm* picnic?"

"Ah, yes." Jake snickered, guessing that Tina's cheeks blushed in the near darkness. "There's a five-year gap between Caroline and me, so when she started dating, my parents hauled me along on all their weekend trips." He paused, turning more solemn.

"They died in sixty-nine and seventy-one, but they did something great, as if they knew they'd never retire. They took all their vacation; get this, and drove a Ford station wagon to Mexico City. Two years later, they took that same jalopy to Banff in Canada."

"It's wonderful they thought to do that."

"Yeah. They didn't have an L.A.-New York mentality like they lived at the hub of the world." Jake paused again. "Sorry, I got off the subject."

"It's okay; this is interesting."

"If you say so. Anyway, they knew every place within a day's drive that was the *opposite* of L.A.—ghost towns, apple orchards, small villages, Death Valley, Lake Arrowhead, and, of course, the ocean, but always at sunset after everybody was gone."

He mused a few seconds then chuckled. "Okay, so one Sunday, I was maybe ten, we took off in the car for the mountains and I asked if we'd be eating at a restaurant or if it would just be 'sperm of the moment' again at some grocery—" He stopped when Tina put a hand over her mouth, covering the first full smile he had seen from her.

"Sorry, you were so serious, then—" She tried to constrain herself, her eyes squinting with the effort, but she burst into laughter.

"Glad you think it's so funny," he said, pretending umbrage but delighting in her unexpected gaiety. "Anyway, after *they* stopped laughing, Mom explained the difference between spur and sperm." He saw Tina muffle her chortles behind both hands. "So, it became 'sperm of the moment' picnics, then 'sperm picnics.'"

Tina practically hooted then pulled a tissue out of her small purse, still laughing. "Okay, I get it." She dabbed some tears. "Don't say it again, okay?"

Jake smiled. "Sperm picnics?"

"That's not funny," she said, catching her breath.

"I didn't know you could laugh like this."

34

She glanced at the driver, who was dutifully ignoring them. "Well, now you know; it's embarrassing."

"No, it's great."

"Doesn't happen often; I don't control it very well." She exhaled loudly. "Just a minute, please." She made a final titter and looked out at the lights streaking by. "All right, I'm over it." Still grinning a little, Tina kept looking out of the window.

Jake leaned across, his shoulder against hers, craning his neck to see a billboard: COMING SOON – EL DORADO VISTA – OCEAN VIEW COLONIALS – $79,995 AND UP. He sat up, their arms still touching; he noticed Tina didn't move away.

"One of our rides," he said, "was down to San Juan Capistrano then here to my cousin's. Back then, L.A. to San Diego was orchards, countryside, and beaches. Won't be long before the Marine base will be the only land left."

"That's a shame. I've missed the ocean so much; I'm so glad we did this." In the flashes of light, he saw she was somber again. "Jake, you told Nacho you learned some Spanish in Mexico and Costa Rica. Traveling?"

"Some, and I was in school in Mexico City for a summer. After I finished my B.A., I tried to do my bit in the Peace Corps, remembering JFK and all that. I was in Texas, then Costa Rica; came home in six months with, uh, humiliating stomach problems. Then I took my fifth year and student teaching; the rest is pedagogical history."

"I want to hear about your teaching and your travels, but do you mind telling me how your parents died?"

An inch or so away from her, he sighed. "Well, you're no stranger to cancer. My parents died two years apart of the same kind, not isolated; they had it all over."

"I'm sorry, Jake. Losing them so close together must have been really hard."

"Yeah. When Mom got it, we knew the score from Dad; Hannah was on the doctors, but I tend to blame L.A. and the damn cigarettes. Smoked into their forties before they quit, and they breathed the crappy air every day, driving to that airplane plant where they worked. They joked that they left town so much just to breathe all the way in."

"Is that partly why you live in Orange County?"

"I guess, but it's just as bad."

"Where would you like to live?"

He combined a scoff with a chuckle. "Oh, I guess a town with a strong sense of community, but spread out and close to some wilderness. To make it a total pipe dream, a place with some tolerance for individual differences."

"I don't think that's so unreasonable. Where would you look?"

"I'm thinking about the Southwest. Plenty of work there, and I like the whole idea of trying out a place for a few years then moving on—kind of a benefit of teaching."

"You also seem pretty dedicated to your work."

"Yeah, so do you, Ms. Linn," he said, grinning. "I do have, uh, a hobby—I write some short stories and verse."

"Really? Then why not teach creative writing?"

"Maybe after I feel like I know what I'm doing. I'll stick with practical writing for now."

"I think you probably have a passion for both writing and teaching, like your father's acting."

He scoffed quietly. "Maybe so."

"Can you tell me more about him?"

"Okay." Jake paused. "Dad's stage name was Jake Dylan; he was into Dylan Thomas. Ergo, my full name—Jake Dylan Friend." He told Tina about a favorite photo of his father and an actress mugging toward baby Jake, used as a stage prop, sitting on a table in diapers and laughing. Jake went on to tell her a little more about his father's acting.

"It must have been fun to be around all that," Tina said. "Is your name Jacob on your birth certificate?"

"Nope, just plain Jake, like it's all *jake* with me."

"What?"

"It means *okay*. One of my dad's old expressions."

"And Friend? It sounds like Quakers."

Jake saw the cabby head for a freeway exit. "Not quite. William Friend, his real name, was raised a Mormon in Cedar City, Utah. My grandparents were Welsh-Irish jack Mormons; the only thing they did that pleased the church was to have six kids. Anyway, during the Depression they moved to L.A. and got lost in the crowd."

"What about your mother?"

"Would you believe her name was Rose Pearlman?"

"Jewish?"

"Yup, and from New Jersey, but not a practicing Jew; though she did speak fluent Yiddish."

"And what about you?"

"I know maybe thirty or forty words."

"I guess I meant the religion."

Jake sniggered. "A gentile-gentile; Mormons and Jews use the same word.

36

I'm just one of the multitudes of half-Jewish agnostics. Does that bother you?"

"No. Tell me more about your mother."

Pleased that his lack of religion didn't seem to be a problem, he described the trouble Rose had when she married William Friend, who was as goy as they come. Rose was ostracized for years by her own mother, Jake's grandma, who actually refused to hold their firstborn, Joyce.

Jake explained that Rose Friend's refuge was her own art, which fit perfectly with the traveling she did with William. An avid amateur photographer, she had her own dark room and specialized in natural scenery.

"Okay," Jake said, "now I think you know way more about my family. What about your mom? It doesn't sound like you two get along so great."

Tina had turned to look out. "Jake, I think we're getting close to the beach."

Man, she cut that off fast.

5

In the rearview mirror of his truck, Jake saw the door of the La Cholla P.D. squad car open, but Jesús got out, not Captain LeBlanc. *Thank God.* Jake put his left arm on the sill and watched him come to the window.

"What the hell happened to you?" Jesús pointed at Jake's arm.

He looked down to see coagulated blood smeared all over his left bicep, some of it stained into the sleeve of his summer shirt. "Guess I scratched it under the seat, searching for my wallet; looks worse than it is."

"If you say so. You find the wallet, Jake?"

"No."

"Jesus. Well, I'm glad you stopped when you did or you'd be in some real trouble."

"I was going to tell LeBlanc the parade was in my way; truth is—"

"Save it. Lucky for you, he's heading south in the old Ford."

"So now what? I've got to get to the hospital."

Jesús pushed his sunglasses up to his forehead; his dark eyebrows furrowed with concern. "What's wrong with the baby, Jake?"

"She's breathing too fast. Serna and the nurses say it's 'high-normal,' some such crap. They think we're troublemakers."

"You and Tina?"

"And María Juana."

Jesús winced. "Not good, she's usually right about these things, even if some of the hospital staff won't admit it. What are your options?"

"Old Doctor McNally, I guess."

"I doubt he's here. What about the university?"

"I'd have to do paperwork, get an ambulance; I'm not sure there's time for all that—I don't know. For starters, I just need to get back there."

"Take you forever in the truck. C'mon, hop in."

"Your car?"

"Can't have you driving around without a license. Let's go." Jesús turned around; Jake jumped out and ran to catch up with him.

"You know what the locals call María?" Jesús asked as they opened the doors of the idling squad car.

"*Curandera?*"

They got into the cool interior and put on their seatbelts. "No, she's not much into herbs, potions and all that." Jesús put the transmission in gear. "They call her *la vigilante*, because she watches over all the babies." As he drove away, Jesús reported on the radio, then hit the siren.

Unaccustomed to the speed, Jake held on tight going down the first hill. *Something's finally going right.* "I appreciate this a lot, Jesús."

"Yeah. Eventually, you have to deal with the tickets; I think I can keep it to traffic violations."

"Thanks again."

"Sure. That's all just small potatoes compared to your kid."

The cabby stopped at the barrier of a closed parking lot. Jake gave him a good tip; Max said he was on all night and left his dispatcher's number.

Sacks in hand, Jake and Tina ducked under an iron pole and started across the lot in the dark. The *whump-thump* of the crashing surf seemed very near; ahead they saw dim outlines of a low building and three squatty palms. Approaching the structure, they ducked under another pole.

"Are we breaking some law?" Tina asked as she stood.

"No, there's a couple cars parked back on the road; look out there." He pointed to a flickering campfire ahead that threw light and shadows on a lifeguard tower. "They just want to keep cars off the beach."

They walked around a cinderblock wall that surrounded the bathroom alcove, where Jake knew there were probably sand showers. On the ocean side of the building, they saw a single light near the phone booth and walked over to it.

"All the comforts of home," he said, turning to her.

Tina pointed at the payphone. "Look." Its metal plating crusted turquoise from the damp salt air, the phone's receiver was hanging in the slot without a cable.

"Hm, that's a problem."

"What do you want to do?"

"It's two or three miles back to the freeway exit; I saw a gas station there."

"That's not very far."

"You want to start back or go on with the picnic?"

"We're so close." She put down the bag of utensils. Tina stood on one leg and pulled off a sneaker. "I came to walk in the ocean." She slipped off the sock then switched legs.

"Isn't it sort of cold for that?"

"I have a sweatshirt on under here." Her footwear vanished under the heavy wrap. "Ready?" she asked, straight faced, picking up a bag.

"Yeah. You're too much," Jake said with an appreciative laugh. "I'll stick with shoes."

Beneath a dense curtain of overcast, they walked onto the beach toward the guard tower. Luminescent streaks of foam in the rolling waves gave off just enough light to make out a fifty-five gallon barrel ahead. On the other side of the tower, they saw a solitary angler near the small fire, fooling with one of those tall, embedded fishing poles.

Tina moved easily in bare feet; Jake kept up until his shoes were full of sand. "Hang on," he said, sitting to remove them. Loaded down with the food sack and his footwear, he trudged on, thinking the dry sand was unexpectedly cold on his feet. Tina waited a few seconds then ran on ahead, leaving the bag between the trash barrel and the water.

Her silhouette set off by the bright foam, she romped in the shallows; he saw the gabán scrunched up away from the water. As soon as Jake's toes touched the wet sand, a chill shuddered up his back. He retreated to dry ground, zipping up the windbreaker and pulling the flimsy excuse for a hood over his head.

He put the food with the other sack and looked across at the fisherman, now bundled in a blanket and carrying the pole away from the dying fire. Tina ran up to Jake, lucent strands of her hair reflecting the scant light and blowing wildly in the breeze toward shore.

"Cold?" she called out.

"I'm okay." He stuffed both hands in his pockets.

"That was so fun, but my calves are frozen; didn't think it would be *that* cold."

"The Pacific isn't very warm here, even in summer."

"Seems strange—palm trees and all." She knelt in the sand, making a sort of teepee around herself with the heavy gabán. Tina gathered her hair under the collar; Jake watched her elbows and arms jostling beneath the material. Then she stood, her feet below in the white sneakers again, no socks. "That's better," she said, and they started to amble slowly away from the tower on firm wet sand.

Over the racket of Jake's coat flapping in the steady light wind, they chatted about their travels for a few minutes until Jake asked if she was getting hungry.

"Sure am." They turned back. "Jake, it's pretty chilly for a picnic; you want to walk out and eat on the way?"

"We could, but somebody left us a little fire." He pointed ahead past the guard tower.

"He's gone? Oh yes, let's do that."

Tina and Jake jogged from there to retrieve the bags, then they circled the tower's ramp. The small fire pit had a log nearby, but the man left no wood to feed the weak flames. They ransacked around in the dark, finding only a sports section in the barrel and some driftwood twigs. Tina twisted the newspaper into kindling, then dumped the utensils into the food sack. She started to wring the bag and extra paper plates like washrags.

After putting on his shoes, Jake rolled the log closer to the pit, watching Tina and noticing that a modest smile had endured on her face since she came out of the ocean. *Like she never had much chance to act like a kid. Her mother's work, I bet.*

He put most of the pile she made on the fire; they sat in the sand, backs to the driftwood trunk, silently holding their hands up to the poor flames for a few seconds. Jake took out the utensils, drinks, fruit, and the thick burritos. They began to peel off the layers of foil.

"Still a bit warm—look at the size of this; I'll have to save some." Tina took a bite. "Yum."

Jake answered after a swallow. "Yeah, real homemade; you can be glad it isn't *picante*." He swigged from one of the two cans of beer he bought.

"Oh, my," she said after the spicy chicken settled in her taste buds. She took a swallow of juice; he opened the pint of fruit, put some on a paper plate and held it between them.

She took a section of orange and ate it. "Thought so, it's hot, too."

"Pico de gallo, another way to warm up."

"It's all so delicious, just a bit hotter than what I'm used to. Those cookies are going to taste good."

They ate quietly for a while, watching the churning waves. Tina wrapped half of her burrito in foil and took another bite of fruit. "Mm, so good." She held up the next piece on a plastic fork near Jake's face. "You know what this one is?"

"Can't see it," he said, and she inserted the cube into his mouth. "Thanks." Jake chewed. "It's *jicama*, a kind of root." He finished the last of his beer.

"Really?"She savored another piece, still with the understated smile. "Jake, this is so much more fun than any restaurant." Tina turned to him. "Thank you."

"You're welcome," he said, his earnestness in contrast to her high spirits. Jake stood up to think, shivered again, and put the dregs of their meager fuel on the fire. He rubbed his hands over the heat.

"Something wrong?" she asked as he sat down.

"Why?"

"Your eyebrows tell all."

"So I've heard." He started to gather the trash. "Don't mind me; I really am glad you're enjoying this so much."

Tina put her leftover burrito in the sack and helped him put everything in, except the cookies and peanuts. They leaned back on the log, watching the surf.

"Jake, just tell me what's bothering you."

"Okay. Earlier, you avoided my question about your mother."

"I know." Her face turned somber in the uneven light. "You had it right; we don't get along, but that's nothing new."

"I probably shouldn't have brought it up. If you don't feel like talking about it—"

"It's okay, a little reality won't hurt." Tina thought for a moment. "My mom has always been in charge of everything—my father, my brother, me; the church. She's the real evangelical; she'd consider your Mormon relatives to be cultists, and the Jewish ones misguided."

"There's probably some truth to that—as long as she knows her brand of religion isn't any better."

"No, there's one perfect way for her. Mom pretends to be accepting of other religions, but she isn't."

"So non-believers must be evil."

"Worse. You wouldn't want to hear."

He picked up the cookies, pulled apart the end of the package and held them out to her. Tina took one, bit into it; Jake did the same.

"Mm, chewy," she said.

"Yeah, stale—just how I like them."

"They're good."

Jake swallowed. "So, you don't get along with your mother because you, uh, don't buy into her, uh—?"

"Ignorance?" Tina tongued some molasses off her teeth. "She just assumes that I agree with her take on Christianity. Jimmy and I are more like Dad."

"Which is?"

"Sure you want to hear all this?"

"I do." Jake's neck and back shuddered; he got up and knelt toward the pit, palms out, coaxing the last of the warmth.

"Remember, you asked for it."

"Okay, I'm duly warned." He smiled, and then sat with her near the log.

"You've heard of the good Samaritan."

"Just the basic idea."

"It's actually one of the best stories. Okay, Cliff Notes version." Tina faced the waves. "Jesus advised this lawyer that he could gain eternal life by loving 'thy neighbor as thy self,' that line everyone knows. So the lawyer asked, 'Who's my neighbor?' Jesus told him about a wounded traveler who was ignored—first by a teacher, then a preacher. So a Samaritan came by, and they were outcasts to most of the Jews. He, of course, saves the traveler, but this is the best part: Jesus asks the lawyer, 'Who is your neighbor—the teacher, the preacher, or the outcast?'" Tina turned to Jake. "The rest is obvious."

"So it's as much about hypocrisy as charity."

"Yes, which is how my father always taught it." She faced the sea again.

"That made your mother mad?" Jake felt his teeth chatter; he stood up to keep moving while he listened.

"She'd just be dismissive, as if Dad was some naive child. She's very intelligent—knows the Bible chapter and verse. The sad irony is she doesn't get the important things. She'd work with Dad for hours on his sermons, but he'd rather have been studying. He was into the similarities between religions.

"I do remember one time Mom was furious with him. She got back from a trip and found out what he preached to some church officials who came by on a pop-in visit. He quoted Jesus telling some spiritual leaders that they were like 'whitewashed tombs—outside beautiful and righteous but inside full of hypocrisy and wickedness.'" Tina sighed. "That's pretty close, I think."

"I never heard that one before; good for Jesus," Jake said, not intending sarcasm as he sat down.

Tina turned to him. "She accused Dad of disrespecting the visitors; he said it was a message we *all* needed to hear. It was one of the only times she couldn't pretend things were just the way she wanted. His next sermon was by the book, but the people knew; they loved him and pretty much feared her." Tina paused, looking away. "I can't believe I bored you with all this."

Jake trembled again, trying not to show it by pressing his elbows into his sides. "It wasn't boring at all. So, how did she treat you and your brother when you were kids?"

"We did mostly what we were told. As long as we acted like good little *mish* kids, she assumed that's who we were. Jimmy inherited her brains—he's Mom's genius, though he never acts like that. He keeps up appearances around her; the rest of the time he's just Jimmy."

"And you're Tina, not Christina, but still in the church."

She looked at him, her normally symmetrical face askew, as if asking herself something. "I tried some Zen and other stuff, but I came back." Tina paused, sighed, and turned to stare at the last of the glowing embers. "I've read a lot about Gandhi and Doctor King, and there's an Anglican minister in South Africa who nobody here has probably heard of—Desmond Tutu."

"I want to hear about him, but I'd like to ask you one more thing."

"My answer is yes, I would like another cookie."

In the near darkness, Jake could barely see the hint of a smile on her face as he handed her the package. "Sorry, that's not my question," he said with a grin. Jake stood, hopping on his toes.

"Jake, you *are* getting cold." She put the cookies down.

"I'm okay; hang on." He quickly removed the jacket, rolled down his long sleeves then put the windbreaker back on, pulling over the hood. "Okay, would you agree that your mother didn't expect much from you?" He stood by the fire pit, hands deep in his pockets.

"Actually, she expected perfection. I'm her disappointment—B's in school, working with Catholics, twenty-four years old and not married. Jimmy isn't either, but that isn't a problem for her."

"That's all such BS."

"You sound like my brother."

"Good for him. I take it he's not a preacher." Jake jogged slowly in place.

"No, but she wanted him to be one. Jimmy has his master's in physics, halfway to his doctorate."

"Good for him again. Now I sort of get that crack you made today."

She creased her brows. "What crack?"

"You said you aren't as shy around your kids, implying that you're on the same intelligence level."

"Well, some of them are very smart, but they aren't old enough to, uh—" She looked down at the ashes.

"To what?" Jake sounded like he dared her to finish.

"I'm not sure."

"I think you're saying they don't know enough to intimidate you. Maybe that's your mother, saying *you're* not smart enough. Sounds like she treated your dad the same way. Don't you think *he* was smart?"

Jake sat down next to her and saw a tear reflecting the light from the waves, curving down her cheek. *Now I've done it.* "I'm sorry I upset you, Tina."

"No, there's no controlling my waterworks." She inhaled, sniffling and looking out to sea again. "My dad *was* smart, but he wasn't ambitious in the way she wanted; that's what really got to her."

"Well, all I know is that she's wrong about you."

"Jake, you don't really know me."

"That's right, I don't." Jake touched the gabán so she would look at him. "But I know enough to recognize an intelligent person when I meet one."

She thought about what he said, drying her face with the edge of her wrap. "I hope you don't expect that to suddenly improve my self-esteem," she said quietly with a touch of sarcasm.

"No, even though it is the truth. And that's not some line I'm using on you."

"Don't worry, I'm quite sure it isn't a line."

"What does that mean?" Jake stood up yet again, arms folded on his chest.

"Using a line on me—that'd be some conquest."

He looked down at her, shaking his head. "Ah, because you don't think you're desirable," he said, and she responded by forcing air through her teeth. "Why are you scoffing, Tina? Look, I'm a male of the species; if I didn't like you, I probably *would* be trying some line. You're a smart, attractive woman, regardless of your mother's so-called morals and her warped ideas of perfection. Well, to hell with all that."

Jake shivered, trying again not to show it while Tina watched the sea. He sat back down. "How do you act when you're around her?"

"Say nothing, do the minimum to keep the peace, and get away as soon as I can. I don't remember really hugging her since I was ten." Tina frowned and chuckled at once. "It's kind of sad, but Jimmy and I sometimes laugh about it when we see each other. He'll say, 'What'll it be, Dad-hug or Mom-hug?'" Tina paused. "I miss Jimmy."

"He sounds like a great guy."

"Yes." She turned to Jake. "My gosh, you're shaking like a leaf."

"I'm okay."

"That jacket's nothing; get under here and get warm."

"You trust me?"

"Oh, I forgot," she said wryly, "you're a male of the species who finds me desirable."

"That's not funny; I do."

"Well, I trust you. It has a wide collar; we can both look out the top."

He scooted closer, she lifted the gabán over him, and they poked their heads up through the opening, facing the water, their sides touching.

45

"Much better, thanks," he said, his teeth chattering.

"You're trembling; you could be hypothermic. I'm just going to help warm you up." She reached over, placing her arm around his other shoulder; he could barely feel it.

"Don't take advantage of me, Ms. Linn." He shuddered again.

"Relax, John Wayne, it's just a Mom-hug. Isn't there some two-headed beast like this in *Alice in Wonderland*?"

Jake chuckled. "There should be." They were quiet for several seconds.

"Is that better, Jake?"

"Feel th-this," he stuttered. Jake searched for her hand, but she found his first; her warmth spread through his fingers. *Man, is it the heat, or because you're touching her?* "Pretty ch-cheap trick t-to hold hands, huh?"

"Glory, you're freezing. You didn't even go in the water; how'd you get so cold?"

"G-guess I'm not dressed for s-sunny San Diego."

Tina found his other hand, bundled all his icy fingers in the sweatshirt material outside her abdomen, then scooted up and put both her arms around him.

My God. "Th-this qualify as a D-dad-hug?"

"Shh, you need to get warm. Look, it's dark as ink; the only light is coming from the water." They stared at the breakers for a couple of minutes while Jake warmed up.

"It is amazing," Jake finally said, the shivers almost gone. "*You're* amazing, Tina Linn."

"Don't get carried away." She held him tighter. "I'm a glorified hot water bottle."

"That's crap. I have a good name for you."

"What? *Ms.* Linn?"

"Nah, it's *Tina, la gabacha Latina*."

"*¿Gabacha?*"

"In Mexico, *gabacho* is more common than *gringo*. Let's see, we'll make it 'Tina Latina' for short."

"Well, I guess that makes you the first person to name me since my mother."

"I name everything I like, even my truck."

"I'll take that as a compliment."

"You should." Jake laughed. "I like you better than my truck."

"Thanks a lot."

Now what, Romeo? "Uh, no more shivering, thanks to you and your tent," he said, and then sighed. "Maybe we should get back."

"If that's what you want."

"You aren't worried about finding a taxi?"

"I'm not worried about anything."

He removed his warmed hands from Tina's solar plexus and encircled her with his arms, holding tight.

"Mm," she said, "that's a Jake-hug, I think."

6

Jake woke up in pitch darkness around midnight, he guessed, naked from the waist down but not cold. She was similarly dressed; he surrounded her with his arms and one leg. The gabán not only covered them but they had tucked one side of it underneath to separate their bodies from the sand.

Man, what in hell have you done? The thought coincided with his low, brief moan.

"Jake, I really do want another cookie."

He let one arm go and his leg. "You're awake?"

"Yes, you snore a bit."

"I do?"

"Well, a little more than a bit."

"Sorry."

"I wasn't sleepy anyway."

"Shall we go up top and find the cookies?"

Tina chortled. "Maybe we should find our bottoms first."

"Uh-oh, are you going to lose it again?"

"No." She sat up in the dark, searching for her clothes. They both got dressed, and then pulled the gabán out from under. They sat in the sand, inserting their heads up through the slit again.

"The two-headed beast returns," she said.

Jake chuckled, then they silently watched a sliver of moon peek in and out of the thinning overcast; it reflected intermittently on the sea.

"It's beautiful," she mumbled, squeezing his arm.

"Yeah, it is." Stretching his legs out, Jake flapped up his side of the gabán and pulled in the cookies, taking out two. He stuck them up between his face and hers.

"Yum," she said, but Jake pinched the cookies together with a finger and thumb, making one molasses glob.

"Koo-gie." His voice was throaty and gruff like the Sesame Street character. Jake took an exaggerated bite.

"Cookie Monster got to share," Tina told him in a falsetto whine.

"Shh, me no have two heads." Jake kept chewing.

"I go get Bob and María," she warned in the high-pitched voice.

"Oh no, not them. Me share with cutie monster." He put the glob to her mouth; she took a bite. "How come cutie monster know Koogie," Jake asked, "but not big-shot cowboy?"

Tina grinned. "Everybody know you, Cookie."

With a second molasses ball, Jake and Tina finished their silly play, then held each other and kissed. His arm around her, they watched the waves silently, mesmerized again by the pounding surf.

"Latina?"

"You weren't kidding about the name?"

"Two names—Latina and cutie."

"Okay, I like Latina, but I'm not—"

"Koogie say yes," he said with the deep tone again, putting his forefinger up through the hole to wag it at her.

"Oh brother."

He lowered his hand; they embraced, watching the ocean again. "Man," he said in a normal voice, "the waves seem like they're really crashing now."

"Maybe it's because we're outside again." They listened and watched, Jake still holding her.

A minute or so later, Tina said, "You started to ask me something."

"Yeah." He exhaled heavily. "Maybe I ask too many questions."

"Go ahead, Jake."

"All right. Uh, I didn't hurt you did I?"

"Of course you didn't. You were very gentle but, um, passionate." She looked at the sea, then let go, except for his hand. "Jake, I should tell you . . . " She sighed. "When this night started I wasn't, uh, a . . . "

"So? You don't have to tell me that." Jake's tone was fervent. "It's dumb the way this works." He paused; she caressed his fingers. "If a man's a virgin, he's not a *real* man, but if a woman's *not* a virgin, you're supposed to be ashamed. It's stupid."

Tina nodded. "Well, believe me, I was ashamed."

"Okay," he said, more calmly, "you don't have to say any more about it."

"Jake, I want to." She heaved another sigh. "I worked on a cruise ship one summer in college." She paused; Jake could just hear her over the breakers. "I was rebelling a lot; decided I had to try, uh, *it*. I don't drink much, but I got pretty drunk with this guy. When I told my roommate, she said I was raped, but I knew what I was doing. He was cold, kind of rough, penetrated once and

49

finished, enough to change my, um, status, and leave me not very interested in sex. I felt empty after the whole thing."

She turned from the sea, tears welling up. "It was so different with you. Like I said, you were considerate, and I, uh, enjoyed it; I didn't even know I could." She lifted the fringe of the gabán to dab her eyes.

Now what do I say? He took her warm hand again. "Uh, Tina, I'm not exactly Don Juan, you know. My, uh, experience—" Jake stopped to scoff at himself.

"Jake, the only thing I—"

"Hang on. You told *me*—so here it is. Mostly, it was a few times with prostitutes. I rationalized that it's just business for them. But there were a couple other women I knew, uh, biblically. Why do they say that, anyway?"

"Well, if it says in the Bible she *knew* no man, it means she didn't have—"

"Oh. Now you must think *I'm* slow."

Ignoring his self scorn, she said, "Jake, do you mind telling me how you felt after being with them?"

"Uh, the truth is, mostly guilty. I crave the physical part of it, like any man, I guess, but I can't stand the whole stupid game. If I felt like somebody thought I used her, I was guilty for days."

She sniffled once. "Well, you didn't use me; I wanted this, too."

My God. He let go of her hand and hugged her tightly with both arms. "I'm not sure what to say, Tina."

"It's okay, neither am I."

He kept one arm around her. "I do know that I already care about you. I don't want this to be the end of it."

Tina turned to him. "Me either, Jake. See? As usual, you *did* know what to say. You're very sweet."

Their lips barely touched when Jake suddenly pulled away, startled. "What the hell was that?"

"What?"

"Something touched my leg." He reached down to his calf. "Jesus, my pant leg's wet."

"High tide!" she shouted, but before they stood all the way up, seawater inundated their shoes and ankles.

"Run!" he yelled, ducking out from under the gabán. Mildly alarmed but laughing, they grasped hands and started sloshing against the water flowing back to sea; Jake saw something floating by. "Hey, there go the cookies." He let go of her to snatch the package but lost his balance, falling to his knees in two or three inches of water. "I got 'em!" Jake yelled, and then guffawed, holding the package over his head as if it were a great prize.

Tina reached down for him. "Way to go, Cookie Monster; get up."

He stood, laughing as she took his hand. The seawater was gone, but the next wave *ka-thumped* behind them.

"Let's go!" she shouted, more enthused than desperate. They ran-trudged together up the soft sand. Jake turned back and saw foam approaching, much higher than the first onslaught; he knew they weren't going to get away.

Damn. "Stop, Tina, brace for it; we can't fall over in this one."

"*I* didn't fall over," she said, snickering. Her other arm darted out from the side of the gabán. She clutched onto him; he dropped the cookies.

This isn't funny anymore. He tried to envelope her tightly as the sea rumbled around and beyond them, above Jake's calves. Then, for a few moments, the water turned calm as a lake; now well over his knees and almost up to her waist. They managed a step or two before the force of the outflow began, trying to sweep them away.

Shit! "Tina, hold on tight, lean into the current." Jake forced his back leg into the sand as a brace; the detritus in the water flicked against his body while the grains around his buried foot started melting away. *Don't lose it, damn it.* The last seconds of backwater seemed like a full minute, but they held their ground.

"You okay?" Tina asked, pulling on his arm as he strained to extract his back calf from the muck.

"I'm fine." He freed himself from the suction. The next wave crashed, but they slogged away to more stable sand and moved faster, making for dry land without looking back. The wave caught them again, but only enough to drown their shoes and make them slosh through the water one last time.

"Made it!" Jake shouted. He and Tina hobbled hand in hand through the dry sand up to the showers, lightheaded from the adventure and each other's company. They laughed at their mostly ineffectual attempts to remove the sand and seawater from their clothes. Convinced that her gabán was ruined, Tina hauled it along anyway as they started hiking across the parking lot.

They moved at a good clip on the asphalt, the vigorous exercise holding off any chills. About halfway back to the freeway exit, a guard on security rounds stopped to give them a ride to the gas station, scolding them mildly for their foolishness.

While they waited for the cab, the clerk let them stand inside where they shared a concoction of hot chocolate and coffee. It wasn't Max who showed up, so they didn't bother to explain to the driver their "drowned rat" appearance or the wet money they laughed about when Jake paid the cab fare at the hotel.

Armando was just turning off the TV when Jake got up to the room at about one-fifteen. "Damn, Skip, you got drunk with her?" he asked when he got a good look at him.

"No, I'm just a tad wet." Jake, still giddy, realized he had a goofy grin on his face.

"Un-frigging believable. Okay, so tell me about it, lover-boy."

Trying to be serious, Jake said, "Tomorrow, okay? I need a hot shower and some sleep."

For Tina and Jake, the second day of the conference was even less professionally stimulating than the first. They spent much of the day together, still chuckling at times over their damp escapade. Separately, they explained the last part of their previous evening to Orie and Armando, who, unimpressed, came up with similar versions of, "I guess you had to be there." Jake and Tina had another laugh when they discovered that their friends had reacted about the same.

Armando also told Jake he had other plans for that night, so he made the gesture of giving up the room for the "love birds." Jake called his cousin again to apologize, setting up a time to have breakfast with him on Saturday.

That evening, Jake and Tina decided they owed themselves some seafood and walked down to the bay for dinner at a small chowder house. Talking at their table until the place closed, they took a taxi back to the hotel.

Jake held the room's door for Tina and followed her inside. "No sand to sit on; guess this will have to do." Jake had left his grey canvas bag on the bed; he walked over to remove it.

Tina put her big flag purse next to a straight-backed chair in the corner, and sat. "Yes, it certainly isn't the beach." She folded her hands on her lap.

This is bothering her. "Want to watch TV for a while?"

"No thanks."

"Shucks, ma'am," he said in a bad Slim Pickins accent. Jake sauntered slowly over to her as if he lugged rocks in his pockets. He took her hand. "I truly am hankerin' to git to know y'all better, ma'am."

"In the biblical sense, sir?" she asked, a smile barely creasing one side of her mouth.

"Gosh, ma'am, I'd be mighty obliged."

"Glory, I'm sleeping with a famous cowboy."

After Jake met his cousin on Saturday morning, the conference finished with two sessions and a salad bar/raffle designed to keep people around. Tina and Jake parted with the understanding that they would speak by phone often, and he would drive up to see her at spring break, which happened to be on the first actual day of spring for both of their school districts. Verbally, they made no other commitment beyond that they cared about each other, deciding independently it would be premature at this point in their relationship to even mention the word *love*.

7

Jake thought it took Jesús less than a minute to drive the squad car to the hospital. He parked at emergency; they went right in and found Ben waiting there.

"Maestro, I am sorry. I come back."

"I see that. Let's go, Ben; there's nothing to be sorry about." Jake passed him and strode right down the hallway, Ben and Jesús behind. "Ben, you must have seen Captain LeBlanc before you got out of the truck," Jake said back to him. "Right?"

"*Sí, maestro.*"

Jake looked at Jesús as he caught up. "My students are afraid of half of the police force."

"They should be," the sergeant mumbled.

The three of them slowed down just before the nursery. The charge nurse puttered in the back room near Emma's incubator; María was with the sleeping twins. Jake knocked lightly on the glass so as not to disturb the babies. María saw his bloody arm, then went directly to the sink. A few seconds later, Jesús held the door for her as she came out.

"*Sargento,*" she said to him.

"*Señora,*" Jesús answered, his tone deferential.

María smiled at Ben; he nodded back, and she walked to Jake with a damp washrag and a towel.

"*No es nada, señora,*" Jake told her as she cleaned the cut. "*¿How is the baby?*"

She finished drying his arm, put the used rag inside the towel, and gave him a tiny tube of ointment and plastic bandages from her pocket. "*Señor Fren, la niña, her breathing is faster, and still she does not move, only her chest. I am sorry; I think she is worse.*"

"*¿And the nurse; what is she doing?*"

"*She said Doctor McNally left permission to increase the oxygen a little. She is doing that now; she already called Doctor Serna. He has not called back.*"

"*He's in the parade with the mayor,*" Jake told her. "*It should almost be finished.*" He put the bandages and tube in his pocket.

"I don't think so," Jesús said, and then changed to Spanish. "*The parade will go slow at the border, señora, then the two mayors speak at the plaza before the fiesta there. It could be hours; it depends on when the doctor checks his calls.*"

María started frowning before Jesús finished. "*We cannot wait; the child is very sick.*"

After María's pronouncement, Jake looked helplessly at Jesús. "Guess I'll start the paperwork to move the baby; I don't know what else to do."

"I can find Serna."

"He might not listen, even to you."

"He'll listen. I'm going." Jesús took a first step to leave.

"*Sargento,*" María said.

He stopped and turned to her. "*¿Señora?*"

"*We need to try in two ways.*" She looked at Ben. "*¿Mijo, do you know the clinic of Doctor Castilleja?*"

"*Sí, señora, but it is Sunday.*"

"*Sometimes he opens anyway. If not, go to his apartment in back. Use my name; he will come with the maestro.*"

"*Señora,*" Jake said, "*the hospital is not going to allow—*"

"*Señor Fren, this doctor has an American diploma, and I have a plan for him to get in.*"

Jake stared at her for just a moment. "Okay. That's good enough for me."

"*Vámanos,*" Jesús said. "I'll drop you and Ben at your truck, then you can follow me to the border."

Jake, Jesús and Ben ran out through emergency and got in the squad car. Jesús put his flashers on, no siren, and sped up the hill, Ben shrinking down into the back seat.

"Are you going to get in trouble for doing this?" Jake asked, holding onto the bar above the door.

"No, I have my lunch hour coming."

"You know anything about this doctor?"

"Just that he's over here sometimes to help the poor. I hear he's a good guy; I don't know anything about his doctoring."

"Do you think María can get him into the hospital?"

"I don't know; she does have her ways."

The new couple had little time to worry about their interrupted affair. Jake and Armando's program had three busy weeks planned before vacation, including an all-day tour for their seniors of the same state university in Los Angeles Jake had attended.

On top of her usual challenges, Tina would be working hard with Orie to help their students survive a school-wide spring pageant and not be disparaged again as "those special ed. kids who ruin everything."

Nevertheless, Jake and Tina chatted long distance three or four times each week, mostly sharing school-related anecdotes and filling each other in on some personal and family matters, including Jake's twenty-sixth birthday. Besides expressing eagerness for the spring vacation time they planned to spend together, they hardly discussed their relationship.

On the Friday school was out, Jake spent the late afternoon cleaning, servicing and packing his truck, wondering how Tina would react when she got her first gander at Loretta, his 1960 Volkswagen dual-cab pickup with a custom snap-on black tarp over the back.

When Loretta was clean, "she" was a shiny, deep forest green with white trim, the colors Jake chose over the original faded tan. To him, the truck was both a fun and practical vehicle—you could haul five people, two next to the driver and three more in back, with all your gear secured behind. He was convinced Loretta's venerable little engine would run forever if he followed his mechanic's decree to change the oil and adjust the valves more often than did most owners.

Because of the truck's lack of power on even the slightest incline, Jake had learned to leave early when driving to out-of-town destinations. He named Loretta for a Beatles lyric he was listening to one day while going thirty up a grade from L.A. to Mount Wilson, traffic lining up behind him. He yelled, "Get back, Loretta," and moved to the side of the road to watch everyone go by.

Since Tina didn't expect him until Monday evening, Jake planned to take a leisurely drive up the coast, camp at night, and meet her in San Francisco after she spent the weekend with her mother in nearby Sequoia City. Tina had given him a vague explanation that Mrs. Linn's "status with the church" had changed, causing her recent move from Redding to the Bay Area. Neither Jake nor Tina knew San Francisco very well, so he made reservations to spend three nights there; they planned to be tourists during the day.

He left Orange County before ten on Saturday morning and didn't finish with the freeways until after Ventura. Heading for Santa Barbara, he observed that the coastline, as in San Diego, was succumbing to development. Jake cleared Santa Barbara and most of the traffic around three o'clock, listening to his eight-track player. When Randy Newman's raspy voice finished *God's Song*, he played it again, wondering how Tina would react to the cynical Lord in Randy's lyrics.

He stopped in Solvang, one of his parents' favorite destinations. They took him there twice for the Danish festivals; Jake especially remembered eating *Aebelskiver*, a sort of handball-sized pancake the locals cooked and sold right in the streets. He found some of the Danish treats at a small café and ordered some for an early dinner.

Jake then took Highway 1, known by long-time Californians as "the old coast road." He was surprised to find mile after mile of pristine beaches until he checked the map and realized he was driving through land controlled by the Air Force for ballistic missile sites. He watched the sun set over the Pacific, decided not to camp, and drove to Santa María to stay the night in a cheap motel.

Up early Sunday morning, he settled for coffee, a roll and an apple as he set out for Highway 1 again. He didn't get far before he came to a sign for the San Luis Obispo mission, recalling how he hadn't paid much attention to the old Franciscan outpost when he was there once with his parents. Jake drove to the mission; this time he read the historical displays before buying a book about Junípero Serra in the nearby town.

He continued up to Morro Bay and stopped at a small grocery to purchase a light "sperm picnic," smiling to himself about Tina's laughing fit in the cab in San Diego. Deciding not to eat off his lap again, he found the nearby state park, put on his coat and ate at a picnic table. He had seen the Morro Bay rock before, but this day the volcanic plug protruded above low-lying fog in the bay like a monolithic shark fin moving through a grey ocean. After eating, he spent a relaxing half hour watching seals and shorebirds through his binoculars.

On Highway 1 again, Jake looked back at the partially cloaked rock until it was out of sight. He disinterestedly passed road signs for the Hearst Castle and enjoyed the twisting ride by picturesque rocky shores, stopping once to beach comb and fool around near the waves, which also reminded him of Tina. At Big Sur, he spent the late afternoon hiking the beach trails before camping that night at the state park. He drank two "tall boys" from a six-pack and slept well to the sound of the steady breakers.

Jake arrived in Monterey Monday morning with several ideas on his mind. He was enjoying the trip more than he expected, and he knew why. Besides the anticipation of seeing Tina that evening, each experience on the journey made him wonder how she would respond if she had been with him. Jake decided to call her midday instead of waiting until he was almost there.

He had only been in Monterey as a child; his notion now was to dedicate the rest of the morning to his favorite writer. In Jake's opinion, John Steinbeck was unjustly eulogized as the author of one of his more trivial works, *Travels with Charlie*. Jake would honor the writer by attempting to visit some of the places that contributed to the vivid settings in his novels.

He decided to take a short drive to Salinas first, where he lost himself for an hour in the Steinbeck library before returning to Monterey. Jake found the cannery district and was surprised how the mostly abandoned factories and grey warehouses still resembled the images he remembered from *Cannery Row* and *Sweet Thursday*.

Walking around the neighborhood, Jake came to a small bookstore where he bought the paperback, *In Dubious Battle*, a short Steinbeck novel he had not read. At a "head shop" next door, he entered through some beaded curtains actually made of caps from beer and soda bottles.

Inside, a bearded man with a blond Afro and a tie-dyed shirt stood by an Earth Day poster. At first doubting the man's radical credibility, Jake inspected the wares and discovered they were mostly crafted from recycled or natural materials. He inquired about the curtains, thinking they would make a cool boundary for his classroom reading area. The clerk, also the owner, said they were easy to put together, demonstrating with some pliers by squeezing two caps onto a shoelace. Jake decided to start saving bottle caps to make his own curtain.

Finding that much of the inventory came from co-ops, Jake bought a small hand-woven Native American basket for Tina. As the owner made change, he wanted to know if the "outasight green truck" was for sale. Jake told him it wasn't, but they chatted about Volkswagens for a while. On his way out, Jake asked where the nearest pay phone was. The man said he was welcome to use the store phone for a local call, or get time and charges.

The proprietor showed him the way through more bottle cap curtains into a small back room, where Jake sat by the phone. He dialed the operator; she went ahead and placed his call to Sequoia City. *Man, I hope Tina answers, not her mother.*

"Six-six-four-oh-oh-one-four." The voice was even crabbier than Jake expected.

Polite, Jake. "Hello, uh, Mrs. Linn, I'm a friend of Tina's, my—"

"I'm sorry, Christina is not available now."

Jesus. "I see. Can you tell me when I might be able to talk to her?"

"No, I can't. Please call back in a few days."

No way. "Ma'am, she and I have, uh, an appointment this evening. Not exactly an appointment—"

"I'm afraid it will have to be postponed. Christina is recovering from a medical emergency."

"What? What kind of emergency? Is she okay?"

"She's recuperating, but it will be two or three days before she's on her feet. As I said, you can call then."

Bull. "Excuse me, Mrs. Linn, I think she'll want to talk to me before that."

"Your name?"

"Jake Friend."

"That's really your name?"

Afraid so, lady. "Yes, you can't tell me what's wrong with her?"

"No, but I've decided to tell her you called."

Thanks a million. "I don't mean to be pushy, but please tell her I'll call again in the morning around ten, if that's a good time."

"If she indeed wishes to speak to you, that would probably work. Good afternoon."

"Ma'am, uh, Tina's condi—" The phone was dead. "I'll be damned." Jake stayed in the chair a moment, his mind racing. He got up, took out his wallet and swept his way through the clicking bottle caps, a five-dollar bill in his hand. He put the money on the counter, called out his thanks and hurried to the truck.

Though he knew he couldn't do anything about Tina until the next morning, Jake took U.S. 101 and headed toward San Francisco as fast as Loretta would take him. On one down slope, he got her over sixty-five; Loretta rebelled with rattles and vibrations Jake had never heard before, so he slowed to sixty.

Debating with himself all possible reasons for Tina's illness, he passed San Jose, drove up the west side of San Francisco Bay and approached Sequoia City around three o'clock. Perturbed by the town's audacity to use *sequoia* in its name, the place reminded him of freeway blight in Los Angeles. Each neighborhood was a middle-class parody of the last, interspersed with blocks of drab warehouses and factories.

He found a chain motel named for the seven bucks a night it cost to stay there years before. Jake paid for one night and took a few of his things into the small, chintzy room, thinking about Tina and what he would do if her mother kept them apart.

Not sure what to do with himself, he put on his jacket and Cubs cap, went out into the cool, cloudy afternoon and walked several blocks to a convenience store. He bought a Bay Area map and a newspaper and was halfway back when hot grease molecules found their way into his nostrils. The source was a corner Chinese restaurant; he entered and ordered some prawns and fried rice. While he waited, Jake drank a beer and found Mrs. Linn's street on the map. He thought about driving by but decided that would be a creepy thing to do. Jake had another beer with his bland food, which wasn't as greasy as it smelled, and satisfying for no other reason than it was warm.

Back at the room, he put his first two found bottle caps on the end table and then tried to distract his rambling, worrisome thoughts about Tina. After reading in the Chronicle about Nixon's boys going to jail and the Giants' spring training woes, he picked up the Steinbeck novella but couldn't seem to get started. He went out to the truck and brought in the rest of his six-pack. Jake turned on the TV and went through the channels, staying with an *All in the Family* rerun. Sipping from one of the tall cans, he lowered the volume and let a gangster movie with spraying bullets, stilted dialogue, and car chases occupy his next couple of hours. He barely paid attention as he finished off the last can of tepid beer and finally went to sleep.

8

Jake slept through the wind-up alarm. He opened his eyes an hour later, disoriented by the orange, white and light brown paint once slathered onto every surface of the Seven Days Motel. His alarm clock had stopped; he turned to the electric one on the end table. *Geez, after nine; get yourself together and call Tina—damn, what a headache. Too many beers, Einstein.*

After he took an aspirin and a slow, warm shower, Jake shaved his neck, gave his beard a quick trim, and put on a blue long-sleeve denim shirt and black jeans. When he finished putting things away, it was five after ten.

The phone to his ear, Jake sat on the bed, got an outside line and dialed. *This should be fun. Polite—if you want to get past the ol' crab.*

"Hello?"

Thank God. "Tina, how are you?"

"*Estoy bien,*" she said quietly, sounding furtive.

Why the Spanish? "Your mother said it was an emergency—I've been going nuts—she wouldn't tell me anything."

"*She exaggerated. She is here, very close. Momento.*"

"I was expecting her to answer."

"*She is leaving now.*" Her voice was still subdued until she changed to English. "Bye, Mom." She paused. "There, she's gone—sorry."

"Tina, what happened to you?"

"I'm okay now, Jake. It's, uh, kind of difficult to talk about."

Like female difficult? Easy, could be anything—a rash, bowels..."

"You there, Jake?"

"Yes, sorry."

"Where did you stay last night?"

He heard her sniff away from the phone. *Is she upset?* "I'm at a motel, a mile or so away. You sure you're all right?"

"Yes. I'll be ready for school next week."

"That soon?"

"I didn't really need to go to emergency." She paused again; he didn't hear any more signs of crying. "But that place did bother me a little."

Jake waited to see if she would explain.

"I haven't been in a hospital for myself," she said, "since I had malaria."

"You had malaria?"

"When I was little. They just put me in there to rest."

*What if this **was** female problems?* He could hear Tina sigh. *Good God, a miscarriage? Calm down, you don't know that.*

"Jake?"

"Yeah, uh, I'm sorry you had to go through it, whatever it was."

"Can you come over here tomorrow? I'd rather talk about it then."

"Sure, Tina. Can I see you that soon?"

"Yes, I've been resting for two days."

"What about your mother? I didn't get off to a good start with her."

"She's speaking at a church luncheon tomorrow in Palo Alto. We can work around her; it's probably not a good time to meet her, anyway. Jake, how was your trip?"

Quick change of subject. He briefly mentioned the beaches and Steinbeck country. "I'll tell you the fascinating details tomorrow, if you want. When do you think I should come by?"

"How about late morning?"

"That's fine."

"Jake, I'm sorry this ruined our plans."

"It doesn't matter."

"You could just head back after I see you. Then maybe we can meet on some weekend."

"If that's what's best for you, but I'd rather wait and then spend more time—if you're up to it."

"I'm ready to get out of here for a while."

"Are you sure?"

"Yes, I need a rest from all my resting."

"I have an idea. When I cancel our reservation for tonight, I can keep the room for Wednesday and Thursday. You could rest there; we could talk, play cards or something, get room service or I could go out and get us, uh, one of my famous picnics. We could just hang out and relax." *You're pleading, Jake.*

"That sounds so fun."

"Uh, great, but we'll see how you're feeling tomorrow." He thought he heard her sob. *Damn.* "Tina?"

"Yes."

"Did I upset you?"

"No, it's my ol' waterworks again. I just appreciate how nice you're being about all this." She made a long, draining exhale. "*Bastante*, no more crying."

"Siesta time, maybe?"

"Probably so."

"What's your mother going to say if you leave for a couple days?"

"After I'm in bed all day today, she won't bother me; she's finally resigned that I make my own decisions."

"I'd rather not chit-chat with her on the phone, so let's set a time. Is eleven too early?"

"Just right, she'll be gone by then. What will you do today, Jake?"

"Touristy stuff, I guess. Can't wait to see you, Latina." *Ugh, corny.*

"*Sí, yo también.*"

Man, that sounds so good. "Uh, I'll let you rest. In case something comes up, I'm at the Seven Days, room one ten."

"Got it. Thanks, Jake—*mañana, a las once.*"

"*Cierto que sí. Adiós, Latina.*"

He hung up and stretched back on the bed. *She was more upset than she showed.* Jake looked up at the soundproofing holes in the ceiling. *My God, if it was a miscarriage, it would've been ours. Of course, you schmuck.* He got up and walked into the bathroom.

How would you deal with it, if she were pregnant? He saw his mellow smile in the mirror. *Yes, it would be good, very good. Jesus, what matters now is if she's okay.*

Over the next twenty-four hours, Jake worried about Tina, constantly at times, although he figured out plenty to do. First, he shook himself from his introspection to find the local map. Jake studied it on his way out to the motel office, where he paid for another night. He came back to the room and phoned the hotel to change their reservations.

Jake had two places on his itinerary for the day—Candlestick Park, the home of the hapless Giants; and then he was going to check out what was going on at Haight-Ashbury and look for something Tina might like.

With his girlfriend not far from his mind, Jake drove up Highway 101 through San Mateo into South San Francisco along one of the oldest stretches of freeway in California, his map claimed.

Dubious distinction. Jake decided to get off at the next exit, where he stopped and glowered at a stretch of tidelands littered with plastic, old tires and rusted metal, the rocks frothy with dun-colored foam.

He returned to the freeway, found his turnoff, drove past more tideland, not as polluted, and then by scrubby undeveloped hilly ground on the way out to Candlestick Park. At a forlorn parking lot, he climbed down from Loretta, zipped up his windbreaker and pulled over the hood. It felt to him like it might be as blustery as that day, years before, when a Giants pitcher was blown off the mound during the All-Star Game and charged with a balk.

Jake looked out at the sullen bay and wondered how it could be so foggy and breezy at the same time. He turned to the massive, austere stadium. A few years before, they tried to close in the structure—a futile attempt to cut off the swirling wind for the new football tenants. The place looked ordinary to Jake, like a fat egg, especially compared to Wrigley Field, Yankee Stadium, and Fenway—the *real* ballparks he visited on his trips to and from Costa Rica. Candlestick was locked and nearly deserted now, save a half-dozen vehicles for staff who were probably sprucing up the place for baseball. A 49ers billboard still promoted a season that was long over.

Stupid football. He drove into the Candlestick Point Recreation Area and from the front seat looked out at the gusty bay through his binoculars. Other than some suburbs in the distance, the tidelands here were nearly pristine; he watched what he guessed were cormorants taking off from the rocks and diving for fish. A kayaker in a wet suit came into his view; Jake put down the binoculars and stared at the determined man, paddling by the small sandy beach. After the kayak glided away, Jake started back to town.

He wanted a bite to eat, but there wasn't even a mini-mart before 101, so Jake got back on the freeway and took the second exit into the city. He found a hot dog stand and ordered a foot-long with the works, chatting with the lonely proprietor, who commented on Jake's Cubs cap. For a half hour or so, they talked about Candlestick, debated the batting statistics of Willie Mays and Ernie Banks, and compared the bleak prospects for both the Giants and Cubs in the coming season.

Before one o'clock, Jake backed Loretta's front wheels down to a curb in a steep residential neighborhood. He zipped up his jacket, checked the street sign, then hoofed his way around, finding plenty of exercise on the city's famed hills. He was impressed that so many of the older homes had been remodeled without violating the original architecture, an approach he hadn't seen much in L.A.

Closer to the city center, Jake found a few blocks of inactive old warehouses and office buildings, reminding him of the post-apocalyptic San Francisco in *On the Beach*. He came to a more active artery where a trolley passed by, rumbling and squeaking, only a half dozen people on the seats, bundled up against the cold.

He followed the trolley tracks into the skyscrapers and watched downcast white-collar workers on the streets hurrying back from lunch. After Jake checked his map, he walked almost another half hour before he found the corner of Haight and Ashbury. The iconic intersection was formed by several old refurbished buildings, each one three squat stories of Victorian architecture, he guessed, lacy and ornate. The upstairs of the side-by-side edifices appeared to be apartments, with storefronts on the bottom floors.

The area was mostly lifeless. Many of the shops were closed or abandoned, and there were no "colorful hippies" in sight, just a few ordinary people as well as a handful of the city's destitute, living out the day on the street. Other than political graffiti here and there and layers of stapled neon-bright posters on telephone poles, Jake thought he could just as well have been on a rundown stretch of Pico Boulevard in L.A. He walked three more blocks and spotted new construction ahead, unmistakably a convenience store or a fast-food joint.

He turned back toward the heart of the "Haight" and found an open boutique. Jake entered the shop and focused right in on a white peasant blouse from Mexico, embroidered in blue and yellow flowers with dark green stems. With that purchase under his arm in a recycled grocery bag, Jake poked around the neighborhood, thinking that the local merchants had an identity crisis. They were having trouble figuring out how to merchandise the so-called counterculture without abandoning it.

Around five o'clock, Jake started back downtown, feeling hungry. He found a taxi, got in and asked the driver about fish and chips. The man assumed he wanted Fisherman's Wharf, but Jake said he just wanted a place nearby. The cabby found a stand and waited for Jake to purchase his deep-fried repast before driving him to a convenience store. Jake bought a six-pack of beer, bottles this time, and rode the few miles in moderate traffic back to the truck.

He climbed into Loretta, felt a pinch in his jeans and emptied some bottle caps he found onto the seat. Jake opened a beer with his pocketknife, saved the cap, and took a long drink. Sitting back, he looked down through a foggy dusk at the settling city. Wondering what Tina was doing, Jake began to ponder the ramifications if she had indeed miscarried. He considered how difficult it would have been for her to go through something like that alone, her mother probably not much help. Jake felt pressure around his eyes but held off any tears. By the time he bit into a piece of fish, it was cold.

9

Back at the motel after his late night and busy day, Jake watched a TV report on the startup of the Alaska pipeline, scoffing at their predictions for minimal impact on the environment. He read the first chapters of *In Dubious Battle* and was comfortably involved for a while in the Depression-era fruit pickers' revolt in the San Joaquin Valley. Thirsty, Jake started out to Loretta to get the six-pack. *And get shit-faced again?* Instead, he bought a diet cola from the motel's pop machine, went back to his book and finally nodded off before midnight.

He woke the next morning before eight, disappointed that it wasn't time to go, so he lolled in bed and read more chapters of the novel. Just after nine, the phone startled him from his reading.

"Yes?"

"Morning, Jake."

"Latina." He did a fair job of containing his enthusiasm. "Good morning yourself."

"You sleep well?"

"Yeah, okay, how about you? How are you feeling?"

"After all this rest, like nothing happened. Jake, just come over when you want; Mom left early on an errand."

"Okay, let's go out for breakfast."

"Yum, I am finally feeling hungry."

"Great. You know a place nearby?"

"There's a couple. You're a ways from here; do you know where Redwood Street is?"

"Yup, found it on my Frisco map."

Tina chuckled a little. "You were right about Frisco, they don't say it up here. See you soon?"

"I'll get together and come over—*una media hora, más o menos.*"

66

"*Está bien.* Bye, Jake."

"Bye, half an hour." *You just said that, klutz.* He threw back the covers and rushed into the bathroom to handle the bare minimum. He stumbled back into the room, stepping into the jeans he had hung on the door the night before with the denim shirt. Jake realized he forgot to brush his teeth; he went back to do that and apply some deodorant. Putting on his shirt, Cubs cap and windbreaker, Jake scrambled outside, vaguely aware that it was another overcast day.

He started the engine and idled it when something else dawned on him. Jake dashed back to the room, dropping the key twice before he made it in to find Tina's gifts. Cursing his clumsiness, he brought two sacks out to Loretta's back seat. Though it was after morning rush hour, the traffic was heavy as he finally drove off.

Jake found Redwood Street, which was mostly apartments; he started counting down the addresses. He spotted 1317 at the end of two off-white stucco duplexes, a straw colored lawn out front. At the center of the otherwise empty yard, a ten-foot pine with brown needles drooped off to one side.

The parking places for the duplexes were taken, so Jake pulled in by a Chevy next door at one of the only regular houses on the block. He got out and walked down the sidewalk to a narrow paved path that bisected the dry lawn in front of 1317 and 1319.

You're actually going to see her; don't mess it up. Jake walked by the pine, noticing that someone had hung homemade paper Easter eggs on the ailing tree. He climbed the three steps and pressed the buzzer; Tina came right away to the door in jeans, a blue KENTUCKY sweatshirt and white sneakers. She seemed serious to him, which wasn't unusual, but she did look pale.

She still looks great. Tina opened the door to let him in, her hair opalescent, though there was no direct sunlight. "Hey, Tina," he said. They embraced but neither of them spoke or moved for a kiss. They finally released and stepped inside, still holding hands. She let go to shut the front door to the cold day, then turned back to him.

"Tina, it's probably the wrong thing to say when you feel so crappy, but, uh, you look really good."

"Thank you, Jake. I'm okay, really."

He took both of her hands. "I missed you, Latina."

She squeezed his fingers. "And I missed you, *Don Joaquín.*"

"What?"

"Well, you gave *me* a name." A spark of a grin showed on her face. "You told me you were no Don Juan, so now you're *el caballero, Don Joaquín.* That's as close as we'll get to *Jake.*" As quickly as she had smiled, Tina turned serious, releasing his hands. "Jake, do you mind if we just leave? I really want to get out of here."

"*Pues, vámanos.*"

"I'll get my coat." Tina went to a hall closet; Jake looked around the small living room and dining area, both painted a flat yellow. It all looked sparse to him: a couple of end tables, TV, and a matching couch with easy chair; all of it of bland design, like rental furniture. Above the sofa, an expensively framed print of the Last Supper was the only decor. A round dining room table—her mother's work station—was cluttered with the phone, a manual typewriter, a crank calculator, and lots of mail, scattered between faltering piles of bibles and other books.

Tina came back, wrapping herself in a bulky dark blue down parka. "Something wrong, Jake?"

"No, I just expected your mother would, uh, I don't know, seem more established."

"I probably didn't explain that this is temporary. She decided to come out of retirement; Mom goes back to Africa in May."

Good. "Is that right?" He turned toward a *yip* he heard from the back yard. "Your mom's dog?"

"No, that's *Fiera*; she's mine."

"What? You didn't tell me you had a dog."

"I'm afraid she isn't much to brag about."

"Fiera the beast? I've gotta see this."

"Fair warning, her name fits."

Tina went to the back door, was gone a minute, and then returned with the dog on a leash, almost pulling her over. Fiera, her tongue hanging out, strained the line to greet Jake, who quickly sized up the mutt. Sorrel brown without any obvious markings, she had the length and height of a full-grown Basset but was more slender like a beagle, and unlike any hound he knew, she had pointy ears.

"*¿Es mala?*" he asked.

"No, hardly."

"Okay, let her go."

As soon as Tina released Fiera, the dog lunged to Jake, who stooped to roughhouse her ears. Fiera licked him wherever she could; her ears somehow relaxed and turned floppy.

"Oh, isn't *that* something, she actually *likes* you," Tina said, her tone wry.

Jake was taken aback a moment by her sarcasm. "In other words, she does this with everybody." He started to stand, but Fiera kept slobbering.

"Afraid so. C'mon, pooch." The dog went to her after a second call; Tina picked up the leash, canine tongue all over her hand. She ruffled Fiera's ears, then pulled her; but the sinewy mutt tugged hard the other way, escaped, and sprinted back to Jake, her claws scraping on the linoleum.

"Sorry, Jake; she's so strong. Probably best if you escort us back out. She'll think it's a walk."

They led the dog through the small kitchen and out the back door into a narrow yard, which was secured all the way around with five-foot chain-link. Tina tied her up; Fiera began yipping as they left.

"Why do you have to tie her up?"

"Believe it or not, she can get out of there—if not over the fence, then under it. I don't think any yard can hold her; the vet told me that's pretty typical of hounds, even mixed ones. He thought she would mellow after she was spayed—no such luck. If we don't turn back, she'll settle down." After entering the kitchen, they stopped to listen; the dog had stopped whining.

"She's a hound mixed with what?"

"Who knows? I got her from some kids outside of a market in Visalia last year. 'Wanna real Germanshepper, lady? Only five bucks.' She was so adorable, I didn't care what she was."

They left the kitchen. "Hold on a sec, Jake." Tina went into another room and came right back. "This is for you. Happy belated birthday." She handed him a rectangular shirt box wrapped in white tissue and blue ribbon. "Open it after we leave, okay?"

"Thanks. I have something from the trip for you—not wrapped, though."

"So? We'll have a little party." Tina didn't sound very enthused by her own suggestion.

Trying hard to be cheerful. "Tina, how did you get the dog over here?" They started for the door.

"Beth, my roommate, bless her heart; she packed us all into her new Mustang."

"New? I thought she worked for the State."

"She's a big shot administrator." Tina took out a key from the same beaded hand purse Jake remembered from San Diego. "It'll be nice to have Mom's car when she goes back to Africa."

"Right. Where's your Cameroon bag?"

"Oh, it's here, full of stuff, as usual." They went out, she locked the door, and Jake offered his free arm. "Thanks," she said, taking his elbow. "Guess I am a bit shaky from lying around." They stepped down and started on the path, but Tina tugged him to a stop. "Which car is yours, Jake?"

"Right there." He pointed to Loretta.

"The green one?" Her voice sounded slightly critical until they got closer. "It's a Volkswagen. I never saw one like this."

"You don't see 'em a lot." They half-circled Loretta; he told her a little about the truck. "You don't mind being seen in it, Ms. Linn?" he asked, raising one eyebrow.

"Are you kidding? It's very cute."

The girl's too much. He opened the passenger side front door. "Okay, Loretta, you passed the test so far." Jake turned to Tina. "Ma-dam." With exaggerated chivalry, he swept his arm toward the seat, then lifted her elbow.

"Gracias, Don Joaquín," she said, attempting a grin.

He put the gift box by her, closed the door, hurried around to the other side and got in, noticing that she had found the middle lap belt and put his binoculars over by the present. Jake clamped his belt and settled in by her, imagining he could feel Tina's warmth through her thick coat. He turned the ignition key. *This is good, very good.*

"Jake, I think I'm jealous of Loretta; she's so pretty, and starts right up," she joked with a half smile. "Tell me about her name." Jake drove off and told her the Beatles story; she gave directions to the diner and asked him to recite all the lines he could remember from *Get Back*. Jake laughed as she made deadpan comments on how each lyric did or did not fit him.

"Maybe you should be Jo-Jo instead of Don Joaquín," she said.

He chuckled again. *She's feeling better.*

Since Jake had the song on tape, she insisted that he play it for her after breakfast. They arrived at the Sequoia Waffle House, parked, and started in. Jake leaned over and picked up a bottle cap off the ground.

"All right, that's about a dozen," he said. Tina wrinkled her fair brows as he put it in his pocket. Jake took her hand. "Just a beer cap. I'll explain later."

Tina ordered coffee, fresh orange juice and an omelet; Jake added a side of pancakes to the same meal. They chatted about Fiera, then Tina asked about his "Frisco" excursion.

As they ate, he described his hiking tour of the city. "…I found you a new hippie item from Haight-Ashbury; it's not as good as a gabán."

"Well, thank you." Tina put her fork down by the half-eaten large omelet. "Orie will be envious," she added.

"Right, but this is something she might like. Can I order something else for you, Tina?"

"No thanks; I'm stuffed." She frowned at her plate. "Jake, I can't just leave this."

"Uh, okay, I'll ask for a box." It was a small thing, but Jake, who never had leftovers at a restaurant, was impressed by Tina's resolve. While he craned his neck to find the waitress, he saw a vacated table nearby with enough potatoes, pancakes and bacon to feed a hungry adult. If not for Tina, he wouldn't have even noticed the waste.

They left the restaurant, Jake holding a paper sack with the small carton inside. They got into the truck, and Tina told him she felt good, suggesting a ride somewhere. Jake said he knew "just the place," where she could see the bay. They started out and, as promised, he put the Beatles and *Get Back* on the eight-track.

"Get back, Loretta," he said, then retraced the streets and freeways to return to Candlestick Point. Jake turned off the tape after he exited 101, where he saw someone walking near the bay, all bundled up. Tina had already zipped up her coat; Jake realized it was even colder and no less windy than the day before.

He headed out for the "Stick," cranking the heat up to maximum. Loretta's feeble heater, never a problem around L.A., now made Jake grumble as he pulled repeatedly at the vent flap.

"Something wrong, Jake?"

"This heater isn't worth crap."

"I have my big coat; I'm fine."

"What about your feet?"

"They're a little cold. I'll live."

"I can get my sleeping bag for your feet, or maybe I should just take you back."

"No. We don't turn around unless we absolutely have to. Remember?"

He chuckled. "We don't, huh?"

"Yes, I want to see this place."

"Okay, if you promise to stay out of the water."

She made a slight smile. "Deal," she said, then scanned the foggy tidelands, serious again. At the ballpark, Jake pulled over, the engine idling.

"This stadium looks so strange out here," she said.

"Especially the way they closed it in for football. Not much of a ballpark anymore."

"You look disgusted."

"Yeah; but I can tell you something cool about this place you're not going to believe." He put Loretta in gear and drove off, telling Tina about the guy he met at the hot dog stand. "Get this, he said the Beatles' last concert *ever* was right here at Candlestick in sixty-six."

"You're kidding."

"No, he even had the article."

"Well, get back, Loretta—that is something."

Jake laughed again, then drove on out to the Point and parked at the shore. A storm threatened in the bay, the fog churning up into leaden clouds. The birds were fishing again, and two beachcombers in layers of clothing leaned forward, inching along over the sand and rocks.

"My gosh, look at those birds dive," she said.

He reached around Tina for the binoculars and gave them to her. "I think they're cormorants." He watched her focus intently on them.

"They're so graceful—just beautiful."

You're beautiful. Don't say that, sap. "Yeah. How are your feet?"

"Freezing. Maybe I will take that sleeping bag."

While she kept watching the birds, Jake got out into a stiff wind, zipped up his jacket and pulled over the thin hood. At the truck bed, he unsnapped a corner, extracted the sleeping bag, and then re-secured the tarp. The wind's relentless chill made him hustle back into the cab. Tina unbuckled her seatbelt, zipped the bag down, and held it open.

"Put your feet in, Jake."

He shivered a little. "Just like ol' times?"

"Not quite. C'mon."

After fiddling with the bag and zipper, they intertwined their lower extremities in the downy cocoon; Jake put his arm around her.

Yeah, much better. Cálmate. "The guy at the stand told me the Point is named after a bird like a sandpiper. They don't nest around here anymore because of the development." He paused, looking in the direction of the mist-shrouded suburbs. "They should save more land, or someday it'll just be this park and the stadium."

"Imagine how wild this was a hundred years ago."

He nodded, and they scissored their legs together for more warmth, watching the turbulent bay close in like a slate curtain. As sprinkles dotted the truck's windshield, the beachcombers looked at the sky and began to wander away.

"This does remind me of your gabán—almost as warm," Jake said. "What happened to it?"

"Shrunk. I made it into a throw for my couch."

"You did?" *Are you going to ask what you really want to know?*

Tina reached for the gift box; she put it in his lap. "Okay, good timing; you need this."

"I get to go first?"

"Yes, please open it."

Jake brought his arm down and pulled the ribbon and thin paper from the white box. He removed the cover to reveal a grinning bear cub logo and CHICAGO in red letters over blue muslin.

Tina watched his face brighten. "The man said it's heavily lined for the Windy City. Look under it."

He found a Cubs stocking cap. "Thanks, Tina; how did you get this stuff so fast?"

"It seems there are a lot of Cubs fans; it wasn't that hard. Put them on, Jake."

"This is just great." He put the coat on over the windbreaker, zipped up, tossed his hat behind, and then pulled the stocking cap down over his ears.

"Good, it all fits, and we certainly know which team is yours."

"Yeah, I think it's also a not-so-subtle message that when I take you somewhere I freeze my butt off."

"Well, maybe a little."

"Now you." He turned around, extracting his legs from the bag and lunging halfway over the seat for the small white sack and grocery bag. He brought the gifts up front, stuffed his legs back in by hers and tightly rolled up the paper sacks. "Pretty fancy wrapping job, huh?" He handed her the small white bag.

She returned one of her pleasant smiles. "Opening is opening." Tina unrolled the top, lifted out the woven grass basket, and carefully inspected it. She silently read the artisan's card. "A lady from one of the coastal tribes made this—the workmanship is amazing. Where did you find it, Jake?"

He told her about the head shop, including an explanation of why he picked up the bottle cap earlier.

"You're going to make your own beaded curtain?"

"If I find enough bottle caps."

"Oh, you will. I love the basket, Jake, but you didn't need to get me two things."

He touched his new hat. "You did." Jake handed her the grocery bag. "C'mon, Latina, open it, *ábrela*."

She unrolled it slowly, raising both eyebrows as if a great mystery awaited her. Tina took out the blouse and held it up. "Glory, this is hand embroidered. It's so tasteful, Jake. I have to put it on."

"Right now?"

"Well, you got to put on your jacket." Tina scooted away a few inches, still in the sleeping bag, and retracted her arms inside the big coat. She turned it backwards and pushed it up over her head, an elbow jabbing Jake softly. A muffled "Sorry" came from inside the bouncing coat. Her bare arm darted out, flinging the sweatshirt in back and snatching up the peasant blouse next to her, all in one motion.

"Man, let me know if there's anything I can do to help out under there," he said.

"Don't be naughty now." Tina's face surfaced, her long hair somehow falling almost back into place. She tucked and jostled, then let the coat fall to her lap, holding out her arms. "Ta-da!"

Jake knew he was right to choose a modest blouse that came up to her neck, but when he saw how nicely she filled the white bodice, he felt himself harden. *Cool it, for God's sake.* "It looks great on you."

"Thank you, Jake, so much. It fits just right. How did you know the size?"

"Lucky guess. C'mon, you'll get cold." He lifted the coat to cover her; she moved it back over both of them; they hugged tightly.

Tina retracted her head a little, looking right at him. "Guess what?" she said, not really asking. "You have orange pulp—*en tu bigote.*"

"Hm?" He raked his moustache with his lower lip.

"Nope, you didn't get it. Guess I'll have to kiss it off of there."

"Now who's being naughty?"

"Isn't naughty." She pecked him below his nose.

"Oh yeah? You have some egg—*en tu barba.*" He returned a quick buss to her chin; they chuckled and fell into a long kiss. Still embracing, Tina and Jake turned their heads to the bay; only the thick clouds and the closest stretch of beach remained visible.

Perfect. For you, maybe—what about her? He released an arm so he could see her. "Are you sure you're okay, not cold anywhere?"

"No. And I feel much better, thanks to you. Only one thing we forgot—molasses cookies," she said, now with an easy grin.

He smiled. *You could ruin the whole day if you ask about it.*

"Jake, you have that telling eyebrow up again."

He moved slightly away. *Go on.* "Yeah. I was thinking about asking you what happened."

"I'd be surprised if you didn't." She took his free hand. "I'm sorry; I've been stalling."

"No, you asked for a day; we can wait longer if you want. What matters most is that you're okay, Tina."

"That's very sweet; always the caballero, Don Joaquín." Moisture welled in her eyes as they met his. "Jake, you probably already guessed I was . . . "

She paused, lowering her chin. "Uh, late for my period—I'm never late—clockwork." She looked at him. "They said it was probably a miscarriage, but they weren't completely sure."

"And you really are all right?"

"Physically, I'm fine." She sighed deeply. "I almost told you on the phone, but you know how I sometimes avoid dealing with things." Tears launched from her eyes, slaloming down both sides of her face. After she dabbed her cheek with a tissue from the purse, he held her for a few moments. "I'm finished crying," Tina said, biting her lower lip.

Jake let go with his outer arm and smiled at her. "It's just your ol' waterworks opening a little."

"That's right." She made a long sniff. "Thank you, Jake." They hugged again, watching the drizzle turn to a steady rain, streaking the windshield. The interior glass fogged up; he wedged open the wind wing before putting his arm back around her; she held his other hand.

"Jake, I've been trying to deal with some guilt."

"Your mother seems pretty good at dishing that out."

"Not over this. I told her it was just 'lady problems.' Even if she suspects I was pregnant, I could fly to Mars before she would talk about it. She'd just stick to her script and pretend it didn't happen."

He saw a single tear bulge then escape from the canthus of her left eye. "Tina, I know we should talk about this, but we can give it a rest for a while if you want."

"No. If I could just stop bawling." Trying to regain composure, she blew her nose lightly in the tissue. "When I was late, I was worried you might think I trapped you."

Jake scoffed. "That'd be some conquest, like you said at the beach."

She thought for a moment. "And I remember what you said—'To hell with that.'"

He grinned at her adamant tone. "Okay, we're even."

Tina looked down at her hands. "Another thing that bothered me—I thought I must have done something wrong to, uh, cause the miscarriage."

"Of course you didn't."

"I guess I know that now."

Jake watched her stare solemnly at the rain. "Tina, I have to admit that yesterday, after I thought you might've been pregnant, it freaked me out some."

"Yes. We should've been more careful."

"No, that's not what I meant." He shook his head. "Let me start over."

"Jake, you won't say anything wrong."

"Yeah, we'll see." He sighed. "When I thought about just the possibility of, uh, us having a baby, the truth is, uh, it . . . " *Say it, klutz.* "It felt right."

She moved into his arms, looking up at him, her eyes puffy. "For me, too, Jake," Tina said around a sob; he embraced her again.

She drew another long sniff through her sinuses and gently pulled his arm down. "Jake, even after they said they weren't sure, I had this uncontrollable wave of sadness at the hospital."

"I'm sorry. I wish I could have been there with you."

She tried to smile and opened her hand, revealing only a soggy little white ball. "That was my last tissue; I'll just have to stop blubbering."

Jake found some napkins in the glove compartment; she wiped her eyes, then exhaled loudly, almost like blowing out candles. "Anyway, I was so upset I made the mistake of telling the emergency doctor how I felt. He told me to relax, that it was probably just 'a normal, very early, spontaneous abortion.'"

"Just like that? Jesus, it's good to get the facts, but that's sounds pretty cold."

"Yes, he was impersonal, but that's okay."

"I don't think so—sounds like a putz to me."

She dabbed her face again. "A what?"

"Another Yiddish word—a *jerk*," he said, irritated and serious.

Tina snickered a little.

"What's so funny?"

"Nothing. Dad and Jimmy stood up for me like that sometimes. I'm a big girl, Jake, but thank you, the support feels good."

"Uh, sure." They hugged again and watched the rain. *Okay, Don Joaquín, blurt out the big one.* Jake took both her hands. "Tina, I've been going nuts these last weeks." *Terrible—spit it out.* He released one hand to softly touch her cheek; she lowered her eyes. "Latina, I, uh, care about you more than anyone, period. Nothing else is more important. I know that's corny, but it's how I feel. I love you, Tina."

She sobbed once, looked at him and said, "*Sí, te quiero, amor.*" They kissed then held each other, but a few moments later, she surprised him by muffling a laugh with her fist.

He pulled his head back. "Tina?"

"Sorry," she said around a self-deprecating grin. "It's embarrassing to say, but I practiced saying that over and over in Spanish when I was fifteen. I was sure I'd never say it and mean it. I do love you, Jake."

Part II

Teddy Bear Cholla

10

Jesús didn't slow the squad car when he saw Jake's truck up ahead. "Okay, Jake, downtown's jammed, so I'll go across the valley. After I drop you two off, stay close. I'll go slower up the hills." Jesús stopped abruptly behind the VW, his tires screeching a little. "Wait, Jake, your wallet—you'll need I.D. on the way back."

"Damn it." *Let's see, I last had it . . . when I called Ben.* "I think I left it at the store."

"Which one?"

"Your uncle's."

"Good. As long as nobody took it, he's probably tried to call you."

Crap, what if he doesn't have it? "Okay, we'll meet you at his parking lot. Let's go, Ben."

Jake and Ben jumped out and got in Loretta. He lost sight of Jesús on the first hill, then drove on to Ortega's market and parked by the squad car. By the time Jake ran up to the entrance, Jesús was hurrying out with the wallet and a six-pack of soda.

"Your lucky day," the sergeant said, holding up the billfold.

"Thanks to you, maybe so." Jake put it in his pocket while Jesús handed him two cans of lemon-lime pop.

"Okay, Jake, stay with me; I'll get you right across the border." They ran back to the vehicles.

"Hopefully, we'll see you at the hospital," Jake said, opening Loretta's door. "Thanks again, Jesús."

"Sure. Let's go."

Jake gave Ben the sodas and followed Jesús down the back streets to the border, where two long lines of vehicles waited to cross into Mexico. With Jake right behind, Jesús drove into a closed lane and spoke to a border guard, who removed the barrier and let them both go through. No one was minding the Mexican entry; seconds later they were stuck in heavy traffic on the tourist blocks, the sidewalks swarming with parade watchers and shoppers.

Damn it to hell. Behind several cars and a ramshackle multi-colored bus, Jake watched the squad car ahead as Ben opened the sodas. Jesús was five vehicles behind the final entry in the parade—1976 Miss La Cholla. Moving at a plowing pace, the tractor gradually pulled the pageant queen's float into a left turn for the plaza.

"Okay, Ben, which way when we get up there?" Jake took a long gulp of the cold pop.

Ben pointed toward Jesús. "The same street, but turn right. Then straight, many streets."

Maybe that place we saw before. "I think I've been there—if we ever get by this light."

"Maestro, you have black, right here." Ben touched his own forehead.

"What?" *Oh.* He pointed to the door pocket. "Yeah, I used my oil rag to dry off." Jake drew the back of his arm across his forehead, just smearing the grease.

After creeping along for two blocks, he made the turn at the PEMEX station. "Damn—finally!" he yelled, passing the small city hall/police building.

Jake accelerated as quickly as Loretta allowed past old La Cholla's handful of middle-class homes, the tops of their walls imbedded with colored glass fragments. He made it up to fourth gear, hardly slowing for the narrow road that dissected block after block of much poorer houses.

After a half mile or so, Ben lifted his arm to say something, but Jake suddenly braked, making a half brodie into a shaded dirt alley by a citron colored two-story building with HOSPITAL in faint black letters on its stucco exterior. He parked behind a blue Karmann Ghia, jumped out, and headed for the door that faced the street.

"No, maestro, Ben said. "The doctor—there." He pointed to a screen door entrance to an apartment behind the clinic; Jake followed him past the dusty Karmann Ghia. A swamp cooler rumbled away in a back window, leaking moisture below into a garden box of purple and yellow violets.

Ben knocked hard on the screen door, Jake standing right behind him. He struck the wood frame again, even harder, then shook his head. "Not here, maestro." Ben tried a third time.

Now what the hell do I do?

After two restful days in San Francisco, Jake and Tina kept up the regular calls between Visalia and Lemon Branch. They didn't work out another rendezvous until three weeks later when Jake drove north on a Friday evening. Tina was coming from Visalia to the Bay Area with her roommate, whose boyfriend was watching Fiera. The plan was for Tina to introduce Jake to her mother the next day.

He turned into the driveway of the Sequoia Waffle House about a half hour before he was to meet with Tina at eleven o'clock. Jake got out; it wasn't very cold and he was wearing a flannel shirt, so he left his jacket in the truck. Walking to the restaurant, he found a bottle cap by a curb, so Jake took a circuitous route to the door, checking the ground for more caps. Someone tapped him on the shoulder and said in a false bass tone, "No bottle cap searching allowed, sir."

What? It's her. He turned, smiling. "Very funny." Tina, in jeans and the blue Kentucky sweatshirt, put her backpack down; they kissed then hugged silently, Jake enjoying the fresh smell of her soft hair.

"You're early," he said, releasing her but still holding hands.

"Yes; so are you. Beth was in a hurry; she wants to stay an extra night with her dad and go back Sunday morning. I told her I thought it would be okay with you."

I'll say. Jake picked up her pack. "Hm, let's see, I was hoping to get weeks ahead on my lesson plans." They walked toward the entrance.

"Of course you were."

"After meeting you-know-who tomorrow, maybe I'll need the extra night to recover."

"Not very nice, but probably true." Tina tugged his hand, pointing at a sign on the door. "Jake, we ate on the trip; did you?"

"Yeah—snacked all the way from L.A."

"They close in twenty minutes; let's just go."

"*Vámanos.*"

"Do you want to pick up something to eat?"

"I'll be fine." They started back to Loretta. "Tina, do you mind if we stay at the Seven Days?"

"No, but there are probably even cheaper places."

"Ah, mediocre I can afford."

Jake drove them to the tacky but clean motel; he rented a room with a king-size bed for two nights and proudly signed them in as Jake and Tina Friend, though he didn't mention it to her back at the truck. He got his pack from the back seat, then handed Tina hers.

Jake showed her to the room. "Tina, before we, uh, go in . . . " He sighed. "I just, uh, want to be here with you. If it's too, uh, if you're not ready yet to, uh—"

"Jake, it's a month now; I was at the doctor's yesterday. Everything's okay," she said, and then blushed as she thought her words sounded a bit eager. "Thank you for asking, Don Joaquín."

After making love, Tina and Jake slept most of the night in each other's arms. He woke up in the morning and felt Tina "spooning" in cozily behind. *Man, don't move; this is the best. Ask her now? Sure, right when she wakes up— very romantic. Maybe after you meet her mom.* Jake saw the clock on the end table. "Wow," he whispered.

"Morning, Jake."

He turned over to her; Tina had ponytailed her long hair before bed, and now she didn't even look disheveled. "Hey, cutie, good morning." He touched her cheek.

"Oh, sure. I must be a sight."

"For sore eyes, as they say."

She kissed his nose. "Jake, what were you just *wow*ing about?"

"Did you see how many hours we slept?"

She nodded. "It was a long week."

"Yeah, I think we were both pooped."

"Beth makes fun of my sleeping; she doesn't think teaching is exhausting."

"It isn't, if your heart's not in it."

She thought for a few moments, frowning. "Jake, how bad do you think it is? How many teachers don't care?"

"More than people think. Our staff has a clique of six or seven, and half of them don't even hide it."

"We have two, just in our wing, who admit they don't like kids. Why do they teach, then?"

"A job, I guess."

"That's very sad."

"Yeah. We'd better get moving."

"I think we have time to eat. Mom said she'll be there all morning."

"Pancakes and eggs?"

"Definitely."

In less than a half hour, they got themselves cleaned up and then dressed in jeans and sturdy shoes; Tina put on a plain white sweatshirt and Jake wore the same flannel. He drove back to the waffle restaurant; they sat side by side in a corner booth Jake requested, about twenty feet from any other customers.

After a veteran waitress in "granny" glasses took their order, Tina unfolded a napkin and put it on her lap. "I could eat the whole omelet."

"Is that why you didn't order anything else?"

"Yes, it's the omelet challenge." She took a sip from what she called her "one daily coffee."

There's time now, Jake. "The coffee okay?" he asked, drinking some water.

"Yes, very fresh. Jake, you never told me how Easter went with your family."

"Fine—all of us, as usual, spoiling Joyce's kids." He shook his head. "When the sisters are all together, their intuition is impressive. They somehow knew something was up; I told them a little about you."

"Oh?" Tina raised her brows. "What did you say?"

"I didn't overstate things, but I did say 'serious.' They went nuts—started teasing me and all that."

Tina snickered, then contrived a frown. "Poor Huey."

Jake scoffed. "Yeah." *Go ahead, chicken.* "Uh, Tina, your mom still doesn't leave until May?"

"The fifth, I think. Why?"

"Uh, I don't know. I just wondered how her, uh, leaving might fit in with any plans we might make." *Geez, what a great start.*

"Plans?" she asked, distracted by the waitress bringing orange juice.

She's not getting it. Of course not, you didn't say anything. He thanked the lady after she placed the two glasses on the table.

"Sure, darlin'," she said to him, walking away.

Go on. Jake took Tina's left hand after she put down her juice. "Latina, I, uh, know it's only been a couple of months, uh, and I'll understand if you want to think—" He stopped when she looked at him, her mouth partly open.

She picked up the napkin to wipe a bit of orange pulp off her lip. "Jake, you're proposing?"

"I didn't think you'd be so surprised." *Screwed this up bad.*

She put her other hand on his. "Well, I just wasn't expecting it right this minute."

"Yeah, my timing could use some work."

She let go, and hugged him around his chest. "You know I love you, Don Joaquín."

Jake surrounded her with his arms. "I love you, Latina. So you'll, uh, marry me?"

"*Claro que sí.*" Still snuggled up to him, she began to weep very softly.

He hugged her more tightly. *This is actually happening.* Jake saw their breakfast coming and let her go. Tina sat up straight, dabbing her eyes with the napkin.

"Everything okay, hon?" the lady asked her.

"Yes, thank you." Tina, her face a little flush, smiled to the waitress as she left. "I'm very happy, Jake."

"Me too," he answered with a sigh, "and relieved."

"Oh, you knew you had nothing to worry about." She checked to be sure no one was coming and then moved back to him. They kissed again then released, both of them looking at their food as if they had forgotten it.

"Glory," she said, "look at this omelet; I think I lost my appetite."

"Tina, I don't even have a ring yet. This is just to hold you over." He took a small jewelry box from his pocket and handed it to her.

"My goodness, Don Joaquín. Gracias." Tina bowed her head shyly before she opened the lid. "It's beautiful, Jake." She held up the thin silver chain; a small, brown inset gem hung at the end, refracting in the light.

He drank some juice. "It's just zircon; they called it sienna zircon. It sort of matches your, uh, root beer eyes." *Too schmaltzy, Jake.*

"My what?"

"I'm afraid I've always thought your eyes are the color of root beer." He made a self-critical snort. "Tina, I'm sorry, none of this was very, uh—"

"Don't be silly," she interrupted and smiled, a full one for her. "Put it on me?"

She handed him the pendant, he undid the tiny clamp and secured it behind her neck, the dark little stone falling to the front of her white sweatshirt.

"It really does match your pretty eyes."

"Well, thank you," she said, making an effort to accept the compliment. Tina pecked him on the cheek.

"Uh, the food's getting cold. Can you try to eat something?"

"Yes, after my coffee."

"I think the road snacking caught up with me. I'm definitely hungry."

"Go ahead, Jake, please."

He started into his breakfast, glad he wasn't looking straight across at her after his botched proposal.

Tina finished the coffee and drank some juice, watching him. "What's wrong, Jake?"

He swallowed and put down his fork. "You deserved something better than this."

"Listen, okay? The usual falderal doesn't mean anything to me. What matters is I'll never forget how sweet and sincere this was. *Gracias, amor.*" After they kissed briefly again, Tina finally picked at her food, gnawing on a wedge of toast while he ate.

"Jake, something else . . . " She paused to sip some water. "I absolutely do not want a diamond ring."

"You're kidding." He forked in a hunk of pancake.

"I'm not. You probably already know that the diamond and gold trade in Africa is infamous for abusing the people. I can tell you some stories about that sometime. I wouldn't want a diamond ring even if you could afford it, believe me," she said with no hint of rationalization, then ate a bite of egg.

"All right. You never cease to amaze me."

She smiled at him around a swallow. "How soon were you thinking for the wedding?"

"Unless you want to wait, how about a couple weeks after school's out?"

"If we keep it simple, that's plenty of time; we could actually try to enjoy it."

"What do you mean?"

"I've been to two formal weddings here; didn't like either one of them. All that pressure to make it storybook perfect for the people who aren't getting married."

"Right, like a performance."

"Exactly. Let's make our wedding for us—no church, some close friends and family; then a party with dancing—just a lot of fun."

"Armando's group could do the music."

"Perfect, Jake!" she said, very enthused. "That's just what I mean."

He smiled back, then finished his juice. "Tina, what about your mother? She'll be gone; that's what I was trying to get at before."

"Just another reason why June works so well. She won't have a chance to pressure us about a church. This might sound cold, but I don't want to tell anyone we're engaged until she's gone. I do care about my mother, but this isn't for her."

"Okay, that's completely your call." He took the last bite of his omelet.

Tina rediscovered some appetite and ate more breakfast, though they again ended up taking her leftovers with them.

Jake drove to Mrs. Linn's duplex on Redwood Street; there was a parking spot out front. When he turned off the motor, Tina didn't move; he looked at her.

"Jake, I told her you're my, uh, boyfriend, and that you're not a Christian. She just changed the subject."

"Well, I'm glad she knows. It's okay; I wasn't expecting her to be thrilled to meet me."

"Good. Let's get it over with."

After they got out and walked up the path, Tina simultaneously opened and knocked hard on the front door. She called, "Mom!"

He followed her in, expecting Tina's mother to be surly, but Mrs. Linn came out of a back room with a preoccupied, neutral expression. Jake guessed that her pasty face had never been stained by makeup; everything about the woman seemed certain and emotionless. Not morbidly fat, she looked contentedly oval and thrifty in her drab clothes—a faded yellow housedress and a linty light grey cardigan that nearly matched her thinning neck-length hair. Mrs. Linn just nodded and veered off for her workstation in the small dining room.

"Mom," Tina said again.

Her mother picked up some stamped letters. An inch or two shorter than her daughter, she spoke to Tina through brown-framed bifocals attached to a black cord hanging from her barely-discernible neck. "Christina, would you take these out and put the flag up when you go, please? He comes before noon."

"Sure, Mom. This is my, uh, friend, Jake Friend."

Jake chuckled at Tina's introduction and started to walk over to shake her hand, but Mrs. Linn turned to her table again. He backed up, stayed with Tina and said, "Uh, it's nice to meet you, Mrs. Linn."

"Yes," she answered. "That is quite a name." Mrs. Linn pushed a bible and a dictionary away from the phone. "Oh, here's that letter for Josephine." She put it with the others and turned around with the mail to face her visitors.

We may as well be selling brushes. "Uh, must be at least ten degrees warmer than the last time I was here."

"Oh? I wouldn't know. Would you two care for some tea? I'm afraid that I'm out of sugar."

"We just had breakfast, but sure," Tina said.

The phone rang; Mrs. Linn grabbed the receiver. "Six-six-four-oh-oh-one-four." She listened for several seconds. "Yes, Rebecca, our group would be happy to." Mrs. Linn wrote on a pad. "And where?" she asked, then answered affirmatively three more times as she jotted. "You're quite welcome, Rebecca." She hung up. "Christina, that was your Aunt Rebecca in Redding."

"I heard."

"Faith, your second cousin, lives here in the Bay Area. Her husband's having back surgery this afternoon. I'm afraid you'll have to excuse me while I make my prayer chain calls."

Tina exhaled audibly through her nose. "How many?"

"Only three, but Mrs. Marsh will insist on talking. Would you still care for tea?"

"No thanks. Maybe we'll drop by later; I'll call if it works out."

"Yes, call first. I'll be grocery shopping this afternoon."

"Okay, see you, Mom."

That's it? "Uh, good to meet you, Mrs. Linn."

"Yes. Oh, Christina." Mrs. Linn walked forward, holding out the letters. Tina took them; she and Jake turned around and walked to the door.

On the way out, Jake heard the phone, then Mrs. Linn: "Six-six-four-oh-oh-one-four." He and Tina single-filed down the stairs to the narrow path.

"That's not quite what I expected," Jake said quietly, following her toward the curb.

"Really? How could it have been any worse?"

"I guess I expected a little hellfire and brimstone."

"Outwardly, she's always low key." Tina put the letters in the mailbox and lifted the red flag.

They climbed into Loretta; Jake put the key in the ignition. "So you're really not going to tell her we're engaged until she's gone?"

Lips pursed, Tina frowned. "That's right. Let's go, Jake; I'm *not* going to cry over her."

New subject—now. He started the motor. "Okay, are we still beach-combing at Candlestick Point?"

"Yes; maybe we'll pick up, uh, a 'sperm picnic' for later." Though she was trying to lighten the moment, Tina made the suggestion solemnly.

"Good idea," he said, chuckling for both of them as he drove off. "What time do you want to get back to your mom's?"

"I don't. She had her chance."

11

In the weeks that followed, the newly engaged couple began discussing over the phone some tentative plans for the future. They agreed that they would like to start a small family and "use" their profession to live in a bilingual community, with Tina returning gradually to the classroom. As for the wedding, they were thinking about a justice of the peace, probably in L.A.

They told their close friends about the engagement as soon as Mrs. Linn left the country in early May. Tina drove south in her mom's big Pontiac to see Jake, meet "the sisters" and tell them the news. Joyce Friend immediately offered her home in Pomona for the wedding at the end of June; Tina and Jake gratefully accepted.

Three weeks after Tina's visit, Jake intended to drive up to Visalia for Memorial Day, but the Friday morning before the long weekend, Loretta's old generator gave out. The truck would be in the shop until after the holiday, waiting for parts. That night, Jake called Tina to tell her what happened.

"You sound pretty happy, considering that Loretta's under the weather."

"Had a beer or two—she's just a truck, right?"

Tina didn't answer right away. "Are you still coming?"

"Sure, I'm catching a ride with Armando tomorrow morning; he's going up to Fresno to see his folks."

"Good. I have something I was going to tell you."

"Did you get around to telling your mother about the wedding?"

"Yes, a couple days ago."

"Did she call me a heathen?" he asked, laughing.

"No. She said congratulations and started talking about her mission—just what I expected."

"Oh well, life goes on."

"Yes." Tina paused. "Jake, that's not what I wanted to tell you. Are you sure you're, uh, okay to talk to me for a minute?"

She thinks I'm plastered. "Tina, Armando and I just had a couple; I'm fine, okay?"

"All right. I'm late again, Jake; I went to a doctor right away this time. He says I'm five weeks pregnant."

I'll be . . . "My God, Tina, you are?"

"Yes, but I was a little embarrassed after he asked all his questions and said it was 'an easy one' to estimate. Clockwork again, I guess."

"And you're feeling okay?"

"Just fine."

"Man, do I, uh, get to say congratulations?" He sounded giddy.

"Of course, Jake. How about congratulations to *us*?"

"Yes, to us!"

"We'll celebrate when you get here tomorrow, okay?"

A sobering thought crossed his mind. "Just a little celebrating, Tina; we have to start being careful, you know."

"Yes, that's true." Chuckling at his sudden seriousness, she told Jake that her local doctor was current on pre-natal care and had given her the latest dietary regimen.

"Good, I guess you'll just have to stop being such a boozer."

"Yes, and knock off all the smoking and drugs."

"I'm so happy about this, Latina."

"Oh? I couldn't tell. Me too, amor."

"Are we going to let anyone know?"

"I just found out today. It's still so early; let's wait a while."

"Sure, whatever you think. It's good I'm not driving; probably get a speeding ticket."

"Not in Loretta," she gibed.

"Yeah, wise guy. Tina, Armando reads me like a book. He'll know something's up."

"Okay, just go ahead and tell him, unless he's seeing Orie."

"No, he plans to visit an old girlfriend." Jake settled down some more; they spoke for another half hour, mostly about her health, their plans for the weekend and how they would meet up in Visalia.

The small house Tina and Beth rented was actually in a town east of Highway 99, so on Saturday she drove her mother's Pontiac through the smoky fields to Visalia. Tina waited for Jake and Armando at a Mexican restaurant known for "the best chile relleno in town." They found her before one o'clock at a secluded table, sitting beneath dark green, cactus-shaped candelabra.

Armando went right over to her. "Sorry, Skip," he said back to Jake, "I get first *abrazos*." Tina stood up; Armando gave her a big hug. "*Felicidades, maestra.*"

Jake tapped him on the shoulder. "Okay, cutting in." He embraced Tina and they kissed.

"All right, you guys, come up for air; I'm hungry," Armando said with a wide grin. During lunch, he and Jake chatted with Tina over a beer while she had juice and watched them eat all three *buñuelos*, the complimentary pastries that came after the meal.

"Another beer, Mando?" Jake asked him.

"Nah, I'm driving."

Jake laughed. "Yeah, and I might have to navigate the Linn barge."

Tina ignored Jake's wisecrack, placed her napkin on the table and looked at their friend. "Armando?"

"*Sí, maestra.*"

"Are you sure that you and your *banda* don't want to be paid for the wedding?"

"No, that's my *very* expensive present." Armando bent his left arm and hit his elbow with the other palm, a common gesture for *codo*, meaning *cheapskate*.

Jake and Tina laughed; then she asked Armando, "Can you handle a wedding march, too?"

"Yes, we have a portable organ."

"And Joyce has a piano," Jake added.

"Either one; I just need the sheet music that Tina wants."

Tina patted his hand. "Gracias, Armando."

"My pleasure, maestra. Okay, guys, I gotta get my fanny up to Fresno." He reached for his wallet.

"Don't even think about it," Jake told him.

"Thanks, Skip. Monday at noon, then, right here."

Tina and Jake saw him to the door, then came back to dance once to the lively local Maríachi. When they went out to the Pontiac, the temperature was in the upper eighties, not unusual for the San Joaquin Valley in late spring. After she asked him to take the keys to the "Linn barge," they got in front and kissed again until Tina chuckled.

"What's so funny?" he asked her.

"I can just picture my mother's face if she saw us making out in her car."

"Imagine if we were in back." He turned, pretending to ogle the spaciousness behind. "Mmm, pretty tempting."

"A bit warm and much too public, don't you think?"

"Yeah," Jake answered with a false pathetic frown.

"So sad, Don Joaquín; maybe I can cheer you up. Beth is gone today, and my doctor said that, um, sex within reason is okay, even recommended." Tina raised her brows invitingly and blushed.

"Not another word," he said, pretending to desperately start the car, fumbling intentionally with the keys, activating the wipers and bumping the horn. He drove away past two teens in the parking lot who gawped at them as if they were old and crazy, making Tina and Jake laugh even more.

They were soon out in the country. "Man, these strawberry fields—forever." When she didn't acknowledge his Beatles reference, he turned to her.

She touched her abdomen. "Jake, I probably shouldn't have had that salsa; it didn't settle very well."

"Heartburn?"

"Guess so; I'll be fine."

He drove on for a mile or so, but she began sobbing very quietly. "Tina, what's wrong?"

"It isn't, uh, heartb—don't know," she told him, clutching herself. "Oh, no. My God," she said around breathy heaves. "I'm . . . cramping, Jake."

Jesus. "Easy, Tina, it still could be the food." *Damn it to hell.* He stopped immediately at the side of the road and helped her lie down on the back seat. Jake saw that the back of her tan skirt was stained. *Oh God, no.*

"Go, Jake," she cried, not very loud.

He scrambled up front, U-turned the car for Visalia and floored the accelerator, passing the strawberry fields and looking for hospital signs. Barely sensible enough not to make things worse, Jake drove through red lights and stop signs at the intersections where traffic was sparse. Tina moaned and made more muffled cries, Jake telling her repeatedly, "Hang in there, we're almost there."

At the hospital, he ran inside for a wheelchair; a nurse came back out with him. He followed them in, carrying Tina's purse and intending to stay with her.

"Sir, I'll take her right in; please stay here at the desk for now. We need you to start the paperwork."

He kissed Tina on the cheek. "It'll be okay, Latina; they'll take care of you now. I'll be right there."

Tina was silent and had stopped crying; the nurse started to wheel her away. Jake turned to the receptionist at the desk.

"Sir," the woman said, "the patient's last name, first name, and middle name, if any, please."

Jake told her, and then began filing through Tina's wallet for the necessary numbers, reading them aloud with abrupt impatience. After several more minutes, they finally let him join Tina and the nurse in the exam room.

"She's going to be fine," the nurse said to him. They had already cleaned her up and Tina was lying there in a hospital gown, her eyes now dry, staring up at the drip flowing into her arm. They had her sign the admission papers and a permission form for Jake to receive her medical information.

He stood there, smiling awkwardly, holding her hand; Tina closed her eyes. After another minute or so, the nurse asked Jake to wait in the emergency lobby. She said that Doctor Ames would come out to see him soon after he gave Miss Linn a more thorough examination.

Jake kissed Tina on the cheek again before he left. He walked down the hall and stood by a plush chair across from a fidgety couple in their late teens. They were listening to an elderly physician with a slouched medium build and curly grey hair. Jake tried to peek at the name badge on the man's lab coat, but the doctor and the couple left in different directions. Jake sat and leaned forward, pinching his brow with an index finger and thumb, his mind jumbled with disconnected thoughts about Tina and their future.

The same doctor, now in green scrubs, approached Jake about twenty minutes later with an encouraging smile and said, "You must be Mister Friend. I'm Doctor Ames."

"Yes, hi doctor." He stood to shake hands; the physician led him into a quiet room with a couch and chair, but they remained standing. Worrying about the doctor's competence, Jake suspected he was about seventy and thought he looked like the pope in hospital scrubs.

"Mister Friend, your fiancée did have a very early miscarriage, but she's doing well now. Christina's resting in her own room, half asleep and just waiting for you." The doctor briefly checked the clipboard he carried. "No complications; there was no excess bleeding, her uterus is clear, and there's no apparent damage. By tomorrow afternoon, she should be ready to leave."

"Then she just takes it easy for a few days?"

"That's right." Ames smiled again. "She asked first about you, then if she could still have children, and whether she could teach next week. I told her you'd be there soon; that yes, she could still bear children; and we'd talk about work later. Next week is her last, right?"

"Yes, Tuesday through Thursday."

"If she's up to it, maybe she can go on Thursday."

"She'll go—believe me. In fact, when you next see her, I'd appreciate it if she hears directly from you that Tuesday and Wednesday are out."

"I'll be sure to do that. Most vital right now is support, even more so since this is probably her second one. A miscarriage is hard on dads too, but we can't fully understand how traumatic this probably is for her. It would be best if someone is with her these next days."

"It's my last week, too; I'll take the time off."

"Very good, Mister Friend. Any other questions?"

"Not yet. Thanks for being so, uh, on top of all this. I'll go on in then, unless she's asleep."

The physician grinned. "I don't believe she'll go completely to sleep until she sees you." He looked at his papers. "Room one forty-two."

"Thanks again, doctor."

Tina's eyes were closed, and she still had an IV attached when Jake walked into the small generic hospital room. He sat quietly in a visitor's chair, but she opened her eyes right away.

Jake stood up and took her hand. "Hey, Latina." He smiled at her, but his emotions pressured his eyes.

She kissed his wrist and said, "Thank you, Jake."

"Didn't do anything."

"I'm so lucky you were here." Before she finished the sentence, tears raced down her cheeks.

He held her in his arms a few moments, his eyes now damp. "I'm so glad you're okay."

They kissed briefly, then Tina spoke quietly. "I have to talk to you, Jake."

Still holding her hand, he said, "Tina, you need to rest and—"

"I know, just a couple things; then I'll probably go right to sleep."

"Okay, only a minute or two."

Before Tina could begin, two nurses started jabbering loudly in the hall. She saw Jake glare at them.

"Jesus Christ," he grumbled, "don't they—"

"Jake," Tina interrupted, "it's all right. Please just close the door."

"Yeah, sorry." Calming himself, he got up, pulled the handle, and then scooted the chair to the bed, taking her hand as he sat. "Okay, cutie, what is it that can't wait?"

"I'm worried about you. You were so excited about the baby coming." She touched her eyes with a tissue.

"Tina, I'm fine now that you're okay. And you heard what the doctor said about having children."

"Yes, he's so much nicer than the last one I had."

"I should hope so." He squeezed her hand. "Kids will happen for us someday, Latina."

She tried to smile. "Okay, Don Joaquín." Tina sighed deeply, wiping her eyes again. "Jake, the other thing is, uh, what about school? I can't just *not* go back to my class before the year's over."

"You don't have to. The doc said if you promise to rest until Wednesday, you can go see them on Thursday."

"He did?" She started crying again. "I'm sorry, Jake. I was so worried about that."

Jake hugged her. "Yes, Ms. Linn, I know you were."

He stayed near Tina for the rest of the day and sat with her all night, eventually falling asleep in the chair.

12

He took Tina home the next afternoon and nursed her until she was on her feet in a couple of days. While he had some time, Jake went ahead as they had planned and started their resignations in motion. Still three weeks before the wedding, they launched a job search through Jake's placement center, which allowed them to register as a "teaching couple."

They applied to four districts in the Southwest and had two leads within ten days. They accepted an interview with a small rural district near the Mexican border in Arizona. Their administrators were coming to Los Angeles on a recruiting trip, just days before the wedding.

Jake and Tina finished up in Lemon Branch less than a week before the interview. They drove to Pomona to finalize wedding arrangements and to stack Jake's possessions in Joyce's garage. Fiera made friends with their white Labrador, so Tina and Jake left the next day without the dog. They drove to Visalia and began moving Tina's things out of her rental into a small storage unit.

Two days later, they headed south in the early afternoon; the temperature rose as they came to the desolate fringes of the Mojave Desert.

"So what did you think of my uncle and aunt?" Tina was asking him about her relatives from Redding who came to Visalia that morning to pick up the Pontiac.

"They're not quite so, uh, intense as your mother."

"Nice adjective, Jake. You don't have to try so hard not to hurt my feelings when you talk about her."

"Is that what I do?"

"Yes. Just be yourself. I'll tell you if I think you're wrong."

"Okay, it's a deal."

They stopped for cold drinks near Bakersfield, then began discussing the fate of their modest belongings. Some of it, they decided, would be sold, recycled, or given away, but the rest, including their books and teaching materials, was too much for Loretta, so they would have to rent a larger truck after they found new jobs.

That topic eventually petered out at the Grapevine, north of L.A. Jake scanned the straw colored tinder-dry hills, perfectly primed for Southern California's next big wildfire. He knew the high desert was sometimes degrees cooler than the basins, but this day it was sweltering at all altitudes. Jake and Tina were in shorts and T-shirts, and had all the windows open; she was looking out her side at a lone scraggly oak. Tired of her hair blowing everywhere, Tina deftly secured it behind her head and turned to him.

"Jake, what about Fiera?"

"What about her?"

"I have a friend who would adopt her."

"Is that what you want to do?"

"No, but you saw how it was, taking her to L.A. A longer trip could be difficult."

"C'mon, she's not that bad."

"You haven't lived with her."

"We'll be okay; she loves riding in Loretta."

"All right; I just hope you don't regret it."

The steep incline made Jake settle his truck at about thirty-five in the right lane where they watched the traffic whiz by. "Can you imagine if the back was full on a grade like this?" he asked.

"Would she make it?"

"Yeah, in second gear." He pointed to the side of the road. "At least we don't have to worry about *that*." A fortyish man in a shirt and tie confidently poured liquid into the radiator of an early-sixties ash colored Chrysler, its yards of chrome shimmering in the sun. "Probably running an air conditioner," Jake added dryly.

"The tortoise passes the ol' grey hare." Tina sipped the last of a large lemonade.

Jake snickered. "You're too funny, Latina. So, what about Loretta? Do we keep her?"

"Don't be silly. If I keep my pet, you keep yours."

He grinned. "Okay, cutie, we'll honeymoon in style with both of them. I know we talked about Oregon, but see what you think of this: Tomorrow, these guys are going to stumble all over themselves to offer us contracts, and—"

"How do you know?" she interrupted.

"They aren't just eager; I think they're desperate, and surprised to have two qualified people who might forsake the land of milk and honey to go down there. If they offer us contracts, maybe we should visit the place before we sign."

"Drive down there after the wedding?"

"What do you think?"

"Sounds sensible, but are we in a position to dictate terms like that?"

"We already have another interview if we want it, and I'm pretty sure these guys will give us time to decide. We could visit Grand Canyon; we'd even have a place to stay in Flagstaff."

"I'd love to see Grand Canyon."

"Then let's do that, no matter what. I'm not worried about finding a job."

"I am, Jake."

"You are? Why?"

"I'm not sure. Tomorrow, do we tell these people we want to start a family?"

"No. It's none of their business."

"Okay, but there's one thing I won't do."

He smiled. "Only one? Let's see, there's no wasting food, no diamond rings, no kids dumped in special ed. Oh, and no turning around, and—"

"Jake, it isn't funny."

"Hey, I love you for those things. Sorry—what were you going to say?"

"I won't quit in the spring because I'm having a baby. After we get jobs, I want to teach the whole year."

"Yeah, of course; we'll be careful."

"Next July would be the earliest, so we have to be *careful* a couple more months."

"Yes ma'am, I'll curb my enthusiasm whenever we, uh, trip the light fantastic."

"What does that mean?"

"Hm, dancing, I think. Can I take it back?"

She laughed at him as they made it to the top of the Grapevine. The downhill air offered no relief; it was even hotter the closer they came to Los Angeles.

They stayed in Burbank that night with Hannah Friend, the unmarried lawyer, and planned to get an early start to the interview the next day. Tina and Jake spent the evening in her air-conditioned home, eating barbecued chicken while Hannah filled them in on the grape boycott and the fall of Saigon, hardly mentioning the wedding. She was the least ebullient of Jake's siblings over the event. Before bed, Jake came down from two large frozen daiquiris he drank and listened impatiently to Hannah's report on the family's moribund lawsuit against the hospital where their mother died.

After breakfasting with Hannah the next morning, they left for Los Angeles. Jake encountered a traffic jam on the freeway, making them a few minutes late for their nine o'clock appointment.

Of the opinion that a necktie wouldn't help him land any job he actually wanted, Jake wore his usual teaching garb for the interview. As always, he felt proud of his bride-to-be but thought she was a bit gussied up in a white blouse, grey skirt, and polished black low-heeled shoes. Tina gave her freshly shampooed hair no extra attention other than the usual thorough brushing that brought out its sheen. She hauled along her big Cameroon flag purse as they made their way across campus.

It was another hot morning, but as soon they were inside, the aggressive air conditioning left even the hallways chilly. They checked in with a secretary, who directed them to a bald man in a tan summer suit, waiting with his coffee by an interior door. He was over six feet; his excess weight made it difficult to tell if he was around forty or fifty.

Jake heard the man burp as they walked up to him. "La Cholla School District?" he asked.

"Mister Friend and Miss Linn?" The administrator lowered the cup from his sunburned face.

"Yes. Sorry—we were stuck in traffic."

The man forced a smile and limply shook their hands. "Jon Munz, Special Programs, and principal for Sofia." He pronounced it SOFE-yuh. "We'll begin with Miss Linn." She walked with him to the unmarked door.

What's this guy's story? Jake saw Tina look back, intimidated, he thought, as she went into the corridor before Munz. *She'll be okay.* He sat in one of the plastic chairs by the door, put down his spiral notebook and opened a thin paperback. He began *The Moon is Down*, the next in his odyssey of Steinbeck's lesser-known novellas. Jake nearly finished a fourth of the World War II story by the time Tina emerged, holding a tissue.

Munz was right behind her. "Mister Friend, we'll need a minute before we see you," the obese administrator said, then left before Jake could stand all the way up. Tina sat down; he waited until she stopped dabbing her face.

"You okay, Tina?"

"Yes. Mister Munz told me in the hall I did fine; who knows what that means? I just hate this sort of thing."

"I'm sure he was right."

She shook her head. "I was okay until they had me explain why special ed.

is important. I said something dumb like every child needs a chance to learn. I talked about Graciela, one of my Down's kids." Tina took a deep breath. "I started crying; it took forever after that."

He put an arm around her. "Tina, take Munz at his word; you probably did better than you think."

"Blubbered my way through." She sniffled, drying her eyes again. "I'm so hopeless sometimes."

"You aren't either. Let's just see what happens."

Munz came out again. "Okay, Mister Friend."

Jake stood, facing Tina. "Sure you're all right?"

She glanced at Munz before extracting a nest of knitting from her purse. "Of course; go ahead."

Jake left the novel with Tina, picked up his notebook, and then followed Munz down a long narrow hall into an interview room, where two more men waited at a ten-foot rectangular table, office chairs all around. There was a pitcher of ice water, napkins, cups, and doughnuts on a desk by the door. Jake's place was obviously behind a single sheet of paper at the head of the long table.

"Help yourself before you take the hot seat, Mister Friend," Munz said, snatching what was probably not his first powdered confection of the day.

"I'll have water, thanks," Jake said, nodding toward the panel members without really looking at them. After he poured the water, Jake put the glass and notebook by the paper, reading its title: INTERVIEW QUESTIONS— ESL/SOFIA. He looked up to see the other two men, who were now standing.

"Mister Friend, I'm Raul Ortega, Superintendent, this is Mike Serna, School Board President." Serna leaned over to exchange handshakes, his grip intentionally tight.

Ortega's grasp was firm but not aggressive. Jake sat, watching the two men take their seats. Finishing the doughnut, Munz wiped red jelly from his mouth with a napkin and pushed his belt below his belly to get comfortable.

As he sipped water, Jake noticed Ortega and Serna both had fair skin and wore neat summer suits; he thought they could pass for Anglo businessmen. Serna was younger, maybe forty, a plump five-eight, with receding brown hair, severe dark brows, and trendy sideburns. Ortega, Jake decided, was one of those timeless seniors who would look fifty for the rest of his life. Slim and almost six feet tall, his age lines vanished with an easy, calm smile; he had a full head of brownish blond hair with tinges of grey. Looking very relaxed as if he might not say another word, Ortega spoke again.

"Mister Friend, is Miss Linn okay?"

"Yes, thank you, she'll be fine," Jake put down the glass.

"Is she always so, uh, emotional?" Serna asked.

Jake detected a slight frown from Ortega in reaction to Serna's question. "She's actually pretty tough," Jake said, "even if she does cry easily."

"Miss Linn seems very dedicated," Ortega interjected pleasantly.

"Yes, she is." Jake saw that Munz was oblivious to the interchange, working his tongue to dislodge dough from his teeth.

"Mister Friend," Ortega said, "the position you're interviewing for is rather unique. We have an old elementary school in Sofía we re-opened last year with two classrooms, one for grades six to eight, the other nine to twelve." Ortega paused. "*Señor, este programa en Sofía,*" he said in rapid Spanish, "*is for youth who are recently arrived to our school district; the majority have not studied much in Spanish or in English. ¿If you understand me, what are the first questions you would have about such a program?*"

Jake answered in Spanish at about the same speed. "*Sí, señor, I understood and I have some questions. ¿Primeramente, please explain to me what the basic educational goals are for the program?*"

"*You both speak very well,*" Ortega said, continuing in Spanish and smiling again. "*Your teaching objectives would be to instruct one of the groups in basic education and teach them English as a Second Language.*"

"*¿Y los estudiantes, how many in the two groups?*"

"Let's return to English now, Mister Friend. Okay then—we want to keep class size below twenty in each room; we'll eventually add rooms, I'm sure. The majority of the students come from around La Cholla."

Only twenty? Perfect. "Do you mind if I ask what happened to the first teachers?"

"A teaching couple. Put it this way: some of our questions today are designed to show us if you are likely to have similar problems, which is about all I can say for now. We'll be happy to answer anything else at the end of your time. The first five questions on your sheet are about your background; please just answer them in order after you have read the page. We will read the second five questions aloud. Please take a few minutes to review all ten of them."

"Sounds good." While the panel members chatted quietly, Jake skimmed the first five questions and found them to be pretty standard. He took his time reading the second five, not surprised that they were mostly about organization and discipline. Jake told them he was ready, then used about ten minutes to answer the five background questions and respond to their follow-ups.

"You speak the lingo better'n me; where'd you pick it up?" Serna asked in a snotty tone. Jake gave him the usual explanation about learning the "bad words" as a kid in L.A., then mentioned his Spanish minor in college, a summer in Mexico City and the six months in Texas and Costa Rica.

Stuttering slightly over the words, Munz read question six, a classic one asking for self-evaluation of "strengths and weaknesses." Jake handled it humbly but with confidence, and then Ortega and Serna read two discipline questions. Jake described the kind of structured plan he knew they wanted; he sensed from them that the school had been beyond unruly.

Munz started the ninth question. "Since the school in Sofia is somewhat isolated from the rest of the district and there isn't an on-site principal, how would you describe yourself in terms of being an independent self-starter?"

Good, this means I'd never see the guy. Jake pointed out similarities between their program and the one he began "from scratch" in California, which was one reason, he said, why he preferred to teach the older group.

"One of the teachers," Munz replied, "will have to be lead teacher and do the paperwork—there's some extra pay in it. Are you willing to do that if you're hired?"

Does he do anything? "Yes, I would do it."

"All yours, Mike," Munz said, eyeing the food again.

Serna spoke up in a brusque tone. "All right, Mister Friend." He cleared his throat and started reading. "Ten: A teacher wants his students to learn about photography. He also wants them to have, uh, a hands-on experience, so he has them take apart and reassemble the school's movie projector. What do you think of this approach? Please be specific with your answer."

Easy. Jake organized his thoughts a moment. "Okay, the basic idea here is a good one. I like its appeal to a sense of discovery and wonder." He paused and saw Serna's frown turn to a complete scowl. *Hold your water, schmuck.*

Jake continued. "For starters, of course, you don't attempt this project with equipment you depend on and are responsible for. You could get serious about this idea only if you can find discarded equipment. Next, you'd need to focus on what you're teaching—photography, mechanical science, mathematics—though I like the idea of using one discipline to support another. Then, what are the specific goals of your instruction? Do you expect the students to be able to—?"

"Excuse me," Ortega broke in, "I'm going to stop you since we're running out of time, and I believe you've already answered this to our satisfaction. Any follow-up, gentlemen?" He looked at the other two. Munz shook his head, and Serna just turned away.

"Okay, Mister Friend, what other questions do you have for us?"

"Well, I think I have a pretty good idea about the job; your brochure answered most of our questions about the community and the district. One thing I didn't see is anything specific about medical facilities. Is the nearest hospital at the university?"

"We need to add that to the brochure, Jon," Ortega said to Munz, then turned to the Board President. "You want to fill him in, Mike?"

"La Cholla," Serna said it, Luh-CHOY-uh, "might be small, Mister Friend, but we are a modern town with electricity and flush toilets." He sneered sarcastically. "We have a small Catholic hospital with a very professional staff, including two local doctors." He finished in a huff, as if daring Jake to ask another question.

"Uh, that's good to know." *Pendejo.* "That's all I have for now."

"Thank you, Mister Friend," Ortega said. "It's quarter to eleven; we should be able to tell you and Miss Linn something by the hour, if you'd care to wait."

"We can do that. Thank you."

"I'll show Mister Friend out," Munz said, getting to his feet.

Why? Jake walked to the door first, opened it and waited for Munz; they started down the hall.

"You did great," the administrator said from behind.

"Uh, thanks."

"Nobody told you this, okay? Miss Linn is in, and you have my vote. Serna doesn't like you, but don't worry about that; he doesn't have any pull with Ortega—a lotta ol' family crap."

"What do you mean?"

"Nothing, just the way it is. See you in a minute." Munz turned and started back. Jake opened the door and walked over to Tina.

She looked up from her knitting. "How did it go?"

He sat down. "I knew it, Tina, they loved you—you're in."

"Really?"

"Yeah, I'm the problem. One of them doesn't like me."

"The school board jerk," she said immediately.

Jake chuckled. "Yeah."

She gritted her teeth. "Well, I don't like *him*."

Man, Tina critical? "What did he say to you, Tina?"

"Nothing. It was *how* he spoke to me, like I was a little girl. And, well—now don't get mad—but he, uh, when we shook hands, he put his other hand in my hair, behind me; the others couldn't see. You know I'm not touchy, Jake, but it was on purpose."

Jake had started shaking his head in the middle of her explanation. "I'll be a son of a bitch."

"It's not that big of a deal; he's just a creep."

"Do you still want to work for these people? I think we're going to get the offer."

"My job is perfect," she said, now more enthused than upset. "Ten or so kids, two aides; Fridays for lessons and all the paperwork. Ortega's nice; I think Munz will be easy to work with. I can ignore the other guy if you can."

"As long as the *cabrón* stays away from us."

"And your job?"

Jake told her he was just as enthusiastic, adding that Munz probably wouldn't even know what they were doing.

"Do you still want to see the place first, Jake?"

"No, I'm not worried about that now, if you aren't."

13

Three days after they accepted their new jobs, Tina and Jake's wedding, as intended, did not much resemble a traditional June ceremony. The bride-to-be decided to have a real pastor, which was okay with Jake, who sat quietly the day before in the office of Joyce's clergyman while Tina answered most of the reverend's nosey pre-nuptial questions.

That evening, Tina was more excited than nervous over the event, her anticipation exacerbated by her brother flying in from New York to be the "father" of the bride. Tina and Jake took a break from the hubbub at Joyce's house and went for a stroll in T-shirts, shorts, and flip-flops.

The neighborhood was about ten years old, street after street of two-story homes on hilly lots barely large enough for small front and back yards. The plain architecture of the light pastel houses repeated before the end of each block. As dusk approached, most places had a few lights on and a silvery TV glow projecting from at least one room.

Walking in the street since there were no sidewalks, Jake let go of Tina's hand, pointing toward a typical two-car garage with a basketball hoop and backboard. "So what do you think of the suburbs?"

"The houses are nice, but I don't think I'd like to live like this."

Thank God. He took her hand again. "And what makes you decide that, Ms. Linn?"

Tina grinned. "You can't call me that much longer."

"If you say so." He pointed to a house with a ten-foot tree out front, fully bloomed in lavender flowers. "So, Ms. Friend, what *don't* you like about this?"

"*Mrs.* Friend to you, sir." She nodded to the same colorful tree. "See this jacaranda? It's one of my favorites, but did you notice there are two on every block, one on the corner and another in the middle? It's all so planned; the owners haven't even changed their yards much."

"Which is what a lot of commuters want, I guess."

They walked on. "I wonder what kind of place we'll find down there," Tina said.

He raised an arm toward the homes. "I just don't want neighbors so close we can hear them fart."

She wrinkled her brow. "I agree, and I think I'm starting to get used to your, uh, graphic images."

"Not original, believe me." Two pre-adolescent boys zipped by them, getting in a last bike ride before dark. "Well, Latina, you certainly hit it off with Joyce's kids."

"They're so fun, creative and—"

"And spoiled?"

"They're not that bad, Jake; they definitely love their unc."

"Yeah, but I'm glad I don't teach younger kids. I don't think I'd handle them very well."

"You might be surprised."

They were silent for a short time, walking by the block's one palm tree. "Your sisters have been wonderful," Tina said. "They've taken care of everything just the way we wanted. Do you think it would be ungrateful if I changed one thing?"

"I doubt it. What is it?"

"Caroline's husband is supposed to pick up Jimmy at the airport in the morning. Would you do it instead?"

"Sure, is there some reason?"

"There won't be any time tomorrow. This way, you'll have a chance to get to know my big brother."

"Okay, I'll tell Joyce and Caroline."

The next morning, Jake took the freeway west through yellow-tinged grey smog to L.A. International to pick up Jimmy at ten o'clock. He took a wrong turn in the airport loop and ended up back on the freeway at nine thirty. Jake exited onto a surface street, turned around, got stuck in traffic, and finally came back onto the loop almost at ten. It took minutes more to park, then he jogged to the terminal but had to slow down in one of the porcelain tunnels because foot traffic was heavy both ways.

Halfway to the gate, Jake heard a *toot-toot* behind him, turned and saw a black man in uniform driving an electric cart and calling in a deep monotone, "Mistah Martin, comin' through," and then just, "Comin' through."

Bull, keep going. The sea of commoners parted for the dignitary, some began to applaud; Jake used the opening to jog forward until the cart caught up with him again.

"Mistah Martin comin' through," came from behind; Jake moved to the right but kept trotting. The crowd was close enough to the wall that the cart made it around Jake, who looked over at the bored driver. In back, the celebrity had his face buried in a newspaper with a picture of Dodger ace, Don Sutton, on the front. *Screw you, Mister Martin, and the Dodgers too.*

By the time he arrived at the gate, Jake was twenty minutes late. Since Tina told Jimmy to watch for *a bearded guy in a Cubs hat,* Jake thought about holding his cap in the air, but there were only a few people hanging around as the agent closed her station.

He saw who he was looking for—a guy in a denim shirt, glasses, and a Mets hat. Tina's habit of calling Jimmy 'big brother' made sense right away when Jake saw he was of average build and an inch or so over six feet tall. Jimmy had straight light brown hair down to his neck, full sideburns, and wasn't nearly as fair as Tina. The two young men said each other's names at the same time, smiled, and shook hands.

"Sorry, Jimmy, I took a wrong turn or two."

"It's okay, but aren't you from here?" His tone was curious, not judgmental. He held a plastic dry-cleaning bag over his backpack.

"Yeah, doesn't help much; L.A. traffic's bad for everybody. Do you have luggage checked?"

"This is it."

"Good, that just saved us a half hour. If you don't need anything, I'd like to get out of this madhouse."

"Right. Let's go."

"I'll hold your suit if you want." Jake took the bag and showed him the way out, neither of them saying much. *A man of few words—like his sister.* Regardless of Jimmy's glasses, Jake noticed his sepia brown eyes were like Tina's, but her brother had long ears and a more angular face. *Sort of like a tall, intellectual elf. Bad, Jake.*

They made it to Loretta, exited the garage, and then Jake felt obliged to communicate. "Jimmy, how did you get to be a fan?" Jake pointed to the Mets hat.

"I came to school in New York in sixty-nine, when—"

"Right, their first Series. Did you know much about baseball?"

"Almost nothing."

"So what interested you?"

"Physics, partly. I heard people talking about Seaver's curve ball."

Jake inched ahead in a midday traffic jam. "And?"

"I didn't believe that the ball could curve."

"Believe me, it curves—never could hit a good one."

"I'm still not convinced it isn't an optical illusion. To me, it's great how the whole game is based on science—physics, geometry, an interplay of time and space."

"Please don't say it's a game of inches."

"No, millimeters." Jimmy smiled for the second time since they met.

Jake returned a grin. "Well, some people think the game has a sort of poetry to it."

"Yes, but so does science. I also like how baseball sometimes helps me break the ice with people—like right now, I guess."

Finally up to ten miles per hour, Jake glanced at his soon-to-be brother-in-law. "So I bet you think Seaver's better than Reuschel," he said, feigning a scowl.

"I know he is, Jake."

Discussing the wedding, their families, and more baseball, they got back to Pomona around one o'clock, three hours before the ceremony. Jake drove into Joyce's driveway; Tina was on the front lawn playing some sort of tag with two of the kids, who ran in to announce Jake's return. Tina scurried over to Loretta's passenger side before Jimmy was on the ground.

"James, Dad-hug." Tina reached out for him.

"Absolutely, Christina." Jimmy took her into his arms; both he and his sister were laughing uncharacteristically.

"Man," Jake said as they let go, "Christina and James? Didn't expect that—your little joke, right?"

The Linn siblings chuckled again before they got Jimmy's things and started for the house with Jake; Tina walked in the middle, holding their free arms. "So, how are you two getting along?"

"Your big brother's okay, mainly because he hates the Dodgers and Yankees."

Jimmy scoffed. "Yeah, I'll let you marry him, Tina, misguided though he is."

"Oh?"

"Yeah, he says the Cubs have a better chance than the Mets of winning the pennant."

"You know they do, Jimmy."

After Jake's retort, Tina's face was beaming as they all walked in the front door.

The ceremony that afternoon filled Joyce's living room, vacant of most furniture except for ten rows of borrowed, unmatched chairs. The well-wishers included a dozen or so of Jake's Southern California relatives, mainly from his father's side, as well as his parents' closest friends. A few Linn relatives from Redding attended, and more than twenty friends of the bride and groom.

At five minutes to four, Tina and Orie waited in a bedroom at the top of the stairs. The bride wore a crown of daisies and a simple white cotton dress she brought from Cameroon; it was embroidered in bright, iridescent colors, a style characteristic of the grasslands region of that nation. Orie, the only bridesmaid, shimmered in her tight, dark blue formal gown, turning the heads of many in the crowd.

The rest of the small wedding party waited near the bottom of the stairs, starting with Jimmy, who would escort Tina across the room. Armando, in his *banda* uniform of black pants, white shirt and string tie, played a classical waltz softly on the piano—the sheet music from *The Sound of Music* wedding march propped and ready in front of him. Jake and a boyhood friend, the best man and keeper of the two silver rings, waited in ordinary dark suits, ready to join Tina, Jimmy, Orie, and the preacher at the double doors that looked out on Joyce's patio.

Two of Armando's musicians, helping out by seating the guests, walked urgently up to their leader to whisper something. Armando stopped playing, got up and spoke to Jake. "Skip, there's a slight problem. Some old guy named Pearlman is making trouble."

Crap. "My uncle; I'll take care of it." Jake went to the front door where another *banda* member was trying to reason with Rose Pearlman's only sibling. Myron, like his nephew, was just under six feet, but thin as a matzo sandwich. He still had much of his dark brown hair, cut short and combed back. Nearing retirement as an accountant for the power company, Myron Pearlman was, in his own words, "an influential businessman."

Jake approached his uncle, whose tan summer suit hung from his bony frame like a bed sheet out to dry on a still day. Freckles and liver spots blemished his jaundiced pale skin; he had a black mole like a curled-up spider on the side of his chin.

"Hello, Uncle Myron," Jake said, trying to be cordial. The musician walked away, relief on his face.

"Jake, about damn time," he snarled, then covered his mouth with the long, pocked fingers of one hand. "What's with all the spicks and *schvartzes* here?" he muttered under his breath.

Jesus. "Friends of ours, Uncle Myron."

"Christ's sake, Joyce should have a place for me," he said in a normal tone, several people turning toward him.

"First come, first served today, as advertised, but I see a spot in the fourth row there. Let me take you over."

Uncle Myron clenched his jaw. "Jesus, some deal."

Jake escorted him to the chair; Myron dusted the seat with his hand-kerchief before sitting between the very pregnant spouse of a musician, and a female friend of Tina's from Kenya, both of whom Jake met earlier.

Good spot for the old kvetcher. Jake touched his guests' shoulders. "This is my Uncle," he said with an impish smile; the women greeted Myron amiably. "Enjoy the wedding everybody." As Jake left, he heard Myron mumble a Yiddish epithet.

Though there had been no rehearsal, the principals in the wedding knew the very loose plan and patiently waited their turns, chuckling good-naturedly at a few minor foul-ups. Jake heard later that his uncle blustered out of the house as soon as the ceremony was over.

At the reception on Joyce's patio, Fiera inhaled every dropped morsel of hors d'oeuvre and wedding cake, Joyce's husband dubbing her, "a brown torpedo vacuum on legs." It became quite the party; the champagne flowed and the revelers danced to Armando's group for two hours before the Friends and Fiera took off in Loretta, looking out windows soaped with bawdy witticisms. Toilet paper fluttered and empty beer cans clattered behind the old green Volkswagen; many of the neighborhood kids stopped playing with bikes or basketballs to gawk from their identical driveways at the passing spectacle.

14

The freeway was only four blocks away, so Jake stopped at a market parking lot to prepare Loretta for the road and to shake off the effects of too much champagne. He put down the coffee Joyce gave him and saw that Tina was crying just a little as she helped him unsnap the tarp.

"I assume those are mixed tears—right, Tina?"

She sniffled quietly. "What?"

"My guess is you're happy with the wedding and sad to be leaving Jimmy." He yanked a snap and looked in the bed.

"Yes, but there's something else." Tina resolutely wiped her eyes with her T-shirt sleeve.

"Hold that thought—can't find anything in here." Pushing aside their gear and luggage, Jake took out a spray bottle and a newspaper. "So what was the 'something else'?"

"It's a strange feeling, being around most of the people we care about for days, and now here we are in a parking lot, driving off to where we don't know anyone."

"Yeah, it's kind of unsettling." He took the pocketknife out of his jeans, put it on the rail and hugged her with one arm. "Wasn't it like this the times you went to Africa?"

"No, it feels a lot different; maybe it's because I didn't care much about the people we left behind."

"Well, we do have one of our friends with us." He let go and pointed to the truck's cab, where Fiera was hanging from a side window, tongue all the way out, waiting.

"Silly dog, she's ready," Tina said with a chuckle.

"Yeah." He handed her the bottle and paper. "If you'll start on the windows, I'll cut all this crap off."

After a few minutes, Jake tossed a string of cans into the bed, and then drank more of his coffee. "That's it, Tina."

"Me too, except this last one." She sprayed over HOT SPRINGS TONIGHT!—soaped onto the rear window. "I won't be able to reach all of it."

He took the paper, leaned way over and wiped. "What did you think of Orie and Armando today?"

"Oh, I know; they danced every time he took a break. She's very impressed by his talent."

"Me too. I knew he was good, but not that good."

After he finished wiping, they secured the tarp and got in; Jake headed for the freeway. "I think it all went pretty well, except for my uncle's bruised ego." Jake explained why Myron was so incensed.

"Jake, I didn't even meet him."

"It's all right. My guess is he won't talk to me for quite a while."

"My glory. That's too bad."

"Not really, though it probably cost us a couple hundred bucks."

"Why is that?"

"He doesn't do presents—strictly cash. He would've probably slipped us some big bills on the sly, and then bragged about it to my other relatives." Jake spotted the Interstate sign. "We can live without his shekels. Okay, that's it— Uncle Myron doesn't get one more second of our honeymoon."

The newlyweds planned on a week in Northern Arizona before they would venture down to the border to check out Sofia, La Cholla, and their new jobs. Using his buddy's place near Flagstaff as a base, Jake and Tina marveled at the enormity of Grand Canyon and the power of the Colorado River, but it was the vermilion gorges of the Navajo Reservation that beckoned them to return someday.

After a Monday lunch with Jake's friend, they headed south through more stunning red rock country, denouncing the area as too commercialized compared to the isolated canyons of Navajoland. During their long descent into the Sonoran desert, they listened to Randy Newman, Credence Clearwater, John Denver, and the Beatles on the eight-track. Jake could have kept up with traffic, but he coasted Loretta at times, especially after they came into the tall cacti.

"The saguaros are amazing," Tina said.

"Yeah, even a lot of the shrubs are green." Jake turned off for a rest area. "Man, the Mojave never looked like this." The temperature was mercifully moderate at around ninety degrees as he and Tina led Fiera out to pee near some brittle white bushes that seemed to grow out of black rock. Jake wondered to himself about the constant buzzing and clicking he heard, like a downed electric line.

They finally rolled into the Phoenix outskirts and were impressed that some of the residential development had preserved acres of desert between home sites. That impression quickly dissolved when they passed industrial sprawl and Levittown-type neighborhoods before coming to the city's center, a concrete confluence of freeways and tall office buildings. Tina turned on the radio; an announcer said it was still before rush hour, but Loretta was soon stuck for ten minutes in smoggy one-hundred-two-degree heat, creeping along in low gear behind an oblivious boy in a maroon Porsche with an A.S.U. sticker, his stereo blasting the "Stones" for all to hear.

Jake cleared the traffic jam, exited, and drove through some suburbs where all activity revolved around the pervasive cars, just like in L.A., except most of the autos here seemed new. Unimpressed by the strip malls, golf courses, and opulent homes with fairway lawns, it dawned upon Jake that all of the unnatural greenery survived on precious water from the same river that awed them over the last few days.

Heading back toward the freeway, they happened upon a local café with a rock garden and the only cacti they had seen for blocks. He parked in some shade; Tina took Fiera out into the weeds while Jake walked back to the café to order drinks and burgers to go. He complemented the owner on her front yard, but she told him, "The place came that way; wish I had a lawn instead."

Eating off of their laps, they left Phoenix and came into miles of hot, humid farmland. "Yuk—looks and feels like the San Joaquin Valley," Jake said, scanning the smoky fields. "But next spring it'll be great to visit here."

"Why? You obviously don't like it very much."

He tipped the bill of his baseball cap toward her. "True, but I do love my Cubs."

"I don't get it." Tina gathered the trash from their late lunch and checked her panting dog.

"The Cubs had spring training in L.A and on Catalina Island for years before they moved here. That's one reason why they have so many fans in L.A."

Tina turned to him. "Ah, now I know why you wanted to come to Arizona."

"My secret's out," he said with a grin.

As the miles went by, the agriculture and turbid air diminished. The closer they came to Tucson, the more the Sonoran desert seemed to regain foothold, the saguaros gradually reappearing by the road.

It was after six o'clock, degrees cooler and much less humid as they watched orange wisps of clouds form above the hills to the west. Jake heard a buzz droning from the desert, the same noise he noticed before Phoenix. "You hear that, Tina?"

"What?"

"It's getting louder, that constant buzzing."

"Locusts, I think. That's how they sound in Africa, anyway. You get used to it."

"I'll be. I never heard them, even in Mexico."

"Well, they do come in cycles—and the bible tells me so." She sang the last six words.

He laughed at her little parody as they came to a billboard for "Old Tucson," a fake town in the saguaros used as a backdrop for Western movies.

Jake pointed out the sign. "There you go, Tina. Guess who must have spent a lot of time in Old Tucson?"

"Hm, would that be the Duke—of York?"

"Geez, how did a mish kid get to be such a wise guy?"

"Oh, I get by with a little help from Jake Friend," she sang, this time at the expense of the Beatles.

"Very funny—you're on a roll," he said with a laugh, approaching a strip of motels north of town. They soon discovered that the downtown area wasn't near the highway; Jake took an exit, and turned back for the motels.

They came to a residential neighborhood, modest stucco houses on large lots, many of the yards rocked in around natural desert plants. A few people poked around the homes as if these were their first moments outside for the day.

Loretta passed a block of small businesses, the sun was still just above the horizon; a bank sign blinked **7:34 P.M.** and **91°**. The next neighborhood was chiefly old frame homes surrounded by flowers and fenced dirt yards. Many families, mostly Mexican-American, were outside, barbecuing under shade trees, the kids playing and hopping around to the steady beat of *cumbias* and *rancheras*.

The truck came to a stretch of open desert; Jake took a gravel side road for twenty yards before stopping to exercise Fiera. They got out into a comfortable warm breeze; Jake was surprised to see a mountain range to the north that appeared to have sufficient altitude for snow. Tina opened the back door; the dog went berserk with her freedom, darting out into saguaros that seemed to reach up to the deepening red sunset.

While they prepared a bowl of water for Fiera, an occasional car passed behind on the road. Hooked together by index fingers, Tina and Jake strolled

113

into the desert through leafy acacia, green skeletal branches of palo verde, and tall wiry stalks of ocotillo, all names they would soon have a chance to learn.

Tina pointed to the ground at a black "hand" slowly crawling by. "Jake, is that what I think it is?"

He looked down from the flame colored sky. "Man, looks like a tarantula to me."

"It doesn't even care we're here."

"We don't want Fiera to mess with it; we'd better get her." Right on cue, the rambunctious dog burst from the brush with a long, sun-bleached rib bone in her mouth.

"She's too excited to have done her business," Tina said, pushing the dog's bowl with her foot. Fiera came right to the water, released the rib to the ground and slobbered the bowl almost dry. She picked up the bone again and turned to them, seeming to smile.

"Okay, baby, give it," Tina said, taking the new treasure and tossing it past the truck, away from the spider's path. They played with Fiera for a few minutes until she finally pooped in the sand. After using the bone to entice the dog back to the truck, Jake drove off for the strip of motels. He had to ask two managers before a third one agreed to accept Fiera, but only with a damage deposit.

After a mid-morning breakfast the next day, they started out and soon passed a small Indian reservation before Jake realized he was on the wrong road. He stopped, checked the map, and then turned Loretta around to get back to an eastbound federal highway, which they took to the next junction before heading south again.

They were back out in open desert, mostly low rolling hills and dry arroyos. The inclines kept Loretta well below the speed limit; only one car passed them on the quiet two-lane road. Her head out the back window, Fiera's ears flapped in the very warm and dry morning air.

The saguaros had become scarce but other desert flora flourished everywhere, especially the palo verde, which in places grew over twice Loretta's height. Jake spotted a squatty barrel cactus, remembering it from school science, then some branchy low cactus with lucent white needles.

"Wonder what the white ones are," he said just as Tina pointed out a sleek bird by the road, sprinting side-by-side with Loretta until darting away into the bush.

"I had no idea roadrunners were that long," she said.

"Me either. Check this." He nodded ahead to a wide billboard, the only manmade object in the entire panorama save the road and power lines. The sign read:

SHANGRI-VILLAGE—5 MILES
ARIZONA'S FINEST RETIREMENT COMMUNITY
TURN ON VALHALA DRIVE TO VIEW MODELS

"Out here?" Tina asked.

"Yeah, I thought Sun City was a Phoenix thing."

Loretta chugged over a moderate rise, catching up to a line of dark blue military vehicles, mostly jeeps and vans. Jake followed them past more billboards and down into to a valley where the Air Force convoy exited at Valhalla Drive. Jake stayed on the road and drove slowly by the development in third gear, wondering if the airmen were on maneuvers. He found out later that for the second time in months he had inadvertently driven close to a ballistic missile site.

Shangri-Village turned out to be row on row of flat three-bedroom homes on standard lots, with tall fencing for residents who didn't face the golf course. To achieve a "territorial" ambience, the houses had faux red tile roofing, each façade with at least one Spanish arch.

About a mile square, the development had replaced the desert with carpets of green turf, flowering exotic trees, and different kinds of imported palms. Jake spotted some of the same tropical bushes he was accustomed to seeing on the streets of Southern California.

Loretta passed the Elysian Shopping Center, where the military convoy mustered at a newly painted parking lot the size of a football field. The enterprises facing the road fulfilled basic needs—a restaurant, groceries, drugs, and a gas station, each one covered with that same red roof. The other side, Jake thought, must have had offices for tax preparation, a clinic and a mortuary. An advertised recreation center for tennis, swimming, meetings and the like was apparently behind one of the green hills on the golf course.

At the southern end of Shangri-Village, giant yellow graders, earthmovers and dump trucks crawled busily over the hills, clearing desert for the next mile of "gracious retirement living." As soon as Loretta rolled by the excavation, they came back into indigenous flora.

"Well," Tina said, "hopefully, we won't need to go back there for anything."

"La Cholla should have what we need." Jake drove on a few minutes and came to what his parents always called "a little wide spot in the road." In this case, it was a cluster of small frame and brick houses, one near the highway and the others off a ways, separated from each other by tall desert growth. Two more miles down the road, the next populated outpost had a small grocery out front. They stopped, bought cold drinks, and munched on the pancakes, sausage and scrambled eggs Tina saved from breakfast.

They passed another wide spot with a produce stand advertising ELOTES/SANDIA. "Mm, cold watermelon sounds so good," Tina said.

He glanced at her. "Some restaurant in near the border should be able to handle that."

"Jake, this is it." A crooked, green rectangular sign by the road had SOFIA written in faded white capital letters.

"Man, not even a speed limit change." He passed the withered shell of a fifties-era gas station and then a closed fruit stand. Another hundred feet or so brought them to a driveway for a small open-air restaurant attached to a cinder-block house. A homemade two-by-ten-foot sign out front said, CHIMICHANGAS – OPEN FRI/SAT AT 5. Above the desert brush beyond the simple house, Jake saw the roofs of two more small bungalows.

"Looks like the only business." He checked his rearview, and then downshifted all the way to second. Fiera sat up on the back seat and stuck her nose out into the warm air again. Jake drove slowly through Sofia, which was turning out to be not much more than a few consecutive wide spots—about two dozen brick or cinder-block houses, a TV antenna on each roof.

For an early Tuesday afternoon in July, the scattered population was relatively active, especially the kids, trying to fit in a full day's play before the heat drove them inside. Mostly in shorts, T-shirts and sneakers, the generally dark-skinned children ran in and out of slamming screen doors while older siblings and relatives hung wash or tended vegetable and flower gardens. Jake noticed "project" vehicles in many yards, parked under shade trees. The cars in the driveways, '60s models or older, were shiny and probably well maintained, he thought.

Some youngsters near the road paused to watch the Volkswagen truck roll slowly by. "I guess we're quite a sight," Tina said, turning back to check Fiera, who had jumped down on the floor, panting again.

"I'd bet not many cars slow down. Then there's Loretta the big kids are probably thinking 'hippies.'"

"Oh well." Tina patted the dog. "Jake, Fiera didn't drink much at the store; she's ready now."

"Yeah, it's getting humid again. I'll find a place to stop." He shifted up to third gear and passed a clump of houses, not finding anywhere to pull off. Jake came to a junction of sorts with a gravel side road and the only street sign in town: SCHOOL RD.

He made the turn. "All right, now we won't have to ask for directions; this should work for the dog, too." The rough road looked more to Jake like a firebreak in the thick Sonoran underbrush. "Good God, I guess the school has to be in here somewhere."

15

Not fifty yards from the highway, a dusty, long-ago-scraped flat five acres materialized from the desert like a mirage. A one-story red brick building stood at its center, a half-acre of lawn and a huge weeping willow out front. "I'll be," Jake said, coming to a stop.

Tina said nothing, both of them still surprised by the isolated school. Jake looked down and saw that the hardscrabble ground by the road had managed to reproduce low mesquite, some prickly pear and the same kind of "white" cactus he saw before. At closer look, he realized each slender green branch was thick with ivory colored quills, giving the false impression that the succulent plant was furry.

Jake put Loretta in gear and drove up to the freshly cut grass and recently trimmed willow tree, its long branches hanging uniformly about five feet off the ground as if it had a "bowl" haircut. The wooden sign posted in the lawn said: SOFIA SCHOOL – LA CHOLLA S.D. A swing set, slide, monkey bars, five wooden picnic tables and a flagpole survived in worn but decent shape on the grass in front of the school. Out in the nearby dry dirt, someone had put in a brick barbecue, two horseshoe pits and a tetherball pole.

Two thin girls with braided raven hair stood there holding the tethered grey ball and gaping at Loretta. One was a pre-adolescent, the other, much younger, had some kind of brace on her leg. A dilapidated light orange Ford pickup waited just off the lawn, LA CHOLLA S.D. stenciled on the door, a power lawn mower strapped into its bed.

"Somebody's here—great." Jake cut the engine and opened his door. "Man, I was expecting everything to be more run down."

"I'll take care of the dog while you check it out," Tina said. "Join you in a minute."

Jake attached Fiera to a longer leash, actually a twenty-foot chain, and left her with Tina. He walked onto the lawn's paved path, waving over to the two girls, who didn't notice him because they were watching Tina pour water for Fiera in a slit of shade by the truck.

The closer Jake came to the school, the more he could tell its advanced age. The masonry between the red bricks was worn, showing gaps and holes; the brown trim around the windows, doors, and flat roof had faded and started to peel. The windowpanes were scratched, chipped and milky, except for two newer ones on each side of the wide-open double front doors.

Just before the stairs, Jake spotted a strange little trove of three identical cola caps in the grass. He bent over, pocketed them, then climbed the four wide concrete stairs and walked into the school.

The lights were off inside, but the sunrays from behind reflected off the heavily lacquered wood floor, casting light all the way down the hall to a GYMNASIUM sign above the closed back double doors. The opaque glass upper halves of seven hallway doors were inscribed with a black number or some block lettering. Brass coat hooks lined both walls, about four feet above the floor on one side, five feet on the other. The nearest doors on the right, labeled OFFICE and CUSTODIAN, were both ajar.

"Hello!" Jake called, his voice echoing some.

"Here. Just a sec," came forcefully from the custodian's room. An elderly man, about five-foot-eight, muscular for his age, entered the hall. His ears protruded from a grey-white crew cut; he plucked a pencil from one ear, inserting it into a front slot on his faded jean overalls. He had a small carpenter's level in one pocket; a beat-up tape measure hung at his side.

"Is that your truck out there?" he asked with a scowl in clear English.

Jake backed off a step as if he were about to go and move the truck. "Yes. Is it in the way?"

"No." The man eyed Jake's cap, beard, white T-shirt, brown Bermudas, and sneakers.

Jake noticed the custodian's closely-trimmed white moustache; he saw some small black moles, barely visible on the man's sun-weathered but only slightly wrinkled brown face. "I'm Jake Friend, new teacher here." He offered his hand to the sturdy old man. "I have the nine-twelve students."

"Figured. *Emilio Montalvo*," he said, not anglicizing his name as they grasped hands comfortably. "Good to meet you," Emilio added, not as hostile.

"Glad to meet you, Mister Montalvo. Do you work here full time?"

"Half, but full time for a second straight summer, thanks to your predecessors."

Predecessors—my, my. "Oh? Why is that?"

"Last summer I had the refurbishing crew." He sighed and frowned at the same time. "This year, well, I'll let you see for yourself." Emilio removed a wad of keys from a pocket and led Jake down the hall.

"The place looks good for its age, outside and in," Jake said before they came to a room with "4" on the glass.

"Yeah, get a load of this—grades six to eight." He opened the door and Jake walked in first, hitting a switch that lit up some glass fixtures above. The back wall had a seam in the middle; to its left, the room was barren. The walls were pungent with a fresh coat of tan paint, the wood floor slick and shiny, and the nearby window had new panes.

The right side was piled high with desks, tables, chairs, and overflowing boxes of books, materials, and equipment. Beyond that, Jake saw bright tempera paint dried all over a sink and splattered onto gouged walls and a cracked green chalkboard. The guts of two broken light fixtures hung down like jellyfish tendrils, and a torn shade leaned on some plywood nailed over the second large window.

Friggin' tornado. Jake walked up to the nearest cardboard box; it was full of blue plastic casing, small pulleys and cables, lenses, knobs, bolts, screws— the remnants of a film projector. *So, the interview question came from this little experiment.*

"You should see the damn floor under there," Emilio stated blandly. "After this side dries, I pull all that over here and do it again. What do you think?"

Jake pointed to the left side of the room. "I think you do excellent work." He faced the custodian. "I also think you have every right to be pissed. So they just up and left it like that in June?"

Emilio scowled again. "It's not that unusual. Seems like there's a teacher in the district who pulls this kind of crap every other year or so. This is the worst I've seen—your room is probably the second worst."

Jake laughed. "Great. That makes my day."

Emilio managed a reluctant smile, exposing crooked teeth and more creases around his mouth and eyes. "You want to see it?"

"Sure, let's go."

They walked down the hall toward the gym, but Jake stopped to look at the wall above the higher coat hooks. Someone had begun a mural, about five by fifteen feet, in a style similar to the Mexican artist, Clemente Orozco. Not a fourth painted, the full sketch showed robust cotton-clad workers with pre-Columbian features, heroically pointing their straw sombreros to show the women and children the way across the desert.

"You like it?" Emilio asked glumly.

"Well, I think the art work is very good, but it looks kind of, uh, romantic."

"Yes, it's just missing poverty, *la migra*, and the damn *coyotes*."

"They started making this last year?"

"No. We had a small arts grant a few years ago. They paid the kids and me a few bucks to start it."

"Really? Wasn't the school closed then?"

"The district rented it to us cheap as a community center; we did the upkeep, paid the utilities."

"Why didn't you finish the mural?"

"Didn't reapply—too many strings; we got tired of working on something so, uh, *falso*. I'll paint it over one of these days."

Jake followed him to room 5; Emilio unlocked the door. "This used to be the old five-six; we didn't have to change much in here last year." They walked in.

As before, everything was moved, but Emilio had yet to paint the dirty walls or varnish the scarred floor on the left side. The mess was similar to the other room, except the lights were intact and neither window was broken. The sink area was filthy, and the stacked materials were in complete disarray, most of them not even boxed.

"Pretty bad," Jake said, "but it's my room now; I'll help you with all this. Looks like a lot of it can be ditched or stored."

"We have storage space in the other two rooms."

Jake pursed his lips in disgust. "For what it's worth, this won't happen again as long as I'm here."

"Good," Emilio said, not sounding very convinced as they left. He locked both rooms, then walked down the hall with Jake. "Want to see your office?"

"I think that can wait; I should check on my wife." They walked out the front doors. Fiera was on her back under the tree, soaking up attention from the girls, who were alternately latching onto Tina and playing with the dog in the grass. Jake noticed the younger girl wasn't letting the bulky leg brace keep her from all the fun.

"I think we've made some friends," Jake said as they walked slowly down the steps together. "Do you live in Sofía, Mister Montalvo?"

"Emilio. My whole life, except four years in the Army and one in school."

Hm, World War II or Korea? Jake walked out on the path with him, gazing at the nearby wilderness.

"It amazes me, Emilio, that the desert is so green here, compared to the Mojave in California."

"More rain, although I think we're behind this year. By now, more cactus should be in bloom."

The smaller girl stayed with Fiera while the older one pulled Tina toward the two men. Jake saw his spouse smiling freely, not the obligatory half smiles she made around most adults.

"*Abuelo*," the girl called, her two pigtails whipping around. "Can she be my teacher?" The pre-teen was neatly dressed in a summer blouse, knee-length shorts, and leather sandals; her pretty, café au lait features radiated around a single flaw, prominent white buckteeth.

"No, *mija*, but you'll see Mrs. Friend at your school."

"I can visit you there, teacher?" she pleaded, still holding her hand as they came close.

Tina patted the girl's arm. "Of course, Rosalinda."

"You hear her Spanish, abuelo? She speaks good."

"Yes, she speaks well, mija. Remember your manners and greet Mister Friend."

Rosalinda finally let Tina go and reached out for Jake's hand. "Nice to meet you," she said shyly.

"A pleasure to meet *you*." Jake smiled, releasing her light touch.

"Mrs. Friend," the old man said, "please excuse *my* manners. *Emilio Montalvo, a sus órdenes.*

"*Mucho gusto, señor.*" Tina smiled and shook his hand.

"*Encantado*," he answered with a slight bow.

Jake glanced over at the little girl tumbling with Fiera and getting her summer clothes grass stained. "You two seem to like our dog," he said to Rosalinda.

"Yes, she's friendly, not like her name." The girl was exuberant again. "I hope you can be our neighbors and we can visit you."

"Rosita," Emilio interjected kindly, "you can go back now with your cousin." She ran off; Emilio turned to Tina. "Thanks for putting up with Rosita's, uh, enthusiasm."

"Not at all. She's wonderful; so interested in everything, a teacher's dream. Is Nora just learning English?"

"No, she hardly speaks at all around strangers. Nora will be one of your students."

Tina's face was pensive; Jake was sure she was already churning over how she could help the child. "Emilio," he said, "from what you and Rosalinda said, I'm guessing you have something to do with the schools besides maintenance."

"I'm a janitor who can fix the easy stuff, and the at-large Board member," he replied, watching the girls.

"Good, so Sofía has a little clout?"

"Very little." He faced the young couple. "Are you folks planning to take a look at La Cholla today?"

"We just have the rest of the day," Jake said, "before we start back tomorrow." He saw Tina smiling toward the kids.

"Plenty of time to get a feel for the place." Emilio shaded his eyes and turned to Tina. "My sister's son, Jesús, is off Tuesdays; I know he'd like to meet you both and show you around."

"We don't want to impose on anyone," she said.

"I'm certain he'll want to do it; I'll call him. Excuse me, I'll be right back." Emilio bowed again to Tina, then turned to go in the door.

Jake and Tina started toward the tree; he grinned at her. "Well done, Latina; you charmed him."

"What?"

"He was pretty grumpy until he met you."

"Ridiculous."

Jake snickered. "I know what I saw."

Tina scoffed and headed for the children. Jake stayed behind, watching her rejoin the girls before he walked out past the barbeque pit. He leaned down to inspect a white-quilled cactus, and then spotted a different kind with skinnier branches and only a few drab spines. Jake compared them, then moved his hand back to touch the white one.

"Don't let that teddy bear bite you," Emilio said from behind.

Jake retracted his finger and stood. "Yeah, they fascinate me. Do you know what this one's called?" He saw that the old man was now wearing a western-style straw hat.

"Just said it; teddy bear *cholla*."

"It is? My Spanish dictionary said *cholla* is another word for skull."

Emilio nodded. "Yeah, but the English dictionary will tell you it's a cactus. Anyway, you're all set. I spoke to Jesús; he's on his way."

"That's great; thanks, Emilio. Uh, do you know anything else about these?" He pointed at the two different cacti. Jake squatted, carefully touching a white needle. "Man, it's sharp all right."

"There are several kinds; I know of only three around here," Emilio said, betraying some enthusiasm in his voice as Jake stood up to listen. "This teddy bear cholla is the most handsome, but they all get flowers. People call them 'jumping cactus' because if you touch one, it jumps onto your hand." He

123

smiled. "Actually, you have to touch it pretty hard—some birds nest in them for protection."

"Incredible."

"They say the Apache threw chollas down from the cliffs onto the Spaniards, then onto the Mexicans and the *gabachos*."

"I'm surprised you let it grow close to the school."

"We didn't before, but they come back fast. When a piece of cholla falls in the dirt, it can take root right there. Our kids know the results of messing with them." He looked at the girls playing with Fiera. "It's dogs that never learn; be sure you have good pliers."

Jake sniggered. "Great, knowing our dog, she'll—" He stopped when he saw a light blue police car come down the road toward the school. "What's this about, Emilio?"

"That's your ride today, maestro."

16

Jake watched the big Ford sedan with L.C.P.D. on the side pull up near Tina and the kids. Little Nora tried to run to the car, limping with a radical gait, her single long braid flopping behind. A man got out and lifted the child for a big hug. He was in his thirties, about five-ten and trim in a T-shirt, jeans, sneakers, and an orange ball cap. Rosalinda ran to greet him as well, then hurried back to Tina.

"Let's go meet my nephew," Emilio said to Jake. They walked together from the dirt onto the grass and started across.

"Can he take us over the border in a police car?" Jake asked.

"Yes, but I didn't know you wanted to do that today."

"It can wait."

Rosalinda ran up, Fiera right behind, to take her grandfather's hand and lead them to the new arrival. "Abuelo, can I take care of the dog while they go to town? Please?"

"You need to ask—"

"I did, I asked teacher and tío Jesús."

"Okay, mija," he said, and she skipped off ahead with Fiera. The nephew, still carrying Nora in one arm, was shaking hands with Tina on the lawn near the tree.

As Jake got closer, he saw black lettering on the officer's white T-shirt: XL - LA CHOLLA P.D.; his cap had a blue Denver Broncos logo. Nora nestled her small dark face into her daddy's shoulder, peeking at Tina.

Jesús greeted his uncle with a pat on the shoulder, then turned his stubbly vacation-day chin to Jake. "Jesús Ramos," he said, putting a hand out, a pleasant smile on his almond-colored face.

"Jake Friend." They shook with firm but friendly grips. "Nice of you to show us around."

"Yes, thank you," Tina added.

"My pleasure. The Superintendent has told me good things about both of you," Jesús said, Nora clinging to him, her black eyelashes downcast.

"He's made us feel very welcome to the district." Jake glanced at Rosalinda and Fiera playing under the tree. "Jesús, how do you want to do this, with the dog and all?"

"Just follow us; you can leave the truck and the dog at my place."

"Okay, will do," Jake said, still unsure about who went where with whom.

"See you there then." Jesús turned to Emilio, putting Nora down. "*Adiós, tío*; thanks for letting her come." Hand in hand, Nora and her father started for the squad car at the child's halting pace.

"Rosita will go with you then?" Emilio asked the Friends.

"Sure, she can start her dog-sitting," Tina said.

Jake reached out to shake the custodian's hand. "Thanks, Emilio. I hope you'll show me more about the desert."

"If it's something I know, maestro." Emilio grinned humbly, then he bowed slightly to Tina again before heading back for the school.

Jake and Tina walked toward the tree. "So, Don Joaquín," she said, "now who charmed the old man?"

"What?"

"You two are already science pals." She couldn't hold back a titter.

"Okay, okay; I think we'll get along fine. Let's get our passenger and that wild dog of yours."

With Rosalinda and Fiera in back, Jake drove out in the dust left behind by the squad car. He followed them back to the other side of Sofia to the small restaurant they saw earlier. Jesús turned off the road, driving by the CHIMICHANGAS sign and through tall green brush over to the far side of an attached cinder-block home.

Jake followed him around to what turned out to be the front of the square house, facing away from the highway. Tall green pickets closed in the lawn and a long bed of roses, blooming in several colors. One crimson variety was trained to climb on an arbor over the front walk. Beyond the flowers, a huge gnarled oak shaded much of the big yard that extended around the grey home to the restaurant.

Jesús left his car idling in the wide dirt driveway next to an old Malibu and a newer Ford truck. He walked back toward Jake as Rosalinda and Fiera jumped down from Loretta. Nora opened the gate and then hobbled in after Rosalinda, who had to duck under some errant rose branches. A short woman in a housedress faced the yard from behind the screen door. She let out a tan part-Chihuahua that ran right over to sniff Fiera's rear end.

126

"Anywhere's fine," Jesús said to Jake, then started back to his vehicle. "*Abuelita* will keep an eye on your dog." In silhouette, the grandma raised her arm.

Jake parked by the Malibu; he and Tina got out, waved to the woman, and saw the kids and dogs already romping across the lawn and into their own world.

The Friends continued over to Jesús, who waited in the squad car, its right-side doors ajar. Tina got in back, Jake in front, separated from the driver's seat by a black console with a clipboard on top. Not accustomed to air conditioning, Jake shivered once after he closed the door.

"That was Emilio's wife, *Alicia*," Jesús yelled over the blasting air. Nodding to the house, he turned down the fan and lowered his voice. "She's everybody's abuelita; you can meet her when we get back. Seat belts, please."

Tina and Jake secured themselves as Jesús started down the driveway. With the exception of some extra switches, a spotlight handle and the silent police radio, Jake thought the squad car was like any austere Ford. He decided that the other cop equipment was locked in the console or the trunk. Jesús stopped at the road to record something on the clipboard; Jake assumed it was mileage.

"No radio on your day off?" Jake asked.

"Right; the car's just a deterrent today." He tilted back his orange cap and looked up at the rearview. "You okay back there, Mrs. Friend?"

"Yes, I'm fine. It's Tina."

Jesús smiled back and made his left turn. South of Sofia, the desert looked about the same as it did to the north. Jesús crossed a bridge over a fifty-yard-wide dry arroyo he called "*Sofia* Wash." He and the Friends exchanged a little information about their backgrounds; Jake took the discussion further by asking about the local history. Jesús said that about half of the eighty or so adults in Sofia were related to Emilio or his wife, who was from another old family, the Ortegas.

"Is she related to the Superintendent?" Tina asked.

"Yes, Alicia's his first cousin."

Jake noticed the desert was turning hilly, and he saw a rail line by the highway. "Are the Ortegas related to the president of the school board?"

"Serna? Probably, if you go way back, but they've had feuds for generations. You may as well know right off the bat—the Sernas and Ortegas have most of the influence here."

Jake realized that Jesús pronounced all the surnames except Serna in Spanish. "And Montalvo, how do they fit in?"

"Emilio is from another of the original families; mostly workers for the Sernas in the past."

"So, you're part Ortega and part Montalvo?" Tina asked.

"Yes, from my mom. My dad's people, the *Ramos*, are latecomers. My wife, *Ana* is a *Morales*; she and I have all the old families covered, except for the Sernas."

Jake grinned. "I'm afraid you lost me."

"It takes a while," Jesús said with a laugh.

Tina spoke up again from behind. "Will your wife be home when we get back?"

"Yes. Ana's shopping for the restaurant—she runs it."

"Maybe we can try it out tonight," Jake said.

"*Cierto que sí*," Jesús answered with another smile.

They left the desert and came to a long cinder-block warehouse with SERNA PRODUCE, INC. painted on the side in four-foot red letters. Some scraggly desert shrubs grew around the rusted wheels of a ramshackle brown boxcar parked on a side rail by the hangar-sized building.

Jake turned to Jesús. "Where's the produce from?"

"Some from here in season, but Serna makes his big money in winter fruit and vegetables trucked in from Mexico."

After the warehouse, they went by a quarter mile of small frame or brick houses with big yards, gardens and trees, resembling the low-income neighborhoods Tina and Jake saw in Tucson. They passed another block of homes, two of them doubling as repair shops; a large house on one street corner was also a small grocery.

Jesús entered downtown; the street sign said, INTERNATIONAL AVE. He drove slowly by the core businesses: a hardware, drugstore, post office, two cafés, a bank, dime store, tavern, coin laundry, mortuary, J. SERNA INSURANCE, a few inactive storefronts, and then, SERNA & LE BLANC, ATTORNEYS. Soaped onto the next window, *CAMBIO DINERO* was the only Spanish besides surnames.

"I see Sernas, but no Ortegas," Jake said.

"Except the supermarket, the Ortegas are more involved in the professions and government—and the schools, of course. The mayor is Serna, but the Ortegas and Montalvos have more votes on the Council."

Jake saw that the block ahead was much different. Bright advertisements in Spanish for dry goods and currency exchange predominated the signage at the last stores before Mexico. After that, two lanes of slow traffic passed a grey structure with five limp flags—three stair-stepped Old Glories, and the Arizona and Mexican flags hanging below.

At the last side street, Jesús turned right, then right again past a one-story yellow brick City Hall building, a vintage black and white squad car parked out front. He saluted with a chuckle, then drove through blocks of poor clapboard houses behind downtown.

Jesús came to a sign for PARK ST., which was wider than International Avenue, and newly paved. He turned left and started up a hill. After two blocks, the older houses gave way to about ten acres of municipal park, then a few middle-income homes. LA CHOLLA SUPER FOODS and its parking lot took up the entire top of the hill.

"So much for driving north for groceries," Jake said to Tina, who just nodded. He turned to Jesús. "I don't see Ortega written on the market, either."

Jesús shook his head. "My great-uncle—he never does that. His old store was downtown; the Sernas fought him about moving it up here. They wanted it over on the next hill, but my tío wanted it right here in between."

"In between what?"

"I'll show you." He took the next street down into a valley of bungalows not quite as old as the houses near downtown. They gained altitude on the other side, driving up to a block of three-bedroom ramblers and functional two-stories.

"Okay," Jesús said, "this is the low-rent side of the Gardens; the Sernas wanted the market over here." At the top of the hill, he turned right on GARDEN DR. and stopped at a black-fenced subdivision with a flower bed surrounding its entrance sign:

LA CHOLLA GARDENS
NO TRESPASSING

Fifty yards or so away, acres of lawn surrounded the first home, a tri-level professionally landscaped English Tudor. Jesús pointed beyond the big house. "Maybe six or seven finished places up in there. A hundred and fifty thousand bucks, at least."

"Serna and friends?" Jake asked.

"Mostly. That's the biggest one, right there. Frankie Serna—he's a lawyer." He glanced up at Tina in his rearview. "Want to see the rest?"

"No, thanks. Jesús, do you mind if I ask you something personal?"

"Fire away."

"Does Nora talk at home?"

"That's a first." He seemed wistful. "It's always her leg people ask about." Jesús cut the motor; he turned to Tina. "She speaks at home, especially with Ana and me, and in Spanish with her abuelita."

Tina's jaw dropped before she spoke. "Both languages?"

"Yes, she understands everything. When she goes out, Nora stops speaking unless she's sure no strangers are around. Hardly says a word in the restaurant."

"How old is she?" Tina asked.

"Just turned six; she's repeating Kinder."

"They've already processed her for special education?"

"Yes, tests, meetings, all that."

Tina thought for a moment. "What did they say she's going to be served for?"

"In general, both physical and mental disability."

Jake had been staring at a perfect bed of white petunias that surrounded the entrance sign, but he was attentive to their conversation before he turned and saw Tina shaking her head in disgust. "Tina's already in teaching mode," he said, attempting humor, but she and Jesús remained serious. *Shut up, Jake.*

"Do you mind telling me about her leg, Jesús?" Tina asked.

"Of course not, maestra." He pushed up the brim of his cap and gazed out. "Nora was born with spina bifida, a relatively mild case, thank God, but with neurological damage and partial paralysis of the left leg. She's had that clunky brace more than a year; I guess it stabilizes her some." He looked in the rear-view again. "They don't agree with me, but I think the brace makes her shyness worse, and I see no improvement when she has it off."

As Tina was thinking, Jake saw fervor in her eyes. "I'll tell you this much," she said, "it's obvious that something isn't right with the school's part in this. After we settle in, I'll begin a reevaluation."

Jesús grinned. "Don't get in trouble now."

"I won't." Tina was still solemn. "I know a little about shyness, how our culture demeans it, but it's not abnormal unless there's constant self-isolation."

"Nora was actually early with her first words, and she wasn't all that late walking. She had it all figured out, then just stopped, maybe when she realized she was different; I don't know. It took six weeks before she walked again." He sighed heavily and started the motor. "I guess we've all been over-protective."

Jesús flicked his radio onto some low static, then turned back onto Garden Drive, away from downtown. "Our two oldest boys, the twins, are eleven now; our youngest boy—" He turned off the radio. "Sorry, bad habit." Jesús looked up at Tina. "Anyway, Nora's first school year was pretty rough—all those strangers, and our boys got in fights when someone made fun of her. It's hard for our boys to understand that the fighting just makes Nora more self-conscious."

"Sounds to me like they have a real good dad," Jake said matter-of-factly as Jesús approached a one-story professional building with a manicured lawn out front.

"We do our best." He sighed again and pointed to the offices. "Both doctors are in there. Oh, and our dentist—another tío of mine." Jesús drove on, descending past a few tidy mid-income homes into a valley with the largest building they had seen in La Cholla.

The hospital had two wings, one made of red brick and perpendicular to a shorter wood-framed addition, which had a recent coat of reddish-brown paint. Like the modest homes across the street, the hospital grounds showed no evidence of the desert, just grass, flowers, and a few mature trees. A life-size white statue of Jesus with outstretched arms stood in the lawn by the newer wing and its attached modular building, where a tall sign proclaimed EMERGENCY in plastic red letters.

A fifteen-foot white cross imbedded in plate glass formed the A-frame façade of the hospital, the vertical line of the crucifix dissecting the double front doors. Enduring time, weather, and birds, a grey statue of Mary holding baby Jesus stood to the left of the entrance.

"*Santa Concepción*." Jake read aloud a painted wooden sign over the doors; it actually said, SAINT CONCEPCION.

"Yeah, Saint Connie's. Our boys were all born here."

"And Nora?" Tina asked.

"The university." Jesús stopped near the entrance.

"With all that glass, it looks like the addition must have been pretty expensive at the time," Jake said.

"My dad told me they had quite a fight about it thirty years ago. The other ward back there is over sixty years old; some said it was good enough; others wanted progress, and now they want a new building again."

Tina leaned forward. "Jesús, can we take a quick look inside?"

"Not much to see, but sure." He parked the squad car right out front; they walked below the cross into an inactive lobby. The layout was simple: a small chapel and a tiny admissions office next to the information/security counter, and three couches on each side. The closest hallway went straight ahead; the one to the left also went straight, then jutted off to the old brick wing. A girl in her early teens waited on a far sofa, reading a magazine.

Jesús waved to the receptionist/operator and a silver-haired man next to her who was wearing an ordinary white dress shirt with a security patch sewn crookedly onto one of his short sleeves. "Jesse," the man shouted for some reason; Jesús nodded and smiled back. Tina took the lead, walking ahead under the sign that said:

PATIENT ROOMS 111 – 118 / MATERNITY

ADMINISTRATION / LABS / EMERGENCY

"They call you Jesse?" Jake asked Jesús.

"In town they do, ever since school."

They walked down the hall by four vacant rooms. The floors shone and the powder blue paint looked recent, but there were drooping electric cords near the ceiling, where brown watermarks resembled continents on an old map. Jake noticed the antiseptic odor was more pungent than in most hospitals; to cover up a lot of old smells, he decided. The only religious trappings he saw were two unimposing crucifixes and an eight-by-twelve-inch portrait of Mary and baby Jesus.

A young red-haired nurse smiled to them as she walked by in light blue hospital scrubs. They came to a see-through room at an intersection of hallways. The crossing corridor connected the old wing from the left to administration and emergency to the right. Inside the nursery's glass walls, they saw five empty incubators and no staff.

"The four maternity rooms are ahead," Jesús said. "That's about it, unless you want to go down to emergency or over to the old wing."

"No, that's good, thanks." Tina said, turning back, the men on either side. "Jesús, it doesn't seem, uh, very busy."

"It is at times; the diocese keeps the place afloat because it serves so many poor people. Years ago, the nurses were mostly nuns—low overhead, I guess. They only have two now, the administrator, Sister Ruth, and another one who minds the chapel."

They came back to the lobby and walked out. "Okay," Jesús said, "I'll show you the schools and the district office—just a few blocks from here." They got back in the squad car; he drove up yet another hill past a bright orange and black twelve-by-eight-foot billboard:

NEXT RIGHT

LA CHOLLA HIGH SCHOOL

HOME OF THE TIGERS

STATE CHAMPS

1957 & 1963 A FOOTBALL

1974 GIRLS A BASKETBALL

"Gotta hand it to those girls; we had to repaint that old sign." Jesús made a turn onto level ground to a campus of three veteran red brick buildings and a newer one built to match. The schools were separated by asphalt and grass, including some mature willows like the one in Sofia. The nearby building was an old two-story high school built around a gymnasium.

Jesús pointed ahead to the new school, the only one with parked vehicles. "That's your building, Tina. K-three, and the district offices are on the far end. Do you want to go in or see more of the town? Whatever you'd like."

Jake glanced at the dashboard. "It's almost four; I guess we should get the dog and start thinking about finding some place that'll take her tonight." He turned to Tina; she nodded back.

"Don't want to be pushy," Jesús said, "but I think we've got that handled for you."

17

That evening, the Friends met Ana, a slight woman whose long hair and black eyes shone like obsidian as she calmly took charge of the seven-table restaurant and put her three extroverted sons to work. Ana prepared the chimichangas like beef or chicken burritos, except fried in lard to a light crisp, then covered with lettuce, salsa, and crumbly white cotija cheese. She used homemade flour tortillas the diameter of pizzas; Jake could barely finish one, and Tina, of course, saved half of hers for the next day.

Emilio's wife, Alicia, whom Jake and Tina had only seen behind the screen door, came by to help Ana. Her hair completely grey, Alicia was much shorter and more wizened than Emilio, although she seemed healthy. Another half-dozen members of the extended family came in after five, most of them helping Ana before they ate.

When Jake noticed there were few paying customers, he realized Tuesday wasn't a regular night; they had opened just for them. The dinner transitioned into an evening-long casual fiesta with more friends and relatives from Sofia and La Cholla dropping in for coconut agua, beer, food, and to meet the new teachers.

Ana was still frying chimichangas after eight o'clock, showing Tina how to make them. With Nora clutching her apron, Ana explained to her daughter how busy she was and that maybe Tina could read to her. The child's eyes, dark as her mother's, focused on Tina. Nora smiled and took Tina's hand, leading her through the restaurant and into the house.

Nora brushed her teeth, changed to pajamas, and brought a dolly and a stack of worn Doctor Seuss books to Tina at the small bed in her alcove-like room.

"I just happen to know all of these, Nora. Which one should we start with?"

Nora held out the most faded and threadbare of the lot, *And to Think that I*

Saw it on Mulberry Street. "This one is my favorite," Nora said, opening the cover eagerly as if to hear the story for the first time.

Determined to hold back tears brought on by this so-called mentally disabled child, Tina smiled and started to read.

After Tina rejoined the adults, one of the uncles brought out his guitar and started everyone singing. The party broke up later after the tío taught Jake some lyrics to *Malagueña Salerosa* and the two of them sang a slow, sentimental and inebriated version of the old love song.

The Friends were escorted to a spare room in Emilio's house fifty yards away while Fiera stayed with Rosalinda at her house somewhere off in the tall palo verde.

"Are you always such a happy drinker?" Tina asked Jake from the bed as he finally settled to remove his shoes.

"What? I guess so."

"You don't ever get depressed or, uh, angry?"

"Not angry anyway. Why?" He took off his shirt.

"I'm just a little bit worried about you."

"I know what an alky is, Tina; my dad's family taught me well." He pinched his two-inch fat roll, grinning. "Check this, maybe I have been overdoing it a little."

"Okay, get your tubby ol' self in this bed."

While breakfasting the next morning on eggs, fruit, and reheated cheese enchiladas, Jake and Tina heard from Emilio that his grandson, Juanito, Rosalinda's father, had three small rentals. After Emilio told them that one place would be available when they returned from California, Alicia came over from the kitchen to whisper something to her husband.

"You two have a visitor," Emilio said. Jake, nursing a headache, went to the door with Tina to find Fiera curled up on the porch; the Friends had a good laugh over their loyal mutt.

After Emilio left for work, Alicia came along to guide Loretta about forty yards into the bush to Juanito's place. Nora was already there with Rosalinda; the two cousins were halfway up the driveway as if they were starting to leave.

"I'm so sorry," Rosalinda said to Jake, nearly crying. "We just now found Fiera was gone."

Tina, sitting in back with the dog, opened the door; Fiera leaped out to lick the girls. "Don't worry, *Rosita*," Tina called, "we should've told you to tie her up."

Rosalinda pointed back at her house, which had a five-foot adobe wall all the way around. "See my daddy's big fence? I didn't think she could get out."

"It's okay, mija," Tina said. "She can get out of anywhere."

"I'm not in trouble then?"

Tina shook her head reassuringly. "Of course not. Hop in and show us the way to the rental." After the girls and Fiera got in back, Rosalinda began begging the Friends to rent the house, citing all the possibilities for visits and dog-sitting. Jake followed her animated directions through the underbrush to yet another small cinder-block house in a clearing. He stopped and ran around the front of the truck to help Alicia get down from the high front seat.

As they walked, the old woman said, "Sorry, no key," in English; Rosalinda told them her dad's painter had it. They looked in the windows at the cottage's gleaming off-white living room walls; the compact kitchen was cluttered with ladders, tarps, and paint cans. Tina and Jake spoke for a moment, then told Alicia they would love to rent it. A cheer from Rosalinda and a squeal from Nora followed, which brought a surprised chuckle from their *abuelita*.

"*Emilio told Juanito he would not send teachers again to rent,*" Alicia said in Spanish, the first full sentence she spoke to them, her words slurred by loose dentures.

Jake raised his brows. "*¿Por qué, señora?*"

"*They ruined this house like the school.* But he likes you two," she added in English, turning back. She took Rosalinda's hand; Nora had already latched onto Tina's.

The Friends' original plan was to make their move to Arizona in August, but after renting the house in Sofia, they decided to return as soon as they could. While Jake and Tina were gone, Fiera would stay with Rosalinda, an arrangement that seemed to please all concerned.

They made it back to Sofia the last week of July, Jake in a small rental truck and Tina driving Loretta. As they began to get things squared away, the relentless hundred-degree heat bothered both of them, especially Jake, but he soon adjusted with the help of the shady oak tree out front and a wheezing swamp cooler that kept the living room in the eighties during the day.

As for Fiera, she found relief in the shade on the back veranda in her drinking bucket, an ordinary mopping pail. She had figured out how to stuff her entire back end into the water, her two front paws out on the concrete slab. She sat there minutes at a time, tongue hanging out, and occasionally lapping water from around her hard belly.

Every evening at dusk when the heat broke somewhat, the desert began to crawl with tarantulas, an occasional diamondback rattler or giant centipede, and worst of all, scorpions as common as stink bugs. The tarantulas were by far the most docile of these, often walking right by Fiera, who would follow them for a while until she became bored. After getting nipped by a scorpion, the dog decided they were worthy of barking, which was fine with Jake, who told Tina he could deal with the spiders and snakes but admitted the scorpions "creeped him out."

One sweltering night that first week, they were lying on top of the sheets in their underwear, reading. Jake was trying to ignore the squadrons of June bugs, mantises, moths and unidentified flying creatures bouncing off the screens of the bedroom windows. He turned and spotted a striped-tail scorpion over their heads on the wall. Jake sprang right to the floor yelling, "Damn it!"

Tina sat up and saw the arachnid above, motionless, as if it had been watching them read. "We'll have to kill it, Jake; we can't leave it wandering around in here."

"No shit." He was surprised by the pique in his voice. "Sorry."

"It's okay."

"Damn thing must be four inches long."

"I don't think so." Tina tried not to smile. "You want me to do it?"

The scorpion hadn't moved. "No, I'll handle it."

"You don't have to prove anything; I'm glad you don't kill things."

"I never said I wouldn't kill something that was after us." He kept one eye on the scorpion as he looked around for a potential weapon. "I'm going out to get something."

It took less than a minute for him to return from the veranda with a garden shovel and a push broom. She was looking in the closet.

"What happened, Tina?" Jake pushed two boxes out of the way.

"I tried to squash it with a book. I hit it hard, but it just fell off and ran in here."

"Why didn't you wait?"

"Sorry. I didn't think it was that hard to kill."

"Man, no one can accuse you of being squeamish."

"Been around bugs and varmints all my life, Jake."

He knelt in front of the closet and started taking out shoes, one at a time, with the broom. As he carefully pulled things out using his left arm, Jake held the shovel above with his right, ready to flatten the formidable little beast. He kept working cautiously for at least ten minutes—no sign of the scorpion. "Nothing else I can take out; now we just wait."

137

"Jake, it's late. Let's sleep in the other bedroom."

"It might just walk right in there."

"I doubt it. I'm going to bed."

"Fine. I'm staying here."

To make Jake's vigil more comfortable, Tina brought him a kitchen stool before she went to bed. He put a lamp near the closet for more light and waited on the stool, shovel at the ready. He kept watch for a while before he started to nod off. After the third or fourth time that Jake woke himself, the creature was there, on the wall in the closet. He stood up stealthily, swung the shovel, but only dealt the scorpion a glancing blow; it fell to the floor and fled. From overhead, Jake came straight down on it, screaming "Eyah!" as the steel shovel clanged on the floor. He repeated the assault three times, "Eyah! Eyah! Eyah!"

Tina stood at the door. "I think you got it, Jake."

"What? Yeah—little bastard." He took a deep breath. "Jesus, I really wanted to get it, didn't I?"

Tina grinned. "Thanks for rescuing me, Don Joaquín."

He stared at the little mess. "Yeah, funny. Talk about overkill."

"Can we go to bed now?"

The next day, as they got ready to leave, he asked her not to tell any of the locals about his scorpion hunt. Tina said she would save the little drama for Hannah's visit at Thanksgiving.

"Drama?"

"Yeah—Hiyah! Hiyah! Hiyah!"

"Hilarious." He chuckled with her on the way out the door.

During their second week in Sofia, the dry, hot mornings continued, but thunderheads formed in the nearby hills in the afternoons, making each day progressively more humid. The monsoonal electrical storms came close enough twice to bring them some brief respite from the heat.

One afternoon, while tossing emptied boxes onto the veranda, Jake saw slate clouds building to the southwest. He brought Tina out to see the lightning bolts arc and stitch between the leaden thunderheads and a hilly horizon. They stood there for a couple of minutes in their tees, shorts and sneakers, watching the storm intensify.

"Pretty far away, we'll probably miss the brunt of it again," Jake said. "Where's Fiera?"

"Already under the bed." They turned to go back inside but heard a low rumble behind them, in the opposite direction from the storm.

Jake turned around. "Is that water?"

"Maybe; I don't know." They walked out across the veranda into the dirt back yard and started toward the noise. Jake had his trusty shovel, using it as a cumbersome hiking stick.

"In case of a scorpion, Jake?"

"Right, smart aleck," he answered with a grin.

The desert was nearly lush with new growth, and more of the cacti were blooming. Jake stopped to show her one kind he had recently discovered. It was called the "hedgehog," a squat succulent with lavender-pink flowers.

They walked on, heading for the noise and passing a tall mesquite. After weaving around palo verde and some grey ironwood, they came to an ocotillo more than twice Jake's height. Each of its lanky, spiny arms had small red blossoms at the tip.

"I didn't know these bloomed," he said, not paying much attention to some loud thunder behind them.

"Such delicate little flowers."

"Yeah. The noise is that way." He pointed past more tall stands of palo verde, which they circumvented before stopping again to listen.

"It *is* water, Jake—rushing water."

They walked quickly out to the edge of the bluff and looked down into Sofia Wash, churning from side to side with at least four feet of brownish-grey, sludgy run-off. All sizes and shapes of limbs, even a few logs, bobbed in and out of the swift current.

Jake pitched a stick into the current and watched it vanish. "Man, wouldn't want to be standing there when that first came through."

"Look at this." She pointed upstream to a blue plastic kiddie pool that sailed by in seconds. "The wash must come right from the hills."

They heard louder thunder, and turned to the storm; a cool breeze blew in their faces. The steel grey clouds had boiled higher in the sky and moved much closer. Jake's peripheral vision spotted something, a white milk carton floating by in the flood. He let go of the shovel, picked up some rocks and managed to throw two of them at the target before it was gone.

"You almost hit it."

"Not really." A loud crack seemed to rip the atmosphere not far behind; Tina and Jake turned into another wave of air, this time it smelled of damp dirt. "Jesus, how could it be that clo—" A roll of thunder obliterated Jake's last word, wobbling the ground. "It's moving fast." He picked up the shovel. "Let's head back."

At first, they just walked from the bluff toward the menacing dark front, thinking they still had time since the sun shone brightly behind them. After another fifty feet or so, Jake's toes tingled, then his legs.

"You feel that?" Tina asked, but before he answered, lightning and thunder crack-boomed simultaneously, electrifying their arm hair. The white bolt appeared to strike near the house; burnt ozone touched their nostrils as the first heavy drops splattered onto the ground.

"¡*Vámanos*!" he shouted; they took off running, Tina in front and Jake lurching along with the shovel. The downpour turned ferocious, striking the ground so hard that the rain ricocheted, spraying up to their bare knees as they ran through the brush. With each zap of lightning, Tina and Jake retracted their necks involuntarily like turtles. Jake yelped once between the strikes; she looked at him quizzically, but they kept going and scurried onto the veranda, completely sopped.

"Thank God the lightning didn't hit here," Tina shouted over the deluge slamming onto the veranda's metal roof. She pulled her drenched hair back and watched the curtain of rain.

Tossing the shovel away, Jake looked immediately at his hand. "Piss up a rope, dumber than the dog."

"What's wrong?" She turned to him and saw a hunk of cholla wedged into the palm of his left hand.

"Barely touched it; Fiera was supposed to be the first one to do this," he called back.

"How do you get it out?" she shouted over the racket, a bit of panic in her voice.

"Emilio said to use pliers."

"Pliers? Shouldn't you go to a doctor?"

"Only if I can't get it all out."

They went into the kitchen and found the toolbox. Jake took some locking pliers and poked the branch to see if the spines were deeply imbedded. "Ouch, damn it."

"Can you do it?"

"I think so. Find the scissors, okay?" She brought them; Jake cut out the cactus parts not in contact with his skin. Six quills remained, practically sewn into the adipose tissue between his thumb and forefinger. He sat at the kitchen table and yanked them out one by one, grumbling an oath with each spine he freed. Tina puttered around with salve, sympathy and antiseptic until he finished the extractions.

The rain had completely stopped, but they heard a second storm approaching from a different direction. Tina checked on Fiera in the guest bedroom, then joined Jake in their room, where he was opening the windows. They took off all their wet clothes and got under the sheet to listen to the next storm.

"Enjoy this cool air while you can, Tina."

"How's your hand?"

"It's fine now—had a good nurse."

"Oh sure."

"I did." He leaned over; they kissed on the lips. He released; she put her damp head on his shoulder. Jake cupped a breast, his member poking her in the leg.

"My, my, that was a quick recovery, Don Joaquín."

"I guess so." He kissed Tina on the nape, tickling her into a slight shiver.

"Before you get too friendly, find one of your little plastic hats; I'm not equipped."

"Man, that sure breaks the mood."

"A few more weeks, amor."

"Right, I know. Now don't go anywhere, cutie." He tossed back the sheet and rushed to the bathroom.

18

That fall, Tina and Jake saw why new retirement communities were developing in the desert. The weather was Chamber-of-Commerce-perfect week after week; some of the insects, arachnids, and snakes hibernated or died, and most of the mammals and birds they wanted to see were still around. The mountains north of Tucson were another bonus; Tina and Jake camped up there twice over fall weekends to enjoy the bright foliage and snow neither of them had experienced much as children.

Jon Munz turned out be somewhat of a surprise to Jake. The supervisor agreed to almost everything his new teacher wanted to do, especially if minimal cost was involved. As anticipated, Munz was often content to leave the program in Sofia to fend for itself, but not out of laziness, Jake decided. The administrator just seemed to have a lot of confidence in the school's small staff.

In August, they had interviewed Rosa Méndez, an accomplished teacher of science and math who was tired of living in Phoenix. To hire her, Munz and Jake had to outvote the high-school principal, who preferred an applicant with coaching experience.

After Jake and Rosa spent weeks sorting, discarding and reorganizing, they set up the program so she could teach her strong subjects to all grades; Jake would do the same with Language Arts and Social Studies. They taught ESL as a part of content classes; Jake did the P.E., and Rosa alternated music and art. For her first art project, Jake got permission from Munz for Emilio to adjust his duties so he could volunteer an hour each day to guide Rosa and the students in revamping the hallway mural.

Jake made a point of not asking for money until he had to have it, but he soon discovered a glaring educational gap for youth who worked during the day. Munz came through again, tapping into federal Migrant funds so they could offer ESL and high school equivalency preparation on Tuesday and Thursday evenings. Rosa and Jake would start the new program in early

November; he gave it an acronym, MAPAS, which stood for Migrant Alternative Program at Sofia. Tina was also going to be involved, volunteering for some Thursday nights, and the program gave Jake five hours of extra salary they would need, as it turned out.

Just after Halloween, a few days before MAPAS started, Tina felt sure enough to tell Jake that she was pregnant. He was usually home first on Fridays, but Tina arrived early from La Cholla in the old Opel Kadett they had bought from a lot in Tucson. She prepared dinner, trying Ana's recipe for lemon pastry, and hesitantly told Jake the news after they ate.

Jake gave her a cursory hug and sat down. "Man, I didn't expect that. You sounded like you had bad news."

"You don't seem very excited about it either."

"Uh, how long have you suspected?" he asked, ignoring his second helping of dessert.

"A while, but I wanted to be pretty sure."

"Are you past where you were the second time?"

"I think so; I haven't seen anyone yet." Tina paused. "Listen to us; we're both so cold about it." Tears welled up in her eyes. "I wasn't going to cry— shoot."

He reached across the table. "Sorry, Latina."

She sobbed, holding his fingers firmly. "There's nothing to be sorry about. You're afraid of what might happen; so am I."

Jake got up and pulled his chair next to Tina's. He put a napkin in her hands, and then held her.

"*Gracias, amor*. I'm okay," she said, wiping the last of the moisture from her face as he let go. "We have to talk about this." Tina made a long sniff, determined to put the crying behind her. "If we make it this time until I start to show, that's when I want to tell people. Except maybe Hannah at Thanksgiving."

"Sure, that's a good idea. What about a doctor?"

"I don't know. The university is so far; we came here to be part of a community."

"And remember our insurance only covers complications. We could probably afford the university hospital, but not the specialists."

"It's good we have two salaries."

"We still might have to borrow. If we use Saint Connie's, Jesús said Doctor McNally is, uh, sort of over the hill—that just leaves Serna's nephew."

Tina nodded. "I heard he went to a top medical school; knows all the latest."

143

"That's something, I guess; he's only been practicing a couple of years. Remember him at the Superintendent's party—the frat boy?"

"Yes, but I don't think he's much like his uncle."

"God, I hope not."

"Maybe I'll give him a try; see how it goes. I'm going to wait another week or two."

"Okay. Can I ask you something about that, Tina?"

"Of course, but about what exactly?"

"Male doctors. Do they bring a nurse in for, uh, O.B. exams?"

She forced air through her teeth, a scoff for her. "Usually not."

"Well, they should. I suppose you don't want me to come to the appointment."

"You can if you want, but I think they'll ask you to stay in the office."

"That doesn't make sense; I'd refuse."

"Maybe you'd better not go then."

"Okay, maybe not for the first one."

"Everything will probably be okay. If not, we'll just have to find a family doctor near the university."

Most of the ten students who began MAPAS at night were sixteen-to-twenty-year-olds from rural Sonora who worked the fields or warehouses in the U.S., living on their own or with relatives. All of them were Mexican citizens; three had completed only primary school, the rest attended or graduated from secondary. Two exceptions were the Hernandez brothers from Mexico City, college prep graduates, twenty and eighteen years old, who lived with their parents and only worked in the summer. All of the first MAPAS students were male, except for one popular and closely guarded twin sister.

On the second night of MAPAS, Jake was at his desk, grading and monitoring practice exams for four students; the rest were in ESL in Rosa's room. A young man walked in with a binder, but he stopped, almost cowering, just inside the door. The others glanced up and went back to their tests.

The new student was an inch or so taller than Jake and so thin his blue flannel shirt and faded jeans sagged from his lanky frame, making him appear more destitute than he probably was. His sneakers were ragged but in one piece and he wore a sweat-stained white baseball hat with a HAWAII 5-0 rainbow on the front. The young man's face and neck were very dark, a combination of genetics and years in the sun, Jake thought, smiling to him.

Solemnly, the newcomer approached, pushing dark brown hair from his forehead. "*¿Maestro?*" he asked quietly.

"*Sí, soy maestro* Friend. *¿Cómo te llamas?*"

"I am *Benjamín Soto*. I can study here?"

The older of the light-skinned Hernandez brothers from Mexico City, Justino, sniggered and said, "*Mojado*" in a low voice. The other students kept working, and the Soto boy also ignored Justino.

Jake stood up to shake hands. "Good to meet you. If you're under twenty-one, you can study here."

"I am nineteen, maestro."

"Okay. Should I call you Ben?" The young man nodded; Jake reached into a tray on his desk and gave him a registration form. "Fill this out, please; let me know if you have questions." Ben sat and started writing; Jake checked the clock. "Okay, guys, time's up—take your break, except Justino; I need to see you."

Justino Hernandez adjusted the collar of his silky royal blue dress shirt while his brother, Ricardo, left with the others, shaking his head. Jake led Justino to the far end of the room, well away from Ben.

"You know why I told you to stay?" Jake asked, just above a whisper. Justino looked sullenly away and ran a comb once through his slick auburn hair. "Answer me," Jake said flatly.

"I know nothing," he grumbled in his heavy accent.

"Yeah, Justino, for a guy who I know is smart, sometimes you act like you know nothing." Jake's voice was still low; Justino just scowled at a map on the wall. "In this school, you don't call anybody *mojado*; you show respect for the other students."

He turned to Jake, his teeth clenched. "Wetbacks get no respect of me."

"Guess I can't change that, but here's the deal: If you want to stay here and get your diploma, then you leave him alone. Is that clear?"

"*Sí.*" Justino looked away, pouting.

"Good. Go on out." Justino left; Jake walked back over to Ben.

"Maestro, the address and *teléfono*—it's my uncle. *Mi papá*, he look for a house."

"That's fine, Ben, tell me if it changes. All right, let's see." Jake took the form and looked at it. "Okay, you finished eight years in Hermosillo; two in La Cholla. How did you learn so much English?"

Ben removed a dog-eared tourist dictionary from his back pocket. "I study this; listen to American radio in the night. I want my English, uh, to be more good."

"You're doing very well; you'll be in the advanced class second hour, with those boys who just left."

"*¿Avanzado?* I need the first class, no?"

"We only have two levels; you'll be fine in there."

"*Gracias, maestro.*" He pointed at the exams. "What they doing?"

Jake explained how they were studying for their high school equivalency degree. " . . . and you can too, Ben."

"Yes, I want this very much."

Within a week, it became obvious to Jake that Ben Soto would become the top student in the MAPAS program. Ben said math was his best subject; he took that exam first, passing it easily, which peeved Justino Hernandez, who had already cleared all the practice exams except for math.

The Tuesday evening before Thanksgiving, Jake was excited about Hannah's visit but miffed because the holiday would interrupt MAPAS just as the students were settling in. He was administering a practice test to two students while the others studied. Ben, who was absent for the first time, finally walked in quietly at break, holding a plastic sack full of bread.

"Hey, miss your ride?" Jake asked; Ben just looked around the empty room. He walked to the reading area, held aside Jake's bottle cap curtains and saw Justino on the couch, flipping disinterestedly through a magazine.

"*¡Soplón!*" Ben shouted, dropping the bag to go after him. By the time Jake rushed through the curtains, Ben held the smaller Justino down by the shoulders on the sofa, cursing him.

"Ben, stop!" Jake yelled, pulling him off. The moment he was free, Justino yanked a knife from his pocket. He pointed it at Ben; a long blade sprang from the handle.

"*Goddamn mojado,*" Justino snarled, standing up, but Jake stayed between them.

"*Pinche soplón,*" Ben said, spitting his words and pointing at Justino as Jake held him back.

"*¡Cálmate!*" Jake ordered Ben, who slowly lowered his arm, glaring at his adversary. Jake turned to Justino. "You're pointing that damn thing at me now. Put it down."

"The *pendejo* jump *me*, man."

"Yeah, but not with a knife. He gets suspended, but unless you want to deal with the cops, put it down."

Justino sneered, closing the knife into his pocket. He walked for the door. "*Mi papá, maestro*, he gonna come."

"Fine, I want to see him; I'll need that knife before you come in this school again."

Justino pushed his way past the others as they walked back in. Ben picked up his plastic bag.

"Get your things, guys, and go to English," Jake told the group. After they left, Jake and Ben went out in the hall and stood below the mural. "What's going on, Ben? First, what's a *soplón*?"

Ben leaned back against the wall, whisking away strands of hair. *Este soplón nos rateó a la migra.*"

A snitch. "He turned in your family?"

"*Sí. Mi papá, my uncle and aunt, and their children—all deported,*" he said in Spanish. "*Ricardo told me. He hates his own brother.*"

Some students came down the hall; Ben took a deep breath. Jake told his new group to go in and study for their next exam; he turned back to Ben. "Okay, so when did Immigration come?"

Calmer now, Ben switched to English. "I go for *pan* in the morning." He held up the sack of bread. "When I come back, the neighbor tell me what happen. I hide; wait for my friend and go work."

"What will you do now?"

"*Mi papá*, I think he stay in *México*; he is here only for me to study. My uncle—*sus niños son americanos*—he come back after the Christmas, I think."

"When he returns, can you stay with him?"

"Yes, but I think I am problem for my uncle; maybe I go back to stay in *México*."

"You want to study here, right?"

Ben frowned. "*Sí, maestro*, but the fight—*Justino*."

"Yeah, you did the wrong thing, but he pulled that stupid knife; he's in more trouble. You're suspended three days—today, tomorrow and Friday."

"The class is only today."

"Funny how that works on Thanksgiving. Where are your things?"

"Only this now." Ben pathetically lifted the bag of bread. "They close the house, but I can find the key. After two, three days, I go back late in the night."

"Where will you stay?"

"My friend at work, maybe."

"I have an idea. See what you think."

19

While Jake's situation with Jon Munz worked out well, Tina's principal was an ambitious new administrator, a former high school math teacher with aspirations to be a superintendent in some big city. After his first official visit, he told Tina that her discipline was a bit lax. At the post-observation, he said her lesson lacked "large-group instruction" and needed more "measurable goals." She knew he was spouting his internship pedagogy and didn't understand what took place in her class. Try as she did to restrain her emotions, a tear escaped one eye; she apologized and dried her face. To his credit, the novice principal asked Tina to describe her methods.

She explained how each student had a separate learning plan. While they did have large-group work, it was the exception, and they measured success more by observed accomplishments than testing. Tina, her two aides, a nurse who was there for one boy, and her parent volunteers sometimes ran what seemed like a circus, she admitted, but they provided a specialized "ring" where each child could learn. The principal insisted that she commit to a goal of more large-group instruction, but he didn't show up in her room again for weeks.

Though Nora was happy in school and a helper for the other students, Tina began the promised reevaluation of the child's educational program. It took until Thanksgiving week for Tina to complete the paperwork and confer with the psychologist, her principal, Munz, Jesús, and Ana. After a Tuesday afternoon meeting with all of them, Tina also had her first appointment with Doctor Serna.

She got home from the doctor's after six, checked the thawing turkey in the sink, and ate an apple to hold her over until eight-fifteen, when she expected Jake to get home from MAPAS. Ana had given her some chicken tamales, one of Jake's favorites; Tina put a few in to steam at eight o'clock. She chopped fruit, took out a chilled bottle of his favorite Mexican beer, and even lit two candles.

When Jake called to say he'd be late, Tina put away the food and sat in their small living room, overcome by a crying jag. He came home before nine thirty, saw the extinguished candles and went into the bedroom to find her lying on the bed in school clothes, facing the wall.

"Tina, I'm sorry. We had some problems tonight."

"What happened?" she asked around a telltale sniff.

"You've been crying."

"What else is new," she stated coldly.

"Something go wrong at the doctor's?"

Tina turned to him. "No, it went okay. The due date is June twentieth." Her frown morphed into a brief grin. "We're pretty fertile; it's a bit earlier than we planned."

Jake sat, taking her hand. "Yeah, but it'll work."

"I'll just be huge by the time school's out."

"What did he say about the baby?"

"Everything seems fine."

"Well, that's all good news then, right?"

"M-hm. I asked about miscarriage; he said it's not likely, though still possible."

"That's great, Latina." They hugged a few moments; he let go. "I blew it; you were going to celebrate, candles and everything. No wonder you were crying; I'm sorry."

"No, something else got to me. I'm sure you had no control over what happened, whatever it was."

Jake winced. "A fight, believe it or not; the last thing I expected from these kids."

"Everybody's okay?"

"Yeah, later for that." He took her hand again. "Did Serna upset you?"

"No. He was actually very professional, up-to-date, but, uh . . . ."

"Yes?"

"You were right; he sure plays up the phony bedside manner, but I think I trust him to do his job."

"You said he was professional. How did he act when, he, uh, exam—"

"No problems there, Jake—very respectful."

"Good. What did he say about me being with you for the birth?"

"Saint Connie's doesn't allow it."

He let go of her and stood up, scowling. "Jesus, some places encourage it now." Jake leaned on the wall, folding his arms.

"I know; I doubt they've even considered it. So, do you think we should go to the university?"

"If we stay here, I'll do what I can, but you're the one who'd have to deal with them the most." Jake sighed. "Maybe that old emergency doc in Visalia would like to semi-retire in Shangri-Village."

"He was so good," Tina said, ignoring the ridiculousness of Jake's comment. She sat up on the bed. "Maybe we'll feel better about everything after a couple more months. If not, there's still time to change."

"Yeah, the next appointment should tell you more. Since that went okay, what was it that upset you today?"

"Nora's meeting." She stood up. "Let's go to the kitchen; we can share our little disasters over some fruit."

They walked out; Jake got a beer while Tina dished up some pico de gallo similar to what they ate on the beach in San Diego. They sat at their small kitchen table; Jake forked a hunk of jícama, dipping it in the spicy juice.

He inserted the cube into his mouth. "Dli-shus."

"Good. Should I heat up the tamales?"

"No thanks, I ate something at school."

Tina pushed her fruit around with the spoon. "Well, Munz turned out to be a savior again."

"How's that?" He took a swig of his Bohemia.

"My principal said January before Nora could move to a regular first grade; the rooms are full. I told them how much I enjoy Nora, but how wrong it is for her to wait; that she reads, for God's sake—I didn't say it like that. Anyway, Munz was way ahead of it; he brought a first grade teacher with him who needs ESL support. He said there's a bilingual teaching aid they use only for duty at the high school. So this teacher accepted Nora; she gets the aid. Apparently, the high school principal is, uh . . . "

Jake laughed while swallowing some fruit. "He's pissed off—too bad. That's more good news, then. What was the upsetting part?" He sipped the beer.

"Well, Munz and Jesús made a big deal about how I supposedly stand up for my students."

"Good for them—that's exactly what you do."

"Jake, the doctor's appointment was on my mind. As much as I want this baby, I felt so guilty when they said those things about me, knowing all along I probably won't be with those kids next year."

"Ah, I get it now." Jake smiled. "Tina, while you're on maternity leave, you can volunteer for some hours with your own class; maybe sub half-day. I bet you'll need to get out of the house anyway; I have a feeling Alicia would love to babysit."

Her mouth open part way, Tina thought about what he said. "Jake, that's such a good idea. I would still know a lot of my kids if I take the class back after next year."

"Sure, if that's what you decide to do."

She smiled and ate her first bite of fruit.

"Uh, not to spoil the mood," Jake said, "but I have to run something by you. I invited Ben over for Thanksgiving dinner."

"So? That's wonderful; we have plenty of food, and Hannah would love to meet him."

"Well, there's a little more to it. Ben's the one who started the fight."

"What? That's hard to imagine."

He told her about Ben's assault on Justino and what motivated it.

"Jake, after Hannah leaves, Ben can stay here as long as he wants, as far as I'm concerned."

He looked at her sheepishly. "I, uh, already told him that. Ben's so proud; he's thinking it over."

"I'll talk to him on Thanksgiving."

"Gracias, Latina."

The next morning, Tina started some Thanksgiving preparations while Jake drove to Tucson to pick up Hannah. He wasn't surprised to see her walk out of the connecting tunnel closely attended by a tall young man in a pilot's uniform. Jake's attractive unmarried sister, now well into her thirties, always had to deal with men falling all over themselves, at least until they heard her opinions.

She was the only Friend sibling with dark hair; her sisters said she was a partial throwback to mother's Semitic genes or to so some putative "Indian blood from one of father's Mormon ancestors." Her skin, however, was almost as fair as Jake's, making her short black hair always seem like a dye job.

Though Jake warned Hannah the weather would be cooler than L.A., she was wearing a canary yellow, light summer dress; she also had an airline blanket wrapped around her torso. Jake couldn't wait to ask her what that was about.

Hannah spotted her brother, dumped the pilot, and rushed over to Jake, her handbag falling from the blanket as she reached out with one arm to hug him. They let go; Jake picked up the purse and held it, smiling.

"Huey, you look so good." Hannah took the bag while holding up the blanket with her other arm. To Jake, she was the same—her dark round eyes, steady wry grin and cute lump of a nose gave her a genial countenance, though she always considered herself to be "all business."

"You look great, Sis. So who was your friend, Ms. Friend, and what's with the blanket?"

She shook her head. "He's some back-up flyboy who came to my rescue." She didn't lower her voice as they started arm-in-arm down the crowded passageway. "He managed to put this blanket on me without feeling my boobs, though he took a damn good look." Hannah, a trim five-four, had always taken guff from her taller sisters for not being sturdy enough to support her heavy breasts.

"What? You lost me." Jake tried not to care that Hannah was drawing a lot of attention.

"The stewardess spilled a whole cup of water right on my chest—actually put out my cigarette. The girl was so embarrassed she brought me towels, a blanket, and junior flyboy to apologize. I dried off in the bathroom; my bra is still sopping."

Jake started laughing as he led her around a corner toward the baggage area. "Did they know you're a lawyer? Maybe they thought you would sue."

"Real funny, Huey. Pilot Bob, who didn't even know his name is a palindrome, sat down and started hitting on me. He decided I wasn't worth the effort after a minute or two of politics—about average," she added with a laugh.

"Good riddance. Do you have a backup slingshot packed?"

"Of course, but I can wait; it's just water."

Jake chuckled. "Yeah, at least it wasn't beer or wine."

"Glad to provide the entertainment." Hannah smiled. "I need a smoke."

On the trip back to Sofia, they filled each other in on their lives. Hannah had a laugh at what she called "the spectacle" of Shangri-Village; then she turned serious and spoke a few minutes about reviving the litigation against their mother's hospital.

"Hannah, you know I'd testify like I promised, but if you start it up again, don't send me copies of all the threats."

"The schmucks have to pay for what they did, Jake."

"I just don't care; the money isn't worth all the BS and stress."

"I told you, they count on people to get tired of the process so they can get away with it."

"Maybe so, but look at us right now. Instead of just hanging out, we're talking about this crap."

"Okay, I won't bring it up again while I'm here."

"Thanks." Jake slowed for Sofia. "We *are* here." He turned in at the CHIMICHANGAS sign.

"You must be kidding."

Ben came over on Thanksgiving morning before noon and knocked on the door. "Excuse," he said through the screen to Jake, "uh, a problem." Ben pointed to the yard; Jake ran out, Tina and Hannah following.

Fiera had yanked Hannah's expensive bra from the clothesline and was tearing around the yard with white nylon stuck over her snout, the rest of the material dragging in the dirt. Jake yelled; the mutt stopped only because a strap snagged on some creosote. Before Jake could get to her, Fiera growled and pulled the elastic back until it snapped like a rubber band, flinging the bra to the top of a tall mesquite.

"Damn it." Jake headed back to the house.

Hannah was on the porch, grinning around puffs on her cigarette. "Look at that crazy mutt." She pointed at Fiera; the dog circled the dark green bush as if trying to decide how to climb it. Tina, her eyes wide open, stood by Hannah while Ben covered a smile with his hand. Jake grabbed his shovel and turned to the dog before he realized everyone was laughing.

"It's okay, Jake," Hannah told him.

"I can get it down, Sis."

Tina chuckled. "He's very good with that shovel."

"Very funny." Jake walked toward Fiera, who was now sitting and looking up at the bra as if she was waiting for a treat.

Hannah snuffed the cigarette with her foot. "Huey, it's shot; just let her have it."

"You sure?"

Hannah nodded. Jake snagged the torn underwear and threw it to the dog. Fiera snatched it up and sprinted away with her new toy and its strange physical properties. She tossed it in the air repeatedly, tugging on the elastic after each catch.

They all watched her, chuckling, until Tina said to Jake, "Your shovel was a little late this time—hi-yah!"

"What's that all about?" Hannah asked.

"Tina's just been *dying* to tell you."

She explained and demonstrated the scorpion's demise to Hanna, taking the shovel and slamming it on the ground. By the time Tina screamed "Hi-yah!" three more times, they were all laughing again.

After Thanksgiving turkey with atypical trimmings like Ana's tamales and Hannah's version of Rose Friend's potato *kugl*, they cleared the table and Ben insisted on doing the dishes. Tina, Jake, and Hannah thanked him and went out in light jackets to walk over to Jesús and Ana's, where they were expected for Mexican cocoa and pumpkin *empanadas*.

"He's such a nice kid," Hannah said, carrying a bottle of wine and puffing on another cigarette. As they started down one of the driveways, Jake explained Ben's situation and told Hannah he might be living with them for a while.

"Where is he staying tonight?"

"With a work buddy in La Cholla, I think. I told him to stick around so I can drive him down there; otherwise he's apt to walk the ten miles."

Hannah flicked off some ash. "Jake, he might sleep in a park or something. That's ridiculous—when he joins us at your friend's house, invite him to stay on the couch tonight."

Jake turned to his spouse. "Tina?"

"Of course, Jake."

"Okay, we'll see what he says." They continued down the gravel lane; the late-fall desert flora around them was almost barren.

"We have something to tell you, Hannah," Jake said.

She stopped, put out her smoke and fingered a pebble from under her heel. "Is it something good about this forest of sticks, cactus and rocks?"

Jake scoffed. "Okay, city girl; we like it here." They walked on.

"Yes, I get that; so what is it?" She saw Tina shy away, moving a couple steps ahead. "What? You guys aren't pregnant, are you?"

Jake smiled and grimaced at once. "We're not getting too excited about it until Tina's further along."

"Of course, after everything she's been through. How far are you, Tina?"

Tina slowed; they walked together again. "More than two months; the date is June twentieth."

"Well, I'll follow your lead and not get too excited, but congratulations, doll." Hannah pecked Tina on the cheek, then slugged Jake in the arm.

"Ouch." He pretended to recoil in pain. "Thanks, Sis,"

"I let him call me Sis, Tina, only because it's a palindrome. Which reminds me—if you tell Caroline and Joyce, they'll start mailing diapers and a ton of other crap before you want it." They came around a bend to Jesús and Ana's place and the restaurant.

Tina sighed. "We haven't told anyone yet, except Ana."

Jake walked a few feet ahead to open the gate. "Yeah, let's keep it like this until we're absolutely sure."

Hannah nodded. "Jake, I need to talk another minute."

"I'll go on in and see if Ana needs help," Tina said.

Hannah gave her the wine. "No secrets, doll, just some sisterly advice."

"Jake can fill me in." Tina walked beneath the pruned rose arbor.

Hannah turned to her brother. "Two things, Jake. First, Uncle Myron is still pissed off."

"He is? He sent us a check, much to my surprise."

"He's taking it out on Joyce; won't even talk to her."

"Ah, now *that's* the ego we know and love."

"Joyce is handling it, but I wanted you to know."

"I'll give her a call and thank her again."

"She'd like that." Hannah paused, sneering at the desert. "Jake, where are you planning to have the baby?"

"A small Catholic hospital in La Cholla or up at the university; we're not sure yet. The guy in La Cholla seems to know what he's doing, but, personally, I think he's a putz."

Hannah shook her head. "I know an O.B. and a pediatrician in L.A. even *I* would go to."

"You thinking about getting pregnant, Sis?"

"Funny, Huey. Point is, that's where you'd probably have to go to be sure of some competence."

"I think we'll be fine here."

"Okay, just keep an eye on them, and hold onto your documents."

Jake rolled his eyes. "Let's go have some empanadas."

Part III

July 4, 1976, La Cholla, Arizona

20

Hannah, who had only been to Acapulco, wanted to go to Mexico on the day after Thanksgiving. Jake told her that the border towns he had been to—Tijuana, Mexicali, and Juárez—were big cities, but old La Cholla wasn't much larger than La Cholla, U.S.A. Jake and Tina had been there to shop and dine, but that's not what interested Hannah, so Jake recruited Ana to show them around.

In light morning traffic, they crossed the border after nods from two inscrutable *federales* who hardly bothered to look up from their magazines. Jake warned Hannah to be prepared for the "third degree" on the way back. He said that between his beard, Tina's long hair, and Loretta, the U.S. Border Patrol was apt to check for contraband in most any cavity, human or automotive.

The first two blocks of La Cholla were a miniature version of the carnivals of commerce Jake had seen on the way into the border cities; he told Hannah that this was "tchotchke heaven." The stands and shops were just opening for the day to sell everything from genuine crafts to pure schlock from Tlaquepaque, Mexico City, and even the Yucatán. You could find exquisite handmade pottery on one shelf, he explained, right above another with a Maríachi band of actual frogs lacquered into stiff grins, their tiny fiddles and horns in perpetual performing position. Jake told her the shops were also full of tourist fare like booze, jewelry, fireworks, sombreros, sarapes, huaraches, and rack after rack of other wool and leather goods.

A few locals puttered around on the next two blocks, some of them opening, and others patronizing the dry goods stores, a pharmacy, two small markets, a laundry, bakery, and a green PEMEX gas station, where an old Dodge waited at a pump. Hannah was chatting in back with Ana, who leaned forward to tell Jake to take a right at the PEMEX, the corner with the only traffic light—Hannah tried to restrain a snicker. After the turn, Ana pointed to a dilapidated two-story office building with POLICIA on its cracked white neon sign; Ana said this was old La Cholla's equivalent of city hall.

The next block had a half-dozen well-kept one-story stucco or brick homes taking up full-sized lots. Several dark-skinned women in full skirts swept with grass brooms in front of heavy wooden doors or black iron gates; at one residence you could see into a lush patio. At the top of every outside wall, the owners had embedded a macabre rainbow of glass shards. After Hannah commented that this home defense method looked "medieval," Ana told her that La Cholla's moneyed class lived in this small area; the women out front were their maids. "Mostly Indians," she added.

The wide street funneled to a narrow paved path through block after block of simple adobes and frame houses, no space between neighbors and most places without sidewalks or yards. Many of the residents were going about their business, a few driving by in old American cars and VW beetles, others walking off for the day, some carrying lunch in colored mesh bags. There were more sweepers, just moving around dust it seemed; Ana said these women lived in the neighborhood.

An occasional two-story place stood out from the small plain bungalows; Hannah pointed one out, a yellow-green stucco with HOSPITAL painted on the wall in fading black four-inch letters. "Maybe you should just have the baby here."

"This is actually more like a clinic," Ana responded, trying not to sound critical of Jake's sister.

"Don't mind me, always a wisecrack."

Jake thought Hannah was almost self-deprecating.

As the road deteriorated to gravel then dirt, it gradually gained some altitude toward a high bluff in the desert ahead, and the houses became huts and lean-tos made of discarded wood, metal, and plastic. Undernourished children, dogs, chickens, and goats gravitated from one hovel to another, not seeming to belong anywhere.

The slum seemed to go on for a mile before Ana asked Jake to make a turn. Not fifty yards past the shacks, they came to a sleepy lane of ten-foot-square pastel cabins between two long, turquoise, frame-built *cantinas* with unlit neon signs. A green neon beer advertisement flickered to life; a thin man in a white apron walked out in front of the first joint to pick up trash and sweep, waving down the road to a fellow barkeep doing his own chores.

Jake stopped; Ana said this was La Cholla's red light district. Without sounding critical, she asked if Hannah had seen enough of real Mexico. Looking embarrassed for one of the only times Jake could recall, Hannah thanked Ana for the tour and said she would like to treat everyone to lunch.

Jake turned around and drove back close to the border; they got out, shopped a little, and walked around the plaza until it was after eleven. They went to a place called La Mina, a half-dug tunnel that passed for a mineshaft, converted years before into a restaurant.

During the meal, Hannah quickly downed two margaritas and lavishly tipped a roving Maríachi, telling Jake to ask them not to play tourist music like La Bamba. When Jake asked what she wanted to hear, Hannah flicked her cigarette and said, "Jesus, Huey, have them play what *they* like."

After what Jake called, "Hurricane Hannah's visit," he, Tina, and their new boarder settled in for the three weeks before the Christmas holidays. Though his work had finished, Ben wanted to pay some rent; Jake told him ten dollars a week would be plenty. Ben's uncle came back in January and found his nephew some part-time work cleaning fields. Ben told Jake and Tina he could now pay seventy-five a month. They negotiated the room and board to forty dollars, with Ben doing some of the maintenance and yard work.

That winter was mild, as expected, though they had one enjoyable day when an inch of snow stayed on the ground for hours. Tina passed the "iffy" months without complications, and remained with Doctor Serna, who cheerily characterized her pregnancy with comments like, "It's going by the book," or "Steady as she goes." He even told Tina he expected her delivery would be the "rolling-off-the-log variety." When Tina reported this to Jake, he said, "Maybe call Joyce for a reality check; she told me she felt like she was going to die with every kid."

On a March weekend, the Friends celebrated Jake's twenty-seventh birthday with a "night on the town" after watching the Cubs play the Cleveland Indians in Tucson. Three weeks later, they were driving down to La Cholla during spring break; it would be Jake's first time to go with Tina to one of Serna's appointments. Looking out at the desert, Jake noticed that the outer branches of the usually dull-green palo verde were in full golden bloom. The dry afternoon air made it feel like summer, he thought, though the temperature was barely in the eighties.

Ben didn't have to work that day and decided to come along. Fiera sat contentedly on Loretta's back seat next to Ben, who was still not accustomed to living with a good-sized, very friendly "inside" dog. Ben had a plastic bag on the seat beside him, his long hair was combed back, and he wore his only dress shirt as well as a new leather belt and some clean blue jeans. He was trying to pet Fiera and also keep the slobber and dog hair off his clothes.

Jake looked over at Tina; her new girth and heavier breasts pretty much filled the peasant blouse he gave her the year before at Candlestick Point. They had finally told their friends of the pregnancy, but Tina continued wearing outfits that camouflaged the coming event.

Recalling how his sisters spoke of Joyce's supposed "glow," Jake was now a believer. The long blonde hair that first attracted him to Tina had somehow gained even more luster, flowing now over her shoulders in the sunlight that streaked through Loretta's windows. There was also a definite natural blush to Tina's cheeks, especially with her more frequent smiles.

"What?" she asked him wryly.

Though Loretta's noisy motor made it unlikely Ben could overhear, Jake mumbled, "You're such a cutie."

"What a laugh. Watch the traffic, please."

Jake smiled lasciviously. "I just hope you're feeling as good as you look."

"Glory, not so loud, Don Juan." She glanced back at Ben, who was watching the countryside.

"What happened to Don Joaquín?" Jake asked, acting hurt.

Tina grinned. "You sound like the other one." She thought for a moment. "Well, Joyce was right; she said the sixth and seventh month were the easiest—I can't even imagine getting any bigger."

Eyebrows hopping, Jake pretended to ogle her. "More for me to hold," he said in a low voice.

Tina furrowed her brows. "Jake, I'm glad you're so enthused about all this, but I didn't expect you to be quite so, uh—what did Hannah say you were full of?"

"Crap?" he asked, chuckling.

She tsked. "No, a Yiddish word your mother used."

"Oh, *schmaltz*—chicken fat."

"That's it. It also means like corny, right?"

"Close enough. I'm preparing for Serna; see if I can be more schmaltzy than he is."

"I think you're just getting excited about the baby."

"Okay—guilty," he said, smiling. They passed the Serna warehouse and Jake saw Ben duck down as they came to a squad car parked off the highway. "I think that's Jesús, Ben—take it easy."

Ben peeked out from behind the seat. "The *jefe* or *Sánchez*, maybe sit in the car with him." Chief of Police, "Whitey" LeBlanc and his minion, Corporal Sanchez, were both fond of detaining farm workers "on suspicion" and without cause.

Jake had his eye on the rearview. "It's not coming, Ben; you're okay." He turned onto Garden Drive and drove up the hill and by La Cholla Gardens to the small medical complex, where he pulled in and parked, five minutes early for the three-thirty appointment.

"Maestro, after the doctor, I stay in La Cholla, okay?" Ben asked from the back.

Jake looked up in his mirror again. "Of course. Can we drop you somewhere?"

"Yes, please." Ben looked like he was going to say where, but didn't. After he left with Fiera on a walk, the Friends started for the office, Tina holding a file folder and Jake lugging her full Cameroon purse.

"Ben looks so handsome in his outfit," Tina said.

"I think he's going to meet his *novia* on the other side."

"That serious? I didn't know."

"He just says 'my friend' with a big smile."

"Well, I hope she's worthy of him."

"Yeah." He reached to open the office door. Jake took his book out of Tina's purse as they entered, then spoke to the secretary—a thin, pale woman in her sixties. When he tried to arrange to join Tina and the doctor after the exam, Jake wasn't sure if he got through to her. He judged that she was actually a receptionist, and barely able to perform those duties. Jake sat down; the Friends were the only ones in the small waiting room until a woman and her son came out after a few minutes. When the receptionist finished with them, she smiled at Tina and opened the door for her.

Reading his novel intermittently, Jake gave up and just waited. Tina finally came out alone, shaking her head and mouthing, "I tried."

Jake walked to the desk. "Excuse me, I explained to you that I wanted to speak to the doctor; can I see him now?"

Taken aback by Jake's pithy tone, the woman's eyes were enormous through her thick glasses. "I'm sorry sir. I left him a note; I'll try to catch him."

"Catch him?"

"He's leaving for a lodge meeting."

Crap. "Okay, go ahead and try, please."

After the woman went inside, Tina spoke to Jake from her chair. "What are you going to say to him?"

"Nothing." He started to pace by the desk. "I just want to hear from his lips how you're doing. I'd like to feel a little more like I'm a part of all this."

"I know, Jake, but try not to make trouble."

Jake held back a scowl. "I won't."

163

Following the receptionist, Serna walked in, tucking a loud Hawaiian shirt into his slacks. Though Jake had met him briefly at the party, he realized now that the doctor was a thinner, much younger version of the fair-skinned, side-burned uncle, but without the sneer. He reached his hand out to Jake. "Mister Friend, that's quite the positive name you folks have," he said with a chortle.

"It's Jake; we met at your uncle's party." He grasped the physician's hand.

Serna, like his uncle, made sure to squeeze harder than Jake before letting go. "Of course, the school shindig; I remember you now."

Like hell you do. "I asked to come in at the end of Tina's appointment to talk to you."

"Yes, sorry about that; I didn't realize Mrs. Friend meant *today*. We don't get very many husbands who are so, uh, attentive and interested in this process."

Gee, I wonder why. "I'd just like to hear directly from you how Tina and the baby are doing."

"Certainly." He made a broad smile, moving right to Tina and patting her shoulder once. "They're doing wonderfully; strong hearts, both of them, and all other indicators are within normal parameters. I'm sure Mrs. Friend can fill you in on the test results." He pointed to her manila folder. "If there's nothing else, I do have a commitment."

That's it? Ask him something.

"Mister Friend?" Serna asked with the same ingratiating smile, taking a step away.

"Uh, yeah, we'll let you go to your meeting. I'll be with her next time; we'll save up our questions."

"That'll be fine; you can come in for the last few minutes of the appointment if you like."

"Yes, I'll be there." *The whole time, schmuck.*

They left the office and saw Fiera running on the lawn to fetch an old tennis ball Ben had tossed.

"Jake, I could use some time in my classroom while you take Ben." Tina released his arm.

"Sure, whatever you need."

"We also have a parcel from Joyce at the post office."

"Right, I'll get it, if it's not too late."

They all got in the truck and Jake dropped Tina off at her school. As he and Ben came down Garden Drive, Jake asked him where he wanted to go.

"The border, maestro."

"How hard will it be for you to get back?"

"One day, maybe two."

It took less than five minutes before Jake stopped at one of the last stores on the U.S. side.

"*Gracias*," Ben said, opening the door, the plastic sack in his hand.

"Sure. Maybe we could meet your friend sometime."

"*Sí, maestro. Adiós.*"

"*Hasta luego.*"After watching Ben walk right up to the border, Jake backed out and drove the two blocks to the post office. He parked twenty yards away in the cool shade of some old maples. Rolling the windows halfway up so Fiera couldn't get out, he turned around to her.

Tie her to the bumper? Only one car here—just go. "Okay, pooch. Stay, I'll be right back." Fiera grunted, then shuddered her whole body as if she were wet.

"That's a good girl." Jake closed the door and ran in; there were two people in line. He got the box in a couple of minutes and ran back out to his truck. For the next several seconds, Jake stared unbelievingly at the shambles before him.

The dog had attacked Loretta's interior and was sitting on the front seat, contentedly chewing on the steering wheel cover. Torn from the ceiling, a beach towel-sized hunk of Loretta's special-ordered tan headliner hung down to the floor. Fiera had gnawed the custom pseudo-leather brown seat covers and sun visors down to foam in places, and only springs remained of the shredded plastic wind-wing knobs.

"Gimme that," he said, pulling on the material in her mouth, but Fiera thought he was playing and yanked back. "Dumb dog, you're in *trouble*!" he yelled, letting go. Fiera turned and jumped on the back seat to chew on her treasures. "I'll be damned." Jake gathered the hunk of headliner so he could see out the back.

He drove up to the school and walked into Tina's classroom, cackling strangely.

She looked up from the forms she was working on. "Something funny?"

"This, my dear, is ironic laughter."

"What's wrong?"

"Your dog is testing our marriage."

"What?" Tina asked, now with eye contact.

"Fiera ate my truck."

"She did what?"

"She ripped up the whole interior during the three lousy minutes I was in the post office."

"My gosh, Jake; I'm so sorry."

"No, you warned me a hundred times; I didn't think she could go quite that nuts."

"You're taking it awfully well."

He exhaled through his lips, horse-like. "She doesn't even know why I'm pissed."

"No, she probably does." Tina stood, putting some papers to take home into a white milk crate. "Where is she now?"

Jake sighed. "Under a tree, tied to the bumper, where I should've put her before."

"How bad is the damage?"

"Loretta's drivable."

"You should've seen your face when you said it."

"Said what?"

"'Fiera ate my truck.'" She tried to cover a short peal of laughter with her hand. "Sorry."

"Yeah, funny, now that it's over." He shrugged then watched Tina pack the plastic container until it overflowed with books and construction paper.

She picked up her purse and looked at him. "Well, let's go see the damage; I'm ready."

"You forgot your folder." Jake pointed to her desk. "You were going to fill me in on everything, remember?"

"Yes, I'm glad you saw it." Tina stuffed the medical info into her big purse.

He hefted the crate; they started for the exit. "So, how badly did I embarrass you at the doctor's today?" Jake asked as Tina reached for the door handle.

"Maybe a little, but you did the right thing." She followed him outside.

"I don't know how you can be so patient with that putz."

"I think he's competent, medically anyway."

"Yeah, guess we can't have everything."

21

The end of the school year went well for Tina, who was very pleased when Nora settled in quickly with her new teacher. The principal gradually concluded that Tina wasn't a "problem," but a knowledgeable educator dedicated to her students. La Cholla School District granted her the standard unpaid maternity leave for the following year and then, on recommendations from Munz and the principal, she was given the option of a part-time contract to teach her own class in the afternoons, which Tina accepted.

As for Jake, his program doubled the previous year's number of high school graduates, including the MAPAS equivalency degrees. The feud between Ben and Justino petered out when Mister Hernandez confiscated the knife, gave it to Jake, and told his son to mind his own business.

Both of the Friends did have one similar hassle. Tina's was partly due to her lack of exposure in Africa to U.S. holidays and patriotic rituals. She had witnessed nationalism running amok in Equatorial Guinea, and though she felt privileged to be a U.S. citizen, Tina held a quiet contempt for bombastic patriotism, no matter the country.

Her school in La Cholla was involved in Bicentennial activities all year, which Tina assumed were optional. Many of her students were part-time "pull-outs" from regular classrooms, and some of the teachers started holding her kids in March for Bicentennial play practices. Reluctant to interrupt their work more than once a week, Tina didn't always let them go.

She met with the teacher of a very needy second-grader whose progress with Tina came to a sudden halt after missing three times in one week. She politely inquired how long the interruptions would last; the veteran teacher fumed, telling Tina that "her kind of attitude" was unpatriotic. The principal came timidly the next day to inform Tina that it was required to release students for the practices.

Jake's run-in came after the high school principal organized a bus trip for "all seventh through twelfth students and teachers to participate in a once-in-a-lifetime event," the impending arrival of the official Bicentennial train in Arizona. Jake informed him over the phone that Rosa would chaperone Sofia's junior high kids and some of the high school students.

"Some?" the principal asked Jake in a scold.

"Yes, a few have already left to work, and four of my equivalency students can't go."

"Why not? The board expects a full turnout."

"I'm taking them that same day for their appointment at the junior college to take their exams."

"Then you can change it."

"No, I can't make them wait until July. This is the last group; they've studied all year."

"We're putting a lot of time and expense into this. It's a Board directive; you don't have a choice."

"I don't think Ortega will hold me to that, especially if it means some students won't stand for their diplomas."

"It isn't a real diploma."

"I disagree."

"You don't care about this trip, do you, Friend?"

"I didn't say that, but these kids' exams are more important."

"We'll see about that."

Superintendent Ortega allowed the MAPAS equivalency students to skip the Bicentennial train. After that, the petty secondary principal had his secretary forward any calls from Sofia to the vice-principal.

Classes were out the second day of June, none too soon for Tina, due in about three weeks and dealing better with her self-described "enormity" than she was with the high temperatures. She had the first fainting spell of her life, and also had to ask Serna for a prescription to alleviate some stubborn rashes in uncomfortable places.

Jake spoke to Rosalinda's father, offering to split costs to upgrade from the old swamp cooler in their rental. Juanito Montalvo said he was about to do it anyway, but it would mean a twenty-dollar rent increase. Jake quickly agreed, offering to help install the new forced-air system. He hoped his limited mechanical experience, maintaining Loretta, would help, but Jake ended up mostly holding the tools for Juanito.

The first storms came the next week, just after they finished hooking up the new air-conditioning. Both the rain and the cool inside air seemed to relax Tina for a day or two until she realized she wasn't "doing anything." She vigorously took up her knitting, and by the time the due date approached, Tina cranked out more booties than the baby could ever use; so, she started crocheting long white and blue stripes—the beginnings of an afghan.

When the baby was a week overdue, they went to Serna, who said everything was "just fine." The doctor expected her to start labor at any time.

Two days later, it was over a hundred degrees again so Jake settled on the sofa with a cold Bohemia, hoping to watch a *M*A*S*H* rerun. That failing, he picked up the newspaper and left the TV on Monday Night Football, turning off the sound. Jake almost nodded off before Tina, crocheting in their new rocker, made a sudden comment.

"There it is again." She looked up from her project. "That definitely isn't kicking."

When her words registered, Jake sat up, immediately alert. "What is it, then?"

"My whole middle constricted; it might be a real contraction."

Jake stood. "Do you think they're serious?"

"I don't think so—far apart; didn't hurt much."

"I could call Serna."

"It's okay, Jake. We'll wait and see what they do."

"Okay—whatever you think." He sat again. "Tina, why is the afghan blue and white? Expecting a boy?"

"No. These are just the colors I had."

The mild contractions stopped after a few hours and didn't return until Friday; it was the second of July. Jake had everything planned—Tina was packed; they would take Fiera to Rosalinda on their way out, and Ben would be home in the evenings to take care of the yard and house. Stronger contractions started that night at about nine, Ben still hadn't shown up, and Jake thought it was too late to bother Rosalinda's family.

Damn, now what'll you do? He took Tina's small suitcase out to Loretta, then hurried back in through the kitchen door.

"Have another one?" he asked; she was on the couch, crocheting again.

Tina put what was now a four-by-six-foot partial afghan on the lap of her sacky blue maternity gown. "About five minutes ago."

"Stronger?"

"A little, maybe."

He jotted on a scrap of paper. "I've been keeping track—that's fourteen minutes apart." He showed her his simple ledger and the wind-up alarm from the bedroom.

"Yes, Jake, I noticed." She nonchalantly kept hooking her yarn. At Tina's last appointment, Jake asked for a specific indicator on the contractions. Serna said to start for the hospital when they were less than ten minutes apart, or to come right away if her "water" broke.

"What can I get for you, Tina?"

"That's the third time you asked in fifteen minutes. You might want to calm down a bit."

"Yeah, you're right." He sat with her on the couch, pretending to watch Walter Cronkite interview some Israeli official about a hijacked airliner in Uganda. Jake chewed on a thumbnail, a habit less than thirty minutes old. The TV interview became just noise and a blur; he turned to her.

"Tina, don't worry about Fiera—got it handled."

"Oh, really? And how did—?" Tina's face distorted for seconds as if a horn had blasted in her ears.

"Another one?"

She exhaled deeply, followed by some shorter puffs. "Yes, Jake."

"That's real good breathing, Tina."

She forced out a couple more breaths. "Thanks a lot. *That* was a good one."

"A lot stronger?"

"No, a little."

"Okay, that was at nine thirty-two and thirty seconds." He wrote down the numbers.

"Nine thirty-two should be adequate, Don Joaquín," Tina said with a slight grin.

"What?"

"You're being very sweet."

He scoffed. "First thing he'll ask is how far apart. That's eleven minutes, thirty seconds. Should we call?"

"Not yet. So how did you handle Fiera?"

"I tied her under the tree; I'll leave Ben a note to take her over."

Tina shook her head a little. "Juanito's coming over now to get her."

"He is? I was thinking it's too late to bother them. "

"They told me to call anytime."

"Oh. Wait, *you* called?"

"So?"

"Well, that means you think it's really happening."

"Sometime tonight, maybe. I think he's outside; go on, Jake."

"You're okay?"

She nodded. "Just fine."

"Watch the clock, all right? Be right back." He ran out to help with Fiera but came back for the dog food. "Be right back," he called again.

"Not going anywhere," she said, but Jake was gone.

A couple of minutes later, he rushed in. "Okay, that's all handled."

"Nine forty or so, a pretty good one."

"What?" He snatched up the scrap of paper. "That's less than ten minutes!" he nearly shouted.

"Okay, Jake, tell him we're coming in."

He dialed the answering service and found out Doctor McNally was on call until midnight. The woman told him that Doctor Serna was in Phoenix and not expected back until after eleven.

"What's the deal?" Jake glared at the phone's base. "We weren't told he would be out of town."

"That's not the way it works, sir."

Crap. "Just a moment, please." He muffled the receiver into the side of his jeans, quickly explaining Serna's whereabouts to Tina. " . . . not back until eleven. We could go to emergency at the university."

"I'm not sure we'd make it in time."

That proof of imminence sunk in right away. "My God," he said, nearly panicked.

"Jake, it'll be okay. Doctor McNally has probably delivered thousands."

He lifted the phone. "Okay, please tell Doctor McNally we're on our way."

"I will, Mister Friend, and Doctor Serna will get the message when he returns."

Great. He hung up and turned to her, but she was waddling away, holding her side. "Where you going, Tina?"

"To pee, if you must know. Everything's fine, Jake; you should get your book—you have a lot of waiting around ahead of you. And maybe you want to change."

He looked down at the dirty tee and jeans he put on earlier to drain Loretta's oil. "Do I have time?"

"Yes, Jake," she called back from the hall.

He put on Bermudas, a pressed summer shirt, and sneakers. Jake found his Cubs cap, a novel he was reading, and the spiral notebook he used for addresses and journaling. They met in the hallway; he took her gently by the arm out to the driveway.

With Tina up front, Jake drove Loretta slowly on the bumpy driveway out to the road and turned left for La Cholla. Her contractions didn't get much more severe on the way in.

At the hospital, a nurse escorted them to a small labor room near emergency. They let Jake stay with Tina because her water still had not broken, though the contractions were now closer and stronger. With each one, he helplessly held her hand and kept a cool washcloth on her forehead until the nurse asked Jake to leave so she could do an exam.

In the hallway a few minutes later, the nurse told him Tina was starting to "dilate nicely" and was on her way to what would probably be a fairly quick delivery. She added that Doctor McNally was already there but asleep, to be woken when "things were moving faster."

Jake went back to handholding and cool washrag duty. Tina's face contorted during the contractions but she didn't make much noise, sometimes even nodding off in between. He tried to make small talk once, but her grimace made him decide to keep his mouth shut.

When Doctor Serna showed up at quarter to twelve in a tuxedo, Tina was wailing with each contraction. Jake had just been escorted out to the hallway again and told it was time for him to go to the "family room."

Jake glowered at him. "Doctor Serna, you were at a wedding?"

"My niece's, but apparently I'm right on time."

Three cheers. "Is there some reason you couldn't let us know you were gone?"

"That's not the procedure, Mister Friend. Everything was covered here," he said with his practiced smile. "Now, if you'll excuse me, I'll go change; we'll see if your new baby is ready to join us."

They banished Jake to the faraway room, where he sat for about fifteen minutes before sneaking back to the hall near emergency, a couple of doors from the labor area. He listened furtively, waited, and then heard Tina cry out even louder than before. *Jesus! Just go in.*

A nurse came out; Jake realized she was new, but he couldn't recall much about the other one, except she was short and wore light blue scrubs. This young woman—tall, heavy, and dressed all in white—told him that Tina's water had broken. She took Jake's arm and directed him like a well-mannered sergeant back to the waiting area.

The small windowless room had two chairs, a sofa and coffee table. After a half hour of flipping through magazines, Jake was sure he could make out Tina's screams very faintly through the air duct. *Who else? The joint's nearly empty. This place is driving me nuts. Why can't I just hold her hand—do something?*

After Jake passed another frantic half hour talking to himself, the burly nurse finally came in to tell him their "big eight-pound girl" had entered the world normally, kicking and screaming. Though the delivery was overdue, she said, there were no unusual complications. Jake was so elated on his way to see Tina and the baby, it didn't register that Serna had not spoken with him. He found out later the doctor went straight home after his long day.

As soon as he hugged Tina and got a first look at the baby, Jake thought their child looked like a chubby, wrinkled old bald man; she even had visible veins on her limbs, but he decided to keep his observations to himself. Tina, who barely acknowledged anyone through her stupor, valiantly attempted a smile for the baby.

Jake held their drowsy daughter, watching her watery, indistinct eyes open slightly behind translucent blonde lashes. *Geez, she could be a redhead.* Like any first-time father, he was awed by the diminutive fingers softly gripping his pinkie; it no longer mattered that she looked so homely.

"See, Latina, everything's fine," Jake said; a solitary tear coursed down her cheek. Thinking Tina was joyful, Jake handed the baby to the nurse so he could hug his wife again. He leaned over but stopped when Tina lowered her chin and looked away, seeming to brood.

The husky nurse pulled Jake several feet to the side, whispering to him that Tina was spent from the delivery and the late hour; she would be fine after a night's rest. The nurse whisked the baby away; Jake went back and held Tina's hand until she was asleep.

He walked down the hall past the nurses' station to the nursery, where a tiny woman, her grey hair bundled in a mesh net, was rocking their daughter. Jake walked around the glass corner and looked in. The woman's pale, oatmeal-brown face, pleated by age, formed a brief smile for Jake. No taller than an average nine-year-old, she bowed her head as she stood up with the sleeping baby, wrapped predictably in a soft pink blanket. The nurse, in salmon-colored scrubs, had to reach up a few inches to place the child gently into a tall open incubator with EMMA ROSE FRIEND, 7/3/76, 1:17 A.M., 8 LBS, 3 OZ printed on its pink card.

22

Jake looked in at Emma, thinking she already wasn't as wrinkled as when he saw her earlier. About three feet away, another baby slept in one of the incubators. She had black hair and fawn-colored skin; her card said: MARÍA ELENA CRUZ, 7/1/76, 6:55 P.M., 5 LBS, 10 OZ.

Jake watched the slight but sturdy woman lean on the door. She came into the hall and took another step as if she were going to walk past him. Her mouth faltering to one side, she smiled with something of a grimace.

"May I speak with you, nurse?"

"*Sí, pero no hablo inglés, señor.*"

She understands it okay. Jake saw her badge; it said, MARÍA R. "*Discúlpeme, señora. ¿You are not a nurse?*" he asked in Spanish.

"*No, I help the nurses.*" Her Spanish was succinct, easy for him to understand. She didn't seem surprised that Jake was bilingual. "*¿You are Señor Fren, no?*"

"*Sí, señora.*"

"*Yo soy María.*"

Feeling somehow compelled to bow to this woman, he kept it to a nod. "*Mucho gusto, señora. I see we have two Marías here today.*" He smiled toward the other baby.

"*Sí. She is the child of my neighbor.*"

"*¿Is she named in your honor?*"

María lowered her chin. "*There are many Marías. Yo soy María Juana.*"

She must take some guff with that name. "*¿Señora, how do you think my daughter is doing?*"

María's neutral expression turned to a slight crooked frown, which vanished immediately as if she had committed some transgression. "*It is not my place to talk of this.*"

He said nothing, his brows slanted inward, showing his puzzlement.

"*Señor, what I know is that she is a very good baby; they say she has no problems.*"

Don't be so paranoid, Jake. He nodded slowly to this old information, covering a yawn with his wrist.

"*I believe maybe you need to rest, señor.*"

"*Sí.*" He chuckled, lowering his arm. "*I can rest in the waiting room.*"

"*¿You live far?*"

"*No, en Sofia. ¿Señora, do you think it is okay if I go home for a few hours?*"

"*Sí. I will watch over la niña until I leave in the morning. ¿The nurse, she has your telephone number?*"

You can trust her, Jake. "*Sí, but I want you to have it, too.*" He yanked a pen from his shirt pocket, jotted the number on a card from his wallet, and gave it to her. "*I will tell the nurse I am leaving. Muchísimas gracias, señora.*"

"*No es nada, Señor Fren.*"

After he told the charge nurse he was going home to sleep, Jake just looked in on Tina, careful not to disturb her rest. He went on out to Loretta and drove up the hill toward La Cholla. *You promised the sisters to call right away—it can wait until daylight.*

He stopped on International at a corner grocery, the only open business in town, where he bought a pre-made chicken sandwich and a diet soda. Jake ate in the front seat, thinking about his new parental responsibilities. He finished the sandwich and raised the can for a drink, looking around at the tape and pins he used weeks before to make temporary repairs to Loretta's interior. *It'll be a while before you can fix her up.*

Jake yawned and started for Sofia, cranking both windows from half to all the way down. Instead of making him more alert, the balmy night air from the desert soothed Jake almost to sleep, his head snapping back up.

"Damn," he said to the dark highway, spotting one of the "wide spots" ahead in his front beams. Jake turned into a driveway and didn't see any lights, so he just parked, leaned back on the seat and listened to a chorus of locusts, crickets, and mourning doves before he fell asleep.

Snippets of dreams raced through his mind, flashing crazily between the Visalia and La Cholla hospitals. Tina was in a bed with wooden posts, recovering from a miscarriage at one moment and giving birth the next. Then Jake could hear her screaming—it all felt familiar but distant, like he was there but not there.

His real hearing picked up car tires crunching in the gravel behind, waking him. Jake groggily looked up at his rearview; it was a squad car, stopping in the grey light after dawn. He glanced ahead through the palo verde at a house not forty feet away.

They must've had their lights off. He looked back again and saw Jesús, in uniform, getting out. *Lucky for you it's him—stay put.*

Jesús came to the window and looked in, his dark brows raised. "Jake, what the heck's going on?"

"Sorry, Jesús; I got drowsy on my way home—had to pull off. Tina had the baby."

"Why didn't you say so? Get outta there for an *abrazo, hombre.* Boy or girl?"

"Girl—Emma, eight pounds," he boasted, opening the door to climb down.

"*Felicidades, amigo.*" Jesús braced Jake's shoulders and shook both his hands before letting go. "Wow, that's a big girl. They're both doing okay?"

"Tina's wiped out, naturally; the baby's doing fine. Man, I had no idea newborns were quite so funny looking."

"Don't say that around the ladies."

"Yeah. What time is it, Jesús?"

He checked his watch. "Seven twenty-five."

Jake yawned. "You're just getting off?"

"Yup, covering a night shift. The new guy quit; we're down to four again. You get any sleep?"

"A little. You must be headed to bed yourself."

"As soon as I tell ol' Mrs. Rangel that hippies aren't after her."

"Please tell her I'm sorry." He put his fist over another yawn. "Guess I'll just go back to the hospital."

"Ana's going to be so excited. When can she visit them?"

"Tina just needs some rest; tonight should be fine."

"She'll probably go tomorrow after the parade. We ran out of some basics at the restaurant last night—going in later. Need anything from the big city?"

"No, but would you mind checking if Ben got back? Just let him know what's going on."

"Sure, Jake. What else can I do?"

"If you don't mind, maybe you could tell Rosalinda or her dad I probably won't get Fiera until tonight."

"You bet; give my best to Tina."

"Thanks, Jesús."

The sergeant got back in and drove to the lady's house; Jake turned around onto the highway. Not sure why he felt so anxious, Jake forced Loretta up to the speed limit. Passing the desert before La Cholla, he noticed the morning sun had already burned off any vestige of cool air. *Another scorcher; they did say a chance of thunderstorms—hope they're right.*

La Cholla, U.S.A. was still waking up to Saturday, one day before its Bicentennial Fourth of July celebration. On the mostly deserted International Avenue, Jake noticed World Series-type bunting hanging from some of the light standards. He turned up Garden Drive, following the familiar route past La Cholla Gardens, the doctor's office, and the turn-off for the schools.

Jake came down the hill and parked in the visitors' lot. He walked under the giant white cross into the hospital lobby and by the information counter, where the lights were off and one of the elderly watchmen was nearly asleep in a chair. Jake didn't see anyone else except an electrician by the doorway to the old wing; the man was muttering to an open panel and its unruly nest of multi-colored wires.

He entered the hall to the right, walked by the four vacant rooms, and then stopped at the nursery to see Emma and the Cruz baby. They were both sleeping; María Juana was working in a back room that Jake didn't notice before. The crossing hallway was empty except for a male orderly in orange scrubs, rolling a food cart over from the old wing.

Jake went on, passing the abandoned nurses' station and two more vacant rooms to the last door on the right. Across the hall from Tina, he finally saw another patient, the sleeping Mrs. Cruz. *Standing room only. Why are they down here on the end?* He walked into Tina's two-patient oblong room with its rolling divider open in the middle. The other bed remained undisturbed; Tina lay in hers, facing the window and stretching her left arm. The open drapes revealed only the white back of sculptured Jesus out on the lawn, and some post-World War II row houses across the street, half hidden by mature weeping willows.

Damn, I should have flowers or something. "Tina?" He approached her, but she didn't answer. "Latina?" Jake went around the bed; she stared out, putting her arm down slowly. He placed his notebook on the sill and put a hand on the bed frame. "Something wrong, Tina?" She glanced at him, breaking her trance; then she turned away again.

He moved his hand to her arm. "Tina, what is it?" She was stiff as the bed rail, and the pewter grey circles under her eyes seemed too dark, like Halloween make-up.

"The nurse brought the baby twice for me to hold," she finally said to the window in a hoarse tone he'd never heard before. "She's not, uh, something's not right."

"What isn't right?"

"She isn't responsive." Tina remained in a tearless daze, glaring out.

"I bet that's not unusual; it probably takes a day or two."

"No, something's wrong."

"Tina, we don't know that. I'll talk to them."

She didn't answer; he thought her arm felt clammy before he let go. "I'll be back, okay?" Again, she didn't respond; Jake walked out and then back down to the vacant nurses' station. He waited there a couple of minutes before he continued down the hall to the nursery.

Jake saw María in the rocker; he walked around the corner to get a closer look. She cooed to Emma, trying to give her some kind of liquid from a bottle. She saw Jake, and then put the baby carefully in the open incubator before coming to the door. Jake had to pull the handle hard for her, realizing the glass door wasn't just heavy, but the air conditioning added some vacuum. María entered the hall.

"*¿How is she, señora?*"

"*She does not drink, Señor Fren.*"

"*¿Is something wrong?*"

"*I do not know. We need to try milk from the mother; but the nurse thinks your wife will not want to.*"

"*I think she will.*"

Not realizing he was chewing his nails again, Jake went back down to Tina; she hadn't moved. He came around in front of her and described the attentive care Emma was getting from María Juana. He chuckled slightly, saying that her name must be a problem at times.

Tina looked past him. "I'm sure it isn't funny to her."

"Yeah, you're right," he quickly agreed, and then told her that María recommended she try to nurse the baby.

Tina thought for several seconds, then looked right at him. "Okay, I'll try."

To Jake, her dry eyes seemed cold and distant. "Be right back." He went out to the station to tell a young nurse what they wanted. She returned in a few minutes with the charge nurse who came on at midnight—the same large woman who had told him Emma was born.

Jake concluded earlier that this nurse was very bright and a bit bossy, the latter because she was so serious about her work. She was constantly on the move; to Jake, she was testament against the generalization that heavy people are indolent. It made sense to him that the charge nurse had so much respon-sibility at a relatively young age, about thirty, he thought.

She had short tawny hair, was at least five-nine, but everything about her was thick—neck, limbs, and torso. If she had any distinctive features, they were hidden in her chubby face. The nurse's pale skin was accentuated by her all-white uniform; it was some sort of milk-colored frock with white support hose and powdery matching shoes.

"Yes, Mister Friend?" she asked in an affable tone, though her expression was neutral, all business. Jake checked her nametag; it read: B. JAWORSKY, R.N."

"Morning. Uh, Tina would like to nurse the baby."

"Good. We usually wait about ten hours, but it's close enough. I was afraid Mrs. Friend wouldn't want to nurse; she's so anxious about the baby."

"You don't think anything's wrong with Emma?"

"I'd like to see her a little more active, but there's nothing alarming. She's such a fine big girl; I'm sure she'll perk up after she drinks."

"Good. Would you mind having María bring Emma? I'd like Tina to meet her."

"We usually bring the babies, but that'll be fine. You do know María doesn't speak much English?"

"Yes. We both speak Spanish."

"Oh," she said curtly and started away. The loose fabric of her tent-shaped dress fluttered; her hosiery made a noise with every stride like sandpaper on wood. Jake got a drink at a fountain and waited.

María soon came toward him, baby-talking in Spanish to Emma as she walked. "*¿Señor Fren, you asked for me to bring la niña?*"

"*Sí, señora. I think my wife is going to feel more calm with you there.*"

"*¿Ella habla español?*"

He smiled. "*Sí.*"

They entered the room, and María sat in a rocker by the window, Jake next to her in a visitor's chair. María calmly and gradually introduced herself to Tina while holding Emma, not rocking, intentionally trying to keep the baby awake. María didn't give Tina a glowing description of Emma's health but quietly reassured her that the baby was "*going to be okay.*"

"*¿Señora Fren, you want to hold la niña?*"

More alert than before, Tina was still glum. "*I will try to nurse her, María,*" she said in Spanish.

"*Está bien.*" María turned to Jake. "*Señor, they have a rule; I do not like it, but you . . .*"

He knew the rest of the explanation. *More bullcrap—don't get María in trouble.* Jake told her he would wait out by the door.

"Gracias, señor. You have to close it, por favor."

Jake went out, shutting the door just as the charge nurse returned. "Thank you," Jaworsky said, stopping in front of him, "I was just coming to see if María told you our rules."

"You're fortunate to have such a good helper. She spoke with Tina a while; it relaxed her some. They just got started."

"Very good." The nurse did a full about-face and started away, stopped, and turned around again. "My shift is finished, Mister Friend; someone new will check back with you soon."

Jake thanked her and waited there not much more than five minutes before María came out with Emma. *"La niña, señor, she will not drink. La señora, she needs you now. I will return to talk to you before I go home."*

María walked away; Jake went right into the room; Tina had assumed the same melancholic position toward the window. He walked around to the visitor's chair and saw her blank, stolid face.

She isn't crying. What the hell? He sat down and looked out the window; nothing there registered in his mind. He decided to follow María's example by not pestering Tina right away. Still mum, Jake just reached over and put his hand on hers.

She looked at him after a few seconds and said, "She's not right, Jake." Tina turned and stared out again. He patted her hand, kissed her on the forehead, got up, and walked out to the nurses' station with his notebook.

The charge nurse was gone; Jake came to a nurse whose badge said, N. RUIZ, C.N.A. She wore an old-fashioned winged nurse's hat and had her walnut-brown hair in a tight bun; he judged that Ruiz was determined to look like a nun. She was about five-five, thin, and in her fifties, Jake guessed; she used no make-up on her plain beige face. Ruiz was too small for her starched loose uniform she kept buttoned to the top, covering her Adam's apple.

Jake asked if Serna had been by on morning rounds; Ruiz told him the doctor was there around seven and gave the baby "a clean bill of health."

See what María says. He hurried to the nursery, where both babies faced the window; Emma was asleep, baby María was boxing and kicking her arms and legs. Jake thought her dark irises looked right at him.

While María Juana cleaned the sink, her replacement, a tall middle-aged woman with pinkish skin, was reading a chart. To match her peach-colored uniform, the new helper wore an orange bow in her dishwater-blonde ponytail.

He tapped lightly on the window with one knuckle; the new lady just glanced at him suspiciously. María saw Jake, dried her hands, then picked up a bulky red cloth handbag by its long strap and came out to the hall after he pulled the door for her again.

"*Gracias, Señor Fren. I wanted to tell you—*"

"*Señora,*" he interrupted, "*perdón, but I have to ask you something first. ¿Did you see the doctor check Emma?*"

"*Sí, he looked at the chart, listened to her heart for a moment, and left.*"

That's it? He bit his thumbnail. "*¿What did you have to tell me?*"

"*La niña, I am sorry, but she is worse since they wrote those numbers on the chart.*" She gazed over at Emma.

"*¿What do you mean?*"

"*It is more than not drinking and too much sleep; that happens* sometimes." She turned to Jake. "*When I carried her to la señora, I noticed she was breathing fast. Also, she does not move much; it worries me that she does not cry.*"

He went right to the glass to look at Emma. *María's not even trained, Jake.* He watched his sleeping child panting in a staccato of short puffs like a puppy left too long in the sun. *Jesus, look at that, and Tina sure as hell thinks something's wrong. So what do you do?* He turned around; María hadn't moved.

"*Señor, I believe she needs help.*"

He nodded. "I'll get the doctor," Jake said, then switched to Spanish. "*Señora, I will have to tell him what you said about Emma. ¿Will that get you in trouble?*"

Scoffing almost imperceptibly, she let the purse go to her feet. "*Don't worry. He is afraid; he thinks I am like a witch. The problem is with a chief nurse—the one who starts now. They changed my hours to separate us.*"

"*¿What is the problem with her?*"

"*Es hombre. He says I am the problem.*"

"I'll bet," he grumbled.

"*¿Mande?*"

"*Nada. ¿Do you have the same schedule tomorrow?*"

"*No, I return today at four in the afternoon.*" She lifted her bag again.

"*I am going to find Serna or McNally to check her by then. See you at four, señora.*"

"*Si diós quiere,*" she said, walking toward the other hallway. "*I will visit Señora Fren on my way out.*"

"*Gracias,*" he called, watching her go. Jake turned to the window; baby María was crying. The helper looked up; the newborn wailed again, and the woman started toward her with a bottle. After Jake saw Emma sleep right through all the commotion, he left with even more urgency.

23

J ake went straight to the assistant nurse, Ruiz, who didn't seem very surprised when he reported the litany of symptoms for Emma. Ruiz said she had to follow the current treatment until the charge nurse came back, but she told Jake to come along while she checked Emma again.

Walking down the hall with her, Jake noticed the monastic nurse's erect posture and a heavy silver cross she had pinned to the front of her stiff uniform so it wouldn't hang in the way. Ruiz entered the nursery, then went to the back room to say something to the helper. The blonde woman peered at Jake again, as if he were suspect. Ruiz returned to the nursery; Jake watched her check Emma's pulse and chest.

Ruiz came out to the hall. "Mister Friend, her breathing is quick, but within normal range; her heart rate is fine, a little slow, in fact. I'll make sure the charge nurse is aware of all this."

"Thank you. You'll tell me when he comes back?"

"If I can. He's also in charge of the old wing, and right now he's in surgery with Doctor McNally."

"McNally's here now? Where, exactly?"

"The main operating room is near emergency."

"How do I let him know I want Emma checked?"

"In case we don't catch him, call the service before he leaves."

"The office number?"

"Yes."

"Why can't you just tell him now?"

"You can only interrupt operations for an emergency, but I'll try to catch him before he goes." She began to walk over to the intersection of the two hallways, Jake following.

"Nurse, can you get me Serna's home phone?"

"No, sir; they don't even let *us* know it."

Crap. "Does anybody have it?"

"Only the charge nurse."

Who must really be a piece of work.

Ruiz stopped, looked to be sure they were alone, then smiled. "Mister Friend, I promise you, as I did to María, to keep a close eye on the baby." She crossed the hallway.

"Thank you very much, nurse." As wary as Ruiz was of breaking rules, Jake was pleased to have her support. "Oh, nurse Ruiz, can I use a phone?" he called to her.

She turned and told him it wasn't permitted, that he had to go to the lobby or to a pay phone by the vending machines. He hurried out to emergency with his notebook; it had the number on the inside cover. Jake used the dollar changer, then called the service, leaving messages for both doctors.

He snooped around and discovered a side door next to a board with MEDICAL STAFF inscribed above. Names with titles were at the left, including the two doctors and a list of nurses and technicians. A white square was lit up by seven names—McNally's, four nurses, and two technicians. Jake sat by the board on an upholstered bench under a SMOKING AREA sign. He waited there for a while, hoping to catch McNally when he checked out.

Jake spent the next hour or so wearing a path between the side door, the nursery, the nurses' station and Tina, who was asleep again. He tried once to get information from the nursery helper; she would only say, "You'll have to talk to the nurses, sir." He watched Emma for at least a few minutes every time he came by; her breathing was still fast, but it didn't seem worse.

He checked again to see if McNally's light was still on, and then found Nurse Ruiz in the nursery. After she invited him to come in, Jake washed his hands and walked over to his daughter. Emma was awake and very still, except her chest contracted like an oblong balloon rapidly losing and gaining air. He touched her soft tiny palm; she grabbed the finger as before, but her eyes seemed glazed. "C'mon, cry," Jake whispered to her. "Cry, Emma." After another minute or so, she closed her eyes; Jake left, keeping himself from crying.

On each of his "rounds," Jake waited several minutes at the in-out board and then a couple more at a door near the operating area. Apparently, an emergency nurse was also in there; her area was vacant, and a sign directed patients to the lobby. Down the hall from the board, he discovered a second side entrance and a punch clock for MAINT/JANITORIAL. He spotted a card in the rack with MARÍA R. at the top. *Right, some janitor.*

Not long before noon, Jake finally found the charge nurse standing at the station, blank-faced and mumbling to Ruiz, who mutely waited at attention, looking like she wanted to get away. He was in his mid-forties, nearly bald, about five-nine and slim, in loose light blue scrubs. Jake approached as Ruiz left; the charge nurse sat down. His badge said, I. MONSON, R.N.; he stared at some papers as if Jake were not there. A day's black whiskers spiked from his chin, blotchy with pink psoriasis.

"Excuse me, you must be the charge nurse."

"That's right." He made no eye contact.

"I'm Jake Friend; I have some concerns about our baby."

"I know." He still didn't look up.

Friggin' zombie. "Her breathing, uh—"

"María," the nurse said, and just continued to read.

"Excuse me?"

Sneering, Monson finally looked up at Jake. "María told you all this."

"No, my wife noticed first."

"María's a troublemaker." He smirked as if Jake should know better. "Doesn't even get that her name sounds like marijuana." He sniggered with a straight face.

"Oh, I think she probably does."

"Mm, so that's the way it's going to be."

What?

Pointing at Jake, Monson's Old Glory tattoo showed on his skinny upper arm. "Look, Mister Friend." He retracted his index finger. "I'll repeat what you already know. You have a big healthy baby who's breathing at high-normal range. That's about it."

Okay, just consider it might not be as bad as María thinks. That would be good, right?

Monson lowered with a sour face as if he had heartburn. "Well?"

"I'd still like McNally to see her while he's here."

"I already gave him the information. He said the baby's levels are okay, and to encourage liquids," Monson said factually, starting to jot something down.

"So he's gone?" Jake was talking to the top of the nurse's balding head.

"That's right."

"I'd like a doctor to check her sometime today."

"Nope, Serna's off Saturdays after rounds; McNally's on call the rest of today." The nurse raised his head slowly. "And the only way *he's* coming back is for an emergency, or if I call him." He went on writing. "We're monitoring the baby, Mister Friend."

How reassuring. "Who's on call tomorrow?"

"Serna."

"Okay, just so you know—I'm not leaving; I'll be watching our baby for any changes."

Monson didn't look up. "Suit yourself. Now let me do my work."

Shit. Jake walked down the hall to Tina; she was still asleep. *Nothing you can do here, either.* He checked Emma, then went back to the pay phone. He called the doctors' service again and insisted on leaving another message for Serna; the woman was short with Jake, telling him the doctor wouldn't get it until the next morning.

Now what? He returned to Emma and stood there watching until his eyes grew heavy. Jake walked out to the lobby and sat on a long couch. A few people came in and out, most of them stopping at the information desk manned by the receptionist and the elderly watchman who apparently didn't know he yelled to everyone. A frail old woman was there to visit with him, or perhaps just to stay out of the heat.

Jake watched a young nun in a full white and black habit glide out of the chapel, the bottom seam of her skirt buffing the shiny linoleum. She saw him, stopped, and then reflexively held her cross. The sister smiled and raised her eyebrows, as if inviting him to talk.

No thanks, lady. He turned away; she left, and Jake stared through the plate glass window at two mourning doves. Taking shade in a maple, they weren't as rotund as other doves he had seen. The parched birds lifted their ash grey wings without opening them—for better circulation, Jake assumed. *Must be young; born in the spring, before the heat—smart.*

Deciding that he was too far from Emma and wasn't resting anyway, Jake went to the family waiting room, took the two straight-backed cushioned chairs and lugged them down to the nursery window. He sat in one, put his feet up on the other and watched Emma, considering a course of action in case she became noticeably worse. The new helper tried the bottle for a while, then made a gesture to Jake with a finger and thumb to indicate that Emma had taken very little.

He walked down the hall to Tina, who was awake, facing the window again. Jake went around to the visitor's chair and saw she was still groggy. "You look a little better, cutie." *Liar.*

She had difficulty focusing on him. "I feel like sleeping all the time."

He saw a tray by the bed, the main dish covered. "Did you eat?"

"A little." She paused several seconds. "That male nurse said to eat or get it in the vein."

"I bet that's how he said it, too."

"I don't remember."

185

"Emma drank a little. The doctor will see her again soon." *Maybe.*

"Good." Tina's eyelids drooped. "Where's María?"

"She's off until four."

"Oh, I forgot." Her eyes were getting heavy again. "Jake, sorry; I'm so sleepy."

"Of course, you rest." He stood, kissed her on the forehead, and moved to the foot of the bed. "I'll check in on you," he said, but she had already closed her eyes.

He walked into the hall. *Jesus, she's beyond sleepy. Ask Serna about that, too.* Jake passed the nurses' station, it was vacant again; he was glad he didn't have to see Monson. He went into the men's bathroom and almost dozed off on the toilet.

Jake washed up and walked back to the nursery, where both babies were asleep; the helper was nowhere in sight, but a man in a white T-shirt and jean overalls stood at the window, staring in. He was about five-six and held a worn green cap at his stomach as he put a gnarled, calloused hand on the glass. His dark, sun-withered face seemed to droop with exhaustion.

Can't tell if he's thirty or fifty. "Is María yours?" Jake pointed from the baby to the man, in case he didn't speak English. The man turned, softening his countenance with a faint smile; Jake decided he was much younger than fifty.

"Yes, María number three," he said in clear English. "María Juana, María Isabel, and now María Elena is almost ready to go home."

"I take it your first María is named after the lady who works here? She's your neighbor, right?"

"Yes." He grinned. "All three are named after her. You must be the other father; María told me a little about you. *Jorge Cruz, a sus órdenes.*" He reached out, now with a full smile; they shook hands.

"*Mucho gusto, Jorge*; I'm Jake."

"She told me you speak Spanish."

"Yeah, *más o menos.*"

"We've known María since we were kids. My wife even wanted to name our boy after her; use her uncle's name, María de Santiago. I talked her out of that one. How's your baby doing? She's sure a nice big girl."

Jake nodded politely. "María and my wife are worried about her a little, but nobody else seems to be."

Jorge sighed. "I can't tell you your business, but if María's a little worried, *I'd* be a little worried."

"Okay, I'll remember that."

"Well, I'm going to get my wife packed up." He turned to go.

"Gracias, Jorge."

"Buena suerte, señor."

Jake watched Jorge walk around the corner and down the hall. Noticing that it was just before two o'clock, he propped his legs up on the chair again, staring at Emma's pulsing chest cavity for a long time before his lack of sleep finally caught up with him.

Jake opened his eyes when he heard the hiss of a closing door. Standing up, he looked at the wall clock. *Man, almost four.* He turned to the nursery.

María was looking up to say something to the blonde woman, who then came out into the hall and turned for the back exits. The other baby was gone; María nodded to Jake, then placed both of her hands on Emma's chest for several seconds. He noticed that María's fingers, light mocha brown and creviced, were very long for such a small woman. She then caressed the baby's arms and feet studiously before feeling around her head. Emma moved weakly to her touch; María glanced at Jake with a trace of a smile.

Well, she must not be any worse. María held up one finger to indicate she would come out soon to talk.

Jake pointed down the hall to show that he was going to see Tina. At the station, a young redheaded nurse's assistant asked if she could help him. After Jake identified himself, she said in an upbeat but serious tone that Tina had been awake a while, crocheting before she went back to sleep. Jake thanked her then looked in on Tina, who was still dozing.

As soon as he returned to the nursery, María started to come out, leaning on the glass door. Jake hurried over to open it for her.

"¿How is your wife, Señor Fren?"

"Maybe a little better, gracias." They moved over to the viewing window.

"I visit her again soon."

"She will be happy to see you. ¿How is Emma?"

"More or less the same. ¿What did the doctor say?"

"I left messages for both of them, two times. I cannot get either one to check her."

The old woman shook her head and tsked, baring her crooked, chipped but clean teeth. *"It is good she is not worse, but she still has problems."*

"Señora, I do not know what else to do."

"I understand." She looked at Emma intently again, then turned back to him. *"The chief nurse is a problem; he is taking a double turn for the holiday."*

187

"Eight more hours?" he asked incredulously in English.

María made an atypical sigh. "*Sí. I will try to work mostly with the other nurses. After he leaves at midnight, maybe the next chief nurse will call the doctor. But I do not yet know which one is coming.*"

"*¿How many chief nurses are there?*"

"*Four. Please do not say this to anyone, but I have confidence only in two of them.*"

"*¿What if Emma gets worse before midnight?*"

"*This Monson will only call if it is very serious.*"

"*¿If she gets worse and he won't call, do you have any ideas?*"

"*They have to bring a doctor if you sign papers to take her from here.*"

"*¿To the university?*"

"*Sí; I hear that is the best place.*"

"*We will probably do that if she is worse. For now, I will leave another message for the doctor.*"

"*Está bien.*" María turned to the baby.

"*¿Señora, do you know where Doctor Serna lives?*"

"*Sí. Los jardínes.*"

"La Cholla Gardens?"

She nodded. "*Eso.*" María stepped toward the nursery door. "*¿Por qué, señor?*"

"*Nada. I just want to know.*" Jake turned and walked quickly toward emergency. *In case I have to go get him.*

24

Jake went to the pay phone and made the call to the service again. He spoke to the same cranky woman; eventually she allowed him to reword messages to both doctors. Jake tried to convey the seriousness of Emma's condition without sounding like an alarmist.

His stomach growled, so he stopped at the four vending machines, the small hospital's only option for hungry visitors. Jake used the changer again, then started feeding coins into a machine with snacks on corkscrew prongs. He saw the glass façade of the machine reflecting the image of SAINT CONCEPCION EMERGENCY from the door behind. Jake selected corn chips, the prong rotated but the bag hung up and didn't fall.

"Shit," he said aloud. *Damn place, nothing works right.* He struck the machine hard with his palm, the glass skewed from its frame, settling at an angle; the bag of chips clunked into the bin below. He stared at his deed unbelievingly, then pushed the bin; it wouldn't open. *Great, mad man, you broke the friggin' thing.* Jake bought root beer and a candy bar from the other machines, walked over to the bench at the medical staff exit and sat by the in-out board without looking at it.

So, what are you going to tell them about their damn machine? He opened the can of soda, peeled back the peanut-caramel bar; took a bite and then a drink. *Just pay for it after all this is over.* Jake nibbled and sipped while glaring at a nearby door sign that said: STAFF HALLWAY ONLY. *Serve them right if somebody who doesn't read English just walked in on an operation.*

He put the soda on the floor, took the rest of the candy out of the wrapper and got up to insert the paper in the side of a black trash cylinder with a chrome ashtray on top. Jake turned back to the bench and saw the light was on by McNally's name. *Didn't see that—damn it.* He left the candy on the pop can and dashed past emergency, then down the hallway to the nursery.

María was trying a bottle with Emma; he opened the door, poked his head in and quietly asked if McNally had been there. She said he hadn't, so Jake went right to the nurses' station, where Monson was on the phone, laughing. It was the first time Jake had seen the man smile.

"The one-five combo hit at ninety to one?" the charge nurse asked some-one gleefully. "What were the odds on each dog?" He paused. "No kidding? Man, a hundred and eighty bucks on a twelve-dollar bet, not too bad."

This is some important crap. Jake stood right in front of the charge nurse and saw a brochure by the phone; it had a photo print of an emaciated greyhound on front.

Looking at Jake, Monson's grin vanished. "I gotta go. Yeah, later." He hung up, pulling out a file drawer from the right side of his desk. "What is it now, Mister Friend?"

"McNally's in the hospital."

Monson fingered through the plastic tabs. "No, I'd bet he's gone by now."

"What? You know I wanted him to check Emma. Why is he here?"

The nurse extracted a file. "Checking the patient he operated on; not that it's any of your concern." Monson looked up. "He called, and I told him there was no change with your baby—which is a fact, Mister Friend."

"Did you talk to María?"

"You mean María?" He pronounced it Muh-ree-uh. "Not if I can help it—I have work to do."

"Yeah, on your damn racing form." Jake turned to go.

"What's your problem, buddy?" the nurse replied as Jake walked away. "You stay the hell outta my face," Monson added in a low grumble, but Jake heard him.

Forget that asshole—maybe McNally's still around. He ran by the nursery back down the hall to the staff exit, but the light was off by the doctor's name.

"Son of a bitch!" he shouted. Jake turned and kicked the black cylinder with his heel; the chrome tray dislodged and clanged onto the linoleum, a wisp of ash and some butts settling onto the floor. He exhaled deeply. *Great, that solves everything.* Jake stood the cylinder upright, replaced the tray, and swept the little mess into his palm.

"What happened, sir?" said a voice from behind. It was the emergency room nurse, a small Anglo woman in her fifties, wearing the ubiquitous light blue scrubs.

"Accidentally knocked it over." He brushed the ash and butts off his hands into the tray. "Why in hell does a hospital encourage people to smoke?"

"Excuse me, sir?"

"Sorry—nothing."

"Are you waiting for someone on staff?"

"Uh, yes, that's exactly what I'm doing."

The woman creased her brows but left, and Jake sat on the bench again, taking a sip of root beer. *No choice, you've gotta give it a try.* Jake got up, threw away the rest of the candy, and started back down the main hallway.

When Jake came to the nursery, María was wielding a huge mop in wide swaths over the floor; he realized she was remarkably fit for her age. Jake motioned for her to come out, then opened the door. She walked into the hallway.

"*¿Any change, señora?*"

She brushed aside a strand of grey hair that somehow had escaped her net. "*Not better or worse, señor.*"

"*I am going to leave for a while, to try to get Serna.*"

"*¿How can you do that?*"

"*I am not sure. ¿Do you have a phone in the nursery?*"

"*Sí, but the bell is shut off.*" María unclipped a pen from her pocket. "*You can call the nurse in emergency; she will come for me if she can.*" Jake handed her his notebook, and María wrote down the number.

"*Está bien, señora. I am going to try to call you every hour to check on the baby and my wife.*"

She nodded. "*I hope you find him, señor.*"

It was nearly six o'clock when Jake turned into La Cholla Gardens; he could feel that it was still around a hundred degrees, though the heat didn't concern him. He drove past the portal and its perfect little flower garden into the development. He came to the lawyer's English Tudor he saw before from a distance; it was grandiose and fussy looking, like some houses Jake had seen in Beverly Hills. This place probably had twenty rooms surrounded by at least five acres of tidy lawn and garden.

Why does anyone need something like that? Screw it; doesn't matter. He drove slowly past two smaller but opulent residences, checking names on the mailboxes. Jake came to a sprawling one-level multi-bedroom home, its siding and shake roof made of stained cedar, with an open four-car garage. A vintage white Corvette convertible and a new blue pickup were parked inside; the last two spaces were empty, lacking even ordinary garage junk like boxes or toys, except for one old bicycle leaning against a wall. Jake stopped to look more closely.

The estate was a "ranch" in every sense; complete with barns, grazing horses, and thousands of feet of white corral fence around the perimeter of about twenty acres. For a porch, the house had a dozen posts the size of tree trunks supporting a fifty-foot wide veranda enclosed by white wagon wheels. A long driveway led up to the place past a half acre front yard of river rock with a windbreak of immature blue spruce and Austrian pine. Mostly lawn and alfalfa took up the far side of the land, save a long strip of flower garden nearer the home.

Out at the curb, a cedar miniature of the house, actually a large mailbox, had SERNAS written cursively on top in wrought iron. *The right Sernas?* Jake took out his binoculars from behind the seat and read the customized frame around one license plate: DOC'S 58 - VETTE ROADSTER.

So now what's your great plan? He drove Loretta about forty yards down the street, parked before the next home under a willow and shut off the motor. *What the hell, just go.* Jake got out, walked back to Serna's place and then up to his eight-foot, heavily varnished, pine front door with a black iron handle. He pressed a button on the wall and heard a series of loud melodic chimes. *Man, that'd wake the dead.* He pressed it again, but no one came to the door. *Crap—wait him out.*

Jake returned to Loretta, put his sweaty Cub's hat on the seat, and waited there in the shade, watching the house. After fifteen minutes or so, some sprinklers started in the pastures, and a short man with a thick roll around his belly rode a lady's balloon-tire bicycle away from the irrigation. In all-white cotton and a straw hat, he coasted into the garage, leaned his bike against the other one, and then walked out past the flower garden.

Jake squinted toward the man. *I'll be, it's Justino's father—talk about overqualified for farm work.* He donned his cap, got out of Loretta, and headed for Mister Hernandez, who stopped on the lawn when he saw his boys' teacher approach.

As he walked, Jake recalled speaking to Hernandez after the fight and finding out that he was once a law clerk in Mexico. He was also impressed that Hernandez didn't look down on recent arrivals, as did some other "settled-in" immigrants. It bothered Jake that Justino had somehow not followed his father's example.

"Maestro, what are you doing here?" Hernandez asked, surprised but friendly. He had a light complexion like his sons, and the man's English syntax was far superior to his pronunciation, which Jake knew wasn't unusual for a bright person learning English as an adult.

He reached out to shake hands. "Hi, Mister Hernandez; I was just waiting to talk to the doctor."

"Ah, let's go to the shade." His sentence sounded like *Les go to di chade.* He pointed to where the house's shadow almost reached the garden; they started that way. "I am Doctor Serna's foreman, maestro. He is on a car trip with his wife and daughter," he said in his thick accent, again with all the right words. "I am not sure when he will return. Maybe after dark."

Damn. "I see." They passed the immaculate flowerbed, thick with tall stalks of white, pink, and magenta cosmos. Entering the shade, Hernandez's long-sleeve white shirt was nearly free of perspiration, while Jake could feel his T-shirt was nearly soaked from the short walk.

Jake turned to him. "I just need to leave him a note. His message service isn't very helpful."

"I can put the note on the door inside the garage before we close up."

"That would be great. How are your boys doing?"

"Ricardo is studying; Justino, he works here with me." He pointed to the barns.

"Oh? And college?"

"He will work all summer for the clothes and things, or he receives no help from me for the college. I want the boy to learn here, too."

Smart man. "I think he will."

"You have the message, maestro?"

He wants to go, Jake. "In my truck. I'll be right back." He walked quickly out of the shade down to the street; Hernandez picked up an iron rod and twisted on some lawn sprinklers. Jake jogged to Loretta, got in and found his notebook. He ripped out a page, put it on the cover and wrote the message:

Doctor Serna,

Sorry to interrupt your Saturday; it was my idea for Mr. Hernandez to leave this note for you. We are very concerned about our baby's condition— one of your staff agrees with us. I know you are not on call tonight, but please call the charge nurse and ask to speak with me in the nursery. Thanks for your time.

Jake Friend

He folded the paper, got out, and started up the street. Both Justino and Mister Hernandez were standing by their bikes when Jake came into the garage. He saw the young man was clothed like his father, except his white shirt and pants were soiled with manure.

"Hi, maestro," Justino said, shoulders drooping, but he looked more tired than self-conscious.

"Hi, Justino. Looks like you're working pretty hard for that college money."

"I think college is easy after this," he answered with a nod, no sign of his usual surliness.

Jake handed the note to Mister Hernandez. "I told the doctor the message was my idea."

"Okay, maestro, I put it on the kitchen door," Hernandez told him, already moving around the Corvette.

"*Gracias, señor*," he said as Justino reached up for the garage door. "Say hi to Ricardo," Jake added, walking away. He crossed the street and saw charcoal-and-white thunderheads loom above the hills, growing straight up into the blue sky. He turned to see Justino and his dad pedal away down the street.

Better call María. He got in, drove out of the development and down the hill, passing the two bikes with a *beep* from Loretta. At the small corner market, Jake called the emergency room nurse on a pay phone. María came on after two or three minutes and told him there was still no change; Monson and Ruiz were the only ones who had checked the baby. He asked if she had a chance to look in on Tina; María said that during her visit la señora ate some dinner and was knitting again.

Jake thanked her, then went inside the store. He chose a turkey sandwich, an apple, and put his hand on a six-pack of beer. *Bad idea. One won't hurt.* He bought the single beer and a diet pop before driving back up to Serna's. The storm was closing in with wind and a few drops of rain when he got there.

By the time he ate the sandwich and enjoyed his beer, a lightning bolt seemed to crack right overhead, followed only seconds later by loud rolling thunder, then a few splats on the windshield.

Geez, nothing safer than a car, right? Facing Serna's closed garage and waiting for the next violent peal from the disturbed atmosphere, Jake let the cool ozone blow across the front seat as he bit into the apple. Moments later, another strike brought with it a slanting torrent of rain. He reluctantly rolled up his windows, leaving the wind-wings open. The downpour pecked Loretta's steel roof like hail on an aluminum awning.

Jake watched the dark house and the weather until the storm eventually moved on. He lowered the windows to enjoy the cool air settling over the neighborhood. It was dusk by the time he drove off to call María.

At the grocery, he waited again for her to come on the line. After reporting no changes, María told him she agreed to cover for a helper who had an emergency. They were letting her off at ten; she would return at six in the morning for the first of two holiday shifts. She told him that Denise, the lady who was on all night, was a helpful person who would answer his calls. María tried to encourage Jake, reminding him that Monson would be gone at midnight.

Jake headed up for the big market, hoping to find some flowers Tina would like. He passed the city park, partly roped off because they were setting up fireworks for the next evening. Jake heard from Jesús that the two La Cholla mayors had worked it out with U.S. Immigration for the citizens of La Cholla, Mexico to cross the border after the parade to enjoy the American fireworks. Captain LeBlanc, Jesús said, wasn't happy about the arrangement.

At Ortega's store they displayed flag-embossed pots of red and white carnations with blue foil stars. Jake paid extra to have the clerk make a special bouquet of red carnations and baby's breath in a white vase; he bought the flowers with a Saturday newspaper from Tucson.

Instead of going back through town, Jake traversed the valley, then drove down to the hospital. He went first to the nursery and watched María trying to feed the baby; she smiled at the flowers for Tina and made a hand gesture showing that Emma had taken a little from the bottle. Jake walked right by Monson and took the bouquet into Tina.

With the television on but muted, Tina was awake and crocheting, her right hand in an up-down motion steady as an oil well pump.

"Hi, Tina." He kissed her cheek and put the flowers on the rolling adjustable table. "Is the afghan going to be for Emma?"

"No, it's too big." She concentrated on the crochet hook as the yarn steadily unwound from the medium-blue skein. Tina glanced up at the bouquet, smiled weakly, and went right back to her project. "Thank you, they're pretty, even if they are dead."

"What?"

"Cut flowers, perfect for funerals."

Good God.

"Sorry." Tina stared at her busy hands. "I probably never told you I don't care for cut flowers."

Jesus, Jake, you knew that. "No, I forgot; I'll find you a live plant."

"Please don't bother."

Jake moved the bouquet to the floor and tried to think of a different subject. Though he didn't want to report his failure to bring a doctor for Emma, Jake decided to tell her if she asked. He tried talking about hospital inanities—the food, noise, nurses and so on—but Tina only looked at him once, as if he were a stranger. Finally, he told her he saw Emma drinking a little more.

She put the hook down, raising her head. "I won't pretend she's okay,

Jake; she isn't. Why don't they listen to María? They just keep saying how big the baby is." She picked up her crocheting and fell right back into rhythm.

"I know; I'm tired of hearing that, too." He paused. "We both trust María, but don't forget she isn't a nurse."

Tina began to tie off a six-foot-long blue strip. "She's only been right all along." She glowered at her work.

"Yeah, it sure seems like it." *She's pissed, just go.* "I guess I'll say good night then; I'll check Emma again on my way out."

Tina started on a white strip. "What good will that do?" Her rhetorical question was barely audible.

Not much. "Uh, I hope you rest okay. I'll see you first thing in the morning."

"Good night." She didn't look up.

He kissed her inert lips just long enough to know she was indifferent. Jake stood up, watching her crochet steadily, as if he had already left.

Jesus. "Uh, you didn't tell me who the afghan's for."

She kept working. "María."

"I'm sure she'll like it." He patted her arm and walked out into the hall with the bouquet at his side.

25

Jake came first to the young redheaded nurse's assistant who was enduring an entire shift with Monson; he gave her the flowers, saying they made Tina sneeze. He left through a side exit to avoid Monson and the nursery, deciding he had pestered María enough for a while.

Driving back to La Cholla Gardens, Jake saw Mister Hernandez ahead in Loretta's headlights, pedaling out to the portal. *Let him go by. Too late, he saw you.* Jake pulled up to Hernandez, who had to jump forward off his rusty bike to completely stop it.

"Maestro."

"Señor, I'm on my way to town," he fibbed. "You want to put your bike in back? I can run you down there."

"*No gracias*. I need exercise." He poked himself in the paunch and grinned.

"Were you just up at Doctor Serna's?"

"Yes, to turn off everything; the rain finish my work for me. He is not yet home."

"Oh," Jake said, as if it didn't matter. "*Pues, adiós, señor.*" He put Loretta back in gear.

"*Adiós, maestro.*" Hernandez waved; Jake pretended he was going downtown, losing him after two blocks. He circled around, drove back up to Serna's and parked under the willow again, though it was dark now and relatively cool.

He sat there a while, focused on Serna's nightlight in the kitchen. Jake tried to divert his thoughts by reading the sports section with his flashlight to find out how the Cubs were doing. After he realized he had perused the Major League standings several times, Jake decided to try to catch María before she left.

This time he called from the gas station's pay phone after filling Loretta's

197

tank. He had made it there just before closing, surprised it was already ten o'clock. Jake got in touch with Denise, María's replacement, who tried to be helpful, as María said she would. Denise reported nothing new with Emma.

Jake drove off for the Gardens again. He turned in at the entrance and drove by the first three homes slowly before he saw Serna's open garage, a dark-colored Cadillac by the Corvette, and some lights on in the house. *It's ten thirty—now what do you do?* He drove up to the willow, turned around, and stopped. *Emma's the same; maybe I'm making too much out of this. Crap, how are you supposed to know? So, right up to the door, or go wait for his call?*

He rolled by the house in first gear, looking in. When he saw most of the lights were off again, Jake kept going, turned left at the portal, and drove down to the hospital. He hurried in and went straight to the nurses' station. Monson raised his head and groaned.

"Well, if it isn't Mister Friend."

"Did Doctor Serna call?"

"Yes. You left a note there, for criminy sake?"

"So? What did he say?"

"What do you think he said? He asked if there were any changes, and I told him there weren't." Shaking his head, Monson checked some papers on the counter.

Back off a little, Jake. He sighed. "All right, do you have my home phone number?"

"Of course." He looked up. "Does this mean you're actually going home for a while?" he asked in a half-hearted attempt at a more friendly tone.

Like you give a damn. "Yeah, I guess so. Did my wife go to sleep?"

"Yes, she finally put the knitting away."

"Okay, I'm going. You'll let me know if there's any change?"

Monson's phone rang. "Yes, Mister Friend; good night." He waved at Jake dismissively and picked up the receiver. "This is Monson."

El pendejo. Jake went down the hall and looked in on Tina; she was snoring very softly, the afghan on her lap. Jake moved closer but didn't touch her. *Jesus, has she ever been through the wringer.*

Holding off tears again, he left the room, passed Monson, and came to the nursery. Jake watched Emma's constant panting until he caught himself daydreaming. He chatted with the lean helper, Denise, who had translucent liver-spotted skin. She was inches taller and years younger than María, but she seemed very frail. Before Jake left, he was impressed that Denise made sure that she had his correct phone number.

He walked outside, climbed into Loretta, and just sat there behind the steering wheel. *Maybe I shouldn't leave. No, Denise is okay. May as well get some sleep; get back here early before morning rounds.*

He debated with himself on the way to Sofia, nearly turning around once. Jake saw lights at Juanito's house and stopped to see if he could get Fiera. As he walked to the door, he noticed there were no rain puddles, and it felt like it was still ninety degrees, bugs flying and crawling everywhere. The Montalvos were watching the end of a Bicentennial special on TV. Jake apologized for the late hour and told them only that Tina and the baby were okay.

Juanito brought Fiera in from the yard; she jumped on Jake, licking him even more than usual, as if he were Tina. He arranged to drop the dog off in the morning, then drove over to the rental; Ben was there, watering in the dark. Jake got out with Fiera; the dog dashed over to Ben, who patiently withstood the same slobbery treatment.

"Hey, Ben."

"Hi, maestro. How is la maestra; the baby?"

"Okay, thanks. Sergeant Ramos told you?"

"No, Señor Montalvo." He kept flooding the tomatoes.

"Kind of late to water; it didn't rain here at all?"

"Only a little. I come here for this; I stay at Mauricio's last night."

"Party time?"

"*Fútbol*, two games; we win Friday and tonight."

"Oh, right, I forgot—good for you guys. Ben, that's enough for now. The rest can wait; come on in."

"Okay, maestro."

After Jake lowered the thermostat, they chatted in front of the TV for a while, Ben telling him he would like to visit the hospital the next day. Before bed, Jake called Monson and had a pithy verbal exchange similar to their previous ones. He hung up and unwound the long line, leaving the telephone in the hall outside their bedroom. While he began to undress for a shower, the phone rang.

Geez, it's almost midnight. He walked to the phone. *Can't be the hospital.* "Hello?"

"Jake, what's going on?"

"Hannah?"

"I called five times; your sisters and I are going nuts—especially them."

"Sorry, just got back. Tina had the baby." He told her the basic information; she interrupted to exclaim or congratulate after each detail. Jake didn't mention there were any problems.

"So tell me what's wrong, Jake."

"What?"

"Jesus, it's me, Huey; what's going on?"

Man. "Okay. Tina and one of the nurses' helpers are worried that Emma's too quiet and breathing too fast, but the nurses say the rate is high-normal. The doctor agrees and won't come back to check her."

"Damn it, you have to make him."

"That's what I'm trying to do." Jake described some of the measures he already tried. " . . . and he's supposed to be there for rounds in the morning."

"I think he's negligent, Jake. You want me to come down there?"

No! "Uh, no thanks, I've got it handled. Do me a favor, Hannah; call Caroline and Joyce but don't mention any complications, especially since we're not sure."

"You're right. They'd go nuts."

"Please tell them, uh, that I'll call soon."

"I'll take care of it."

"Thanks, Sis. I don't mean to cut you short, but I should get some sleep."

"Good idea. Jake, you have to promise to keep in touch, or I'll just fly down there."

"All right, I'll call when I know something new."

After they disconnected, Jake took a shower and went to bed. Fiera somehow knew it was okay this night to jump up on the sheets and rest her moist snout right on Jake's arm. He rubbed her ears and fell asleep.

Jake dreamt again; this time he was driving around a posh suburb, looking for Serna until Loretta was stopped by a flash flood of bizarre detritus gurgling down a wash. He saw frolicking swimmers float by in a huge round plastic swimming pool followed by a Pontiac bobbing up and down, some Linn relatives smiling and gawking out of the windows like tourists. Then came an entire dislodged front yard with Mister Hernandez dressed in a business suit, pruning trees as he passed by. Finally, Jake watched a flotilla of white corral fencing; Ben and Justino were clinging to the wood for their lives.

Jake's alarm went off before six; he had set it to coincide with María's coming back on duty. He sat up with vague images in his mind of white fences in a turbulent arroyo. *Man, that was weird.* Jake made himself get up right away. He put on Bermudas and a clean summer shirt, then called emergency and was relieved to hear the same helpful nurse answer. He asked for María and waited for her again.

"Mister Friend," the emergency nurse said, "María can't get away."

"Is something wrong?"

"She's just very busy. I asked about your daughter; they said she's about the same."

"Thanks, nurse." *That's good, I guess.* "The doctors' rounds are about seven, right?"

"There are no Sunday rounds, Mister Friend—only if they're called in."

"What? No one told me that."

"I'm sorry, sir."

Damn it to hell. "It's not your fault." His mind went blank, as if he'd been struck in the head; he felt lost and isolated for several moments.

"Mister Friend?"

Jesus, pull yourself together. "Yes, sorry. Uh, please tell María I'll try to be there before nine. Thank you."

"You're welcome. I'll let her know."

"Bye." He hung up. *Go get the bastard.* Jake woke Ben to tell him he would call later. He asked Ben to drop off Fiera at the Montalvos.

On the drive to town, he was watching the dawn of what would be a hot Fourth of July when he heard a dull thumping under the back of the truck. *What the hell?* Jake pulled over, got out and found a rear tire almost flat.

"Piss!" he yelled to the desert, "up a goddamned rope." *Focus, for God's sake.* He jumped back in and coasted off the slight crown to level ground, well off the road. After Jake started fooling with the jack, lug wrench and the spare, he heard a twig snap in the nearby palo verde; his nose picked up a thick wave of musk. A car zipped by; Jake heard a grunt. He looked up and thought he saw a sow and two half-grown piglets, backed into some dead branches not even ten feet away. Jake realized they were hairy with pointed noses; the snarling mother had a white collar of fur.

My God, javelina. Bad timing—gotta go. The mother was pissed and didn't back off, so Jake put his tools down in the dirt, backed slowly away from the cornered animals and quietly said, "It's okay, momma, I won't bother you." Before Jake's heel touched the asphalt, the mother peccary thrashed off into the bush, her babies behind. He ran back down to Loretta and changed the tire with no problems.

Jake drove into town, up the hill, and turned into La Cholla Gardens. He parked under the same willow, glaring at a dull kitchen light in Serna's otherwise dark home.

When another light comes on, go to the door. He waited; it was after seven thirty when one of the bedroom shades brightened. *Give them enough time to wake up.* Jake got out of Loretta, stealthily left the door ajar so it wouldn't make noise, and leaned on the truck's bed.

No damn excuses—he's going to listen. After a few minutes, he began walking up the street. Before Jake got to Serna's, a La Cholla squad car approached. The officer wore dark glasses, though the sun hadn't cleared the hills.

Great, it's Sánchez. Jake had seen the corporal previously only from a distance, knew he was very short, and guessed he was sitting now on some sort of pillow or booster. Jesús had confided to Jake that Sanchez was a south Texan who wished he had never left the military, for all the wrong reasons. Jesús, a veteran himself, also told Jake that he always tried to be on different shifts from the corporal.

The officer U-turned and stopped his vehicle between Jake and Serna's place, rolling down his window. Jake took some slow steps toward him. Sanchez, about thirty, wore his flat-brimmed hat like a Marine, its strap back on his neck below a buzz cut. Reflective sunglasses covered about a third of the corporal's small, light-tan face.

"What's yr' business here, sir—ain't you a teacher?" he asked, his nose wrinkling as if he smelled something bad.

"Yes. Is there some problem, officer *Sánchez*?" Jake pronounced his surname in Spanish.

"It's Sanchez." He said, SANN-chiz. "How come you know my name?"

My kids all know your name. "You work with my neighbor, Jesús Ramos."

"That right? So what's yr' business here?"

"Uh, I'm just going to visit Doctor Serna."

"It's before oh-eight hundred. You tellin' me he's expectin' a visit?"

"No, I just need to talk to him about a problem at the hospital."

"That a problem he wants to hear about?"

Damn. "Yes, I think so, but you'd have to ask Doctor Serna." *Yeah, go get him for me.*

"Nope, ain't gonna happen. You need t' call the doc for permission to be here."

"I've been trying to call him for more than a day."

"That's sorta too bad; this here's private property. That's yr' green truck over there," he stated, craning his skinny neck out for a better look at Loretta.

"Yes."

He sniggered. "Guess it's a truck—surprised you ain't painted no flowers on it. Believe I seen it in town with wetbacks."

Friggin' yokel. "Yeah, my students; I smuggle them over the border."

Sanchez lowered his glasses enough to reveal squinty olive-green eyes. "You ain't bein' no wise-ass with me, are ya', teach?"

That was stupid, Jake. He sighed, shook his head and turned to the flaring sunrise just over the horizon.

Sanchez fingered his sunglasses back in place. "Y'all listen good. Yr' gonna go climb right up in that piece-a-crap VW an' just drive it on outta here."

"Wait a minute, officer, I just need—"

Sanchez pointed at him. "What you need is to go now, before yr' under arrest for trespassin'."

Shit. "All right, I'm leaving."

26

Jake dialed Ben from Ortega's store, taking bites of a frosted doughnut, then a gulp of coffee, cold from all the milk he put in it. After he told Ben he was on his way, Jake left yet another message with the service. He drove on home, trying to think of some other way to contact either doctor.

Ben, dressed in his good clothes and reeking of strong aftershave, impressed Jake with the implied importance of his visit to Tina. On the ride back to the hospital, Jake tried to take his mind off Emma and Tina, telling Ben about the javelina and asking about his soccer team. He parked near an ash grove by the visitors' lot so Loretta's interior wouldn't be scalding when they returned.

Jake got his book and notebook from the back seat; they walked across the already searing asphalt into the hospital, then down the hall to the nursery. María was preoccupied in the back room; Emma wasn't with two new babies out by the window.

What the hell? Easy, she's probably in with Tina. The newborns were twin boys surnamed Flores, the card said, delivered after five A.M. by Doctor McNally. *No wonder María's so busy.*

Ben followed Jake to the nurses' station, where he was glad to see that Jaworsky, the nursing prodigy from Friday night's graveyard shift, was back on duty. In her flowing white garb again, the hefty young woman smiled at Jake as he approached.

"Good morning, Mister Friend. I called your house a while ago." She looked briefly askance at Ben.

"Is there something wrong?"

"Nothing serious. After the delivery this morning, Doctor McNally checked your daughter. As a precautionary measure, he decided to put her on some intermittent oxygen to relax the breathing a little. She's in an enclosed incubator, but the doctor says everything is still within normal range. Like I said, it's precautionary, nothing to be alarmed about."

"Okay, well, I'm glad he checked her. What do I have to do to get Serna to follow up?"

"I know this is a very busy day for him, like it is for most everybody."

What? "Oh, the Bicentennial; I sure don't want to disturb *that*."

"Mister Friend, that tone isn't helpful."

Easy, Jake—they finally did something. "You're right. I do appreciate everything you have been doing, nurse."

"Thank you."

"We're getting pretty frustrated with Serna. After I talk to Tina, I think we'll want to change to McNally."

"He's no longer on call and could be out of town."

"But you don't know for sure?"

"No. Please believe me, Mister Friend, we do have things well in hand." She sounded as confident as she did on the first night. "Unless things change, this can wait until Doctor Serna's morning rounds tomorrow."

Maybe, maybe not. "Okay, one more question please. Did you explain to my wife about the oxygen?"

"Yes, but I had to tell her twice to be sure she understood." Jaworsky paused, pulled Jake aside, and then spoke very softly so that Ben couldn't listen. "Mister Friend, she acted like she didn't want to hear it. She hardly speaks to anyone, except María. I'm concerned about her."

Good. "What is it that's concerning you?"

"After a normal birth, depression usually comes later, if at all, but she's already showing some classic signs."

"Except you said 'normal birth.' She doesn't think the baby's normal; that's why she's so upset."

"There's no medical reason to support that. Perhaps you could help us to dissuade her."

"No, I won't try to dissuade her of anything."

Jake's bluntness didn't upset Jaworsky as much this time. "That's up to you. I believe she's awake and crocheting again."

"Okay; thanks. I'll be back." Jake took a step before he remembered Ben was with him. "Let's go, Ben."

"Excuse me," the nurse said, "visiting hours for non-family—"

Jake turned to her. "He lives with us; I think that qualifies as family."

"Very well," Jaworsky answered with a shrug. Jake and Ben continued down the hall.

Not a word from her if he was blond. He showed Ben into the room. Jake was sure Tina saw them in her peripheral vision, but she kept crocheting bright red yarn onto the six-foot-square blue and white afghan.

"Hi, Tina." Jake pecked her on the cheek. "Ben's here."

Still with deep circles under her eyes and scant color in her face, Tina just glanced at her visitor. "Hi, Ben."

Ben, apparently upset by her appearance, shook Tina's hand. "*Felicidades, maestra*," he mumbled. Tina forced a doleful-looking smile as she made a red border begin to appear on one edge of her project.

Geez, still out of it. Jake put his book and notebook on top of some yarn in her big purse. "Tina, I thought maybe they'd give you a roommate. There are twins in the nursery."

She ignored the comment, attentive to her crocheting.

Idiot, she doesn't want to hear that. "Man, I can't believe you decided to go Bicentennial with the afghan."

"María brought in her extra red yarn," Tina said, continuing to work. "All I can do is add a border. She doesn't know it's for her. Please don't tell her."

"Right, I won't." *Get to the point, Jake.* "Tina, I think we're finally getting somewhere with Emma, but we need to talk about it."

"Maestro," Ben said, "I go now." Not waiting for an answer, Ben bowed slightly to Tina and said, "Maestra."

Tina forced a weak smile. "You can stay, Ben."

"Thank you, no. *You need to talk*," he said in Spanish. "I go to the truck." He turned for the door.

"Ben, it's cooler in the lobby," Jake told him. "I'll be a little while."

"*Está bien, maestro*; I wait in the truck."

Ben left; Tina put down her project and finally looked right at Jake. "María said the oxygen isn't helping."

"What? When did she say that?"

"Maybe a half hour ago; she was only here a minute."

Damn it to hell. He turned, glowering outside at the back of the statue of Jesus on the lawn. *Yeah, invite people into this place.*

Tina nearly startled him by speaking louder than before. "So, do you believe us now?"

"Yes, I'll try again to get Serna."

"How?"

"One way or the other, I'll get him."

"Go on then, Jake, do what you can."

"Are you going to be okay?"

"Me? I'm not the one who's sick." Tina scowled a little and resumed working on the afghan as Jake hurried out of the room.

The next hour would later come back to Jake as a jumbled montage of María's overwrought face, Emma's nearly limp body, Loretta hurtling downhill, and Ben jumping out before Jake could stop. After that, mostly in red, white, and blue, it was the impervious Doctor Serna waving to the Bicentennial crowd; then sullen clowns and whining Brownie Scouts followed by the sweaty atonal high school band startling the Mexican cowboys' proud horses. Jake would recall the light blue police car behind him, red lights flashing, accelerating up Garden Drive in pursuit of Loretta; and his relief upon seeing Jesús get out of the squad car. Then the mad dash over the border; the last image from probably the most frenzied hour of his twenty-seven years was of Ben, knocking futilely on Doctor Castilleja's door.

After Jake and Ben finally gave up and walked quickly away from the doctor's apartment, they suddenly stopped when they heard the door rattle. "*Paciencia, paciencia, mi paciente,*" came faintly from inside before the door opened. Ben ran back, Jake right behind. Doctor Castilleja, about Jake's height but not as heavy, stood there in charcoal slacks, a short sleeve white shirt, not tucked in, and bare feet, holding a thick manual of some kind.

Thank God. Ben can explain—less confusion.

"*Mijo,*" the doctor said through the screen to Ben in Spanish, "*it seems you have interrupted my nap to bring me a tourist.*"

"*Perdóneme, doctor, not a tourist; this is my teacher from the other side. He speaks Spanish.*"

The doctor pushed open the screen door. "Oh? *Buenas tardes, Señor, uh . . .*"

"Friend, Jake Friend. Doctor *Castilleja.*" Jake reached out. If the doctor were not wearing bifocals, Jake thought he could pass for Armando's older brother, complete with black hair down to his neck and a full rakish moustache.

They shook hands; Castilleja turned to Ben with a grin. "*It always pleases me, mijo, when one of our neighbors from the north can pronounce my name.*"

"*Con permiso, doctor,*" Ben said seriously, "*I need to tell you we were sent by María Juana Robles and . . .*"

During Ben's rapid explanation, it dawned on Jake that this was the first time he heard María's last name. He watched the doctor's face turn grave when Ben told him the baby was sick and they couldn't find Serna.

"Okay, come in out of the heat," Castilleja said in English with a barely discernible accent.

"So, you'll help us, doctor?" Jake asked.

"If they let me, Mister Friend. While I put on my shoes, you can tell me what's going on with your child. Something to drink for you two?"

Jake stepped forward. "No thanks; we just had something." As soon as they walked in, the doctor left the small living room, which was maybe ten degrees cooler than the building's shade outside. Ben and Jake sat on a hard couch covered with a light blue chenille bedspread.

Having been in a few of his students' homes, Jake noticed this simple apartment was missing some things he had seen in the other houses. Instead of a gallery of religious trappings and family photos, there was just one framed glossy on the doctor's TV/stereo console. It was a shot of Castilleja's parents, Jake assumed, standing proudly with their son in front of the multi-colored University of Mexico library building. The rest of the room had a college ambiance, including a Bob Marley poster, a print of Picasso's Don Quixote, and hundreds of books and record albums on shelves made of planks and bricks.

The doctor came back with his shoes, the shirt tucked in, carrying an old-fashioned black medical bag. He also had on a white, flat-brimmed sunhat, not like the cowboy-style straw hats Jake had seen around La Cholla.

As soon as he returned, Castilleja started grilling Jake on the baby's condition. He sat in an armchair to put on his brown socks and shoes, keeping up the inquiries. Finally, he stood up and asked, "Was your wife overdue?"

"Yes, almost ten days. Does that mean something?"

"Perhaps. Have they done X-rays?"

"I don't think so, doctor."

"*Hijo*," he said, pursing his lips as he picked up the medical bag. "I believe that's something we would have done by now here in the Third World."

27

They left the apartment, hurried past the doctor's Karmann Ghia and got in Loretta. Jake backed up quickly into the road and headed for town, Ben in the back seat. Castilleja put the bag by his feet and looked around at the pins and duct tape holding the interior together. Jake saw the doctor's hat had a chin cord that fell to his chest like a necklace.

"I like your truck, Mister Friend, but what happened in here?"

"Our dog had a few bites. Doctor, do you have any ideas about what's going on with Emma?"

"I have one or two, uh, hunches, I think is the best word. But I don't believe it helps to guess before I see her."

Makes sense. "Right." He continued down the road as fast as he could without drawing attention. After a minute or so, Jake asked, "How free are you to be over there for a while today?"

"It should be fine, Mister Friend, as long as things stay quiet here. I am on call today but forgot to let our police know where I'm going. I need to call them when we get there."

Jake nodded. He finally came to the pavement, then the light, and turned left toward the border.

"Maestro," Ben called, "I get out now, please."

Jake slowed and looked in his rearview. "Ben, maybe they'll let you cross since you're with us."

"No, maestro, and I will use the time you need."

He's right. "Okay, Ben—where?"

"*Aquí*, the market."

Jake pulled over at a curb two blocks from the border; Ben got out.

"Thanks for your help, Ben," Jake called.

"*Nos vemos, maestro*—tomorrow maybe. *Adiós, doctor*." Ben waved, and backed away.

Castilleja waved back as Jake pulled out into the traffic, which was light going north but still congested in the other direction.

"Do you have any problems crossing up here?" Jake asked as they went by the tourist shops.

"Depends, especially since I don't have a pass today."

Great. Jake drove slowly through the border to the shortest of three open lines on the American side and waited behind two cars. The officer let the first one go but seemed to have a lot of questions for the next car, a family in a Dodge station wagon with Oklahoma plates. *Crap, let 'em go; they're from Tulsa, for God's sake.*

"Uh, I think we have some bad luck here with this new inspector," the doctor said. "This could take a while."

"Should I back up and move to another lane?"

"No, that's asking for trouble."

Jake put the transmission in neutral and waited. *Damn it all.* He watched the intense young officer in his tidy uniform—grey trousers and a pale blue blouse with a round navy blue patch on one short sleeve. Wearing a "captain-style" flat cap with a shiny bill, he was an inch or two shy of six feet tall, blond, with a nickel-size brown mole on his face. *Great, one of the Waltons with a crew cut.* After a couple more questions, the Oklahomans were cleared; Jake pulled forward between two booths and into shade from the portal.

The young man leaned into the window; Jake saw a gold U.S. Immigration insignia on his cap, and a badge over the left pocket. The other side had a dull brass name badge that said, T. T. MEACHAM. "Happy Fourth, sir," Meacham said, not happy.

"Afternoon, officer." Jake spoke as deferentially as he could, but Meacham turned away, his eyes poring over Loretta. Jake raised a brow, looking at the doctor.

"Citizen of what country please, sir?" the inspector asked from behind.

Jake turned right back to him, accidentally slamming his upper arm into the door. *Ouch, damn it.* "United States, officer."

"Resident of Arizona?"

See my license plate, John Boy? "Yes. Sofía, Arizona—ten miles from here."

"How long were you in Mexico, sir?" He saw Jake's smudged forehead.

"Uh, maybe forty-five minutes."

"And what purchases are you bringing back?"

"None, officer, I—"

"Have you been in some sort of altercation, sir? Your arm's bleeding."

210

Jake looked down and saw the cut had opened. "It's just a scratch from when I reached under the seat."

"Were you putting something there, sir?"

So stupid, Jake. "No officer, I was looking for my wallet."

"Hope you found it, sir," Meacham warned, removing a small green notebook from his left chest pocket. "Your driver's license, please." Jake took out his wallet and held up the license to the young man, who jotted some information, then leaned in the window again. "Citizen of what country please, sir?" he asked Castilleja.

"La Cholla, Mexico," the doctor answered, anglicizing the words.

"Do you have one of today's fireworks passes or a local card, sir?"

"Not today, inspector."

"They're issuing the passes at your plaza; you'll have to go back and get one, sir."

"Officer," Jake said, "can I please explain? He's—"

"Sir, your passenger will have to get out, then I'd like you to pull this vehicle off to the right." He pointed to a concrete island. "Stop there, please, and turn off the motor; stand by the vehicle and wait for instructions." He spoke to Castilleja again. "Please leave the vehicle, sir, and return to the other side."

"Okay, inspector." The doctor opened his door.

Shit! "Wait a sec, he's a doctor; I'm taking him—"

"Sir, I'll ask you to comply now, please."

Watching Castilleja start away with his bag, Jake turned to the officer. "You *don't* understand," he said in a shrill tone.

"Sir, this is your final chance to comply." Meacham smirked as if he hoped Jake's disobedience would continue.

Damn it all. "All right, I'm doing it." He turned Loretta into the inspection area, parked, and saw the doctor talking to a different officer. Jake took a napkin from the glove box and got out to wait by the door. He saw Meacham in the booth; another inspector was already in his lane. Jake took María's medicine and bandages out of his pocket, wiped off the cut with the napkin and treated it.

He looked up, the doctor was gone. Meacham, now in sunglasses, hurried back to Jake. "Okay, sir, please stand back from your vehicle."

Don't make more trouble—you'll be here all day. He waited in the shade and watched Meacham unbutton most of Loretta's tarp. The inspector rifled through the tools, camping gear, even Jake's trash.

Good, John Boy's sweating. He saw Castilleja and a much older officer in an ordinary tan cowboy hat walking in Jake's direction from the nearby office; they were laughing about something. *What's going on?*

As they came closer, Jake noticed that the senior officer had likely stretched government regulations with his trimmed grey sideburns and a stiff, white handlebar moustache. The man's forest green uniform, however, looked complete—black shiny boots, neat trousers, and a short-sleeve shirt with bars on the epaulets. The revolver in his black leather holster set him off completely from the scurrying inspectors.

"Mister Friend?" the officer asked him. J. R. WILLITS was the moniker on his polished name badge.

"Yes, officer." Jake saw Meacham join them.

"You and the doctor are free to go on over."

"Sir," the young inspector said, "I haven't checked the vehicle's interior yet, sir."

"You can take your lane, Meacham. See you later, doc," Willits said to Castilleja, and started back to the office. The doctor helped Jake snap down the tarp; they got in the truck and entered La Cholla, U.S.A.

"How'd you pull that off?" Jake asked, driving through downtown at the legal maximum.

"Well, in both of our countries it often comes down to who you know or how much money's in your pocket. Next time, you might want to refrain from saying that you were under the seat," Castilleja said with a chuckle.

"Yeah, no kidding. So, how much do I owe you?"

"No, no. Agent Willits and I go way back. Put it this way, I have a Georgia friend who'd call Jim Willits 'good people,' just like we say in Spanish."

"Oh." *Georgia?* Not wanting somebody like Corporal Sanchez to complicate things, Jake increased his speed to exactly four miles per hour over the limit until he turned left on Garden, and Loretta began laboring up the hill.

"Ah, the drawback of a Volkswagen, I know it well," the doctor said.

Don't know this guy from Adam. "Uh, yeah, but your Karmann Ghia's a lot lighter."

"Same engine; I might beat you by five miles an hour."

"Doc, do you mind telling me where you studied and practiced?" *Jesus, Jake.* "Sorry, that sounds bad; it doesn't really matter."

"It's okay, Mister Friend. I am a product of the public schools of La Cholla, the University of Mexico, and then UCLA. After my residency, I worked six years in L. A., then four *en el campo* in Central America, and now in La Cholla for almost five years, I believe it is."

"Man, you've really been around. Did you like L.A.? I'm from there."

"Well, to be honest, after my divorce, I couldn't think of one good reason to stay in the area—not to demean your hometown."

"Hardly. I don't go back except to see my family." Jake drove by La

Cholla Gardens. "With your background, you must have come back here on purpose."

"Yes, a border kid for good, I guess, but I don't have to sell *chicle* anymore." He grinned. "Seven years in West Los Angeles left me with enough money to live here for as long as I wish, and with people who both want and need my help."

Jake nodded at Serna's office as he drove by. "Too bad Doctor Serna doesn't share your, uh, enthusiasm."

"Doctor Serna is young and has many strings attached to him, if I'm using that expression correctly. And he does have all the latest training; I have hopes for him."

"That's one way of looking at it, I guess." *Forget Serna.* "Doc, I want to thank you for giving this a shot, no matter what we run into up here."

"I'll do what I can, Mister Friend."

"Uh, how often have you been in this hospital?"

"The diocese has me over to do free clinics, and a few of my patients end up here. Once in a while, I come over to see them during visiting hours."

"Without declaring that you're their doctor?"

"Right, then they go to my clinic after they get out."

"I see." He cleared the last summit, the hospital below; Jake accelerated downhill, over the limit.

"Mister Friend, does your wife also teach here?"

"Yes, special ed."

"Good for her. You both do very important work. It's obvious that Ben has a lot of respect for you."

"He's a great kid; nearly all of my students are great kids."

"Funny how that works when respect goes both ways," he said as Jake took the corner to the hospital too fast, braking hard during the turn and missing Castilleja's last comment.

"Okay, finally," Jake said, driving right through the lot to the emergency entrance. He parked there, they got out and rushed inside.

28

Jake took him to the payphone, making sure the doctor had plenty of change and the hospital's number. While Jake waited, he bit his nails again, noticing it was after one-thirty. He leaned on the wall, glaring at the snack machine he broke the night before.

Castilleja finished his call, and Jake led him quickly down the now familiar hallway past the staff rooms, labs, and the administrator's office to the nursery. María was gone; charge nurse Jaworsky was in the back room, watching over Emma in the incubator. The Flores twins slept in the open incubators out front.

What'll she say about the doc? She's not Monson; she might listen.

Jake knocked on the window; the nurse came out by the twins and saw Doctor Castilleja and his black bag. Her eyes opened wide for a moment; she moved to the back of the nursery to the wall phone to make a brief call, and then walked slowly out into the hall, looking suspiciously at the doctor.

"And who is this, Mister Friend?" Jaworsky looked beyond Jake, down the corridor.

She knows who he is—easy, Jake. "Doctor Castilleja, this is charge nurse Jaworsky." Castilleja smiled, but Jake spoke up before the doctor could express any niceties. "Can you tell me where María is, nurse?"

Jaworsky turned to answer, her round face pouty. "She has a long break between shifts—she spent half of it with your baby. Her niece came for her; María's due back at two."

"Oh. How is Emma doing?"

Jaworsky's tense face seemed to soften; she ruminated over a response, then sighed before she spoke. "Mister Friend, I'm afraid that she is ill after all."

What? "Has something new happened?"

"No, but she should've perked up by now." The nurse looked down the hall again, then at the doctor, who dropped his floppy hat on a chair. "It seems you were right to be concerned."

"María and my wife were right, not me."

"Well, I'm no longer satisfied with the situation."

"That's good. So here's a real doctor; let's *do* something—" Jake stopped when one of the hospital's grey-haired watchmen walked up in tan summer slacks. Jake remembered the askew patch on his sleeve.

"Can I help, Bonnie?" the guard shouted from three feet away.

Great, this guy. Jake faced the nurse.

"Everything's fine, Wally," she called back. "Please just stay here until we resolve this." She glanced at the doctor, who put the black bag down by his hat.

"Yes, ma'am," Wally yelled, backing off some steps.

"Mister Friend," Jaworsky said, "I left an urgent message for Doctor Serna. I've yet to hear back but expect him to call soon and—"

"Nurse, maybe I can be of some assistance," the doctor interjected, sounding very courteous. "For now, perhaps you can just update me on the baby's condition?"

Jake saw Jaworsky's jaw drop slightly upon hearing the doctor's near-perfect English. "Um, I'm sorry, I can't do that."

Bullcrap. No—easy, Jake. "Listen, nurse, you've been one of the most helpful people around here. Can you just update *me*? Then the doctor can listen in."

She looked away to process the suggestion. "Okay, I don't see why not." Jaworsky went back in for the chart.

"Very tactful, Mister Friend."

"No, it's true; she's the best they have." He paused, sighed, and then shook his head so hard that it shuddered. "This is just so crazy."

"Take a few deep breaths. For now, this is better than nothing."

The nurse came out, read the data to Jake and gave a summation of the baby's condition.

Castilleja read her badge to recall the name. "Very thorough, nurse, uh, Jaworsky. I can't be sure, of course, but I might have a pretty good idea of what's going on with her."

"Oh?" She looked around as if she were violating some cardinal rule. "What do you think it is?" she mumbled.

"The symptoms are very consistent with meconium aspiration."

Her eyes big again, Jaworsky didn't ponder very long this time. "That should have been taken care of in the delivery room."

"Take care of what? What kind of aspiration?" Jake asked both of them.

"Meconium," Castilleja answered. "The baby might have breathed in her own feces before she was born." He turned to Jaworsky. "Nurse, I'm sure you're aware that there are cases of meconium aspiration which are not apparent right away, even if everything seems normal."

Jaworsky again allowed the information to sink in before she spoke. "Yes, I know, but I've never seen it. So, she might need a trachea tube and suction?"

"Probably. If meconium is the problem, hopefully it's only in her airways."

"Or what? How serious is this?" Jake asked, his pitch rising.

"I see this quite a lot, Mister Friend. It is missed most often with babies born at home without a doctor; it can lead to various lung conditions, some very serious."

"Jesus, let's *do* something."

Castilleja turned to the nurse. "As you know, we need X-rays and a blood test to be sure about this."

"Which neither of us can authorize."

"Of course. But if the baby has aspirated meconium, time is very important."

"I *am* expecting Doctor Serna soon."

"And if it's hours before he gets here?" Castilleja replied evenly. "Consider this. Perhaps no one would know the difference if I guide you on the suction procedure from the hallway; as you know, it isn't difficult. If the baby doesn't have meconium blockage, no harm done."

The nurse's brawny shoulders stiffened with incredulity. "I know things are done differently down there, doctor, but you can't be serious."

"Yes, he's serious," Jake said. "The hospital probably wouldn't even know it happened."

"We are small, Mister Friend, but there's other staff here today besides María. Believe me, they'd know."

Jake held his palms up in supplication. "Can't you trust them to support you for doing the right thing?"

Jaworsky scoffed. "Sister Ruth runs this hospital." She glanced at Wally and lowered her voice. "And she's *not* Mother Teresa; I'd probably be fired, and then blackballed from working anywhere else."

"You're right, nurse; I apologize for my, uh, presumption," Castilleja said. "I have a suggestion. Perhaps you could begin preparing for the procedure— the room, equipment and the baby—so it can be done as soon as it is authorized?"

She looked at Emma for several seconds. "Yes, okay, I'll do that, just in case." She gestured for Wally to come closer, then turned back to Castilleja.

"Nurse," the doctor said, "I'd keep the oxygen at the highest level Doctor McNally cleared, and someone should be with the baby to monitor her until she's examined."

"Wally," she yelled again, pointing at the nursery entrance, "please stand right there."

"Oh? Okay," the old man called back on his way to guard the glass door.

"Nobody goes in except medical staff or María." She looked at her wristwatch. "And she's late for the first time ever—what a day." Jaworsky started around the nursery's see-through corner. "I'll be right back," she shouted to the watchman.

"Yes, ma'am," Wally said in a normal tone, probably thinking that he was muttering. He pulled a chair over near the door and sat down, smiling meekly at Jake and the doctor, who walked a few feet away together.

"Damn it, we're not getting anywhere." Jake looked in at Emma.

"Don't give up on María, Mister Friend."

"Yeah, you're right. How much time do you think we have before Emma could get worse?"

"Without more information, there are too many variables to know anything for sure. She's what, about thirty-six hours old?" Castilleja frowned at Jake's nod. "If it *is* meconium, she could be critical by now; it's also possible there's just a blockage that could be easily remedied. More likely, it's something in between."

"What happens if I just move the old man aside and let you in?"

"In the ten minutes it would take for the police to get here?"

"Yeah, you're right." Jake stared toward Emma; his mind felt vacant. "There must be something I can do," he finally said quietly to the doctor.

"Mister Friend, here's the nurse already; she's doing what she can."

Moving as quickly around the corner as her stout frame could manage, Jaworsky followed the nun-like older nurse, Ruiz, who pushed a dresser-sized stainless steel compartment on wheels into the nursery. Jaworsky stopped at the door when she saw the doctor cross the hall to get a drink from the fountain.

She spoke to Jake, again lowering her voice. "I think your doctor's right. I'll deny I ever said this, but you-know-who probably missed this one; I should've spotted it sooner. We also just heard that Sister Ruth is coming, though I certainly didn't call her. Doctor Serna *must* be on his way by now."

She walked into a flurry of medical implements, towels and plastic tubes; Jake couldn't see much else from the hallway. Castilleja came back to the glass to watch; Jake told him that Jaworsky agreed with his diagnosis. Ruiz stayed in the back room with the baby.

The charge nurse came out with a paper in hand. "Mister Friend, this is a standard permission form, in case we get that far. I'm not sure it's even required for this, but if it is, Doctor Serna will consult with you." Jaworsky handed him the paper and lowered her double chin to look in the pocket of her white frock. "Darn, lost my pen."

"Got one." Jake removed a retractable ballpoint from his pocket. He knelt and signed the form on the linoleum.

Jaworsky took the paper as Jake stood up. "Okay, Mister Friend, we—" She broke off her sentence when she saw a small group heading her way from emergency. "Now the fun's going to start," she said, and then went back into the nursery.

A tall, slim woman in severe black glasses and a tan dress to her ankles moved briskly down the hall several feet ahead of a tow-headed priest, who was walking with María. They passed by the lanky woman when she stopped to unlock an office door.

Of slight build and only a few inches taller than María, the priest wore dark grey slacks and a short-sleeve black shirt with a classic notched white collar. A three-inch burnished gold crucifix hung to his chest over a forest green sash.

He looked to be in his forties to Jake, who was not encouraged by the small man's sour expression; he hoped the pastor was just cranky from the pink sunburn on his face. Jake took a step toward María, but she moved right behind Wally to enter the nursery.

"*Buenas tardes, Doctor Castilleja*," the priest said very quietly, his Spanish anglicized.

"Father Paul, good to see you." The doctor sounded polite, as he might to any casual acquaintance.

The priest turned solemnly to Jake. "I assume you are Mister Friend."

"Yes, father." Jake reached out; the small man shook hands indifferently.

"María tells me we have a problem here, Mister Friend." Father Paul's eyes drooped as if he had missed his regular nap.

What's this guy's deal? "Uh, we just want our baby cared for. Obviously, the sooner the better."

"Yes, here comes Sister Ruth; she'll get to the bottom of it," he said, still not showing much concern. The sister carried manila folders under one arm; her eyebrows were pointed down and in like a stereotypical school nun about to punish a miscreant child. She had black hair trimmed into a bowl-like pageboy across her fair forehead. Behind dark rims, the sister's partially rounded blue eyes led Jake to judge her ancestry was both Asian and

European. She seemed more youthful as she came closer, probably about the same age as Father Paul, who had backed up to lean against the wall.

"Good afternoon," she said with a business-like glance at the doctor before turning to Jake. "I am Sister Ruth Lee. Mister Friend?"

"Yes, sister, I—"

"One moment, please," she said, sounding to Jake like a telephone operator. She opened a folder and started reading.

Crap. Jake exhaled audibly; the sister shot him a quick sneer. He turned to the glass and saw Ruiz come out of the back room. María said something to the nurse, extending her neck as if pointing down the hall. Jake saw Ruiz check to be sure her supervisors weren't watching. She grasped María's arm as you would to a long-time friend; Jake was sure she said, "*Sí, señora.*" Ruiz came out, bowed piously to the pastor and nun, and then hurried around the corner.

Sister Ruth cleared her throat. "So, it is your wish, Mister Friend, not to wait for Doctor Serna and to have Doctor Castilleja attend to your daughter?"

"Yes, absolutely."

The sister spoke to her open folder. "Doctor, I assume your license remains current in California?"

"It does, sister."

"This is very irregular; I need to speak with Nurse Jaworsky." Not waiting for a response, she walked into the nursery and had María take Jaworsky's place with Emma.

While the charge nurse came out to talk to Sister Ruth, Jake stared at María as she hovered over Emma, massaging each of her limbs, one at a time. *C'mon, Emma, fight it, whatever it is.* He got so close to the glass that the brim of his Cub's cap bumped the pane.

"She's something," Castilleja said from a couple of feet behind.

"Sorry?" Jake replied; he had nearly put the others in the hallway out of his mind.

"María—right now, she's doing what she can to encourage circulation; very appropriate treatment." Castilleja changed to a whisper. "Father Paul told me in his gruff way that she pulled him right out of a meeting."

"I'll be," Jake said under his breath. "She had a plan, all right; I wonder if they'll let you in."

Castilleja kept a very low voice. "It's a big step from my free clinics— we'll see." He took a business card from his wallet and jotted something on it. "Take this, Mister Friend, in case you need it." The doctor slipped the little cardboard into Jake's shirt pocket, but he didn't read it because Jaworsky was changing places with María again. The sister came out to the hall and walked directly to the priest, still by the wall.

While those two chatted, Jake took out the doctor's card and skimmed it. He looked up to see the sister and father turn in his direction, but she remained silent, deferring to her superior.

"Go ahead, Sister Ruth," the priest said.

"Nurse Jaworsky believes the baby is approaching critical status; my nursing experience leads me to concur. We have decided to allow Doctor Castilleja to examine the child after parental permission is granted and—"

"That's great; thanks," Jake broke in. "Can we please get on with it then?"

"Yes, as soon as you sign forms to hold the hospital legally harmless from Doctor Castilleja's treatment of the baby. Are you willing to do that, Mister Friend?"

"Of course. I have no problems with the hospital." *Except Serna.*

"Very well, then. I need to get those forms from my office." Though she had remained staid, the sister now sounded self-satisfied. "I'll be back right away." She took a few steps, then abruptly stopped when she saw someone enter the far end of the corridor. Sister Ruth turned back to Jake. "Well, I believe this changes everything." She continued on to her office.

29

Castilleja, the father, Wally and Jake saw that it was Doctor Serna walking toward them, still in his gaudy Bicentennial shirt, deck shoes, tennis shorts, and Panama hat. The sister avoided him, entering her door and closing it. Serna's ingratiating smile endured until he passed the offices and figured out the identities of those in the entourage outside of the nursery.

Jake watched the young physician's face harden as he came closer. *Too bad they found him.* He saw Jaworsky leave the nursery.

"What's going on?" Jake asked the charge nurse as she moved right past him.

"I have to get some things from the labor room." She hustled her large frame up the hall toward emergency, passing Serna and saying, "Doctor, be right back."

Serna scowled at the preoccupied nurse, then morphed his face into another smile. He half bowed and said, "Father Paul" to the priest, who barely nodded. Serna walked up to Jake, removed the white hat, slapping it on his leg as if it were dusty. "So you did it, Mister Friend; you managed to bully both my staff and our police," he said matter-of-factly, not even acknowledging Castilleja.

Jake pointed right at him. "They think our baby's critical, goddamnit."

Serna took false exception to Jake's oath by wagging a forefinger. "Now, Mister Friend, no need for profanity; right, father?" The doctor turned to the priest.

Father Paul kept his place on the wall, arms folded. "The sister might have a question or two for you, doctor." He watched Sister Ruth leave her office.

Serna turned right back to Jake. "So, *they* think she's critical? Let me reassure you, Mister Friend; that's very unlikely." Acting as if he just became aware of Castilleja's presence, Serna smiled at him. "Doctor, good to see you; I'm sorry somebody wasted your valuable time and brought you over here. But since they did, please tell me what led you to conclude that the baby is critical."

Castilleja winced a little. "I haven't examined the child, doctor, but—"

"Hm, is that so? In that case, maybe everyone can go about their business, so I can go about mine. I'll change my clothes, Mister Friend, and be right back to re-examine your daughter."

Not if I can help it. Before Jake decided how to respond, the doctor walked away.

With less decorum than he showed for Father Paul, Serna said, "Sister Ruth," as she approached. Jaworsky was following her about ten feet behind, lugging a white valise.

"I'll need to meet with you later, doctor, when this is over," the nun told Serna.

He gave her a condescending grin. "Whatever you think, sister." Serna walked on by her. Sister Ruth came up to Jake, no paperwork in hand. Nurse Jaworsky cut between them into the nursery.

"Well, Mister Friend," the sister said, "things have worked out after all."

The hell they have.

"Mister Friend?"

Think, Jake. "Yes?"

"Uh, we will be leaving now." Sister Ruth looked at Castilleja, who picked up his bag and hat. "Thank you, anyway, doctor." She turned to the priest. "Ready, Father Paul?" The somber pastor didn't move from the wall.

"Uh-uh," Jake grumbled. "Hold on."

The nun faced Jake again. "Sir?"

"I want Castilleja to check the baby."

"That's no longer necessary," she answered gruffly.

"Yes it is." He saw her stiffen even more.

"No, I'm sorry; we can't agree to that now."

"Is that right?" Jake paused. "Well, I called my sister in L.A. this morning. She's a lawyer; I gave her the whole story, and it's her professional opinion that Serna has been legally negligent. Second time, now," he told her, pointing, "I don't want Serna in charge of our baby, especially since the doctor I *do* want . . . " He pivoted his index finger from the nun to Castilleja, " . . . is standing right there."

Sister Ruth remained silent for a moment. "That all sounds like a legal threat, Mister Friend. A few minutes ago you were going to sign those forms."

"Yes, and I'm still willing to sign them as long as Doctor Castilleja is in charge." Jake couldn't see Ruiz behind him, stopping a patient in a wheelchair at the intersection of the hallways.

"Do you want your baby cared for—" The sister halted her irate question when she saw Ruiz and the patient. "Or not?" she finished weakly.

Eyebrows furrowed with urgency, Tina pointed from the wheelchair to Castilleja. "We want our baby cared for by *this* doctor."

Jake turned to her. "Tina." *My God.* He smiled and walked over; Tina reached out. He put his arm around her terry cloth light blue bathrobe.

"And this is what you think is best for the child, Mrs. Friend?" Sister Ruth asked, stern again.

Tina hugged Jake's side. "Yes, we agree it's what's best for Emma."

She said Emma's name. Jake smirked at the nun.

"Mister and Mrs. Friend," the sister began pompously, "I don't know how you expect us to condone this when we have our own doctor—"

"Sister," Jake interrupted, "if we have to, we'll move Emma in an ambulance with Doctor Castilleja to his clinic; that's a reality, not a threat. Now *this* is a threat: If we're forced to do that, my sister will sue both Serna and your hospital when this is over."

He didn't wait for a reaction from Sister Ruth, who stood there, bewildered. "Okay, enough fooling around," Jake said, letting go of Tina. "Doctor, please go in and examine our daughter." Castilleja took tentative steps toward the nursery as Jake removed the card from his pocket, flicking it with a finger. "I'm going to the payphone to call the *Mexican* ambulance." He sounded ironic and sarcastic at once.

Jake faced Castilleja, who had stopped to wait for a reaction from the father or sister. "Doctor, can the ambulance get across the border all right?"

"With a call from the hospital." Castilleja moved closer to Wally, who stood up and looked to the sister for guidance.

Jake spoke to the priest. "Father, will you help us with that call?"

"No, Mister Friend, it won't be necessary." Father Paul turned calmly to Castilleja. "Go ahead, doctor, do whatever you can for the child."

"We need chest X-rays right away, and a blood test," Castilleja said as Wally pulled the door open willingly.

"Arrange for that immediately, sister," the priest said.

"But father—"

"Now, please, sister; then you can go get those liability papers."

The doctor was already at the nursery sink, washing his hands. Ruiz and the sister entered; the nun told María to switch with Jaworsky again. Castilleja went in the back room with Ruiz and had everyone don a surgical mask.

Jake rolled Tina to the window, explaining what he could about meconium aspiration. " . . . and there could be lung problems, Tina. That's about all I know so far."

"It sounds awful."

"Castilleja said he deals with it a lot. He's on top of it; he'll explain more when there's time."

Tina had to stretch her neck to see the doctor examining Emma with his stethoscope. While the sister and the charge nurse spoke near the sink, Ruiz and María followed instructions from Castilleja.

"Finally," Tina said toward the glass. "At least Emma has a fighting chance now."

"Damn right she does." Jake put his arm around her again. "That's the second time you said it."

"What?"

"Emma's name."

"Oh," she mumbled, still watching the doctor.

Jake released her and walked across the hall to the priest. "Father Paul, thank you very much."

The pastor made a slight bow to Jake, then watched Serna walk quickly down the hallway, now in scrubs over a shirt, tie and suit pants, as if he had no intention of staying for long. His black wingtips ticked on the linoleum.

Get lost, doctor. Jake joined the old watchman in front of the nursery door.

Serna came up to them and spotted Castilleja inside. "What's going on here?" He glowered right in Wally's face.

"I believe you're not needed right now, doctor," Wally shouted.

Jake felt the adrenaline warming his face and skull. "In other words, stay the hell out."

The doctor scoffed aloud at Jake. "Guard, please do your job; have Mister Friend move."

Wally cupped one ear. "What's that, doctor?"

"Get this man out of my way," Serna shouted back, not keeping all the anger out of his voice.

"Oh. Sorry, doctor, the hospital would need cops for that." Wally pointed to the hallway. "Here's Jesse, anyway." Jesús had come in and walked most of the way down to the nursery.

"About time, sergeant," Serna said to him. "Please clear this doorway so I can get to my patient."

Jesús nodded to the priest, then the others; he looked in the nursery. "I don't think so, doc." He stood near Wally and Jake. "The sister's in there; I'd say it's up to her and the father to tell me what to do."

Serna snapped his head around to the priest. "Father, what's the meaning of all this?"

The priest turned slowly to Serna. "We are honoring the parents' request to have Doctor Castilleja examine the baby."

His calm veneer gone, a vein bulged in the doctor's forehead. "She's *my* patient. This is outrageous and probably illegal," he said to Father Paul, trying to contain his ire.

"Doctor, feel free to complain about our decision to the diocese."

The sister had come out of the nursery in time to hear the end of the exchange between Serna and the priest. "I suggest that you calm down, Doctor Serna."

"Maybe when someone listens to me," he fumed. "There's no medical reason for this intervention. I have been monitoring the baby's progress all along."

"Doctor, it seems at least one of those points is questionable. If Doctor Castilleja's preliminary diagnosis is correct, I suggest we *all* pray for the baby's illness not to be severe." She nodded toward the nursery.

Serna scoffed again, not as vociferously. "So what is this diagnosis?"

"We're waiting for him to finish the examination and view the test results and X-rays, but he believes it is meconium aspiration."

"What?" As soon as he said that, the doctor turned pensive. Moments later, his mouth and eyes opened briefly like a witness to a sudden auto accident. Serna heaved an anguished sigh.

"Perhaps you should be praying too, doctor," the priest said softly.

Serna was introspective again, seeming to mull over everything at once. "Christ almighty," he finally muttered, then peeked guiltily at the priest. Serna lifted a hand and gripped his forehead for several moments. "Sister," he said, his voice feeble, "since you're covered here for now, I guess I'll be at home."

"I would appreciate it if you would stay. Doctor Castilleja wants to confer with you as soon as he comes out."

Serna looked at her solemnly. "Oh."

"If it's all right with the Friends."

He looks pathetic; *too damn bad*. Jake had already moved over by Tina. He touched her arm. "What do you think?"

"If that's what Doctor Castilleja wants," Tina said distractedly, now on her feet and staring into the back room.

"I guess you're right." Jake turned. "Okay, sister, whatever *our* doctor wants." He scowled at Serna.

"Good." Sister Ruth faced the doctor. "All this will likely save you some trips, Doctor Serna. We'll probably have some fireworks accidents this afternoon."

Serna walked slowly away. "I'll be at my desk," he uttered, his head halfway down as if listening to the clicks of his metal taps on the polished floor.

The sister dismissed Wally and headed back for her office.

Jesús came over to the Friends. "I have to take off; be sure to call me if you need anything."

Jake held the sergeant's shoulder. "We appreciate all you've done."

"My pleasure."

Tina turned away from the nursery and sat in the wheelchair again. "Yes, thank you, Jesús."

"Sure. Oh, Ana will probably drop by in the morning, if it's okay."

"That'll be fine." Tina sounded less than enthused.

"Jesús, do you know if Fiera has been in any trouble?" Jake asked.

"She got out once." He held back a grin. "Showed up with a dolly, all chewed up. Don't worry; she's fine—entertaining everyone." Jesús turned more serious. "Okay, I'm off; good luck with everything."

"Thanks again." Jake turned back to Tina. They watched Doctor Castilleja tapping on Emma's chest with a forefinger. The sister brought the forms right back from her office; they signed them, and she left again.

María came out to the hall and pulled a chair over to Jake. "*Señor Fren, you need to sit, too. I am afraid it is going to be a long time.*"

Tina got up from the wheelchair and embraced her; Jake put a hand on María's shoulder. He saw Tina just staring past the tiny woman into the nursery; it was Jake who had to hold back the tears.

Father Paul came over; the Friends sat down, and Tina said, "Father, thank you for what you did."

"I think we've done what we can on a secular level." He kissed his green sash; María went to him, and they prayed together.

Over the next hour, Tina and Jake waited and watched as the doctor was assisted by most of the hospital's current shift, including three nurses, María, and a technician with a rolling X-ray machine that barely fit through the doors. As Sister Ruth predicted, Doctor Serna was summoned on the P.A. system to the emergency room. The father of the twins visited his children and chatted a while in Spanish with the Friends and Father Paul. The man left, saying his whole family would pray for the baby.

Minutes after the technician finally returned with a large X-ray envelope, Ruiz came out to the hall with a mask still on her face; she hurried toward emergency, carrying the X-rays. Jake and Tina turned to Father Paul.

The priest spoke in his usual subdued tone. "I'll see what's going on." He started up the hallway.

"Thank you, father," Tina and Jake said almost simultaneously. They waited again, watching María go back and forth three times between the twins and the back room. On María's third trip out, Castilleja followed her to the nursery in his blue scrubs. He removed the mask and gloves, then walked quickly toward the hall.

Jake pushed Tina's wheelchair over to the nursery door to meet the doctor. To Jake, Castilleja's dark eyes seemed ambivalent, a conscious effort to be professionally neutral about the baby. *Jesus, what's he thinking?*

"Mrs. Friend, we haven't actually met." He briefly took her hand.

Tina spoke solemnly. "Thank you for being here, doctor."

"Of course." He paused, then looked at both of them. "Unfortunately, my preliminary diagnosis was correct. I removed meconium from her airways with suction, but some matter was already deeply aspirated; we don't know how much. On the X-rays, the lungs show streaks and marks where the lining is damaged, one cause of her labored breathing. She's also running a fever now, which we're treating, of course. For being in such serious condition, she is relatively stable; we will know in a few days if we caught this in time."

Overwhelmed by the information, the Friends didn't respond right away. Jake moved around the chair and took Tina's hand; the doctor turned to see Serna, Father Paul, and Ruiz just starting down the hallway.

"Could she die from this, doctor?" Jake finally asked.

Now with a frown he couldn't hide, Castilleja faced Tina and Jake. "Serious complications with the lungs are possible, including pneumonia. Her late delivery may have had something to do with the aspiration, but it's helpful that she's a big girl with developed lungs. Most likely, she will either improve or decline very gradually while we treat and stabilize her for a couple days before a transfer to the university, unless the pediatrician recommends that she come immediately. Hopefully, there won't be any sudden or severe complications with her breathing."

Hopefully? Good God. Jake let go of Tina, chewing one of his nails again.

"So what is included in the treatment, doctor?" Tina asked, just above a whisper.

"Doctor Serna and I still need to consult with the pediatrician." Castilleja paused; he saw that Serna and the others were more than halfway there. "Actually, I would like Doctor Serna to give you the specifics on our treatment up to now."

"What do you mean?" Jake's face reddened with his question.

Tina clutched Jake's upper arm, pulling on him a little. "What's your reasoning, doctor?"

"I won't be able to do the follow-up on your daughter, Mrs. Friend. I'll be needed at home soon, and you need someone right here to expedite her treatment and the consultations with the university."

Just a minute. "What about Doctor McNally?"

"I don't think you will want to wait for him. I suggest you give Doctor Serna another chance, Mister Friend."

Tina squeezed Jake's wrist, looking right at him. "We need him for now, Jake." Her tone was quiet but firm.

Goddamnit. He clenched his teeth. "Jesus," Jake said, just before Serna, the priest and nurse Ruiz came within earshot. *You bastard*, he wanted to say to Serna, but Jake just glared at him.

The young doctor looked like a mourner, his face pallid and drawn, no sign of his recent anger. Holding the X-rays, he lowered his head to avoid eye contact with anyone before he entered the nursery with Ruiz and Castilleja. The priest walked over to the Friends.

"I'm still not comfortable with this, father." Jake's eyes were daggered toward where the physicians and Ruiz stopped to wash up and put on masks and gloves.

"Mister Friend, I believe you and your wife have done everything you can."

"I guess." He moved Tina up to the glass.

"Well, I'm going now," the priest said. "I'll be back tomorrow to check up on things."

Tina turned to him, her face bleak. "Father, if we need to, can we get in touch with you?"

"The sister will be here for a while, and María knows how to find me at Saint Teresa's—boy, does she ever," he added with just a crease of a grin.

"Uh, thanks again, father," Jake said, glaring into the nursery.

Father Paul raised his open right hand in an informal blessing and walked away.

30

As Father Paul left, Tina glanced up at Jake, who was still glowering at the hubbub on the other side of the glass. The Friends silently watched the doctors and nurses in the back room, their surgical masks puffing when they spoke. Serna, now wearing glasses, moved his stethoscope over Emma's chest. Tired of stretching her neck to see, Tina stood up by Jake.

They watched for another ten minutes or so, hardly speaking except for occasional guesses about what was going on. Doctor Serna came out to the nursery; Castilleja remained with the baby. His mien serious, Serna removed the gloves and mask and made a phone call at the back wall. Tina sat in the wheelchair again, Jake standing by her.

The doctor finished the call, walked into the hallway with a chart, and came over to them, reading. Jake and Tina only saw Serna's mussed black hair until he looked up from his clipboard. Eyes bloodshot and anxious through black rims, the doctor's shoulders slouched under his rumpled blue scrubs.

Serna's demeanor didn't jibe with Jake's image of him as the cocky young doctor of backwater medicine . . . *and damned if he isn't a lot older than I am.*

Glasses in hand, Serna pinched the bridge of his nose hard; it left a white mark in his skin for seconds. "Lost my contacts—not used to these." He sighed. "Mister and Mrs. Friend, I owe you an apology—"

"I don't want to hear it," Jake interrupted, "just give us the rest of the information."

"All right." Serna lifted his glasses and retreated to the clipboard. "You already know, as Doctor Castilleja suspected, that your daughter aspirated meconium." He stopped, glancing up at Jake.

Worried, doctor? "Go on, with something we *don't* know."

Serna held the paper closer. "After he removed some matter from her airways, she began breathing a little easier, though the rate is still rapid. Unfortunately, she aspirated meconium into her lungs before birth, we now believe. The patches on the chest X-ray indicate chronic lung disease, which is causing respiratory distress."

"I think we've heard all of that, too," Jake scolded.

"I wanted to be sure." Serna glimpsed over his rims before directing his eyes back to the clipboard. "Okay, her treatment: We often see lung problems with premature babies, not late-terms like your daughter, but our approach will be similar. As you know, the fever indicates infection; we don't know how widespread. Her temperature is holding for now at about a hundred and two; we've started antibiotics. We are also administering a drug that should eventually give some relief to the lung damage and improve her breathing. She's still receiving monitored oxygen therapy, but we're changing now to a ventilator. We also hope, of course, these measures will help to prevent pneumonia."

"And how likely is pneumonia?" Jake asked.

"It's possible; we can't put a number on it." Serna removed the glasses and tortured the top of his nose again. "We're very thankful Doctor McNally started some oxygen last night. It gave her a head start."

"Yeah, we're thankful, too." Jake narrowed his eyes almost to a squint. "And I bet your lawyer's thankful."

Serna took in a full breath as if his own doctor had just advised him to do so. "I know you're upset with me, Mister Friend, but it's for your baby's sake I'm glad Doctor McNally took the precaution."

Bull. "Just go on."

"Certainly." He looked blandly at his information. "I just called for a consult with a pediatric specialist at the university, Doctor Lowell; we will be speaking to her within the hour." He straightened his neck while staring inside toward the back room. "I think she'll agree that we should continue trying to stabilize the breathing and fever, and to increase nutritional intake before she can be moved." He turned back to them. "She's being fed intravenously."

Tina cleared her throat. "Doctor, what if she does get worse?"

"Depending on the symptoms, Mrs. Friend, we'd likely have to go ahead and move her." He paused. "I do hope you understand there were no clear indicators of meconium aspiration when she was born."

"That's great, doctor." Jake's nostrils flared. "There were plenty of *indicators* before she was a day old."

"Yes," Serna said, long-faced, "which is why I was trying to apologize."

Tina spoke softly to Jake. "I need to talk to you."

"Right now?"

"Please."

Serna took a few steps, putting his hand on the door to the nursery and looking back at Jake. "I'll check back with you in a few minutes."

"Your track record doesn't give me reason to believe that," Jake said. "I'd like to speak to Doctor Castilleja when he has a chance."

"I'll tell him." Serna went back in the nursery, his posture still slumped.

"Something wrong?" Jake asked Tina abruptly.

She looked up at him. "No, but I think Serna is sorry for how he handled everything."

"Well, I don't."

"I know, Jake, but you're not just mad, you're furious." She stood to take his arm, but he moved away.

Jake looked inside at the doctors. "Damn right I'm furious; you're not exactly a barrel of laughs yourself." He exhaled deeply. *For God's sake, Jake.*

Tina sat back down in the wheelchair. "You're right; I haven't been much help."

He turned to her, shaking his head. "Tina, I'm sorry I said that. You *did* help; you came down here with Ruiz and confronted them. That was hard for you."

"Not this time." She stood again, sliding in her soft slippers on the slick linoleum over to Jake. Tina took his hand and they stared inside at the increasing array of tubes, lines, and monitors around their child.

"María was right about you, too," Tina finally said.

"How's that?"

"She told me how you've been trying so hard to handle things. She didn't say it, but she meant that I was acting like you didn't care. I'm so sorry, Jake."

"Forget it; I'm not the one who gave birth to an eight-pound baby."

"Let's just keep concentrating on what's best for her, like you've been doing. That's all I meant about your anger with Serna; I don't excuse what he did, but we do need him."

"Yeah, I'll bite my lip when he's around, but I'm keeping an eye on him."

Tina squeezed his arm. "Thanks, Don Joaquín."

He smiled briefly, patting her hand. "It's helpless time again. I wish there was something we could do."

"Like the father said, we're doing what we can."

Hand in hand, they sat down at the window again and watched. María came out after a few minutes and shared some information, though it was mostly old news. They thanked her for what seemed like the fiftieth time, encouraging her to continue the updates.

Over the next half hour, the nurses drifted away, Castilleja stayed with Emma while Serna came out with María to check up on the twins. Jake heard

231

Ruiz announce on the P.A. system for Serna to take a call. He spoke on the nursery phone for at least ten minutes, then went in to confer with Castilleja before the older doctor walked out to Jake and Tina in the hall.

"Mister and Mrs. Friend," Castilleja said, "the fever is the same; her breathing rate has increased slightly, not enough to say she's getting worse. We just heard from the pediatrician; she concurs with our treatment and agrees we need to stabilize your daughter before we consider moving her. I'm afraid that's all I have for now."

"Doctor," Tina said before Jake could speak up, "can we see Emma?"

"Of course. We're pretty much down to monitoring."

Good, she really needs this. "Uh, Tina can go in alone; it'll be less hassle in there. I'll see Emma later." *When Serna's gone.*

"Okay, you'll need to scrub, Mrs. Friend." He looked at Jake. "Doctor Serna said you wanted to talk to me?"

"Yes, uh, I had a couple of questions. You covered one of them; I forgot the other one. Oh, how long do you think you can hang in here with us?"

"Things are calm at home so far. I'll try to be here at least until the Bicentennial fireworks; wouldn't want to miss that." A sardonic grin broke below Castilleja's moustache; then he was serious again. "After I go, Mister Friend, you're going to have to trust Doctor Serna."

Jake sneered, glancing up at the wall clock. "Six fifteen; I have a few hours to get used to that idea."

"Yes." Castilleja turned to Tina. "María will come out for you, Mrs. Friend." Tina nodded back.

"Doctor," Jake said, "I might go to the lobby for a cat nap. You'll know where to find me if I'm not here."

"Good idea. And Mrs. Friend, I suggest you go to your room for some rest after you see the baby." Castilleja smiled. "No charge for all that good medical advice."

Jake raised his brows. "That reminds me, doctor, we want to pay you at U.S. rates for all your time."

"Considering the work that you and Mrs. Friend do, I won't take a *peso*. Believe me, it's my honor." He walked back into the nursery.

"He's quite a guy," Jake said to Tina. "We're lucky to have him."

"Yes, we are."

María came out and took her in to get ready. When Tina walked by the Flores twins, she didn't look at them—intentionally, Jake thought. After she was ready with the gown, mask and gloves, Tina turned to Jake, her eyes heavy as if she had been weeping, though he hadn't seen her cry for days. She made a passing wave to him with a gloved hand before María escorted her into the back room.

He watched Tina peer into the incubator for a minute or so. Jake felt certain that she longed to smile at Emma, but he could tell by the top half of her face that Tina remained somber. *Jesus, I can't take any more of this.* He got up, knuckling a tear out of the corner of one eye.

Jake walked down the hall to the vending machines, put a quarter in for another peanut-caramel bar, sat on the bench and ate it, deciding against going to the lobby. He stood and saw a blur of lights from the in-out board as he walked out. *Damn thing meant so much a day ago.*

He made his way back to the nursery, glanced at Tina, sat down and propped his feet up, pulling the brim of his cap down over his eyes. Counting backwards from five hundred, Jake consciously breathed in and out sixteen times before he lost his place.

Jake was startled awake by another call on the P.A. for Doctor Serna, who hurried out of the nursery and down the hall. It was just after seven o'clock; María rocked one of the twins, and Castilleja was on the phone. Tina was gone, and Monson had replaced Jaworsky; he stood by Emma's incubator, watching her.

Damn, I thought Jaworsky was on until midnight. Stay away from this schmuck or you'll get pissed again. He forced a smile for María as she brought the Flores baby back to an open incubator by the window. The other twin was awake; María changed his diaper, then put him back near his sleeping brother. Jake watched the alert baby boy seem to check out everything above. *When will Emma do that?*

He saw Doctor Serna come down the hall as quickly as he left, and then go right back in with Castilleja. *Now what?* María came to the door; Jake again pulled it open for her. *"¿Is there some problem, señora?"*

"Señor Fren, you need to talk to the doctors. The breathing is not worse, but they say her heart is slower."

"¿That is something good, no?"

She frowned. *"I only know that breathing and the heart are not always together. I am sorry, but the doctors are worried. They want the X-rays again."*

What? *"¿Señora, is my wife in her room?"*

"Sí, she told us not to wake you."

"*I will return in a moment.*" Jake rushed around the corner almost into a tall cart with a few messy dinner trays. He skirted around it and ran down the hall. He found Tina sitting in the visitor's chair in a white hospital gown; she was asleep with the crocheting in her lap. *Don't bother her yet.*

By the time Jake visited the bathroom and then jogged back to the nursery, Emma's incubator and Ruiz were both gone. Serna was speaking seriously to Monson near the twins while Castilleja and María were in back, moving some equipment. *Jesus, what's going on?* Serna finished with Monson and came out to Jake with a form in his hand. "Where's Emma, doctor?"

"To save time, we had nurse Ruiz wheel her down to X-ray. Mister Friend, the baby's symptoms have changed—both her heart rate and blood pressure have dropped, and there's some cyanosis—uh, her skin color isn't good. All this is indicative of a collapsed lung; we're doing another X-ray to be sure."

"My God, how serious is that?"

"She's definitely in distress, but we're preparing a procedure to help her."

"What procedure?"

"We have to insert a tube between the ribs to remove the air from her chest cavity and allow the lung to gradually re-expand."

"Right through her skin?"

"It sounds worse than it is; this procedure is safe and usually successful."

"Usually? What if it isn't?"

"It's not likely, but we would have to move her right away to the university, perhaps by helicopter."

"Jesus."

"Do you want to speak to Doctor Castilleja?"

"No, do I need to sign that?" Jake pointed at the form in the doctor's hand.

"Both of you, preferably. The X-ray should be here in ten or fifteen minutes." He gave Jake the paper.

"Okay, I'll take this to her." He ran down to the room and found Tina still dozing in the chair. *Damn, you have to wake her.* He signed the form, but made himself wait, actually timing a couple of minutes on the wall clock while chewing his nails and hoping Tina would stir. He walked over, kissed her gently on the cheek and said, "Latina?"

Her eyes fluttered. "Hi, amor." Tina showed a hint of a smile, more than he'd seen in days.

"Hey, cutie. Sorry to wake you."

"It's okay. I just dropped off; I think it relaxed me some to see Emma."

Damn. "I have a little bad news—sorry."

Tina blinked, then focused on him with an intrepid stare. She listened to his explanation of Emma's lung problems, then said, "She's made it this far; give me your pen, please."

Tina signed; Jake told her he'd come back when they began. He returned to the nursery, where Ruiz was pushing the closed incubator into the back room; Monson, Serna and Castilleja were all in there, preparing. María, wearing gloves and a surgical mask, came out to check the sleeping twins. She saw Jake and started toward the hall, lowering her mask. He walked over to meet her.

"*¿What can you tell me, señora?*" Jake let go of the door as she came out.

"*They are still waiting for the X-rays, Señor Fren. To be truthful, la niña, well, she needs the help of both God and the doctors. I am praying for her when I can.*" María briefly closed her eyes and crossed herself. "*I am sorry to be so grave.*" She looked inside at the physicians. "*¿Do you pray, Señor Fren?*"

"*No, señora.*"

She looked at him again. "*Su señora, I think she prays for both of you.*"

"*Sí, that is probably true.*"

"*I will pray with her when I can.*"

"Uh, *I am sure she would like that.*"

They turned toward Emma; Jake saw Castilleja checking her with his stethoscope, Monson just standing there.

María might know why he's here. He raised his brows toward the back room. "*Señora, I thought you didn't work the same hours as Monson.*"

"*It is a holiday schedule. He hates me even more now, but he is quiet. I think he is worried about his job—Doctor Serna scolded him.*"

He did? "*¿Por qué?*"

"*They think I did not understand, but he told Monson that he deserves part of the blame for your baby. I had to go find the sister to stop the argument.*"

"Really?" he said in English.

"Um, *sí, señor.*"

"*¿Is the sister still here?*"

"*No, but she arranged for the baby to go to the university when the doctors say so.*"

"*Muy bien, señora; it helps us a lot to know that.*"

María turned her head when she heard footfalls in the other corridor.

"*The X-rays are here, señor.*"

31

The technician rushed the X-rays inside and left after a couple of minutes. The two physicians came out to the nursery together; Castilleja said something quietly to María, who was with the twins again. Monson sneered at her from the back room as both doctors walked out to Jake.

"Mister Friend, we're certain now that she has a collapsed lung," Castilleja said. "We need to start right away on the procedure."

Good God. Jake handed him the signed form. "Is there anything to worry about with the procedure itself?"

Serna took the question. "No, not at all. It should take us only about ten minutes. If she responds well, then we can transfer her in a couple days."

Jake turned to Castilleja. "How will you know?"

"We want her color, heart rate, and blood pressure to normalize."

"And the breathing?" Jake saw Castilleja wait to let Serna speak, but he didn't.

"That will probably take longer," the older doctor answered, "but we hope it will start to improve."

"And if all that doesn't happen?"

"There are emergency procedures that can be done at the university," Castilleja said. "I don't think it serves any purpose to describe them now." He sounded slightly miffed. "We should get started."

"Of course, go ahead. I'm going to get Tina."

Jake hurried down the hall again to her room; she was still sitting in the chair in her gown. She looked up from the crocheting.

"It's a collapsed lung for sure, Tina. They're starting; it'll only take about ten minutes; I can tell you more in the hall."

"You go. Just come for me when it's finished; you can tell me everything then."

"You sure?"

"It won't help anything if I rush down there; I need to go to the bathroom anyway."

"Okay, see you in a little while." He went directly to the nursery, then waited and watched, though he could only see the backs of Serna, Castilleja, and Monson.

Doctor Serna finally came out to Jake, attempting a reassuring smile before he spoke. "The procedure went fine, Mister Friend."

"Do you know anything yet?"

"Just that air is draining from her chest. Now the waiting is on again."

"We'll need to be updated on everything when I bring Tina back."

"Of course. Is there anything else we can do now for you and your wife?"

Guilt trip—use it. "As a matter of fact, there is. Can you arrange to move Monson back to the nurses' station and leave nurse Ruiz in there?"

Serna nodded. "Yes, I can do that."

"You don't want to know why?"

"That won't be necessary." Serna went right back in to calmly but literally tell Monson where to go. The male nurse walked out and scowled at María; he went into the hall, ignored Jake, and stomped around the corner. María looked out at Jake with that crooked grin he had only seen two or three times. She then frowned and rapidly made the sign of the cross, apparently castigating herself for gloating.

Easy on yourself, María; he deserves it. On the way back to Tina, Jake met Ruiz in the hall; they smiled in passing.

He came to Monson, who stiffly pretended to be looking at some papers on the counter. Jake walked by and said, "Now you have time to find a dog for the next race."

Tina was sitting on the edge of the bed in her robe and slippers when Jake walked in.

"They're finished, Tina—so far, so good." He sat on the bed, put an arm around her, and filled her in on what Serna said about the air draining. "They'll give us the latest when we get there, then we just wait some more."

"Okay. I only need a minute."

"I'll go get your wheelchair from the hall."

"At least let me walk out to it." Tina got up and shuffled to the sink. She washed her hands and gave her long hair a few brush strokes before banding it quickly into a ponytail. Jake took Tina's hand, led her out to the wheelchair, and then rolled her down the hall past Monson. They looked in the nursery; Serna was on the phone.

Jake checked the back room. "Just Ruiz and María—I don't see Castilleja." He stood behind the wheelchair again.

"Maybe he finally took a break." Tina watched Serna finish the call, then come right out to her. "How's Emma, Doctor?"

"Not noticeably worse, Mrs. Friend, which is the minimum of what we expect at this point. We hope the heart rate and blood pressure will gradually improve over the next few hours; that would mean the lung is re-inflating. After that, she will probably have the tube in there for at least two days. Then we hope to move her when she's more stable." Serna paused. "Questions?"

"Yes. Where's the doctor?" Jake asked bluntly.

"He just left in a taxi; he was called to his clinic for an emergency. He said to tell you he'll be back to visit when he can. I'll be consulting with him on the phone." Serna looked in the nursery, then turned back. "Are you and I going to be okay here, Mister Friend?"

"It's not like I have much choice."

"No, I guess not."

The two men exchanged self-conscious glances. Serna sighed before speaking to Tina. "Mrs. Friend, do you want to wait someplace more comfortable?"

"I don't know." She turned to Jake.

"Uh, we'll let María know if we decide to wait somewhere else," Jake said to Serna.

"Sure, that's fine." The doctor went back into the nursery.

"Jake, I feel like a vulture sitting here, but my room is too removed from everything."

"The lobby's actually closer."

"Okay, let's go out there."

María had returned to the twins; Jake raised a forefinger to ask for a minute of her time. She stopped bundling up one of the babies and met Jake outside the door.

"*¿Señor Fren, he told you la niña is not worse, no?*"

"*Sí, gracias. ¿How are your twins doing?*"

"*Bien.*" They walked toward Tina. "*Señora Flores is ready to nurse. She will not allow Monson to bring the boys.*" She shrugged her small but sturdy shoulders as they came to Tina. "*I said nothing to Señora Flores.*"

Jake snickered without smiling. "*Señora, we just want to let you know that we will be waiting in the lobby.*"

"Oh," María said, giving Tina's hand a soft pat. "*I will tell the doctor and nurse Ruiz.*"

Jake managed a smile. "*Gracias, señora. I am going to come by here every half hour or so.*"

"*Está bien, Señor Fren.*"

Holding a mask to her face, María went all the way into the doctor to give him the message. She came back out to her two small charges; Tina and Jake waved to her before he pushed the wheelchair away.

"Jake, I forgot the afghan and my purse; your things are in there, too."

He left her at the corner and walked quickly down the hall, ignoring Monson. Jake hustled back to Tina a couple of minutes later, the big purse and the afghan filling his arms. He put it all on her lap, noticing how the red, green, and yellow Cameroon colors clashed with the pile of red, white, and blue that Tina could barely keep from falling to the floor. He rolled her toward the lobby, passing the four rooms at that end of the ward; they were still spic-and-span, and vacant.

A young couple and an elderly woman sat in the lobby near the door to the other wing. Wally, alone at the counter, asked the Friends about the baby; they yell-chatted with him for a minute or so. Jake noticed it was almost eight-thirty and there was still some light outside. They settled off by themselves on the sofa nearest their hallway and began waiting yet again.

Two feet or so away from Jake, Tina worked so diligently on the afghan that her singular activity began to irritate him a little. He just stared at the same page in his book, getting up after twenty minutes to mosey down past the nursery, making sure María, Serna, or Ruiz could spot him if they needed to. On his second trip, nurse Ruiz smiled at him again, which annoyed Jake because he thought it was false optimism. After Jake's fourth sojourn, he came back and sat by Tina and began gnawing at a thumbnail.

"When did you start biting your nails?"

He dropped his hand as if it didn't belong to him. "Damn—recently."

"Are you okay?"

"Just nervous." He saw that Tina was tying off and snipping around the red border of the afghan.

Tina looked up. "Anything different down there?"

"No, Ruiz is around most of the time, and María's still back and forth between the two rooms. She gets off soon—what a long day for her. She said she'll come by to see you before she leaves."

Tina pursed her lips slightly. "Bless her heart."

"Yeah. I saw Serna go to his office; I'll talk to him on my next trip." Jake saw that it was dark outside; he checked the wall clock. "It's been over an hour and a half now." He watched her trim the yarn for several moments. "I don't know how you can do that; I can't read one lousy page."

"It doesn't take much concentration." She put the scissors on her lap and looked at him. "Jake, I was wondering about something."

"What is it?"

"Why did they believe you before when you said we'd sue them?"

"Oh, that. Before you came, I lied that I had just called Hannah. I told them that she said Serna was negligent, which was true; except she said it last night."

"I see. So your sisters don't know everything that's going on?"

"Hannah just knows about the breathing problems, not the procedure. She called Caroline and Joyce; they think everything's fine."

"You didn't call my family, right?" Tina was staring down at her lap.

"No, I didn't call anyone."

"I want to keep it like that until we know more." She stood, leaving the scissors on the sofa.

"Yeah, except Hannah; she's apt to fly over here." He checked the clock again. "I should call her, but it can wait."

"Jake?"

He turned to her. "Yes?"

Tina was holding up the afghan like hanging out a sheet on a clothesline; it drooped down to the floor and spread a few feet away. "It's finished."

"It's huge. Looks, uh, very patriotic."

"It looks pretty silly to me."

"María suggested the colors. She'll love it."

"But what should I do now?" Tina held up the project again, then tears flowed over her cheeks.

"Jesus, Tina." He took the afghan, pulled up the rest from the floor, and tossed it all on the sofa. Jake put his arms around her as they sat down.

"I'm sorry—so sorry." She began to weep.

"For what? There's nothing to be sorry for."

"I—I—just am," she answered around heaving sobs.

"It's okay; just let it out. You've been holding it in for days."

"I—didn't—know—what—to—say." She struggled to breathe between words.

"To who?"

"You—everybody."

"It's okay, Latina." He held her a minute or two until the crying diminished some and she pushed lightly on his chest. He backed off a bit, caressing her face with one hand.

Tina inhaled a long sniff, sat up, and began gathering all the red, white, and blue material. "I'll be all right."

"Yeah, you will." He watched her begin to fold the afghan. "You could make the border wider, and add some fringe, couldn't you?"

"I suppose so; María brought plenty of yarn." She faced the hallway. "Jake, my God, here he comes." Tina put down the afghan on her other side; Jake held her with one arm as Serna walked up to the sofa.

"Are you all right, Mrs. Friend?"

She had taken a tissue from her purse and was dabbing her eyes. "Yes, doctor, I'm fine. How's Emma?"

Though he was trying to be professional, Serna couldn't hold back a slight smile. "The breathing is the same, but her heart rate and blood pressure are a little better, enough to be reasonably sure that the lung is beginning to re-inflate. I hope this is the start of a turnaround for your baby."

"Thank you," Jake said, holding Tina as she wept quietly to the good news.

"You're welcome." Serna looked up. He, Wally, and four other people in the lobby *oohed* and *aahed* with delight at a red pyrotechnic bloom that lit up the plate glass panes of the hospital's A-frame façade.

Jake and Tina, still embracing, didn't turn around to watch a single burst from the ten-minute Bicentennial display.

32

Three days later, the baby's heart rate and blood pressure had stabilized enough that they went ahead with the transfer to the university. The day before, Jake took Tina back to the house in Sofia.

After they moved Emma, Jake stayed at the university's pediatric intensive care facility for hours, until he was satisfied that he understood everything and the baby was settled in. On his way back to Sofia in the late afternoon, he encountered an intense downpour; it obliterated his visibility, and Jake had to turn off to wait it out. He found a solid gravel road, drove in about twenty yards, and stopped Loretta by a wash.

It was a welcome respite from the stress of the previous week; he swiveled both wind wings open a crack, sat back, and watched the thunderstorm pass, waiting longer than he had to. Jake rolled down the windows, inhaled the cool, fresh air, and listened to what was now just a steady drizzle tapping softly in the standing water.

He got out and walked by dripping palo verde and mesquite over to the wash, which was about a hundred feet wide but only had a few large puddles. Jake watched, waited, and was about to leave when a three-foot swell of dun rainwater roiled down the arroyo. He waited for something interesting to float by, but saw nothing more than bobbing branches before he left.

Jake pulled into the driveway in Sofia, passed the restaurant, and drove slowly through the desert undergrowth to the rental. He was glad to see that a storm, maybe the same one, had hit there and thoroughly watered their yard and garden. After Jake parked, he walked around some mud and noticed that it was still relatively cool outside.

He went in and found Tina resting on their bed, lying toward the wall in her robe. The afghan was folded and stacked on the dresser; she had left scissors, a crochet hook, and a skein of red yarn on top of it.

"Hi, amor," Tina said. "Look what you've done." She turned toward him, revealing Fiera, "spooning" into Tina's other side, her head up, panting toward Jake with her goofy dog smile.

"I'm jealous. That's my spot."

"Oh?" Tina grinned. "Well, there's nothing stopping you; Ben took off for a couple days."

"Nah, I might get too frisky." He sat on the bed.

"Pretty soon, Don Joaquín." Tina patted his hand, then held it. "How's Emma doing?"

"Nothing new since I called you. 'Relatively stable,' like they keep saying; they're still concerned about the breathing not slowing down enough. The pediatrician said to check in with her at five-thirty, before she goes." He glanced at the alarm clock. "Half an hour."

"I was hoping she'd be doing even better by now."

"Yeah, I know. At least she's in the right place."

Fiera couldn't control her innate affability any longer; she jumped down and came around the bed to lick Jake's hand. He rubbed her pointy ears; they drooped, as always, into the relaxed, floppy mode.

"Crazy mutt." Jake lifted one of the dog's ears.

"She doesn't do that for just anybody, you know."

"Right. Listen to who's feeling a little better."

Tina nodded. "I am feeling better."

Jake looked over at the afghan. "I see you added more red to the border."

"Yes, it's finished for sure."

"Does that still upset you?"

"No. I'm not sure why it did before."

The phone rang in the hall; Jake got up to answer. Tina followed him, but she walked right by into the bathroom, leaving the door open.

"Hello?"

"Mister Friend?" It was a subdued female voice.

"Yes. Doctor Lowell?" *Wait, I was supposed to call her. Easy, it's probably nothing.* Jake was holding the receiver away a couple of inches, but he could hear her grave, apologetic tone. *Oh, God, no.* Jake made himself put the phone to his ear. *No, no, no!*

" . . . and I'm afraid there's no easy way to say it. Your daughter passed away a few minutes ago."

No, goddamnit! He was vaguely aware of cramping in his chest. "Jesus, doctor, not just like that."

"I'm so sorry, Mister Friend. Her breathing rate spiked after you left; we couldn't get it under control. We did everything we could."

Not enough, damn it.

When Jake didn't answer, the doctor continued solemnly. "It was likely pneumonia, Mister Friend. We'd have to do an autopsy to be completely sure."

What? The hell you will.

"Mister Friend?"

"No autopsy; leave her be, please." Then Jake heard himself say, "Thank you, doctor." He hung up the receiver, glared at it, then picked up the base and carried the telephone back to the kitchen, the long cord trailing behind. Jake kept on going right out the back door, the line catching in the screen.

"Shit!" he screamed, yanking on the cord. The phone slipped from his hand and fell to the concrete; its casing cracked like an egg. *Finish the job.* Jake grabbed his shovel and slammed it down on the device three times, like he did to the scorpion months before, but now he was silent, his tears falling into the shattered mess of wires, metal, and plastic.

Jesus—Tina. He tossed the shovel, then stumbled in a daze back inside to the hallway. Jake saw her on the bed, facing the wall again. "Tina," he said, scooting in behind her.

"Shh, I heard the call, Jake." She turned and they held each other, both of them crying. Fiera jumped up on the bed and stayed with them most of the night.

Just after dawn, Tina and Jake lay awake, embracing silently for nearly an hour before they got up and morosely took care of some daily chores, barely communicating. Taking Fiera out, Jake found the remnants of the telephone and realized he couldn't start on the burial arrangements without it. After the dog's walk, he and Tina made themselves discuss their immediate plans. Jake then went out to Loretta, notebook in hand, got in, and drove off for his school, crying again.

In the boys' lavatory, Jake slapped cold water on his face, then went into the office. Charging the calls to their home number, he was able to arrange for the burial in La Cholla the following afternoon. Next, he called Jesús; who of course offered his condolences and support. Jake explained what would and would not take place the next day, and asked Jesús to pass the information on to the handful of local people who needed to know.

Dreading the family calls, Jake started with Jimmy in New York, who took the news with that immutable Linn calmness, asking Jake to have Tina call him when she was up to it. Jimmy graciously took on the task of calling their mother and some other Linn relatives.

Okay, now Hannah. She'll handle all the Friends, then screw this for a while. He last spoke to his sister to explain all the particulars before the baby's transfer. Jake called and gave Hannah the news as factually as he could. Her normally tough persona fell apart right away, and she had to excuse herself. Jake waited for her, staring at some overdue supply orders for the new school year. *That crap was important a week ago.*

"Huey, I'm sorry. My bawling isn't helping anything."

"It's all right; you needed to do it."

"You sound like you're handling this as well as could be expected," she said around a final sob.

"I'm just cried out. Hannah, are you up to passing all this on to the rest of our family?"

"Of course I will."

"I really appreciate it."

"Jake, I can fly over and be there by Sunday."

"Thanks, Hannah, but we're going to have the burial right away—tomorrow; just the two of us."

"Oh, okay; I see. You have to do what's best for you guys." She paused. "Does that leave time for an autopsy?"

"No, it doesn't."

The line was quiet for seconds. "Jake, I wish I could say it's hard to believe that this happened again."

"That *what* happened again?"

"There's a specific name for your doctor's negligence. It's called 'preventable human medical error,' and there's plenty of legal precedent to nail him. You did keep all the documents?"

Jesus, Hannah. "I have no idea."

"That's okay. We'll be able to retrieve most of what we need, and you have some ideal witnesses. I'm proud of how you stood up to him, not to mention the hospital."

"Hannah, the hospital came through for us when it counted."

"I don't agree, but we can concentrate on the doctor, if that's what you want to do."

"No, I don't think so."

She was silent again for a few moments. "Jake, you're not going to let him off the hook, are you?"

"I guess we are. And don't tell me they get away with it because people like me don't go after them. I don't give a damn."

"Okay, Jake. Have you thought about the other people this doctor could harm someday?"

"Yeah, that does bother me, but Tina thinks he learned something. I'm going to trust her judgment."

"Jake, please don't decide this while you're grieving. Do yourself a favor and let them do the autopsy. Then you can think about all of it later."

Shit. "Hannah, just listen." He paused to organize his thoughts. "If we sue Serna, you'd be expecting Castilleja, María, and Tina to testify. I sure as hell am not going to put them through a legal circus like Mom's."

"Great, so now you're upset with me."

"Not really. I'm glad you brought it up; then we won't have to discuss it again."

She sighed loud enough for Jake to hear. "So, that's the end of it?"

"How can I make it any clearer, Hannah?" He realized that he sounded angrier than he wanted to.

"Okay, Jake." She tried to muffle a sob.

Happy now, schmuck? He waited for her to come back on.

After a long sniff, she spoke. "Huey?"

"Hannah, I didn't mean to bark at—"

"No, it's my fault for pushing all that on you at a time like this. I'm sorry."

"Forget it; I know you're just trying to look out for us."

"Yes, but maybe I'll learn to butt out once in a while." She paused. "Huey, what will you guys do now?"

"As soon as we can, we'll try to get on with our lives."

33

The burial took place the next afternoon at the town cemetery on a hill in the middle of La Cholla. The Friends requested that only themselves and the two officials be there. Wearing their everyday school clothes, Tina and Jake watched the funeral director in his formal black suit place the impossibly small coffin in the ground.

Jake took out a short poem he rewrote ten times the night before. He finally gave up on the revisions, knowing it would never be right, never be adequate; never be appropriate. Standing on freshly-cut grass with Tina in the shade of an old elm, Jake read it aloud anyway, barely able to say the eleven words:

> *Mother Earth,*
> *Take this girl*
> *Never given*
> *From your omnipotent womb.*

The Friends held each other a short while, then walked hand in hand down to the dirt parking lot. Jake saw someone standing in a dark suit and tie by the truck's bed. A Karmann Ghia was parked about twenty feet behind Loretta where Ben, in his best clothes, stood behind the doctor.

Her eyes swollen but dry, Tina said, "Good, I'm glad they're here."

"Yeah, me too." Jake and Tina walked a little faster, as if concerned that the doctor and Ben would leave.

"Mister and Mrs. Friend," Castilleja said as they approached, "we just wanted to pay our respects. Please forgive the intrusion."

"No intrusion, doctor. We're glad to see you both." Jake let go of Tina to shake hands with him. She walked over to Ben, who looked desolate as Tina hugged him.

Jake went to his student and put an arm around him. "It's okay, Ben." Jake let his arm down. "We want to thank you both for everything you did."

The doctor nodded with his eyes closed, then looked at Tina. "I'm so sorry I wasn't able to do—"

"No," she interrupted, "you were wonderful; you don't need to be sorry for anything." Tina hugged him with both arms, then let go, weeping a little. She hurried up to the front door of the truck. Jake thanked the doctor again and told Ben they would see him later at the house. He walked over to Loretta and climbed in.

Jake drove out of the cemetery, Tina sitting silently beside him on the bench seat. He had called María that morning to ask to drop by; they found her place after a few minutes on one of the oldest streets in town, a row of clapboard houses on large lots, each poor structure surrounded by shade trees and gardens.

María's small yellow house, closed up to the heat, had two picture windows in front and a huge swamp cooler chugging away at the side beneath a magnificent old weeping willow, the ends of its whip-like branches sweeping along the ground. The house had no lawn out front, just a narrow stepping-stone path between María's two gardens, one of them a wanton display of bright blossoms, including six-foot sunflowers at the far end. Her other garden was bountiful with all sorts of vegetables, the corn tassels at the back even taller than the sunflowers.

Both front windows of María's house were draped inside with white material; Jake saw a birdcage through a gap in one curtain. He parked, they climbed down; Jake opened the back door. He lifted out a bulky package the size of a large laundry basket, but it was light, wrapped all around in white tissue. Jake followed Tina on the path up to the front door; she pressed the buzzer, then took the screen's handle to let him go first.

María came to the door in a black cotton housedress; her withered features drooped even more than usual, but without any tears. "*Señor, Señora Fren. Please come in.*" She ignored the parcel Jake carried.

They thanked her, and entered; she showed them to a sofa covered with an orange throw. María said she would be right back, then walked through an alcove on the way to her kitchen. Her four blue parakeets and two canaries chattered away in three cages, basking and preening in the streak of sunlight allowed in by the gap in the curtains.

Jake put the package on the other side of Tina, and sat next to her on the soft cushions. Several prints of sunflowers and daisies brightened three of María's light green walls; real cut flowers and live plants occupied almost every table and nook. Family pictures in white frames covered another wall above a table with numerous stand-up photos of graduations and weddings. If she owned a radio or TV, she didn't keep either in her living room.

María's religious shrine in one corner displayed four lit white candles in glass holders, a six-inch ivory Virgin, and a simple, non-ghastly wooden crucifix.

"As I expected, very homey," Tina said.

"Yeah." He got up and walked over to see the birds just before María ambled in from the kitchen holding a tray with three frosty glasses of citrus *agua*, a lime wedge on each rim. Jake told María he liked her birds, and then carried the drinks for her over to a coffee table in front of the couch. Tina and Jake thanked her as they took their refreshments and María sat down with hers, opposite them in a heavy, padded wooden rocker.

"*¿La niña, she is buried?*" María asked Tina bluntly.

"*Sí, señora.*"

"*¿No service?*"

"*No, no service.*" Tina lowered her head.

"*¿Will you pray with me, Señora Fren?*"

Tina put down her glass, as did María, they moved over to her shrine and stood next to each other. María grasped and kissed some beads she carried, crossed herself, and murmured toward the religious icons. Tina closed her eyes.

Jake stood up out of respect and shuffled slowly to María's photo gallery. *All the damn praying sure did us a lot of good. Jesus, to each his own, Jake.* He found a snapshot of María standing at the center of a score of smiling family members, a busy barbecue taking place in the background. *They definitely know how lucky they are to have her.* His vision blurring, Jake turned to see María and Tina come back to sit down. He returned to the sofa.

Tina, her own face damp, saw Jake's tears as he sat; she took his hand. "You okay?"

Jake attempted a smile. "No, not really," he mumbled, and then lifted his glass for a drink.

"*¿Señor y Señora Fren, are you planning to stay and teach here?*"

Jake put down his glass and took a deep breath to dampen his emotions. "Uh, *no, señora; we have decided to leave after we find new jobs.*"

"*I am sorry to hear that, but I believe to stay here after something like this, you need to have family nearby. ¿Will you go back to live near them?*"

"*No, we are not going to do that.*" Again, Jake tried to smile.

"*I am sorry,*" María said, "*this is something I do not understand.*"

After dabbing her eyes with a napkin, Tina took a sip of her drink, and put the glass down. "*Señora, this is for you.*" Tina touched the thin white paper next to her.

"*¿Señora Fren, a gift on a day like this?*"

"*Sí, María. Thanks to you, we were given a chance to save our child.*" Tina's tears flowed again. "*We think of you as family; when we have a daughter someday, she will have your name.*" Tina stood and took the package to María, hugged her, then sat back down with Jake.

María pulled out a fold in the tissue and saw the afghan. "*It is very beautiful. I saw you work so hard on this, señora.*"

"*Sí, María. Maybe because of that, you will remember us.*"

"I no forget," María said, speaking for the first time in English to Tina and Jake.

END

About the Author

Terry Lloyd Winetsky grew up in Los Angeles. He has taught English, Spanish, and ESL to people of all ages. After surviving a brain aneurysm in 1998, Winetsky retired from full-time teaching and began writing literary and historical fiction. He continues volunteer work with adult farmworkers in Central Washington.

The first three books in his *American Teachers* series are *Grey Pine, Maria Juana's Gift,* and *Los Angeles, 1968: Happy Ranch to Watts,* all now published by Pen-L Publishing. The fourth book in the series, *Belagana-Belazana*, is partially based on his years of teaching in the Navajo Nation in the 70's. Tentative publication will be in mid 2016. The author lives near Yakima, Washington.

Contact Terry at **TLWinetsky.com**

More on the American Teachers Series at **www.AmericanTeachers.info**

Don't miss the rest of T. Lloyd Winetsky's
American Teachers Series!

*A series with backstories that reveal bitter cynicism
and uplifting idealism in American education.*

Book I: Based on real events, *Grey Pine* is a gripping story of one man's struggle to survive amidst the chaos of the forces of nature and the workings of a troubled mind. May 18, 1980, the eruption of Mount Saint Helens: Phillip Stark, a bright and innovative young science teacher who attempts to treat the ash fall as an opportunity for experiment and wonder is constantly thwarted by the resulting havoc in the community, and his own personal demons.

    Grey Pine is a gritty account of post-Vietnam America that chronicles social ills not unfamiliar to us in the present day: youth suicide, clinical depression, racial tension, alcoholism, and the malaise from an unpopular war.

Praise for *Grey Pine*

"Amidst the ashes, Phillip really wants to live and thrive and as I read deeper into the book, I couldn't help but cheer him on. As I read the first fifty pages, I wondered if I could keep up with the intensity of his voice, yet the more I read, the more I liked his character and wanted him to succeed in realizing himself. This book was a great read." – Jillian A. Ross

---

Book III: Not your feel-good story of "white teacher saves the ghetto," ***Los Angeles, 1968*** is a novel partly based on first-hand experience and real events in a volatile urban setting, a slice-of-life account of a young man's gradual maturation toward personal commitment.

    After Dr. King is assassinated, the increased tension leads to dramatic showdowns for Allen, who finds both an unlikely savior and an unexpected calling.

Praise for *Los Angeles, 1968: Happy Ranch to Watts*

"This author is in his characters and writes from the heart. He ably transfers his passions into words. Congratulations on another great book!" – Barb Dixon

FIND MORE GREAT READS AT PEN-L.COM

Dear Readers,
If you enjoyed this
book enough to review
it for Goodreads, B&N,
or Amazon.com, I'd
appreciate it!
Thanks, Terry

Find more great reads at
Pen-L.com